STEAMPUNK

Ann & Jeff VanderMeer | *editors*

Steampunk

TACHYON PUBLICATIONS | SAN FRANCISCO

Cover design by Ann Monn | cover image by Insect Lab
Interior design & composition by John D. Berry
The text typeface is Paperback, designed by John Downer

Tachyon Publications
1459 18th Street #139
San Francisco, CA 94107
(415) 285-5615
www.tachyonpublications.com

Series Editor: Jacob Weisman

ISBN 13: 978-1-892391-75-9
ISBN 10: 1-892391-75-9

Printed in the United States of America

9 8 7 6 5 4 3 2

"Preface: Steampunk: 'It's a Clockwork Universe, Victoria'" © 2008 by Ann and Jeff
VanderMeer. Original to this anthology. | "Introduction: The 19th-Century Roots of Steam-
punk" © 2008 by Jess Nevins. Original to this anthology. | "Benediction: Excerpt from *The
Warlord of the Air*" © 1971 by Michael Moorcock (Ace Books: New York). | "Lord Kelvin's
Machine" © 1985 by James P. Blaylock. First appeared in *Asimov's SF*, Mid-December 1985.
| "The Giving Mouth" © 1991 by Ian R. MacLeod. First appeared in *Asimov's SF* March 1991. |
"A Sun in the Attic" © 1985 by Mary Gentle. First appeared in *Despatches from the Frontiers of
the Female Mind*, edited by Jen Green and Sarah LeFanu (The Women's Press: London). | "The
God-Clown Is Near" © 2007 by Joseph E. Lake. First appeared in *Dark Discoveries*, Summer
2007. | "The Steam Man of the Prairie and the Dark Rider Get Down: A Dime Novel" © 1999 by
Joe R. Lansdale. First appeared in *The Long Ones* (Necronomicon Press: West Warwick, Rhode
Island). | "The Selene Gardening Society" © 2005 by Molly Brown. First appeared in *The
Mammoth Book of New Jules Verne Adventures*, edited by Mike Ashley and Eric Brown (Carroll &
Graf: New York). | "Seventy-Two Letters," © 2000 by Ted Chiang. First appeared in *Vanishing
Acts*, edited by Ellen Datlow (Tor Books: New York). | "The Martian Agent, A Planetary
Romance" © 2003 by Michael Chabon. Reprinted by permission of the Mary Evans Agency.
First appeared in *McSweeney's Mammoth Treasury of Thrilling Tales*, Issue No. 10 (Vintage: New
York). | "Victoria" © 1991 by Paul Di Filippo. First appeared in *Amazing Stories*, June 1991. |
"Reflected Light" © 2007 by Rachel E. Pollock. First appeared in *SteamPunk Magazine #3*. |
"Minutes of the Last Meeting" © 1998 by Stepan Chapman. First appeared in *Leviathan 2*,
edited by Rose Secrest and Jeff VanderMeer (Ministry of Whimsy Press: Tallahassee, Florida).
| "Excerpt from the Third and Last Volume of *Tribes of the Pacific Coast*" © 1995 by Neal
Stephenson. First appeared in *Full Spectrum 5*, edited by Jennifer Hershey, Tom Dupree, and
Janna Silverstein (Bantam Spectra: New York). | "The Steam-Driven Time Machine: A Pop
Culture Survey " © 2008 by Rick Klaw. Original to this anthology. | "The Essential Sequential
Steampunk: A Modest Survey of the Genre within the Comic Book Medium" © 2008 by Bill
Baker. Original to this anthology.

CONTENTS

*To Jacob Weisman and Jill Roberts,
with respect and affection*

PREFACE
Steampunk: "It's a Clockwork Universe, Victoria"

ANN & JEFF VANDERMEER

One of the joys of steampunk lies in its gadgetry, of course, but people sometimes forget that it also provides adventurous entertainment and has led some writers to use its trappings for experiments and alchemies well off the beaten track. In this anthology, we've tried to provide a blend of the traditional and idiosyncratic, the new and the old, while remaining true to the idea of steampunk as dark pseudo-Victorian fun. You'll find stories about mechanistic golems, infernal machines, the characters of Jules Verne, and, of course, airships. You'll find your way into alternative histories, other planets, and even a show-down between a dark rider and prairie steam men. You'll see the influence of Verne, naturally, but also H. G. Wells and others.

Along with the fiction, we've invited three experts — Jess Nevins, Bill Baker, and Rick Klaw — to provide you with context about steampunk, from its origins to its influence on movies, television, comics, and the Internet. These three dedicated purveyors of knowledge can do a far better job than your humble editors in explaining these delicate and important matters. In addition, you'll find copious lists of further steampunk to explore. For even more information on steampunk, seek out the online *Steampunk Magazine* (*www.steampunkmagazine. com*), a virtual cornucopia of interesting steampunk fiction, fact, and speculation.

However, one fact we must draw your attention to is that some of the best steampunk has been written at the novel length. That's primarily why you won't find K.W. Jeter, Tim Powers, William Gibson, and Bruce Sterling in this anthology: their steampunk stories are all novel-length, and we definitely invite you to seek them out. We also highly recommend Thomas Pynchon's recent steampunk homage, *Against the Day*.

The other truth is that this steampunk anthology, while capturing the permutations of steampunk over the past thirty years, represents just the first step toward capturing the best the field has to offer. The idea of steampunk has so entered the mainstream that a second volume including just stories written in the past decade would be a rich and various thing. (The all-original anthology, *Extraordinary Engines*, forthcoming from Solaris Books and edited by Nick Gevers, does its part by showcasing next generation steampunk.)

Now please enjoy the multitude of entertainments that await you, and remember: It's a clockwork universe, Victoria...

STEAMPUNK

Introduction:
The 19th-Century Roots of Steampunk

JESS NEVINS

Steampunk came to prominence in the 1980s and has recently achieved a new popularity. The first generation of steampunk stories and novels began appearing in the late 1970s, but the genre went through a proto phase in which novels like Ronald Clark's *Queen Victoria's Bomb* (1969) and Michael Moorcock's *The Warlord of the Air* (1971) had the basic elements of the genre but lacked its core conceits or ideology. Steampunk's first generation culminated with Gibson and Sterling's *The Difference Engine* (1990), still the finest expression of the genre yet written. The second generation of steampunk writers followed Gibson and Sterling a few years later and took the genre in a number of different directions.

However, any history of the genre must go farther back than the 1960s. A proper history of steampunk must begin in the 19th century with dime novels, for it is there that steampunk's roots lie, and it is dime novels which the first generation of steampunk writers were reacting against.

The American cult of the scientist and the lone inventor grew through the 19th century, and examples of it can be found in relatively mainstream writers like Edgar Allan Poe, Nathaniel Hawthorne, and Oliver Wendell Holmes (in *Elsie Venner*, 1861). But the image of the lone inventor as a heroic protagonist (as opposed to the Gothic-influenced villains and anti-heroes of Mary Shelley and Fitz-James O'Brien) gained a surprisingly large amount of its power, within science fiction and without, from the Edisonade.

The term "Edisonade" was coined by John Clute after the "Robinsonade," or stories about lone travelers stranded on remote islands, in the vein of Defoe's *Robinson Crusoe*. An Edisonade is a story in which a young American male invents a form of transportation and uses it to travel to uncivilized parts of the American frontier or the world, enrich himself, and punish the enemies of the United States, whether domestic (Native Americans) or foreign. The Edisonades appeared in dime novels as both serials and as complete novels.

The first Edisonade was "The Huge Hunter, or the Steam Man of the Prairies." "The Huge Hunter" was created by Edward S. Ellis, a New Jersey schoolteacher and principal, and appeared in *Irwin P. Beadle's American Novels* #45 (August 1868). The hero of "The Huge Hunter" is Johnny Brainerd, a hunchbacked dwarf. He is the teenaged son of a widow living in St. Louis. Brainerd is a good student at school, loved by the other students and the teachers, and he has a knack for invention. When he runs out of things to invent (including a clock which keeps perfect time and a working telegraph), he complains to his mother, who suggests that Brainerd build "a man that shall go by steam." Brainerd is inspired by this suggestion, and after several weeks of thought and false starts he succeeds in creating the "Steam Man," a man-shaped steam engine capable of moving at thirty miles per hour. Brainerd designs a covered wagon for the Steam Man to tow and then sets off for the western frontier. He befriends the titular "Huge Hunter," Baldy Bicknell, and the pair use the Steam Man to frighten off natives, locate and extract a lode of gold, and then (after blowing up the Steam Man to kill a group of attacking "red skins") return to St. Louis as rich men. The story ends with the statement that Brainerd will "construct another steam man, capable of more wonderful performances than the first."

Ellis never wrote a sequel to "The Huge Hunter," and it passed without comment during its initial appearance, but when the story was reissued in 1876 it sold well and attracted notice. Frank Tousey, the publisher of the Tousey family of magazines, saw how well the reprint of "The Huge Hunter" was selling for his rival, Beadle House, and decided that he wanted something similar. He commissioned Harry Enton, one of the writers for the Tousey dime novels, to write something like "The Huge Hunter." Enton's response was "Frank Reade and His Steam Man of the Plains," which appeared in *Boys of New York* #28 (February 28, 1876). Frank Reade is a slim, pale, "not over-strong" thinker who builds a Steam Man similar to (but better than) Brainerd's. Reade, his Steam Man, and Reade's cousin Charley Gorse travel to the western frontier and fight Indians, bad men, and buffalo, and enrich themselves in the process. Three sequels followed the next four years. In these stories Reade had further adventures on the frontier and produced further steam engines and variations of steam men and steam horses.

Enton quit the series over Tousey's refusal to give Enton credit for the stories — Enton had been signing them "Noname," a Tousey company pseudonym — and Tousey approached Luis Senarens, a teenager who had already been published in various Tousey dime novels, to write further Frank Reade stories. Senarens wrote "Frank Reade, Jr. and His Steam Wonder" (*Boys of New York* #338, February 4, 1879). In the story Frank Reade is comfortably middle-aged and retired, tending to his steam-powered garden, but his son, Frank Reade, Jr., is an even greater inventor and creates new machines powered by electricity. He travels to the western frontier with an electric Steam Man and has adventures similar to his father and to Johnny Brainerd. In the following 178 stories, Reade, Jr., has further adventures, both on the American frontier and around the world, using a variety of electricity-powered vehicles and weapons.

Luis Senarens claimed to have received a fan letter from Verne following Senarens' first Frank Reade, Jr. story. It is unlikely, though by no means impossible, for Verne to have been aware of Senarens' work, and certainly Senarens was not above an outright lie in his favor. For his part, Senarens was an avowed fan of Verne, and in addition to claiming that Verne was a fan of his, Senarens did Verne the dubious favor of stealing his ideas, using Verne's *Steam House* (1879–1880) and the *Albatross*, from *Robur the Conqueror*, as models for some of Frank Reade, Jr.'s vehicles.

The success of the Frank Reade, Jr. series inspired several imitations, including Fred Hazel's "The Electric Horse" in *The Boy's Champion* (1881–1883), Luis Senarens' Jack Wright (120 stories, 1891–1896), Philip Reade's Tom Edison, Jr. (11 stories, 1891–1892), and Robert Toombs' Electric Bob (5 stories, 1893). Parenthetically, this series of imitations is one of the larger reasons for considering the Edisonade as science fiction. The content of the Edisonade was scientific, of course, and made use of possible extrapolations of current technology. But, more important to critics, the writers of the Edisonades were aware that they were writing something distinct from ordinary fiction. As has been argued elsewhere, it may not be possible for science fiction to have existed as a separate genre before the concept of science fiction was articulated, but the writers of the Edisonades knew that they were writing stories like Ellis' and Senarens', and like Jules Verne's, and not like mainstream fiction writers'. This consciousness of writing in a distinct mode, with accepted tropes and formula, is relevant to discussions of definitions of science fiction, and is why the Edisonade deserves inclusion into the ranks of science fiction.

The Edisonade genre was successful for twenty years, but the changing tastes of the audience and the greater availability of inexpensive reading material doomed it. By 1896 the genre had peaked and was in decline. The dime novel publishers moved away from prolonged serials or stories involving series characters and began publishing shorter series which avoided regularly appearing characters. With the closing of the American frontier the setting for the Edisonade story was forced to shift, and it became the hidden cities of Lost Races (lost, forgotten, or hidden peoples surviving in remote areas long past the time when they died out in reality) and more overtly science fictional environments, such as fictional lands and other planets, rather than real countries.

In the 20th century the Edisonade mutated and split into two parallel (and interbreeding) species. The first variety was the Adult Edisonade. The Adult Edisonade was the Edisonade in mainstream science fiction, written for adults and intended to be consumed by them. Its protagonists were usually adult male inventors, and while the stories retained an America-centric attitude and the politics remained xenophobic, the themes changed. Garrett Serviss' *Edison's Conquest of Mars* (1898) is a recasting of H. G. Wells' *The War of the Worlds*, with Edison replacing the British narrator. In the novel the setting changes from England to Mars, and the accidental triumph of Terran biology over the Martians is replaced by an overt and thorough victory by force of arms, as Edison leads a human fleet to Mars and destroys the Martians. In Cleveland Moffett's *The Conquest of America in 1921* (1915), Edison responds to a German invasion of America by creating technologically advanced torpedoes and sinking the German fleet. The Adult Edisonade is a logical development following the emergence of science fiction for adults, but the Adult Edisonade was also influenced by the work of Jules Verne, who twice wrote proto-Edisonades. In *20,000 Leagues Under the Sea* (1869–1870) and *The Mysterious Island*

(1874–1875) Captain Nemo is a threat in his submarine, the *Nautilus*, and in *Robur the Conqueror* (1886) and *Master of the World* (1904), the mad aerialist inventor Robur threatens the world from his airship. In both cases the premise of the story — man creates machine which he uses as a weapon against the world — provided a template for later Adult Edisonades. But Verne's protagonists are misanthropes and isolationists, quite unlike the expansionist Americans of the dime novel Edisonades. What 20th-century science fiction writers took were the trappings of Verne and the ideology of the Edisonades.

The other version of the Edisonade, which appeared alongside the Adult Edisonade was the juvenile variety, typified by the Tom Swift stories. Created by Edward Stratemeyer and Howard Garis, Swift appeared in thirty novels from 1910 to 1935 and spawned numerous direct imitations from Rick Brant to Tom Swift, Jr. Tom Swift, like Johnny Brainerd and Frank Reade, Jr. before him, is a plucky American boy, but unlike his predecessors Swift has a living father who is an active part of his life. Swift's adventures are, if not benign, far less malign and blood-drenched than Brainerd's, Reade's, and the others, and the innocence of Swift *et al.* is of a humbler and less privileged sort.

The Juvenile Edisonade, while never a major branch of science fiction, has continued on into the present, in modified form, in works like the cartoon *Dexter's Laboratory* and the film and TV series about "Jimmy Neutron: Boy Genius." The Adult Edisonade is somewhat more vital, continuing on in media from comic books to space opera of the more pulpish variety. The Heroic Engineer of pulp science fiction, and his descendants in contemporary science fiction, is in a direct evolutionary line from Verne's work and from the Edisonade.

Steampunk's relationship with the Edisonades is less obvious than that of mainstream science fiction, but as strong. Proto-steampunk works like Clark's *Queen Victoria's Bomb* and Moorcock's *The Warlord of the Air* appeared in the 1960s and 1970s, but steampunk as a full-fledged genre began in the late 1970s and early 1980s when science fiction took a recursive turn and began incorporating themes, motifs, and tropes from its own past to a much greater degree than previously. Cyberpunk emerged as a reaction to and conversation with many of the assumptions and biases of science fiction in the 1940s and 1950s, while space opera, heavily influenced by its pulp origins but altered to reflect the times, gained renewed popularity in the 1980s. For its part steampunk turned to the 19th century and the Victorians — and, consciously or unconsciously, the Edisonades.

The attraction of the surface elements of the Victorians, the trappings and visual style, is obvious, but the 19th century has a further appeal for modern writers. More so than other historical periods, the 19th century, especially the Victorian era (1837–1901), is an excellent mirror for the modern period. The social, economic, and political structures of the Victorian era are essentially the same as our own, and their cultural dynamics — the way in which the culture reacts to various phenomena and stimuli — are quite similar to ours. This makes the Victorian era extremely useful for ideological stories on subjects such as feminism, imperialism, class issues, and religion, as well as for commentary on contemporary issues such as serial murderers and overseas wars. Stories about the way in which women were treated in the Victorian era can easily be written to address how women are treated today, and without the authorial straining of allegorical novels set in previous historical eras.

Historical fiction set in the 19th century often makes use of the era's ability to portray contemporary issues in Victorian garb. Even writers as apparently non-ideological as George MacDonald Fraser and Patrick O'Brian have acute things to say about modern attitudes, and say them to, and via, the Victorians in, respectively, the Flashman and Aubrey & Maturin novels. Steampunk writers do this, and go beyond this, by making steampunk an argument with the science fiction of previous generations — in this, as in other ways, steampunk is cyberpunk's half-brother — and also with the Edisonade.

Few if any of the steampunk writers would have read the Edisonades, and it was only the first generation of steampunk writers, beginning with James Blaylock, K.W. Jeter, and Tim Powers in the late 1970s and ending with Sterling and Gibson's *The Difference Engine* in 1990, who were doing the arguing. Just as second generation cyberpunk writers like Neal Stephenson and Jeff Noon stepped away from cyberpunk as an ideological genre, second generation steampunk authors have changed steampunk from an argument to a style and a pose, even an affectation. But, however unconsciously, first generation steampunk writers used steampunk to invert the ideologies of the Edisonades. Without too much exaggeration this inversion can be compared to what Claude Levi-Strauss described, in his *The Raw and the Cooked* (1970), as an axis of human culture, running from "the raw," the products of nature, to "the cooked," the products of human creation. Cooking, a quintessentially human activity, takes the basic elements and creates a meal, so that civilization is achieved through the act of cooking — or, more abstractly, through refinement, the winnowing out of the unhealthy, the crude, and the wild.

The Edisonade is American. Steampunk, though written by writers of many nationalities, is English. (Even Japanese steampunk anime, like Katsuhiro Otomo's *Steamboy* [2004], is English in its fashions, manner, and style.) The Edisonade is about setting out for the frontier, about exploring new, rural territory, mastering it, despoiling it, and then returning home. First-generation steampunk is an essentially urban genre, usually set in London. The Edisonade is a dynamic genre, the characters always in motion, always traveling, the backdrop changing from scene to scene. Steampunk is often static, limited to London's confines. One of the core assumptions of the Edisonade is that the inventor is larger than his inventions, that man is the master of the machine, that one sufficiently clever and inventive man can conquer, can master, can own. Nothing is beyond the Edisonade inventor's grasp — he has merely to reach for it. The wearied revelation of steampunk — and this is a reaction not just to the Edisonade but to much of 1940s and 1950s science fiction — is that the machinery of society and life is too much for any man to control or master, and that those who reach too far will have their outstretched arms caught in a metaphorical mangler.

The Edisonade's primary characteristics are technological optimism, exploitative capitalism (via the acquisition of wealth that is usually owned by native peoples or exists on their land), juvenile daydreams (the brilliant boy or teenager, with adult men serving him, becomes master of the adult world and is acclaimed and respected), and the vicarious exercise of bigoted wish-fulfillment (a white American defeats the non-white enemies of the United States, inside the borders of the U.S. and outside). But despite these elements, the genre also has a peculiar innocence to it. For all that the Edisonade portrays white boys using advanced technology to kill non-white men and loot their treasure, the Edisonades never betray a sense that there is any blood in the corpses or real pain in their deaths. The Edisonade's audience were children, juveniles, and barely literate young men, and the stories are dreamlike in their lack of logic, rudimentary literary qualities, and crude imagination. And like dreams, the Edisonades never display a consciousness of their own ideology.

Steampunk is a genre aware of its own loss of innocence. Its characters may be innocent in the context of their worlds, but steampunk writers are all too aware of the realities which the Edisonade writers were ignorant of or chose to dismiss. If the worlds of the steampunk writers are not dystopian, they are polluted, cynical, and hard, quite unlike the clean and simple worlds of the Edisonades. Accompanying this lack of innocence is an anger and a rebellion against much of what the Edisonade's stood for. (Hence the "punk" half of "steampunk.") The Edisonade is a propagandist genre, beating its drums for America, for geographical expansion, for manifest destiny, for the theft of other people's (singular and plural) property. The boy inventor is no rebel or outsider; he is what capitalism approves of and validates, the robber baron in larval form.

Steampunk, like all good punk, rebels against the system it portrays (Victorian London or something quite like it), critiquing its treatment of the underclass, its validation of the privileged at the cost of everyone else, its lack of mercy, its cutthroat capitalism. Like the punks, steampunk rarely offers a solution to the problems it decries — for steampunk, there is no solution — but for both punk and steampunk the criticism must be made before the change can come. The Edisonades could not have conceived of steampunk. Steampunk is well aware of the Edisonade boy inventor, and kills him, as villains must be killed, by the end of the story.

It might be objected that the preceding only holds true for first generation steampunk, and that much or even most second generation steampunk isn't primarily English, urban, static, or melancholy. But most second generation steampunk is not true steampunk — there is little to nothing "punk" about it. The politics of the punk position have largely disappeared from second generation steampunk, and most of it is more accurately described as "steam sci-fi" or, following John Clute, "gaslight romance." The authors of the Edisonades would have loathed first generation steampunk, but they would have approved of second generation steampunk, with its steam machines used against the American natives in Westerns, and steam-powered war machines being used in the service of the British army conquering Mars. (In that sense steampunk has returned to its roots.) This abandonment of ideology is an evolution (or, less charitably, an emasculation) that is inevitable once a subgenre becomes established — witness how cyberpunk went from a dystopic critique of multinational capitalism to a fashion statement and literary cliché. But its loss is nonetheless to be mourned.

Benediction:
Excerpt from *The Warlord of the Air*

MICHAEL MOORCOCK

Considered one of the godfathers of steampunk for his 1970s explorations of Victoriana involving all sorts of airships, Michael Moorcock's *The
Warlord of the Air*, excerpted here, puts the reader right into the action,
envisioning an alternative British Empire in conflict with the world. It's hard
to gauge the influence of any one novel or author, but we can't help but
think Moorcock's work must have been in the minds of many of those for-
mally labeled "steampunks" in the 1980s.

I THOUGHT AT FIRST that I saw a massive bank of black cloud moving
over the horizon of the hills and blotting out the pale sunshine. With
the cloud came a great thrumming sound, like many deep-voiced
gongs being beaten rapidly in unison. The sound grew louder as the
cloud began to fill the whole sky, casting a dark and ominous shadow
over the Valley of the Morning.

It was the allied air fleet of five nations.

Each ship was a thousand feet long. Each had a hull as strong as
steel. Each bristled with artillery and great grenades which could be
dropped upon their enemies. Each ship moved implacably through
the sky, keeping pace with its mighty fellows. Each was dedicated to
exacting fierce vengeance upon the upstarts who had sought to question the power of those it served. A shoal of monstrous flying sharks,
confident that they controlled the skies and, from the skies, the land.

Ships of Japan, with the Imperial crimson sun emblazoned on their
white and gleaming hulls.

Ships of Russia, with great black double-headed eagles glaring from
hulls of deepest scarlet, claws spread as if to strike.

Ships of France, on which the tricolour flag spread on backgrounds of blue was a piece of blatant hypocrisy; a sham of republicanism and an affront to the ideals of the French Revolution.

Ships of America, bearing the Stars and Stripes, no longer the banner of Liberty.

Ships of Britain.

Ships with cannon and bombs and crews who, in their pride, thought it was to be a simple matter to raze Dawn City and what it stood for.

Shark-ships, rapacious and cruel and arrogant, their booming engines like triumphant anticipatory laughter.

Could we withstand them, even for an instant? I doubted it.

Now our ground defenses had opened up. Shells sped into the sky and exploded around the ships of the mighty air fleet, but on they came, through the smoke and flame, careless and haughty, closer and closer to Dawn City itself. And now our tiny fleet began to rise from the air-park to meet the invaders — fifteen modified merchantmen against a hundred specially designed men-o'-war. They had the advantage of the recoilless guns and could "stand" in the air and shoot much longer and more accurately than the larger vessels, but there were few weak points on those flying ironclads and most of the explosive shells at worst only blackened the paint of the hulls or cracked the windows in the gondolas.

There was a bellow and fire sprouted from the leading British air-ship, HMAS *Edwardus Rex,* as its guns answered ours. I saw the hull of one of our ships crumple and the whole vessel plunge towards the rocky ground of the foothills, little figures leaping overboard in the hope of somehow escaping the worst of the impact. Black smoke curled everywhere over the scene. There came an explosion and a blaze of flame as the ship struck the ground and its engines blew up, the fuel oil igniting instantly.

Shaw was staring grimly through the window, controlling the formation of his ships through a wireless telephone. How hard it had been to make an impact on the enemy fleet — and how easily they had destroyed our ship!

Boom! Boom!

Again the great guns roared. Again an adapted merchantman buckled in the air and sank to the earth.

Only now did I wish that I had accepted a commission on one of the ships. Only now did I feel the urge to join the fight, to retaliate, as much as anything, out of a spirit of fair play.

Boom!

It was the *Rover*, spiraling down with two engines on fire and its hull buckling in half as the helium rushed into the atmosphere. I watched tensely as it fell, praying there would be enough gas left in the hull to let the ship come down relatively lightly. But that was a hundred tons of metal and plastic and guns and men falling through the sky. I closed my eyes and winced as I thought I felt the tremor of its impact with the ground.

I was in no doubt of Korzeniowski's fate.

But then, as if inspired by the old captain's heroic death, the *Shantien* (the *Loch Etive*) offered a broadside to the Japanese flagship, the *Yokomoto*, and must have struck right through to her ammunition store for she exploded in a thousand fiery fragments and there was scarcely a recognizable scrap of her left when the explosion had died.

Now we saw two more ships go down — an American and a French — and we cheered. We all cheered save for Una Persson who was looking bleakly out at the spot where the *Rover* had disappeared. Von Bek was in animated conversation with the major and did not seem to notice his mistress's grief. I went over to her and touched her shoulder.

"Perhaps he is only wounded," I said.

She smiled at me through her tears and shook her head. "He is dead," she said. "He died bravely, didn't he?"

"As he lived," I said.

She seemed puzzled. "I thought you hated him."

"I thought I did. But I loved him."

She pulled herself together at this and nodded, putting out a slender hand and letting the tips of the fingers rest for a moment on my sleeve. "Thank you, Mr. Bastable. I hope my father has not died for nothing."

"We are giving a good account of ourselves," I said.

But I saw that we had at most five ships left from the original fifteen and there were still nearly ninety allied battleships in the sky.

Shaw looked up, listening carefully. "Infantry and motorized cavalry attacking the valley on all sides," he said. "Our men are standing firm." He listened a little longer. "I don't think we've much to fear from that quarter at the moment."

The invading ships had not yet reached Dawn City. They had been forced to defend themselves against our first aerial attack and, now that our gunners were getting their range from the ground, one or two more were hit.

"Time to send up the *Fei-chi*, I think." Shaw telephoned the order. "The Great Powers think they have won! Now we shall show them our real strength!" He telephoned the soldiers defending the building housing Project NFB and reminded them that on no account should a ship be allowed to attack the place. The mysterious project was evidently of paramount importance in his strategy.

I could not see the hangars where the "hornets" were stored and my first glimpse of the winged and whirling little flying machines was when they climbed through the black smoke and began to spray the hulls of the flying ironclads with explosive bullets, attacking from above and diving down on their opponents who, doubtless, were still hardly aware of what was happening.

The *Victoria Imperatrix* went down. The *Theodore Roosevelt* went down. The *Alexandre Nevsky* went down. The *Tashiyawa* went down. The *Emperor Napoleon* and the *Pyat* went down. One after another they fell from the air, circling slowly or breaking up rapidly, but falling; without a doubt they were falling. And it did not seem that a single delicate *Fei-chi*, flown by only two men — an aviator and a gunner — had been hit. The guns of the foreign ships were simply not designed to hit such tiny targets. They roared and belched their huge shells in all directions, but they were baffled, like clumsy sea-cows attacked by sharp-toothed piranha fish, they simply did not know how to defend themselves. The Valley of the Morning was littered with their wreckage. A thousand fires burned in the hills, showing where the proud aerial ironclads had met their end. Half the allied fleet had been destroyed and five of our airships (including the *Shan-tien*) were now coming in to moor, leaving the fighting to the *Fei-chi*. Evidently the shock of facing the tiny heavier-than-air machines was too much for the attackers. They had seen their finest ships blown from the skies in a matter of minutes. Slowly the cumbersome men-o'-war turned and began to retreat. Not a single bomb had fallen on Dawn City.

Lord Kelvin's Machine

JAMES P. BLAYLOCK

James P. Blaylock was one of the original members of the steampunk movement as labeled by K. W. Jeter in the 1980s. His "Lord Kelvin's Machine," later expanded into a novel, may be the quintessential steampunk story, with its combination of darkness and diabolical invention and cosmic scope. A delight to read, it also displays Blaylock's signature style, both subtle and entertaining.

PROLOGUE
South America

Langdon St. Ives, scientist and explorer, clutched a heavy alpaca blanket about his shoulders and stared out across countless miles of rocky plateau and jagged volcanic peaks. The tight weave of ivory wool clipped off a dry, chill wind that blew across the fifty miles of Antarctic-spawned Peruvian Coastal Current, up from the Bay of Guayaquil, and across the Pacific slope of the Peruvian Andes. A wide and sluggish river, grey-green beneath the lowering sky, crept across broad grasslands behind and below him. Moored like an alien vessel amid the bunch grasses and tola bush was a tiny zeppelin, silver in the afternoon sun and flying the Union Jack from a jury-rigged mast.

At St. Ives' feet the scree-strewn rim of a volcanic cone, Mt. Ocapaxi, fell two thousand feet toward steamy, open fissures, the entire crater glowing like the bowl of an enormous pipe. St. Ives waved ponderously to his companion Hasbro, his gentleman's gentleman, actually, who crouched some hundred yards down the slope on the interior of the cone, working the compression mechanism of a Rawls-Hibbing Mechanical Bladder. Coils of India rubber hose snaked away, disappearing into cracks in the igneous skin of the mountainside.

A cloud of fierce, sulphur-laced steam whirled suddenly up and out of the crater in a wild, sighing rush, and the red glow of the twisted fissures winked abruptly out, replaced by misty darkness. St. Ives nodded, satisfied, and consulted a pocketwatch. His left shoulder, recently grazed by a bullet, throbbed tiredly. It was late afternoon. Long shadows cast by scattered, distant peaks obscured the hillsides roundabout. On the heels of the shadows would come darkness.

The figure below ceased his furious manipulations of the contrivance and signaled to St. Ives, whereupon the scientist turned and repeated the signal — a broad, windmill gesture, visible to the several thousand Indians massed on the plain below. "Sharp's the word, Jacky," muttered St. Ives under his breath. And straightaway, thin and sailing on the knife-edged wind, came a half dozen faint syllables, first in English, then repeated in Quechua, then giving way to the resonant cadence of almost five thousand people marching in step. He could feel the rhythmic reverberations beneath his feet as he turned, bent over, and, mouthing a quick, silent prayer, depressed the plunger of a tubular detonator.

He threw himself flat and pressed an ear to the cold ground. The rumble of marching feet rolled through the hillsides like the sound of an approaching express or the rushing passage of a subterranean river. Then, abruptly, a deep and vast explosion, muffled by the crust of the Earth itself, heaved the ground in a tumultuous wave, and it appeared to St. Ives from his aerie atop the volcano as if the grassland below were a giant carpet and that the gods were shaking the dust from it. The marching horde pitched higgledy-piggledy into one another and collapsed all of a heap. The stars in the eastern sky seemed to dance briefly, as if the Earth had been jiggled from her course. Then, slowly, the ground ceased to shake.

St. Ives smiled for the first time in nearly a week. His man Hasbro strode up the hillside toward him carrying the Rawls-Hibbing apparatus, and together they watched the sky deepen from blue to purple, cut by the pale radiance of the milky way. On the horizon glowed a misty semi-circle of radiance like a lantern hooded with muslin — the first faint glimmer of an ascending comet.

CHAPTER 1
Dover

The tumbled rocks of Castle Jetty loomed black and wet in the fog. Below, where the grey tide of the North Sea fell inch by inch away, green tufts of waterweed alternately danced and collapsed across barnacled stone, and brown penny-crabs scuttled through dark crevices as if their sidewise scramble would render them invisible to the men who stood above. Langdon St. Ives, wrapped in a greatcoat and shod in hip boots, cocked a telescoped spyglass to his eye and squinted north toward the Eastern Docks.

The mist swirled and flew, now covering the sea and sky in an opaque grey-green curtain, now tearing itself into transparent lace. There, some hundred-fifty meters distant, the steamer H.M.S. *Ramsgate* heaved on the groundswell, its handful of paying passengers having hours since wended their way shoreward toward one of the inns along Castle Hill Road — all the passengers, that is, but one. St. Ives felt as if he'd stood atop the rocks for a lifetime, watching nothing at all but an empty ship.

He lowered the glass and gazed down into the sea. It took an act of will to believe that beyond the strait lay Belgium and that behind him, a bowshot distant, lay the city of Dover. He was overcome suddenly with the uncanny certainty that the jetty was moving, that he stood on the bow of a sailing vessel plying the waters of a phantom sea. The rushing tide below him bent and swirled around the edges of thrusting rocks, and for a perilous second he felt himself pitch forward, nearly flinging the glass away and tumbling headfirst from his perch.

A firm hand grasped his shoulder and the vertigo passed. He caught himself, straightened, and wiped beaded moisture from his forehead with the sleeve of his coat. "Thank you."

"Certainly, sir. Steady-on, sir."

"I've reached the limits of my patience, Hasbro," said St. Ives to the man beside him. "I'm convinced we're watching an empty ship. Our man has given us the slip, and I'd sooner have a look at the inside of a glass of ale than another look at that damned steamer."

"Patience is its own reward, sir," replied St. Ives' manservant.

St. Ives gave him a look. "My patience must be thinner than yours." He pulled a pouch from the pocket of his greatcoat, extracting a bent bulldog pipe and a quantity of tobacco. "Do you suppose Kraken has given up?" He pressed the curly black tobacco into the pipe bowl with his thumb and struck a match, the flame hissing and sputtering in the misty evening air.

"Not Kraken, sir, if I'm any judge. If our man went ashore along the docks, then Kraken followed him. A disguise wouldn't answer, not with that hump. And it's an even bet that he wouldn't be away to London, not this late in the evening. For my money he's in a public house and Kraken's in the street outside. If he made away north, then Jack's got him, and the outcome is the same. The best — "

"Hark!"

Silence fell, interrupted only by the sighing of wavelets splashing against the stones of the jetty and by the hushed clatter of distant activity along the docks. The two men stood barely breathing, smoke from St. Ives' pipe rising invisibly into the fog. "There!" whispered St. Ives, holding up his left hand.

Softly, too rhythmically to be mistaken for the natural cadence of the ocean, came the muted dipping of oars and the creak of shafts in oarlocks. St. Ives crouched, then stepped gingerly across to an adjacent rock and clambered down into a little crab-infested grotto. He could just discern, through a sort of triangular window, the thin grey line where the sky met the sea. And there, pulling into view, was a long rowboat in which sat two men, one plying the oars and the other crouched on a thwart, wrapped in a dark blanket and with a frazzle of black hair dropping in moist curls around his shoulders.

"It's him," whispered Hasbro into St. Ives' ear.

"That it is. And up to no good at all. He's bound for Hargreaves', or I'm a fool. We were right about this one. That eruption in Natvik was no eruption at all. It was a detonation. And now the task is unspeakably complicated. I'm half inclined to let the monster have a go at it, Hasbro. I'm weary of this world of late." St. Ives paused tiredly, the rowboat having disappeared into the fog, the night having drifted into silence.

"There's the matter of the ale glass," said Hasbro wisely, grasping St. Ives by the elbow. "And a kidney pie, unless I'm amiss, is required. We'll fetch in Bill Kraken and Jack on the way. We've time enough to stroll 'round to Hargreaves' after supper."

St. Ives squinted at Hasbro, as if suddenly bucked by the idea of a pie and a glass of ale. "Of course we do," he said. "I might send you lads out tonight alone, though. I need about ten hours of the best to bring me around. Sleep, that's the tune the piper's playing. In the morning I'll wrestle with these demons."

"There's the ticket, sir," said the stalwart Hasbro, and through the gathering gloom the two men picked their way from rock to rock toward the warm lights of Dover.

"I can't imagine I've ever been this hungry before," said St. Ives, spearing up a pair of rashers from a passing platter. "Any more eggs?"

"Heaps," said Bill Kraken through a mouthful of cold toast, and he reached for another platter at his elbow. "Full of the right sorts of humors, sir, is eggs. It's the unctuous secretions of the yolk that fetches the home stake, if you follow me. Loaded up with all manners of fluids."

Jack Owlesby paused, a forkful of egg halfway to his mouth. He gave Kraken a look and cleared his throat.

"Sorry, lad. There's no stopping me when I'm swept off by the scientific. I've forgot that you ain't partial to the talk of fluids over breakfast. Not that it matters a bit about fluids or any of the rest of it, what with that comet sailing in to smash us to flinders — "

"Harrumph!" coughed St. Ives, seeming to choke, his fit drowning the last few words of Kraken's observation. "Lower your voice, man!"

"Sorry, Professor. I don't think sometimes. You know me. This coffee tastes like rat poison, don't it? And not high-toned rat poison either, but something mixed up by your man with the hump."

"I haven't tried it," said St. Ives, raising his cup. He peered into the depths of the dark stuff and was reminded instantly of the murky water in the night-shrouded tidepool he'd slipped into on his way back from the tip of the jetty the night before. He didn't need to taste the brew; the smell of it was enough. "Any of the tablets?" he asked Hasbro.

"I brought several of each, sir. It doesn't pay to go abroad without them. One would think that the art of brewing coffee would have traveled the few miles from the Normandy coast-to the British Isles, sir, but we all know it hasn't." He reached into the pocket of his coat and pulled out a little vial of jellybean-like pills. "Jamaican Blue, sir?"

"If you would," said St. Ives.

Hasbro dropped one into the upheld cup, and in an instant the room was filled with the astonishing, heavy aroma of real coffee, the odd chemical smell of the pallid facsimile in the rest of their cups retreating before it.

"By God!" whispered Kraken. "What else have you got there?"

"A tolerable Weiner Melange, sir, and a Mocha Java that I can vouch for. There's an espresso, too, but it's untried as yet."

"Then I'm your man!" cried the enthusiastic Kraken, and he held out his hand for the little pill. "There's money in these," he said, plopping it into his full cup and watching the result as if mystified. "Millions of pounds."

"Art for art's sake," laughed St. Ives, dipping the end of a white kerchief into his cup and studying the stained corner of it in the thin sunlight shining through the casement. He nodded, satisfied, then tasted the coffee, nodding again. He bent over his plate and addressed Bill Kraken, although his words, clearly, were intended for the assembled company. "We mustn't, Bill, give in to fears about this...this...heavenly visitation, to lapse into metaphysical language. I woke up fresh this morning. A new man. And the solution, I discovered, was in front of my face. I'd been given it by the very villain we pursue. Our only real enemy now is time, gentlemen, time and the excesses of our own fears."

St. Ives paused to have another go at the coffee, then squinted past his cup and resumed his speech. "The single greatest catastrophe now would be for the news to leak to the general public. The man in the street would dissolve into chaos if he knew what confronted him. Let us take a lesson in reverse from the otherwise admirable tale of Mr. H. G. Wells. His science was, I fear, awash with error, but that was no real fault of his. He was a literary man first, and a scientist afterward. But he was fearfully wide of the mark in underestimating the common man's susceptibility to panic." St. Ives stroked his chin, staring at the debris on his plate. "I'm certain that science will save us this time, gentlemen, if it doesn't kill us first. The thing will be close, though, and if the public gets wind, great damage will come of it." He smiled into the befuddled faces of his three companions. Kraken wiped a dribble of egg from the edge of his mouth. Jack pursed his lips.

"I'll need to know about Hargreaves," continued St. Ives, "and you'll want to know what I'm blathering about. But this isn't the place. Let's adjourn to the street, shall we?" And with that the men arose, Kraken tossing off the last of his coffee. Then, seeing that Jack was leaving half a cup, he tossed Jack's off too and mumbled something about waste and starvation as he followed the rest toward the door.

Doctor Ignacio Narbondo grinned over his tea. He watched the back of Hargreaves' head as it nodded above a great sheet of paper covered over with lines, numbers, and notations. Why oxygen allowed itself to flow in and out of the man's lungs Narbondo couldn't at all say; the man seemed to be animated by hatred — an indiscriminate loathing for the most innocent things. He gladly built bombs for idiotic anarchist deviltry, not out of any particular regard for causes, but simply to create mayhem, to blow things to bits.

If he could have built a device sufficiently large to obliterate the Dover cliffs and the sun rising beyond them he'd do it without hesitation. He loathed tea. He loathed eggs. He loathed brandy. He loathed the very art of constructing infernal devices.

Narbondo looked round him at the barren room, the lumpy pallet on the ground where Hargreaves allowed himself a few hours miserable sleep, as often as not to lurch awake at night, a shriek half uttered in his throat, as if he'd peered into a mirror and seen the face of a beetle staring back. Narbondo whistled merrily all of a sudden, watching Hargreaves stiffen, loathing the melody that had broken the discordant mumblings of his brain.

Hargreaves turned, his bearded face set in a rictus of twisted rage, his dark, shrunken eyes blank as eclipsed moons. He breathed heavily. Narbondo waited with raised eyebrows, as if surprised at the man's reaction. "Damn a man that whistles," said Hargreaves slowly, running the back of his hand across his mouth. He looked at his hand, expecting to find Lord knew what, and turned slowly back to his benchtop. Ignacio Narbondo smiled and poured himself another cup of tea. All in all it was a glorious day. Hargreaves had agreed to help him destroy the Earth with out so much as a second thought. He'd agreed with a certain amount of relish, in fact had expended a moment's effort to twist his face into a contorted smile. Why he didn't just slit his throat and be done with life for good and all was one of the first great mysteries of the twentieth century.

He wouldn't have been half so agreeable if he knew that Narbondo had no intention of destroying anything, that his motivation was greed

—greed and revenge. His threat to cast the Earth forcibly into the path of the approaching comet wouldn't be taken lightly. There were those in the Royal Academy who knew he could do it, who supposed, no doubt, that he might quite likely do it. They were as foolish as Hargreaves and every bit as useful.

The surprising internal eruption of Mt. Hjarstaad would throw the fear into them. They'd be quaking over their rashers at that very moment, the lot of them wondering and gaping. Beards would be wagging. Dark suspicions would be mouthed. Where was the doctor? Had he been seen in London? Not for months. He'd threatened this, hadn't he?—an eruption above the Arctic Circle, just to demonstrate the seriousness of his intent. The comet would pass close enough to the Earth to provide a spectacular display for the masses—foolish creatures. The iron core of the thing might easily be pulled so solidly by the Earth's magnetic field that the comet would hurtle groundward, slamming the poor old Earth into powder and all the gaping multitudes with it. What if, Narbondo had suggested, what if a man were to give the Earth a bit of a push, to propel it even closer to the approaching star and so turn a longshot into a dead cert, as a blade of the turf might put it?

Well, Dr. Ignacio Narbondo was that man. Could he do it? Narbondo grinned. His demands of two weeks past had been met with a sneer, but Mt. Hjarstaad would wipe the sneers from their faces. They'd wax grave. Their grins would set like plaster of Paris. What had the poet said about that sort of thing? "Gravity was a mysterious carriage of the body to cover the defects of the mind."

That was it. Gravity would answer for a day or two, but when it faded into futility they'd pay, and pay well. Narbondo set in to whistle again, this time out of the innocence of good cheer, but the effect on Hargreaves was so immediately consumptive and maddening that Narbondo gave it off abruptly. There was no use baiting the man into ruination before the job was done.

Wiping the lanky hair from his eyes and reaching for his coat, Dr. Narbondo rose and stepped silently from the room, carrying his teacup with him. On the morning street outside he smiled maliciously at an orange sun that burned through evaporating fog, then threw the dregs of his tea, cup and all, over a vine-draped stone wall and strode away east up Archcliffe Road, composing in his mind a letter to the Royal Academy.

—❖—

"Damn me!" mumbled Bill Kraken through the fingers mashed against his mouth. He wiped away furiously at the tea leaves and tea that ran down his neck and collar. The cup that had hit him on the ear had fallen and broken on the stones of the garden. He peered up over the wall at the retreating figure of the hunchback and added this last unintended insult to the list of villainies he'd suffered over the years. He'd have his turn yet.

Why St. Ives hadn't given him leave to merely beat the capers out of this devil Hargreaves he couldn't at all fathom. The man was a monster; there was no gainsaying it. They could set off one of his own devices — hoist him on his own filthy petard, so to speak. His remains would be found amid the wreckage of infernal machines, built with his own hands. The world would have owed Bill Kraken a debt. But Narbondo, St. Ives had insisted, would have found another willing accomplice. Hargreaves was only a pawn, and pawns could be dealt with easily enough when the time came. St. Ives couldn't afford to tip his hand.

Kraken crouched out from behind the wall and slipped away in Narbondo's wake, keeping to the other side of the road when the hunchback entered a stationer's, then circling round to the back when Narbondo went in at the post office door. Stepping through a dark, arched rear entry, a ready lie on his lips in case he were confronted, Kraken found himself in a tiny, deserted room. He slid behind a convenient heap of crates, peeping through slats at an enormously fat, stooped man who lumbered in, tossed Narbondo's letter into a wooden bin, and lumbered back out. Kraken snatched up the letter, tucked it into his coat, and in a moment was back in the sunlight, prying at the stickum with his index finger. Ten minutes later he was in at the front door of the post office, grinning into the wide face of the postman, and mailing Narbondo's missive for the second time that morning.

"Surely it's a bluff," said Jack Owlesby, scowling at Langdon St. Ives. The four of them sat on lawn chairs in the Gardens, listening with half an ear to the lackluster tootings of a tired orchestra. What would it profit him to alert the *Times*? There'd be mayhem. If it's extortion he's after, this won't further his hopes by an inch."

"The threat of it might," replied St. Ives. "If his promise to pitch the Earth into the path of the comet weren't taken seriously, the mere suggestion that the public be apprised of the magnetic affinity of the comet and the Earth might be. It's pale in comparison; I grant you that. But the panic that would ensue if an ably stated message were to reach the right journalist..."

St. Ives paused and shook his head, as if such panic wasn't to be contemplated. "What was the name of that scoundrel who leaked the news of the alien threat four years ago?"

"Beezer, sir," said Hasbro. "He's still in the employ of the *Times*, and, we must suppose, no less likely to be in communication with the doctor today than he was then. He'd be your man, sir, if you wanted to wave the bloody shirt."

"I rather believe," said St. Ives, grimacing at the raucous climax of an unidentifiable bit of orchestration, "that we should pay this man Beezer a visit. We can't do a thing sitting around Dover. Narbondo has agreed to wait four days for a reply from the Academy. There's no reason to believe that he won't keep his word — he's got nothing to gain by haste. The comet, after all, is ten days off. We've got to suppose that he means just what he claims. Evil begets idiocy, gentlemen, and there is no earthly way to tell how far down the path into degeneration our doctor has trod. The next train to London, Hasbro?"

"Two-forty-five, sir."

"We'll be aboard her."

CHAPTER 2
London and Harrogate

The Bayswater Club, owned by the Royal Academy of Sciences, sat across from Kensington Gardens, commanding a view of trimmed lawns and roses and cleverly pruned trees. St. Ives peered out the window on the second floor of the club, satisfied with what he saw. The sun loomed like an orange just below the zenith, and the radiant heat glancing through the geminate windows of the club felt almost alive. The April weather was so altogether pleasant that it came near to making up for the fearful lunch that would at any moment arrive to stare at St. Ives from a china plate. He'd attempted a bit of cheerful banter with the stony-faced waiter, ordering dirt cutlets and beer, but the man hadn't seen the humor in it. What he had seen had been evident on his face.

St. Ives sighed and wished heartily that he was taking the sun along with the multitudes in the park, but the thought that a week hence there mightn't be any park at all — or any multitudes either — sobered him, and he drained the bottom half of a glass of claret. He regarded the man seated across from him. Parsons, the ancient secretary of the Royal Academy, spooned up broth with an enthusiasm that left St. Ives tired. Floating on the surface of the broth were what appeared to be twisted little bugs, but which must have been some sort of Oriental mushroom sprinkled on by a chef with a sense of humor. Parsons chased them with his spoon.

"So you've nothing at all to fear," said Parsons, dabbing at his chin with a napkin. He grinned at St. Ives in a satisfied way, as if proud of himself. "The greatest minds in the scientific world are at work on the problem. The comet will sail past us with no commotion whatsoever. It's a matter of electromagnetic forces, really. The comet might easily be drawn to the Earth, unless, of course, the Earth's magnetic field were forcibly suspended."

"Suspended?"

"It's not unknown to have happened. Common knowledge has it that the magnetic poles have reversed themselves any number of times, and that during the interim between the establishing of new poles, the Earth was blessedly free of any electromagnetic field whatsoever. I'm surprised that a physicist such as yourself has to be informed of such a thing." Parsons peered at St. Ives over the top of his pince-nez, then fished up out of his broth a tendril of unidentifiable vegetable. St. Ives gaped at it. "Kelp," said the secretary, slathering the dripping weed into his mouth and chomping away lustily.

St. Ives nodded, a shiver running up along his spine. The pink chicken breast that lay beneath wilted lettuce on his plate began, suddenly, to fill him with a curious sort of dread. His lunches with Parsons at the Bayswater Club invariably went so. The secretary was always one up on him, simply because of the food. "So what, exactly, do you intend? To *hope* such an event into existence?"

"Not at all," said Parsons smugly. "We're building a device."

"A device?"

"To reverse the polarity of the Earth, thereby negating any natural affinity the Earth might have for the comet and vice versa."

"Impossible," said St. Ives, a kernel of doubt and fear beginning to sprout within him.

"Hardly." Parsons waved his fork with an air of gaiety, then scratched the end of his nose with it. "No less a personage than Lord Kelvin himself is at work on it, although the theoretical basis of the thing was entirely a product of James Clerk Maxwell. Maxwell's sixteen equations in tensor calculus demonstrated a good bit beyond the idea that gravity is merely a form of electromagnetism. But his conclusions, taken altogether, had such terrible and far-reaching side implications that they were never published. Lord Kelvin, of course, has access to them. And I think that we have little to fear that, in such benevolent hands, Maxwell's discoveries will lead to anything but scientific advancement. To more, actually — to the temporary reversal of the poles, as I said, and the switching off, as it were, of any currents that would attract our comet. Trust us, sir. This threat, as you call it, is a threat no more."

St. Ives sat silently for a moment, wondering if any objections would penetrate into Parsons' head past the crunching of vegetation. Quite likely not, but he had to try. Two days earlier when he'd assured his friends in Dover that they'd easily come across Ignacio Narbondo, he hadn't bargained on this. Was it possible that the clever contrivances of Lord Kelvin and the Royal Academy would constitute a graver threat than that posed by the hunchbacked doctor? It wasn't to be thought of. Yet here was Parsons, full of talk about reversing the polarity of the Earth. St. Ives was duty bound to speak. He seemed to find himself continually at odds with his peers.

"Have you read the works of young Rutherford?"

"Pinwinnie Rutherford of Edinburgh?"

"Ernest Rutherford. Of New Zealand. I ran across him in Canada. He's done some interesting work in the area of light rays, if you can call them that." St. Ives wiggled loose a thread of chicken, carried the morsel halfway to his mouth, looked at it, and changed his mind. "There's some indication that alpha and beta rays from the sun slide away along the Earth's magnetic field, arriving harmlessly at the poles. It seems likely, at a hasty glance, that without the field they'd sail in straightaway—we'd be bathed in radioactivity. The most frightful mutations might occur. It has been my pet theory, in fact, that the dinosaurs were laid low in precisely that same fashion — that their demise was a consequence of the reversal of the poles and the inherent cessation of the magnetic field."

Parsons shrugged.

"All of this *is* theory, of course. But the comet is eight days away, and *that's* not at all theory. It's an enormous chunk of iron that threatens to smash us into jelly. From your chair across the table it's easy enough to fly in the face of the Academy, but I'm afraid, sir, that Lord Kelvin will get along very well without you — he has in the past."

"There's a better way," said St. Ives simply. It was useless to lose one's temper over Parsons' practiced stubbornness.

"Oh?" said the secretary.

"Ignacio Narbondo, I believe, has showed it to us."

Parsons dropped his spoon onto his lap and launched into a choking fit. St. Ives held up a constraining hand. "I'm very much aware of his threats, I assure you. And they're not idle threats, either. Do you propose to pay him?"

"I'm constrained from discussing it."

"He'll do what he claims. He's taken the first steps already."

"What has this to do with your 'better way'?"

"He intends, if I read him correctly, to effect the stoppage of certain very active volcanoes in arctic Scandinavia via the introduction of petrifacting catalysts into open fissures and dykes. The subsequent detonation of an explosive charge would lead to the eruption of a chain of volcanic mountains that rise above the jungles of Amazonian Peru. The entrapped energy expended by such an upheaval would, he hopes, cast us like a Chinese rocket into the course of the comet."

"Given the structure of the interior of the Earth," said Parsons, grinning into his mineral water, "it seems a dubious undertaking at best. Perhaps — "

"Are you familiar with hollow Earth theory?"

Parsons blinked at St. Ives. The corners of his mouth twitched.

"Specifically with the work of McClung-Jones of the Quebec Geological Mechanics Institute? The 'thin-crust phenomenon'?"

Parsons shook his head tiredly.

"It's possible," said St. Ives, "that Narbondo's detonation will effect a series of eruptions in volcanoes residing in the hollow core of the Earth. The stupendous inner-Earth pressures would themselves trigger an eruption at Jones' thin-crust point."

"Thin-crust point?" asked Parsons in a plonking tone.

"The very Peruvian mountains toward which our man Narbondo has cast the glad eye!"

"That's an interesting notion," muttered Parsons, coughing into his napkin. He stared out the window, blinking his eyes ponderously, as if satisfied that St. Ives had concluded his speech.

"What I propose," said St. Ives, pressing on, "is to thwart Narbondo, and then effect the same thing, only in reverse — to propel the Earth temporarily out of her orbit in a long arc that would put the comet beyond her grasp. If the calculations were fined down sufficiently — and I can assure you that they have been — we'd simply slide back into orbit some few thousand miles farther along our ellipse, a pittance in the eyes of the incalculable distances of our journeying through the void."

St. Ives sat back and fished in his coat for a cigar. Here was the Royal Academy, unutterably fearful of the machinations of Ignacio Narbondo — certain, that is, that the doctor was not talking, as it were, through his hat. If they could trust to Narbondo to destroy the Earth through volcanic manipulation, then they could quite clearly trust St. Ives to save it by the same means. What was good for the goose, after all... St. Ives took a breath and continued. "There's been some study of the disastrous effects of in-step marching on bridges and platforms — military study mostly. My own theory, which abets Narbondo's, would make use of such study, of the resonant energy expended by a troop of synchronized marchers..."

Parsons grimaced and shook his head slowly. He wasn't prepared to admit anything about the doings of the nefarious doctor. And St. Ives' theories, although fascinating, were of little use to them here. Then there was this man Jones. Hadn't he been involved in certain ghastly lizard experiments in the forests of New Hampshire? "Very ugly incident, that one," Parsons muttered sadly. "One of your hollow Earth men, wasn't he? Had a lot of Mesozoic reptiles dummied up at a waxworks in Boston, as I recall, and insisted he'd found them sporting in some bottomless cavern or another." Parsons squinted shrewdly at St. Ives. It was real science that they'd ordered up here. Humanity cried out for it, didn't they? Wasn't Lord Kelvin at that very moment riveting together the carcass of the device that Parsons had described? Hadn't St. Ives been listening? Parsons shrugged. Discussions with St. Ives were always — how should one put it? — revealing. But St. Ives had gotten in out of his depth this time, and Parsons' advice was to strike out at once for shore — a hearty breaststroke so as not to tire himself unduly. He patted St. Ives on the sleeve, waving the wine decanter at him. St. Ives nodded and watched the secretary fill his glass to within a centimeter of the top. There was no arguing with the man. And it wasn't argument that was wanted now anyway. It was action.

The manor house and laboratory of Langdon St. Ives sat some three quarters of a mile from the summer house of William Thomson, Lord Kelvin. The River Nidd ran placid and slow between, slicing neatly in two the broad meadow that separated the grounds of the manor from the grounds of the summer house. The willows that lined the banks of the Nidd effected a rolling, green cloudbank that almost obscured each house from the view of the other, but from St. Ives' attic window, Lord Kelvin's broad, low barn was just visible atop a grassy knoll. In and out of that barn trooped a platoon of white-coated scientists and grimed machinists. Covered wagons scoured along the High Road from Kirk Hammerton, bearing enigmatic mechanical apparatus, and were met at the gates by a man in military fatigues, who poked his head in under tarpaulins in search, perhaps, for unwelcome sightseers or for agents of Doctor Ignacio Narbondo.

St. Ives watched their comings and goings through his spyglass. He turned a grim eye on Hasbro, who stood silently behind him. "I've come to a difficult decision, Hasbro."

"Yes, sir."

"I've decided that we must play the role of saboteur, and nothing less. I shrink from such deviltry, but far more is at stake here than honor. We must ruin, somehow, Lord Kelvin's machine."

"Very good, sir."

"Doing so, of course, necessitates not only carrying out the plan to manipulate the volcanoes, but implies utter faith in that plan. Here we are setting in to thwart the effort of one of the greatest living practical scientists and to substitute our own feeble designs in its stead — an act of monumental egotism."

"As you say, sir."

"But the stakes are high, Hasbro. We *must* have our hand in. It's nothing more or less than the salvation of the Earth, secularly speaking, that we engage in."

"Shall we want lunch first, sir?"

"Kippers and gherkins, thank you. And bring up two bottles of

Double Diamond to go along with it — and a bottle or two for yourself, of course."

"Thank you, sir," said the redoubtable Hasbro. "You're most generous, sir."

"Very well," mumbled St. Ives, striding back and forth beneath the exposed roof rafters and knuckling his brow. He paused and squinted out into the sunlight, watching another wagon rattle along into the open door of Lord Kelvin's barn. Disguise would avail them nothing. It would be an easy thing to fill a wagon with unidentifiable scientific trash — heaven knew he had any amount of it lying about — and to dress up in threadbare pants and coat and merely drive the stuff in at the gate. The guard would have no inkling of who he was. But Lord Kelvin, of course, would. A putty nose and false chin whiskers would be dangerous things. If any members of the academy saw through them they'd clap him in irons — accuse him of intended sabotage, of seeking the destruction of the world. He could argue his case well enough in the courts, to be sure. He could depend on Rutherford, at least, to support him. But in the mean time the Earth would have exploded. That wouldn't answer. And if Lord Kelvin's machine were put into operation and were successful, then he'd quite possibly face a jury of two-headed men and a judge with a third eye. They'd be sympathetic, under the circumstances, but still…

He paused and pressed his face into his hands. They'd have to brass it out — stride in grinning, offering their services. Parsons would be there. Would he have them pitched out? Quite possibly. But in the meantime, between the four of them, they'd surely see some opportunity, some little chink in the armor of Lord Kelvin's apparatus. Who could say what it would consist of? Subtlety, thought St. Ives as the top of Hasbro's head hove into view on the steep stairs, was worth a fortune.

The vast interior of Lord Kelvin's barn was awash with activity — a sort of carnival of strange debris: of coiled copper and tubs of bubbling fluids and rubber-wrapped cable thick as a man's wrist hanging from overhead joists like jungle creepers. A vast globular device shuddered beneath laboring welders and riveters square in the center of the floor, and Lord Kelvin himself, talking through his beard and clad in a white smock and Leibnitz cap, pointed and shouted and squinted with a calculating eye at the dread machine that piece by piece took shape in the lamplight. Parsons stood beside him, leaning on a brass-shod cane.

At the sight of Langdon St. Ives standing in the sunlight outside the open door, Parsons' chin dropped. St. Ives glanced at Jack Owlesby and Hasbro. Bill Kraken had disappeared. Parsons raised an exhorting finger, widening and squinting his eyes at the same time, with the curious effect of making the bulk of his forehead disappear into his thin, grey hair.

"Parsons!" cried St. Ives, getting in before him. "Your man at the gate is a disgrace. We sauntered in past him mumbling nonsense about the Atlantic Cable and showed him a worthless letter signed by the Duke of Windsor. He tried to shake our hands. You've *got* to do better than that, Parsons. We might have been anyone, mightn't we — villains of any sort at all. And here we are, trooping in like so many ants. It's the great good fortune of the Commonwealth that we're friendly ants. In a word, we've come to offer our skills, such as they are."

St. Ives paused for breath and bowed almost imperceptibly. Parsons sputtered like the burning fuse of a fizz bomb, and for one dangerous moment St. Ives was fearful that the old man would explode, would pitch over from apoplexy and that the sum of their efforts would turn out to be merely the murder of poor Parsons. But the fit passed. The secretary snatched his quivering face back into shape and gave the three of them an appraising look, stepping across so as to stand between St. Ives and the machine, as if his gaunt frame, pinched by years of a weedy, vegetarian diet, would somehow hide the thing from view.

"*Persona non grata*, is it?" asked St. Ives, giving Parsons a look in return, then instantly regretting the action. There was nothing to be gained by being antagonistic.

"I haven't any idea how you swindled the officer at the gate," said Parsons evenly, holding his ground, "but this operation has been commissioned by His Majesty the King and is undertaken by the collected members of the Royal Academy of Sciences, an organization, if I remember aright, which does not count you among its members. In short, we thank you for your kind offer of assistance and very humbly ask you to leave, along with your ruffians." He turned to solicit Lord Kelvin's agreement, but the great man was sighting down the length of a brass tube, tugging on it in order, apparently, to align it with an identical tube that hung suspended from the ceiling fifteen feet away.

"My Lord," said Parsons, clearing his throat meaningfully, but he got no response at all, and gave off his efforts when St. Ives seemed intent on strolling 'round to the opposite side of the machine.

"*Must* we make an issue of this, sir?" Parsons demanded of St. Ives, stepping along in an obvious effort to cut him off and casting worried looks at Hasbro and Jack Owlesby, as if fearful that the two of them might produce some fearful device of their own with which to blow up the barn and exterminate the lot of them.

St. Ives stopped, surprised to see Bill Kraken, grimed with oil and wearing the clothes of a workman, step out from behind a heap of broken crates and straw stuffing. Without so much as a sideways glance at his employer, Kraken hurried to where Lord Kelvin fiddled with the brass tube, grasped the distant end of it, and offered his services. In a moment he was wrestling with the thing, hauling it this way and that to the apparent approval of his Lordship, and managing to tip St. Ives a broad wink in the process.

There was clearly no way of getting around Parsons short of knocking the man down, and such an action hardly seemed justifiable. "Well, well," said St. Ives in a defeated tone, "I'm saddened by this, Parsons. Saddened. I'd hoped to lend a hand."

Parsons, seeming mightily relieved all of a sudden, cast St. Ives a wide smile. "Thank you, sir," he said, limping toward the scientist, his hand outstretched. "If this project were in the developmental stages, I assure you we'd welcome your expertise. But it's really a matter of nuts and bolts now, isn't it? And your genius, I'm afraid, would be wasted." He ushered the three of them out into the sunlight, grinning now, and stood atop the knoll, watching until he was certain the threat had passed and the three were beyond the gate. Then he called round to have the gate guard relieved. He couldn't, he supposed, have the man flogged, but he could see to it that he spent an enterprising year patrolling the thoroughfares of Dublin.

CHAPTER 3
London and Harrogate Again

It was late evening along Fleet Street, and the London night was clear and unseasonably warm, as if the enormous moon that swam in the purple sky beyond the dome of St. Paul's were radiating a thin, white heat. The very luminosity of the moon paled the surrounding stars, but as the night deepened where it fell away into space, the stars winked on and brightened and thickened in such a way as to remind St. Ives that the universe wasn't an empty place after all. And out there among the planets, hurtling toward Earth, was the vast comet, its curved tail a hundred million miles of showering ice blown by solar wind along the uncharted byways of space. St. Ives could see it. Tomorrow or the next day the man in the street, peering skyward to admire the stars, would see it too. Would it be a thing of startling beauty, a wash of fire across the canvas of heaven? Or would it send a thrill of fear through a populace still veined with the superstitious dread of the medieval church?

The shuffle of footsteps behind him brought St. Ives to himself. He wrinkled his face up, feeling the gluey pull of the horsehair eyebrows and beard, which, along with a putty nose and monk's wig, made up a very suitable disguise. Coming along toward him was Beezer the journalist, talking animatedly to a man in shirtsleeves. Beezer chewed the end of a tiny cigar and waved his arms to illustrate a story that he told with particular venom. He seemed unnaturally excited, although St. Ives had to remind himself that he was almost entirely unfamiliar with the man — perhaps he always gestured and railed so.

St. Ives fell in behind the two, making no effort to conceal himself. Hasbro and Jack Owlesby stood in the shadows two blocks farther along in an alley past Whitefriars. There was precious little time to waste. Occasional strollers passed; the abduction would have to be quick and subtle. "Excuse me, Mr. Beezer is it, the journalist?"

The two men stopped, looking back at St. Ives. Beezer's hands fell to his side. "'At's right, pappy," came the reply. Beezer squinted at him, as if ready to doubt the existence of such a wild figure on the evening street.

"My name, actually, is Penrod," said St. Ives. "Jules Penrod. You've apparently mistaken me for someone else. I have one of the twelve common faces."

Beezer's companion burst into abrupt laughter at the idea. Beezer, however, seemed impatient at the interruption. "Face like yours is a pity," he said, nudging his companion in the abdomen with his elbow. "Suits a beggar, though. I haven't got a thing for you, pappy. Go scrub yourself with a sponge." And with that the two of them turned and made away, the second man laughing again and Beezer gesturing.

"One moment, sir!" cried St. Ives, pursuing the pair. "We've a mutual friend."

Beezer turned and scowled, chewing his cigar slowly and thoughtfully. He stared carefully at St. Ives' unlikely visage and shook his head. "No, we don't," he said, "unless it's the devil. Any other friend of yours would've hung himself by now out of regret. Why don't you disappear into the night, pappy, before I show you the shine on my boot?"

"You're right, as far as it goes," said St. Ives, grinning inwardly. "I'm a friend of Doctor Ignacio Narbondo, in fact. He's sent me 'round with another communication." Beezer squinted at him. The word "another" hadn't jarred him.

"Is that right?" he said.

St. Ives bowed, clapping a hand hastily onto the top of his head to hold his wig on.

"Bugger off, will you, Clyde?" Beezer said to his friend.

"My drink..." came the reply.

"Stow your drink. I'll see you tomorrow. I'll buy you two. Now get along."

The man turned away regretfully, despondent over the lost drink perhaps, and St. Ives waited until he'd crossed Whitefriars and his footsteps faded out of earshot before he spoke. He nodded to the still scowling Beezer and set out in the wake of the departed Clyde, looking up and down the street as if to discern anything suspicious or threatening. Beezer fell in beside him. "It's about the money," said St. Ives.

"The money?"

"Narbondo fears that he promised you too much of it."

"He's a filthy cheat!" cried Beezer, eliminating any doubts that St. Ives might have had about Beezer's having received Narbondo's message.

"He's discovered," continued St. Ives, "that there are any of a number of journalists who will sell out the people of London for half the sum. Peabody at the *Herald*, for instance, has agreed to cooperate."

"The filthy, scum-sucking cheat!" Beezer shouted, waving both hands over his head.

"Tut, tut," admonished St. Ives, noting with a surge of anxious anticipation the darkened mouth of the alley some thirty feet distant. "We haven't contracted with Peabody yet. It was merely a matter of feeling out the temperature of the water, so to speak. You understand. You're a businessman yourself in a way." St. Ives gestured broadly with his left hand as if to signify that a man like Beezer could be expected to take the long view. With his right he reached across and snatched the lapels of Beezer's coat, then brought his left hand around and pummeled the startled journalist square in the back, catapulting him into the ill-lit alley.

"Hey!" shouted Beezer, tripping forward into the waiting arms of Jack Owlesby, who leaped in to pinion the man's wrists. Hasbro, waving an enormous bag, appeared from the shadows and flung the bag like a gill net over Beezer's head, St. Ives yanking it down across the man's back and pushing him forward off his feet. Hasbro snatched at the draw-rope, grasped Beezer's shoulders, and hissed through the canvas, "Cry out and you're a dead man!"

The struggling Beezer collapsed like a sprung balloon, having an antipathy, apparently, to the idea of being a dead man. Jack clambered up onto the bed of a standing wagon, hauled open the lid of a steamer trunk, and along with St. Ives and Hasbro yanked and shoved and grappled the feebly struggling journalist into the wood and leather prison. He banged ineffectively a half-dozen times at the sides of the trunk, mewling miserably, then fell silent as the wagon rattled and bounced along the alley, exiting on Salisbury Court and making away south toward the Thames.

A half hour later the wagon had swerved around the Embankment and doubled back through Soho as St. Ives set a course toward Chingford. Hasbro, always prepared, had uncorked a bottle of whisky, and each of the three men held a glass, lost in his own thoughts about the warm April night and the dangers of their mission. "Sorry to bring you in on this, Jack," said St. Ives. "There might quite likely be the devil to pay before we're through. No telling what sort of a row our man Beezer might set up."

"I'm not complaining," said Jack Owlesby, grinning gamely at St. Ives.

"It was Dorothy I was thinking about, actually. We're only weeks finished with the pig incident, and I've hauled you away again. There she sits in Kensington wondering what sort of nonsense I've drummed up now. She's a stout woman, if you don't mistake my meaning."

Jack nodded. If Dorothy knew, in fact, what sort of business they pursued this time, she'd have insisted on coming along. Jack thought of her fondly. "Do you know — " he began, reminiscing, but the sound of Beezer pummeling the sides of the trunk cut him off.

"Tell the hunchback," shrieked a muffled voice, "that I'll have him horsewhipped! He'll be sulking in Newgate Prison by the end of the week, by God! There's nothing about him I don't know!"

St. Ives shrugged at Hasbro. Here, perhaps, was a stroke of luck. If Beezer could be convinced that they actually *were* agents of Narbondo, it would go no little way toward throwing the man off their scent when the affair was over, especially if he went to the authorities with his tale. He hadn't, after all, committed any crime, nor did he contemplate one — no crime, that is, beyond the crime against humanity, against human decency. "Narbondo has authorized us to eliminate you if we see fit," said St. Ives, hunching over the trunk. "If you play along here you'll be well paid; if you struggle, you'll find yourself counting fishes in the rocks off Southend Pier." The journalist fell silent.

Early in the pre-dawn morning the wagon rattled into Chingford and made for the hills beyond, where lay the cottage of Sam Langley, son of St. Ives' long-time cook. The cottage was dark, but a lamp burned through the slats in the locked shutters of a low window in an unused silo fifty yards off. St. Ives reined in the horses, clambering out of the wagon at once, and with the help of his two companions, hauled the steamer trunk off the tailgate and into the unfastened door of the silo. Jack Owlesby and Hasbro hastened back out into the night, and for a moment through the hastily opened door, St. Ives could see Sam Langley stepping off his kitchen porch and pulling on a coat. The door shut and St. Ives was alone in the feebly lit silo with the trunk and scattered pieces of furniture.

"I'm going to unlock the trunk — " St. Ives began.

"You sons of…" Beezer started to shout, but St. Ives rapped against the lid of the trunk with his knuckles to silence him.

"I'm either going to unlock the trunk or set it afire," said St. Ives with great deliberation. "The choice is yours." The trunk was silent. "Once the trunk is unlocked, you can quite easily extricate yourself. The bag isn't knotted. You've probably already discovered that. My advice to you is to stay absolutely still for ten minutes, then you can thrash and shriek and stamp about until you collapse. No one will hear you. You'll be happy to hear that a quantity of money will be advanced to your account, and that you'll have a far easier time spending it if you're not shot full of holes. Don't, then, get impatient. You've ridden out the night in the trunk; you can stand ten minutes more." Beezer, it seemed, had seen reason, for as St. Ives crouched out into the night, shook hands hastily with Langley, leaped into the wagon and took up the ribands, nothing but silence emanated from the stones of the silo.

Two evenings earlier, on the night that St. Ives had waylaid Beezer the journalist, the comet had appeared in the eastern sky, ghostly and round like the moon reflected on a frosty window, just a circular patch of faint, luminous cloud. But now it seemed to drop out of the heavens toward the Earth like a plumb bob toward a melon. St. Ives peered into the eyepiece of his meager telescope, tracking the flight of the comet for no other reason, really, than to while away the early dawn hours. There was nothing to calculate; work of that nature had been accomplished weeks past by astronomers whose knowledge of astral mathematics was sufficient to satisfy both the Royal Academy and Doctor Ignacio Narbondo. St. Ives wouldn't dispute it. His desire, beyond a simple fascination with the mystery and wonder of the thing, was to have a look at the face of what might easily be his last great nemesis.

The glow of the lights of Leeds, and to a much lesser extent the lights of Kirk Hammerton, obscured the clarity of the heavens, and the billows of cloud along the northern horizon threatened at any moment to roil up across the sky and cover the sky utterly. His telescope, with its mirror of speculum metal, had been a gift of Lord Rosse, and through it St. Ives had seen years past the strange lunar activity that had led, very nearly, to his death, and to his final cataclysmic parting of the ways with the Royal Academy of Sciences. The telescope, however, was wasted here. He could have seen the comet clearly enough through the window. His brass spyglass alone was sufficient to turn the thing into a monster hurtling among the planets. But his fascination with the simple presence of the deadly star drew him to his observatory as a curious child is drawn to the edge of a deep and terrifying precipice.

Hasbro packed their bags in the manor. Their train left Kirk Hammerton Station at six. Dr. Narbondo, St. Ives had to assume, would discover that same morning that he'd been foiled; that Beezer, somehow, had failed. The morning *Times* would rattle in on the Dover train, ignorant of pending doom. The doctor would try to contact the nefarious Beezer, but Beezer wouldn't be found. He's taken ill, they'd say, repeating the substance of the letter St. Ives had sent off to Beezer's employers. Beezer, they'd assure Narbondo, had been ordered south on holiday — to the north coast of Spain. Narbondo's forehead would wrinkle with suspicion and the wrinkling would engender horrible curses and the gnashing of teeth. St. Ives smiled. The doctor wouldn't have an inkling of who had thwarted him.

But the result of the mystery of the disappeared journalist would, quite likely, be the immediate removal of Narbondo and Hargreaves to the environs of northwestern Scandinavia. The chase, thought St. Ives romantically, would be on. The comet loomed only a few days away, barely enough time to accomplish their task.

A door slammed in the manor. St. Ives slipped from his stool and looked out through the west-facing window of his observatory, waving to Hasbro who, in the roseate light of an early dawn, dangled a pocket watch from a chain and nodded to his employer. In a half hour they were away, scouring along the highroad toward the station in Kirk Hammerton, St. Ives, Hasbro, and Jack Owlesby, bound for Ramsgate to board the zeppelin that would transport them to the ice and tundra of arctic Norway. If the labors of Bill Kraken were unsuccessful, they'd know two days hence.

Bill Kraken crouched in the willows along the River Nidd, watching through the lacey tendrils the dark bulk of Lord Kelvin's barn. The device had been finished two days earlier, the ironic result, to a degree, of his own labor — labor he wouldn't be paid for. But money wasn't of particular consequence anymore, not like it had been in the days of his squid merchanting or when he'd been rescued from the life of a lowly peapod man by the charitable Langdon St. Ives. He wanted for nothing now, really, beyond the success of the night's mission.

In a cloth bag beside him wriggled a dozen snakes, collected by Kraken in the high grass beyond the manor house. In a wire screen cage beneath the snakes were a score of mice, hungry, as were the snakes, from days of neglect. A leather bellows dangled from his belt, and a hooded lantern from his right hand.

No one, apparently, was on the meadow. The Royal Academy was glad to be quit of Ignacio Narbondo, who had taken ship for Oslo, word had it, to effect his machinations. But the Royal Academy would be in before him; they would reduce his threats to drivel. Why he hadn't followed through with his plan to alert the press they couldn't say, but it seemed to be evidence that his threats were mere bluff. This latest turn had lightened the atmosphere considerably, it seemed to Kraken. It had lent a sort of holiday air to what had been a business fraught with suspicion and doubt.

He bent out from under the willows and set out across the meadow carrying his bundles. It would do no good to run. He was too old to be cutting capers on a meadow in the dead of night, and if he tripped and dropped his mice or knocked his lantern against a stone, his plan would be foiled utterly. In an hour both the moon and the comet would have appeared on the horizon and the meadow would be bathed in light. If he were sensible, he'd be asleep in his bed by then.

The dark bulk of the barn loomed toward him; the pale stones of its foundation contrasting feebly with the weathered oak battens above. Kraken ducked along the wall toward a tiny mullioned window beneath which extended the last six inches of the final section of brass pipe — the very pipe which Kraken himself had wrestled through a hole augured into the barn wall on that first day he'd helped Lord Kelvin align the things.

What, exactly, the pipe was intended to accomplish, Kraken couldn't say, but somehow it was the focal point of the workings of the device. Beyond, some twenty feet from the barn and elevated on a stone slab, sat a black monolith, smooth as polished marble. Kraken had been amazed when, late the previous afternoon, Lord Kelvin had flung a ballpeen hammer end over end at the monolith, and the collected workmen and scientists had gasped in wonder when the hammer had been soundlessly reflected with such force that it had sailed out of sight in the general direction of York. That it had come to earth yet not a man of them could say. The reversal of the poles was to be accomplished, then, by emanating the collected magnetic rays developed in Lord Kelvin's machine toward the monolith, thus both exciting and deflecting them in a circuitous pattern, sending them off, as it were, astride a penny whirligig.

Kraken squinted through the darkness at the monolith, doubly black against the purple of the starry night sky, and wondered at the wonderful perspicacity of great scientists. Given a thousand years — two thousand — Kraken couldn't have thought up such a machine, let alone engineer the building of one. But here it was, primed for acceleration on the morrow. Could Kraken, a man of admittedly low intellect, scuttle the marvelous device? Kraken shook his head, full, suddenly, of doubt. He'd been entrusted with little else than the material salvation of humanity…. Well, Kraken was just a small man with a small way of doing things. He'd seen low times in his life, had mucked through sewers with murderers, and he'd have to trust to low means here. That was the best he could do.

He quit breathing and cocked an ear. Nothing but silence and the distant hooting of an owl greeted him on the night air. He untied the bellows from his belt and shook them against his ear. Grain and broken biscuits rattled within. He shoved the mouth of the bellows into the end of the brass tube and pumped furiously, listening to the debris clatter away, down the tilted pipe. Long after the last of the grain had been blown clear of the bellows, Kraken continued to manipulate his instrument, desperate to send the bulk of it deep into the bowels of the machine. Haste would avail him nothing here.

Satisfied, he tied the bellows once again to his belt and picked up the mouse cage. The beasts were tumultuous with excitement, stimulated, perhaps, by the evening constitutional, or sensing somehow that they were on the brink of an adventure of powerful magnitude. Kraken pressed the cage front against the end of the tube and pulled open its little door. The mice scurried roundabout, casting wild glances here and there, suddenly curious about a heap of shredded newspaper or the pink ear of a neighbor. Then, one by one, they filed away down the tube like cattle down a hill, sniffing the air, intent suddenly on biscuits and grain.

The snakes were a comparatively easy case. A round dozen of the beasts fled away in the wake of the mice, anxious to be quit of their sack. Kraken wondered if he hadn't ought to wad the sack up and shove it into the tube, to make absolutely sure that the beasts remained within. But the dangers of doing so were manifold. Lord Kelvin or some particularly watchful guard might easily discover the stopper before Kraken had a chance to remove it. They mustn't, said St. Ives, discover that the sabotage had been the work of men — thus the mice and snakes. It might easily seem that the natural residents of the barn had merely taken up lodgings there, and the hand of Langdon St. Ives would go undetected.

It was very nearly within the hour that Bill Kraken climbed into bed.

But his dreams were filled that night with visions of mice and snakes dribbling from the end of the tube and racing away into the darkness, having consumed the grain and leaving nothing behind sufficient to foul the workings of the dread machine. What could he do, though, save trust to Providence? The shame of his failure — if failure it should be — would likely be as nothing next to the horrors that would beset them after Lord Kelvin's success. God bless the man, thought Kraken philosophically, picturing the aging lord, laboring night and day to complete his engine, certain that he was contributing his greatest gift yet to humankind. His disappointment would be monumental. It seemed almost worth the promised trouble to let the poor man have a go at it. But that, sadly, wouldn't do. The world was certainly a contradictory place.

CHAPTER 4
Norway

The bright April weather had collapsed in a heap before St. Ives and his man Hasbro had chuffed into Dover, and the North Sea was a tumult of wind-tossed waves and driving rain. St. Ives huddled now aboard the Ostende Ferry, out of the rain beneath an overhanging deck ledge and wrapped in an oilcloth, legs spread to counter the heaving swell. His pipe burned like a chimney. Occasional drops, swirling in on the wind, drove into his face, and the orange coal in the pipe bowl hissed and sputtered. He peered out at the roiling black of the heavens, equally dark thoughts drawing his eyes into a squint and making him oblivious to the cold and wet. Had this sudden turn of arctic weather anything to do with the experimentation of the Royal Academy? Had they effected the reversal of the poles prematurely and driven the weather suddenly mad? Had Kraken failed? He watched a grey swell loom overhead, threatening to slam him into paste, then sink suddenly into nothing as if having changed its mind, only to tower up once again overhead, sheets of flying foam torn from its crest and rendered into vapor.

His plans seemed to be fast going agley. The zeppelin he'd counted upon for transport had, been "inoperable," or so he'd been told. The fate of the Earth itself hung in the balance, and the filthy zeppelin was "inoperable." They'd all be inoperable by the end of the week. Jack Owlesby had stayed on in Ramsgate where a crew of nitwits fiddled with the craft, and so yet another variable, as the mathematician would say, had been cast into the muddled stew. Could the zeppelin be made operable in time? Would Jack, along with the flea-brained pilot, find them in the cold wastes of arctic Norway? It didn't bear thinking about. One thing at a time, St. Ives reminded himself. They'd left Jack with a handshake and a compass and had raced south intending to follow Narbondo overland, as it were, trusting to Jack to take care of himself.

But where was Ignacio Narbondo? He'd set sail from Dover with Hargreaves hours earlier; there could be no doubt about that. But the ticket agent could find no record of his having boarded the Dover-Ostende ferry. St. Ives had described him vividly: the hump, the tangle of oily hair, the cloak. No one could remember having seen him board. Had he somehow discovered that agents were at work to foil his efforts? Did he suspect that Beezer had been abducted, that his mail had been interfered with?

It was conceivable, just barely, that St. Ives had made a monumental error, or that Narbondo had tricked the lot of them, had been one up on them all along. He might at that moment be bound, say, for Reykjavik, intent on working his deviltry on the volcanic wastes of the interior of Iceland. The world was vast, full of trackless wilderness. Here was St. Ives, bobbing on the sea like a tin soldier aboard a cork boat, vainly supposing that from his vantage point on the heaving deck he could somehow anticipate the movements of a madman — two madmen. If he and Hasbro arrived in Ostende and there was no word of Narbondo, what then? If no porter or ticket-taker, no vagabond or bun seller, no cleaning woman or constable had seen the hunchback, what would they do? Go on, St. Ives decided.

But in Ostende the rain let up and the wind fell off, and the solid ground beneath his feet lent a steadiness of purpose to St. Ives once again and settled his topsy-turvy stomach. In the cold station a woman stirred a cauldron of mussels in a wall niche, dumping in handfuls of shallots and lumps of butter. Aromatic steam swirled out of the iron pot in such a way as to make St. Ives light-headed. "Mussels and beer," he said to Hasbro, "would revive a body."

"That they would, sir. And a loaf of bread, I might add, to provide bulk."

"A sound suggestion," said St. Ives, striding toward the woman and removing his hat. She dumped open mussels, black and dripping into a roughly woven basket lined with newspaper, heaping up the shells until they threatened to cascade to the floor. She winked at St. Ives, fished an enormous mussel from the pot, slid her thumbs into the hiatus of its open shell, and, in a single swift movement, pulled the mollusc open, shoved one of her thumbs under the orange flesh, and flipped the morsel into her open mouth. "Some don't chew them," she said, speaking English, "but I do. What's the use of eating at all if you don't chew them? Might as well swallow a toad. Do you know what I mean?"

"Indubitably," said St. Ives. "It's the same way with oysters. I never could stand to simply allow the creatures to slide down my throat. I fly in the face of custom there."

"Aye," she said. "Can you imagine a man's stomach, full of beasts such as these, whole, mind you, and sloshin' like smelts in a bucket?" She canted her head at St. Ives as if expecting an answer, then dipped again into the cauldron and tossed another mussel down, grimacing almost immediately and rooting in her half-filled mouth with a finger. "Mussel pearl," she said, holding up between thumb and forefinger a tiny opalescent sphere twice the size of a pinhead. She slid open a little drawer in the cart on which sat the cauldron of mussels, and dropped the pearl in among what must have been thousands of the tiny orbs, picking at her back teeth thereafter with a bent fingernail. "Can't stand debris," she said, grimacing.

The entire display rather took the edge off St. Ives' appetite, and the heap of mussels in his basket, reclining beneath a coating of congealing butter and bits of garlic and shallot, began to remind him of certain unfortunate suppers he'd consumed at the Bayswater Club. He grinned weakly at the woman and looked around at the hurrying crowds, wondering if he and Hasbro hadn't ought to join them.

"Man in here this afternoon ate one shell and all," she said shaking her head. "Imagine the debris. Must have given his throat bones some trouble, I dare say."

"Shell and all?" asked St. Ives.

"That's the exact case. Crunched away at the thing like it was a marzipan crust, didn't he? Then he took another, chewed it up about halfway, saw what he was about, and spit the filthy thing against the wall there. You can see bits of it still, can't you, despite the birds swarming round. There's the smear of it against the paint. Do you see it there? Bit of brown paste is all it amounts to now."

St. Ives stared at the woman. "Big man?"

"Who?"

"This fellow who ate the shells. Big, was he, and with a beard? Seemed ready to fly into a rage?"

"That's your man, gents. Cursed vilely, he did, but it weren't at the shells, it was at the poor birds, wasn't it, when they come round to eat up what your man spit onto the wall there. You can see it there, can't you? I never — "

"Was he in the company of a hunchback?"

"Aye," said the woman, giving her pot a perfunctory stirring. "Greasy little man with a grin. Seemed to think the world is a lark. But it ain't no lark, gentlemen. Here you've been, wasting my time this quarter-hour, and not another living soul has bought a shell. You've frightened the lot of them off, is what I think, and you haven't paid me a penny." She glowered at St. Ives, then glowered at Hasbro.

"What time this afternoon?" asked St. Ives.

"Three hours past, say, or four. Might have been five. Or less."

"Thank you," said St. Ives, reaching into his pocket for a handful of coin. He dumped a half crown into her outstretched hand and left her blinking, he and Hasbro racing through the terminal toward the distant exit, each of them clutching a Gladstone bag in one hand and a basket of mussels in the other. The streets were wet outside, but the clouds were broken overhead and were taking flight in the grey dusk, and the wind had simmered down to a sort of billowy breeze. A bent man shambled past in trousers meant for a behemoth, clutching at a buttonless coat. St. Ives thrust his basket of mussels at the man, meaning to do him a good turn, but his gesture was mistaken, for the man peered at them with a look of mingled surprise and loathing in his eyes, fetching the basket a swipe with his hand that sent the entire affair into the gutter. St. Ives strode on without a word, marveling at how little space existed at times between madness and the best of intentions. In a half hour they were aboard a train once again, in a sleeping car bound for Amsterdam, Hamburg, and, finally, to Hjorring where on the Denmark ferry they'd once again set sail across the North Sea, up the Oslofjord into Norway.

St. Ives was determined to remain awake, to have a look at the comet when it arced in over the horizon some time after midnight. But the sleepless night he'd spent in the observatory and the long hours of travel since had worn him thin, and after a tolerable meal in the dining car, and what might likely turn out to be, on the morrow, a regrettable lot of brandy, he dropped away at once into a deep sleep. The comet rose in the sky and fell again without him, slanting past the captive earth.

In Oslo, Hargreaves had beaten a man half senseless with the man's own cane. In Trondheim, two hours before the arrival of St. Ives and Hasbro on the express, he'd run mad and threatened to explode a green-grocer's cart, kicking the spokes out of one of the wheels before Narbondo had hauled him away and explained to the authorities that his companion was a lunatic bound for a sanatorium in Natvik.

St. Ives itched to be after them, but here he sat, becalmed in a small, brick railway station. The doctor couldn't know that he was so closely pursued. He'd stop in a village for a meal and St. Ives and Hasbro would be upon him as he shoved down a forkful of codfish. St. Ives stared impatiently out the window at the nearly empty station. A delay of a minute seemed an eternity, and each sighing release of steam from the waiting train carried upon it the suggestion of the final, fateful explosion, which Doctor Narbondo, perhaps having finished his codfish quite happily by now, might at that very moment be effecting. Hasbro, St. Ives could see, was equally uneasy at their motionless state, for he sat hunched forward on his seat as if trying to compel the train into flight. Finally, amid tooting and whooshing and three false starts, they were away again. St. Ives prayed that the engineer had understood his translated request that they make an unscheduled stop on the deserted tundra adjacent to Mt. Hjarstaad. Surely he would; he'd accepted the little bag of assorted coffee tablets readily enough. What could he have understood them to be but a bribe?

Darkness had long since fallen, and with it had fled the last of the scattered rainshowers. Ragged clouds pursued by arctic wind capered across the sky, and the stars shone thick and bright between. The train developed steam after chuffing along lazily up a steepening grade, and within a score of minutes was hurtling through the mountainous countryside. St. Ives was gripped once more with the excitement and peril of the chase. He removed his pocketwatch at intervals, putting it back without so much as glancing at it, loosening his collar, and peering out across the rocky landscape at the distant swerve of track ahead when the train lurched into a curve, as if the engine they pursued might be visible a half mile farther on. The slow, labored climb of steep hills was almost instantly maddening and filled him again with the fear that their efforts would prove futile, that from the vantage point of the next peak they'd witness the detonation of half of Scandinavia: crumbling mountainsides, hurtling rocks. But they'd creep, finally, to summits void of trees, where the track was wafered onto ledges that fronted unimaginable precipices, the train scouring away again in a startling rush of steam and clatter.

They thundered through shrieking tunnels, the starry sky going momentarily black, then reappearing in an instant only to be dashed again into darkness. And when the train burst each time into the cold Norwegian night, both St. Ives and Hasbro were pressed against the window, peering skyward, relieved to see the last scattered clouds fleeing before the wind. Then all at once, as if they'd been waved into existence by a magic wand, the lights of the aurora borealis swept across the sky in lacey showers of green and red and blue, like a semi-transparent Christmas tapestry hung across the wash of stars.

"Yes!" cried St. Ives, leaping to his feet and nearly pitching into the aisle as they rushed howling into another tunnel. "He's done it! Kraken has done it!"

"Indeed, sir?"

"Absolutely," said St. Ives animatedly. "Without the shadow of a doubt. The northern lights, my good fellow, are a consequence of the Earth's electro-magnetic field. It's a simple matter — no field, no lights. Had Lord Kelvin's machine done the job, the display you see before us would have been postponed for heaven knows how many woeful years. But here it is, isn't it? Good old Bill!" And on this last cheerful note, they emerged once again into the aurora-lit night, hurtling along beside a broad cataract that tumbled down through boulder-strewn gorge.

Another hour's worth of tunnels, however, began to make it seem finally as if there were no end to their journey, as if, perhaps, their train labored round and round a clever, circular track, that they had been monumentally hoaxed one last, fatal time by Dr. Ignacio Narbondo. And then in an effort of steam they crested one last, steep summit. Away to the west, far below them, moonlight shimmered on the rippled surface of a fjord stretching out of the distant Norwegian Sea.

Tumbling down out of the rocky precipices to their right rushed the wild river they'd followed for what seemed an age, the torrent wrapping round the edge of Mt. Hjarstaad and disappearing into shadow where it cascaded, finally, into the vast emptiness of an abyss. A trestled bridge spanned the cataract and gave out onto a tundra-covered plain, scattered with the angular moon shadows of tilted stones.

Between two such shadows lay a strange and alien object — a sizeable steamer trunk, its lid thrown back, its contents removed. Beyond, a hundred yards distant, lay another, yanked over onto its side. The train raced past both before howling to a steam-shrieking stop. St. Ives and Hasbro pitched their bags out onto the icy plain and leaped out after them, the train almost immediately setting out, north, toward Hammerfest, leaving the world and the two men to their collective fate.

St. Ives hurried across the plain toward the slope of Mt. Hjarstaad. A footpath wound upward along the edge of the precipice through which the river thundered and roiled. "I'm afraid we've rather announced our arrival through a megaphone," shouted St. Ives over his shoulder. "Let us hope," he huffed, "that the doctor is too anxious to culminate his exertions to pay us any real heed."

"Perhaps the roar of the falls…" shouted Hasbro at St. Ives' back. But the rest of his words were lost in the watery tumult as the two men leaped up the steepening hill.

St. Ives patted his coat, feeling beneath it the hard, foreign bulk of his revolver. With the exception of certain loathsome bugs, he had an aversion to the killing of anything at all, and he wondered as he edged along the trail, peering past tumbled rock, listening to the unfathomable roar of the maelstrom below, whether he could deliberately shoot either of the madmen that labored above them, even if the consequence was the delivery of humankind out of their wretched clutches.

There was a shout behind him. A crack like a pistol shot followed, and St. Ives threw himself onto his face, rolling against a carriage-sized boulder. A hail of stones showered roundabout, and an enormous circular rock, big as a cartwheel, bounded over his head, soaring away into the misty depths of the abyss.

Above, leaping from perch to rocky perch, was a man with wild hair and beard — Hargreaves, there could be little doubt. St. Ives rolled to his knees, drew his revolver, steadied his forearm along the top of a rock, and fired twice at the retreating figure. His bullets pinged off rocks twenty feet short of their mark, but the effect on the anarchist was startling — it was if he'd been turned suddenly into a mountain sheep.

Again St. Ives set out up the footpath, but Hasbro, following Hargreaves' lead, pursued a course across the granite hillside, gesturing to St. Ives as he disappeared into shadow. St. Ives, pressed against the stony wall of the path, crept along carefully, grimly imagining himself following the course of the plummeting stone and wondering at the fate of the redoubtable Hasbro. Ice crunched underfoot, and the hillside opened up briefly on his right to reveal a steep depression in the rock — a sort of conical hole at the bottom of which lay a black, silent tarn. The water brimmed with reflected stars washed with the blue-red light of the aurora.

Abruptly he rounded a sharp bend and there above him, perched on the rim of the smoking crater and hauling on the coils of a mechanical bladder, was the venomous Hargreaves, the steamy reek of boiling mud swirling about his head and shoulders. Ignacio Narbondo capered beside him, dancing from one foot to the other like a man treading on hot pavement.

They were too distant to shoot at. Anything farther off than forty feet confounded St. Ives' aim. Where was Hasbro? How in the world were either of them to interfere with the rapidly culminating shenanigan above without racing into the muzzle of a gun? St. Ives was struck with the awful loneliness of the cold night, of the arctic wind slanting across the hillsides, of the black and grey landscape and the unearthly beauty of the northern lights.

He slid two bullets into the empty chambers of his revolver and stepped forward, intent upon simply brassing it out, come what may. The anarchist grappled now with a Gladstone bag. His curses reached St. Ives on the wind. Narbondo raged beside him, looking hastily back and forth between the approaching St. Ives and his fumbling companion. St. Ives smiled grimly and pressed on, pistol aimed, shouting into the wind for Narbondo to give off.

But the doctor was oblivious to his exhortations. He peered suddenly skyward, his forearm thrown across his brow as if to shade his eyes from moonlight. St. Ives followed Narbondo's gaze, vaguely conscious of a low hum, droning, it seemed, in the back of his ears. The

crescent moon bobbed along above the aurora, and below it, dropping into a pale blue wash of color, was the dark, ovoid silhouette of a
descending zeppelin.

"Hooray!" cried St. Ives, forgetting himself momentarily and understanding Narbondo's anxiety. Emboldened, he took a determined step
forward, hearing the crack of Hargreaves' pistol almost at the same time
that the bullet struck him in the shoulder. He cried out and dropped to
his knees, his revolver spinning away into the void. A shriek followed,
and St. Ives looked up to see Hargreaves, pistol smoking in one hand
and the Gladstone bag gripped in another, lurch round, teeter for a
moment on the edge of the crater, and topple off, disappearing utterly
into the mouth of the volcano, Narbondo making one futile grab at the
bag clutched in Hargreaves' disappearing hand.

A prolonged but diminishing shriek ended moments later, followed by a thunderous explosion — the volatile contents of the bag
having been detonated by the fires of Mt. Hjarstaad. St. Ives clutched
his shoulder as Hasbro stepped out of the shadows above, leveling his
pistol at the furious Narbondo in a manner that implied he'd brook no
nonsense — that Narbondo was an ace away from following Hargreaves
into the pit.

Narbondo shrugged, and seemed to slump, half raising his hands in
resignation. Then, without so much as a backward glance, he bolted
down the footpath toward St. Ives, gathering momentum, running
headlong at the surprised scientist. Hasbro aimed the pistol, but a
shot was impossible. St. Ives would be imperiled. Narbondo leaped
along in great springing strides, his face contorted now with fear and
wonderment. St. Ives threw himself sideways, and Narbondo whirled
past in uncontrolled, headlong flight.

It seemed certain that at the bend in the footpath he'd find himself
plummeting into the abyss, but such was not to be. He tripped, tumbled, bounced shrieking against a rock, and caromed back into the
hillside, head over heels, sliding across the steep, scree-slippery slope
into the black water of the tarn. The reflection of the moon and stars
on the surface disintegrated, bits and pieces dancing wildly. But by the
time Hasbro, hat in hand, had made his way down to where his master
stood staring into the depths of the pool, the surface was placid once
again. "He's gone," said St. Ives simply.

"Will he float surfaceward, sir?"

"Not necessarily," replied the scientist. "I rather believe that the fall knocked the wind from him. He'll stay down until he bloats with gasses — until he begins to rot. And the water, I fear, is so cold as to slow the process substantially, perhaps indefinitely. We could wait a bit just to be certain, but I very much fear that waiting would be injudicious." And with that St. Ives nodded at the horizon where glowed a great arc of white fire. As the two men watched, the flaming orb of the comet crept skyward, enormous now, as if it were soaring in to swallow the puny Earth at a gulp.

Hasbro nodded quietly. "Shall we fetch their equipment, sir?"

"We'll want the lot of it," said St. Ives. "And to all appearances, we'll want it quickly. We've a long and wearisome journey yet before us." He sighed deeply. His shoulder began suddenly to ache. He turned one last time toward the tarn which had stolen from him the satisfaction of confronting the defeated Ignacio Narbondo. "I very much suspect," he said in a low and measured tone, "that our villain has found an icy and not undeserved grave, no less fitting than that of his accomplice. It almost seems choreographed, doesn't it, by some higher authority?"

Hasbro stood for a moment as if in silent contemplation, then replaced his hat and set off up the path, leaving St. Ives to welcome Jack Owlesby, whose hurried footfalls scuffled up the trail behind them.

The Giving Mouth

IAN R. MACLEOD

Ian R. MacLeod's explorations of magic in a "gaslight" pseudo-Victorian mode are best known through such novels as *The Light Ages* and *House of Storms*. His short fiction is masterful for its nuance, subtlety, and emotional impact. What makes "The Giving Mouth" an interesting addition to this anthology is the vein of steampunk invention inserted into a setting more reminiscent of a traditional feudal society.

I was a child before I was your King. And even though the redbrick tower where I lived with my parents had many windows that gazed over the Pits, I was raised in what you think of as poverty. Each morning I woke on my pallet of stale straw to the scream of the shift whistle and the clang of the pit wheels. The sound was as familiar to me as birdsong, but the shock of the grey light and mineral stench always came like a physical blow.

Put simply, I was a dreamer. And righteous youth made me certain that my dreams were real. I was convinced that there was a better world than the one I found myself in — and not as some abstraction, but tangible as the grit in my hair and the dirt in the seams of my clothing. Sometimes I could almost see it shimmering at the corners of my eyes; on saints' days when the wind came from the right direction — from the east, and not too strong — when the church bells rang and the underworkers donned ribbons to roam the fair camped in the dust before Castleiron.

But I could only pretend. Everyone knew that there had always been mines. That since the day that the Great Beast first spewed out this mineral Kingdom, Castleiron had always risen like a fist from the green moat at the floor of the valley. And that liveiron and plain iron and copper and zinc were all that separated us humans from the fleas we plucked from our skin.

I remember that on the afternoon when my story truly begins I had been wandering in the marshes between the slagheaps and the Pits where the water's rainbowed oil and exposed minerals made grasses and flowers in colours of dream. Copper green. Cobalt blue. Oxide red. A lonely place, usually pretty, although often things nested and grew there that sent me stumbling away in disgust. So I was always looking around in the wash of light, half in joy, half in fear. And glancing up that afternoon, I saw a figure sitting atop a drift of ash thrown up by the summer gales and honeycombed by the burrowings of a copperworm. A face angled up towards the white sun, eyes quivered shut. Just a girl. But she was bathed in light made pure at every angle of cloth and limb. Everything about her was separate. And although part of my mind still knew that she was some underworker crawled up into the light for a few hours, escaping as I tried to escape, that part was drowned in greater knowledge.

I stared. It seemed quite impossible that my gaze wouldn't break the bubble of her perfection. But there she sat, beautiful and unperturbed, glossy coils of hair at her shoulders stirred like ivy by the wind from the Pits. Eventually, afraid the vision would burst inside me, I turned and ran back towards my tower.

Fool that I was, I tried to explain all this to my father that night.

He was standing with his palm pressed against a window high in the tower, in the big empty room he liked to call his study, looking out, his lips trailing white from the cigarette he was smoking like an old man's beard. He heard my footsteps by the door as I crept by towards places even the servants had forgotten about. I froze at the sound of his voice, but he was only saying Well Son and How Are You. Come Right In. Here into this big room. He turned, outlined against the flickering light, the cigarette bright at his mouth, glowing red in his eyes. I didn't flinch as he reached out to pat my shoulder, didn't shiver with relief as he thought better of it.

And how are you, Son?

I didn't answer. He asked me again. Bittersweet smoke puffed into my eyes. It was hard to make out his face but I knew that he would be putting on his smile, the one that bared teeth the colour of soot-browned ice. It hovered with the smoke in the air between us, unresolved. I squeaked Fine, Pop, Just Fine in a voice that was notched half-way towards breaking.

Something bumped the window. A white nocturnal creature, falling dead from the glass and tumbling down the drop of the tower like spit. I looked out beyond in the direction my father had been staring. The furnaces glowing down the valley, a thousand dogends dropped amid the mines. Up beyond Castleiron, the headlights of a steamhorse hauling some load up the Great Road briefly ribboned the cliffs gold. People living, sweating, burrowing, sleeping...

My father crushed his cigarette beneath his boot. He immediately started up another, the match flame making his face first handsome, then old, then hideous. His lips putted wetly. He puffed in silence. I waited. I was unused to his company. When he wasn't working, cursing the underworkers or snatching half-done tasks from the hands of the servants, he spent his time up here alone. I had little contact with him apart from the hotly unreal occasions when he chose to discipline me. Dreamer that I was, I liked to suppose that, up here where the furnaces bled across the moon, my father might also dwell on better worlds than this. And with the image of the girl in the marshes still pouring through my blood with a power I could only just begin to understand, it seemed like a time for saying things that didn't usually have words.

So I spoke. I could taste the corroded air. Hear the dusty sigh of a furnace engine. And doubtless I sounded like the fanciful, half-satisfied child that I was. But still I believed in the truth of my feelings. And I would like to think that there was some poetry in my expression, that it was that which made my father react as he did. For although children may dream of other worlds, every adult has had childhood stolen from them. Even my father was filled to the brimming with hidden dreams.

He nodded and drew on his cigarette with that hasty and somehow furtive gesture that — like his smile — was all his own, pooling red shadows in his hollowed cheeks. He waited without interruption for me to finish.

"What you're telling me, Son," he said, "is that you think what you see out of this window is wrong? That nothing is as it should be. Is that exactly right?"

No, of course, not *exactly*. But still I nodded.

"And where do you think all this is going to get you?"

"I ..." the jaggedly precise tone in his voice was enough to make me hesitate " ... I don't know. It's just a feeling."

"Just a feeling." He took a long drag on his cigarette. A golden worm trembled at his mouth. "Hold out your hand."

I was no fool. I did as he said. I watched and waited as he ground the cigarette out in my palm. And I stood for as long as I could while he beat me. Then I crouched. Then I lay. My father wanted to teach me a lesson, and for once he did. He was a man raised from this Kingdom, risen from the gritty soil. When he looked out of the window of this room he liked to call his study, he saw the world as it was and admitted no room for love or hope or beauty. Not in himself, nor in anyone else who came close to him.

I realised later as I lay sobbing in my pallet splattered with droppings of moonlight that tonight had been a bad time to approach my father about anything. He was a dour man at the best of times, but tomorrow Queen Gormal had decreed that all the nobility should attend Castleiron. No one who had received that command would rest easy tonight.

I stood outside the tower with the servants next morning, shivering in the dusty wind as our best steamhorse was led from the stables to carry my parents down the valley to Castleiron. My father's jaw was clenched tight. My mother looked white and ill. A bruise — remnant of a week-old argument — was fading to orange on her cheek. I was more than old enough to have an idea of what they might expect at Castleiron. How the Queen would harangue them from the throne set within the cavernous skeletal mouth of the Great Beast that had spewed out this Kingdom and all the riches beneath. How they would have to watch as the royal sentinels hauled some poor wretch from the crowd. How the noblest houses of this land would all stand stiff-faced as the daggers flashed and agony pattered the stones.

You will understand by now that my father kept himself to himself. He had no more time for the other noble houses than he had for the excesses of Queen Gormal. And my mother was a quiet woman who shared his bed when he demanded and checked the books and placated the servants when his brutality went too far. They were trapped by their high birth in the machinations of Castleiron, but in their different ways they were both well equipped to ride the various bloody tides. In his own sullen way, my father managed to keep balance from the more severe swings of power even when the rooks that nested in the abandoned mines near our tower were absent for days as they feasted on the bodies hung out as example from the walls of Castleiron.

That morning, after my father had climbed aboard the steamhorse and hauled my mother up after him, he looked around at the grey landscape and sniffed the sulphurous air. His colourless eyes travelled over the flaking brick of the tower, the upturned faces of the servants. For a moment, I imagined that he was taking in what he thought might be his last glimpse of home. But then his gaze settled on me as I stood unconsciously rubbing my freshening bruises, cupping my fingers around the weeping blisters on my palm. In an instant I realised that my punishment was not yet finished.

He cracked his lips into a smile. Teeth like discoloured ice. A sudden gust of wind batted a scrap of ash into his face. He pushed it away and it tumbled into the sky.

"Come on, Son," he said, a grey smear now on his cheek. "About time you grew up. Hop aboard."

I stepped forward. He held out thin fingers. They were tight on my wrist, jerking me up like a rope.

The steamhorse sighed and tensed its copper flanks. The gears span and the flywheels strained. I gripped my mother's waist as we left the tower behind. Through the slagheaps. Burrow openings to the corrugated realm of the underworkers. Towards Castleiron. Ashlar stone black as coal. My stomach coiled like a slug in acid as we crossed the stinking green moat. In the cold shadow of the courtyard other steamhorses hissed and idled their gears. We joined the thin drift of nobility under the rusted archway that led to the State Rooms. I looked around, breathing the ferrous reek of power, my curiosity battling with my fear. In those declining times when the daylight plundered all dreams, the soot-encrusted ceilings and rotting drapes still had a kind of beauty, albeit one that was not pleasant to behold.

Queen Gormal had arranged a banquet that filled the tables stretched far back into the mildewed darkness of the Great Hall. Through some quirk, my father and my mother and I were destined to sit close to the throne, our faces illuminated in the glare of the smoking sheep's head lanterns chained from the weary roof. The food was actually quite good by the sour standards of that time. It had been the custom of her predecessor Cardinal Reichold to compel the nobility to eat substances too vile for easy description whilst he rocked with laughter on the throne and sipped lemon tea, but Queen Gormal wished to impress us all with her generosity. She had set before us silver platters steaming with heart of agront, hot pickled turnip and salt loin of lamb.

The jaws of the Great Beast yawned up towards the dim ceiling. Only something so huge could have dwarfed the Queen as she sat overlapping her throne, set like a white epiglottis inside the skeletal throat. She was as round as a snowberry and twice as bitter. She was eating. Not one to waste energy, she had an eater machine clamped over her face in much the same manner as a hound might wear a muzzle, although with the opposite intention. Some inventor had cast its prototype in liveiron decades before, the intention being to help those who were too weak or ill to work their jaws and swallow. But the device had been taken up instead by those such as the Queen who wished to avoid the effort of working their throat and jaws as they ate. Two sentries had put aside their ceremonial halberds to load choice items from the feast into the hopper at the front.

I drank the hot wine from the goblet at my side and worked at the food left-handed. I was old enough to relish the ease the unaccustomed tartness of the wine brought to my bruises and my anxiety. But the grease-smeared faces, the clangourous music and the squelching of the eater machine all struck a false note. These were worse than average times. Out in the flatlands to the east beyond the forest where the Great Road met farms and fields and the sky was reportedly blue in summer, close to where mythical Ocean was said to support the land, there was reported to be a Blight. Not canker or insect or disease but a half-creature that flapped from tree to tree like sheeting caught in a storm, that dragged itself moaning through the fields and orchards, drawing away nutrition and flavour. That enveloped the cattle whole and sucked on them like a baby at the nipple, leaving their meat rancid and off-white. At night it howled against the church bells and was rumoured to slide through the windows of hovels to suck the minds from those who were sleeping, leaving the bodies behind, breathing and empty.

It all sounded like the kind of story that starts with a grain of deceit and grows tumourous in the retelling, yet only two days before my mother had purchased one of the first of the year's crop of cabbage from the market beneath Castleiron. Almost fresh from its journey west on the trains of steamhorses, it had seemed a bargain, yet the cooking of it had filled our tower with a stink redolent of the smell that came from the straw of my pallet on the hottest of days. And when we tried to eat it the texture of the plump leaves was like gritty snow. I guessed that in this banquet Queen Gormal was using up the last of the previous year's stores in the kind of binge that the weak use to try to stave off the future. In any event, the signs were bad.

So it seemed to me that this meal might be the last decent one any of us would have for some time. And for all the falsity of the celebration I was determined to enjoy it. Whilst others shouted and banged their goblets and dropped morsels of their food to the stone flags where the rats of Castleiron scurried them away, I kept my head down and chewed every last scrap down to the peel and the marrow and wiped up the remaining juices with a slab of bread until I could see my face staring back at me from my plate. Making the most of the rare sense of well-being brought on by the wine and a full belly, I leaned back on the bench and looked around. My mother — normally a delicate eater — had virtually finished too and was dabbing grease from her lips with the corner of her sleeve. The sounds of eating were quietening along the huge tables and many were already climbing over the backs of the benches to stagger behind the screens and make use of the privy buckets. I reached for a dried apple from the pile in the centre of the table, then drew back in surprise when I saw that the food on my father's plate was virtually untouched.

I looked at him. His face was the colour of a slagheap. I risked asking him if he felt alright.

"I cannot abide the sweet meaty flavour of the agront," he growled. "The juice of the thing has soaked through everything on this dish."

I nodded, even though I knew nothing of the sort. I rarely ate with my father in our tower and the pinkish flesh of agront harvested wild from the mountainsides around the valley was rare and expensive. But admittedly it did not do to think of the plant's nocturnal habits and its questing mouth when you were eating, nor of the strange florescence it brought to the stools.

I looked along the flickeringly lit table, sprawling with shadows. My father's full plate was already obvious amid the ruins of the banquet.

"Look," I said to him. My palm was throbbing and I could still feel the bruises from my beating but I was bold with the wine. "Pass what you can over to my plate and drop the rest on the floor. We can't be seen —"

My voice trailed off the sudden wave of silence as Queen Gormal smashed her goblet against the iron arm of her throne. She waved the sentries to unclasp the bolts and flywheels of the eater machine from her face.

"Now," she spoke. A pretty almost songlike voice that was at odds with almost everything else about her. I risked glancing up at the throne. My heart kicked me twice in the chest, then seemed to stop. Her arm was raised and her index finger was pointing straight at my father. Some odd corner of my mind that was still ticking over noted how the rings she wore sunk deep so that even the stones barely showed, how the clamps of the eater machine had mottled her face like ringworm.

"You," she crooned, "you who have not eaten. Stand up."

My father hesitated a fraction, just to make certain that she did indeed mean him. But there was no doubt. He climbed to his feet awkwardly, his knees bent forward by the edge of the bench. All jollity had died. The whole hall was brimming with a silence broken only by the squabbling rats and the puttering lanterns. As with every other audience, the time had come for the screeching of agony and denial. I saw that the sentries who stood beside the jaws of the Great Beast were resting their hands on their knives and smirking like kids who couldn't wait to open a present.

"Tell me why," the Queen said, her cheeks trembling, "you have chosen to revile my hospitality."

"Your Majesty," my father spread his nicotined hands; an unconscious gesture of helpless innocence that fitted the man as badly as an undersized coat. "The taste of agront — even agront of this undoubted excellence — is like a poison to me. Just as you yourself —"

"Shut up!" Trickles of oily moisture that could have been tears or sweat or the juices of what she had been eating ran down her cheeks and settled in the folds of her neck.

My father let his hands drop. My mother gave a burping sob and stifled it with her hand.

The Queen leaned forward in her throne, out of the mouth of the Great Beast, squinting at him through the smoky light. "I hardly recognise you. What house are you of?"

Hemmed in by the table, my father just managed a bow. More inappropriate than ever now, a half-smile drew shadows across his face. Glancing up at him, this lonely creature of fear and power, I felt a sick frisson of joy that he had come to this. I hated myself for the feeling, but I couldn't help it: I hated my father still more. "The redbrick tower, Your Majesty."

She slumped back. "Then eat the agronts."

Whispers rippled down the tables into the yellow depths of the hall. Was that all? To eat the agronts? The luck of the man! Why I would eat —

Slowly, my father shook his head. "No, Your Majesty. I will do your bidding on any other matter. But as I have explained in all humility, the taste is abhorrent to me."

She sat rigid. Even the rats seemed to quieten. Yet his face was set firm.

The Queen gripped the edges of the throne. Her mountainous breasts began to tremble and the facets and chains of her necklaces flashed red. Then she opened her mouth and let out a barking yelp, a sound oddly similar to that which the agront itself made when it was immersed in boiling oil. She yelped again. He face reddened. There was a long and excruciating pause before anyone realised that she was laughing. But as soon people began to force grins to their lips she waved her hand for silence.

"Well, my lord of the redbrick tower. You have the stupidity to honour your stomach above your Queen —"

" — Majesty, I — "

" — and yet you also seem to have a stubborn bravery about you that these swine around you lack." She put out a pink tongue to draw the saliva back from her chin. "Sir, we have a task for you. You will have heard of the Blight that haunts the edge of our lands. Doubtless some plot of those who would lay all bounty to waste. But so far wizardry has failed. I command you, oh lord of the delicate stomach, to don your armour and go on Quest. I command you to slay the Blight."

My father bowed. "Willingly, Your Majesty." He obviously realised that, virtual death sentence that this was, it was as good as he was likely to get. And at least it avoided the indignities that the sentries would inflict with their knives.

She waved him to sit down. And the pudding was carried forth steaming from the kitchens. Orangebark on a bed of sweet lettuce. My father ate his portion with mechanical absorption, his grey jaws tensing and untensing like liveiron.

The family suit of armour had hung for decades from hooks in a high and draughty corner of our tower, greased with rancid goose oil to keep it from rusting. I remember first stumbling across it on some early exploratory jaunt through the rambling stairwells and dusty rooms — and how the sight of it gleaming black as a sloughed snakeskin had robbed me for nights of my sleep. When the wind howled down from the Ferrous Mountains and the tower rattled like a dry poppyhead, the suit would sway and clang in the darkness, filling my dreams with the clamour of cracked bells.

The morning after the banquet my father commanded my mother and myself to watch as he was clad in the suit. The servants muttered and trembled as they puzzled over how it should be reassembled. Every poitrel and plate was black as the kitchen caldrons. My father struck out at them and clanged and howled his impotent rage. But slowly the task was accomplished. His thin body was swallowed in iron.

He clashed his way out into the bitter air. His heavy sabots sunk deep into the ash. The rooks were cawing, circling. The waiting steamhorse was chuffing restlessly. It had its fill of the best coal in the stables and although it was too stupid to understand the importance of the journey, it sensed that something unusual was afoot. Its headlights glowed. Its piston arms were hot with anticipation. My father lumbered over. Pushing away all offers of help, he climbed aboard. He looked loose and heavy as a sack of clinker.

He donned his helmet and creaked up the visor. His white, bitter face peered down at us like some martyr looking out from the devouring mouth of a dragon. He shouted to my mother. She fumbled matches and a cigarette, coughing as she drew on the flame to get it alight. She passed it up towards him. He seized it in his gauntlet and sat there smoking clumsily through clenched lips. I think the thing that angered him more than anything was realisation of how foolish he appeared inside the armour. It really did look as though it had eaten him. He tried to say something, but his words were lost in the sigh of idling pistons and the hiss of the boiler. He threw the cigarette into the dust. Before he let the visor clang down I had one last glimpse of his face. It was twisted in disgust.

A clanking automaton, less flesh and blood than the steamhorse itself, he let in the gears. The steamhorse tensed it wheels. The whistle screeched and it rumbled away between the slagheaps trailing a flag of sparks and steam, off towards the Great Road and the forest and the flatlands to do battle with the Blight. Dogs and children followed for a while in his tracks, but my mother and I remained standing beside our tower where the rooks cawed and circled the grey air that — amid the scents of coal and toil — carried the fading odours of tobacco and goose grease. We turned and hugged each other in a brief, stiff embrace that at least avoided the necessity for words. Then we went inside to wait for news.

The harvest in the flatlands was a nightmare. My father must have passed the straggling trains of steamhorse-drawn waggons as he headed along the Great Road, each hopper brimming with glossy apples, parsnips as long as your arm and mountains of blackberries dribbling juice into the mud. As always, most were destined for the salt vats, the presses, the smoke houses and the drying racks, but those which did find their way to the markets soon spread panic. The apples had the texture of pustules, the parsnips had the flavour of ancient dung: or so it was said by those who claimed the dubious enlightenment of such comparisons. In any event, they were indisputably foul and gave no nourishment.

The minewheels still turned. The smokestacks poisoned the sky. By some irony a new seam of liveiron was struck that promised the finest pedigree of steamhorse in decades and these were prosperous times for underworkers, with bonus hours for anyone fit enough to work them. But the fresh money chased fewer and fewer goods. What remained of last year's supplies were bought for figures — and, increasingly, other types of currency — that only the most wealthy or the most desperate could afford to pay.

We were fortunate in our tower. My mother invariably expected the worst and she always saw to it that the larders were full. Now that my father was absent she could make the most of her pessimist's satisfaction at being right.

Late autumn fell in filthy torrents from the sky. The bricks in our tower oozed the smell of the ancient river clay from which they had been made. I would stare for hours from the window of a forgotten room I had taken to thinking of as my own, watching the mines claw through the mud, still thinking of that girl I had seen sitting on the drift of ash above the marsh, her face tilted to the sun. Although my room was far distant from the place in the tower that my father had liked to call his study, sometimes I would look around me with a start. But then I would smile. Even in this grim season, there was a fresh sense of ease about the tower with my father gone. I was free to dream of things that never were. Worlds of pretty and of gold. And to watch the puddles along the empty track that led towards the Great Road.

I remember the morning that my father returned. Several weeks before, I had discovered a stock of his old cigarettes. I suppose that curiosity must have driven me to try them, but even now I cannot say what made me persist in breathing the foul smog that was quite different from what I expected and yet so reminiscent of my father. But I did persist. And I was smoking as I stood with my palm pressed against the streaming glass of my own empty room. I had grown used to it, almost to like it, although the bitter grey still stung my eyes. My thoughts were anywhere but on the world outside the window. But I instantly heard, faint but unmistakable over the rain, the chuff of the steamhorse and the squelch of iron wheels pulling through the jellied mud. I crushed out my cigarette and half-fell down the tumbling stairways. Into the sooty rain.

It was a steamhorse. With redgold livery showing through the rust. And there was my father, fully suited and balanced atop the iron saddle, water steaming off the oiled plates of his armour. I splashed out towards him, still half hoping that it wasn't true. I grabbed the raised stirrups of the steamhorse. As I looked up, the rain streaming into my eyes, the breastplate dropped from his chest. I had to jump backwards as metal tumbled by. White flesh showed. Then my father fell too, half-naked into the mud. The visor broke up over his face. He was smiling. The steamhorse ambled on through the rain towards the tower, shedding what remained of the suit.

I bellowed for the servants to pick up the body and the jigsaw trail of armour. Cowering at my threats, they did as I commanded. They stripped him in the rain. He was like one of the dead chicks that the rooks tossed out from their nests each spring. But he had no beak. And he was breathing. He was smiling. As my mother sobbed and chewed

her knuckles the servants formed a makeshift stretcher. They carried
him through cold halls, along damp corridors, up stairways. His limbs
rolled off the stretcher and scuffed the steps. I ordered them to take
him to the room he had liked to call his study, to place him atop a table
beside the window where he used to stand. And then I drove them all
away.

I looked into eyes that were the no-colour of rain. At least that
hadn't changed. I touched his bony chest and felt the birdcage flutter
of his heart, the stirring of his lungs. The Blight had taken him: pushed
him through to another world. That smile came from somewhere deep
within, boring a hole right through me, up through this tower, the rain,
up to the place where sunlight beamed blue over candyfloss. There
was no sign of damage or injury but he didn't even smell the same.
Certainly not the sour and disappointed aroma of sweat and cigarettes
that I associated with my father's body...that I had come to associate
with myself.

How pleasant it would be to tell that I set out clad in greasy armour
and mounted aboard a steamhorse to overcome the Blight. And imagine your pride to know that your King was a hero. But in truth if there
had been a knife in my hand I would have killed my father. Driven the
steel in hard and again. I hated that smile. It was everything that he
had denied in himself and in me.

But I told myself that I was head of the household now. And I was
afraid that violence would only make me more like him than I already
was. Losing your father — even in a way such as this — simply brings
you face to face with who and what you are. That was the most hateful
thing of all.

I let him live. I screamed for the servants. He was thin now beyond
malnourishment. I ordered them to search every room in the tower
until they found an eater machine to feed him. And I saw to it that they
did so.

On Saint Ely's day the moat froze solid around Castleiron. Both despite
and because of the privations of the winter and the Blight, it was a
signal for jollity. The pit wheels stopped turning. The church bells
boomed. Children clambered through barbed wire to tie ribbons to the
steamhorses grazing the coal seams at the head of the valley. Feeling
sick with myself, I stood at a window in my own empty room, watching

the dark streams of underworkers emerge from their chaotic dwellings and spread through the frost like ants in sugar. But to her credit
my mother forced her swollen legs up the stairways in search of me.
Freed from the threat of my father, she had become a different, more
forceful person. While I moped and cursed the servants, she ran the
tower.

I turned from the window as I heard her dragging footsteps. I drew
on my cigarette, blinking through the haze and the shadows. She stood
in the doorway, and her expression bore more than frustration at my
weary indolence. There was anger and fear. Before I had time to argue,
she shouted that no son of hers was going to spend his days like this.
No way was she going to let it happen. She was right, of course; saints'
days were too rare to waste. She nagged me into boots and woollens.
Not that I agreed at the time, but I was still half a child and going outside seemed like less trouble than arguing.

Outside, the chimneys were topped for once by no more than pinkish sky. With the wagons and the pumps all still, my feet crunched loud
on the clinker path. The valley resounded with huge silence, like the
last echo of a struck gong. I walked over the shifting slagheap, picking
my way down between the tin flaps that covered the passageways to the
underworkers' dwellings, on through the maze of the Pits. I was drawn
by the sounds of life, of people, not specifically of voices and movement, but the indeterminate rumble that a crowd gives off as readily as
the smell of close flesh. People laughing and talking and squabbling,
people spending money they didn't have and making happy fools of
themselves.

There was a fair close to the ice, on the flat wasteland that spread
before Castleiron which people — in place of any number of more
accurate descriptions — called the Meadow. The stall holders had
taken their customary pitches. I let the flow of the crowd draw me
down the breath-smogged passages, past brass incubi and shawls
of woven steel for the wealthy, cast-iron whistles and cheap trinkets
for the poor. A liveiron automaton stumbled through the crush, his
unoiled legs creaking and the glow almost gone from his headlights,
offering the attractions of a tent where the curious could talk with the
still-animated severed head of Cardinal Reichold. I had no money, but
many of the sights were free. A copperworm from the deepest mines
coiled around the quivering form of a dancer. A down-at-heel magi-

cian was offering Lightening Bolts While You Wait although the peeling sign failed to suggest any useful purpose. Further on, the food stalls were more thinly spaced than I remembered from previous fairs and the miasma of cooking meats and burnt toffee was replaced by the thinly rancid smell, unpleasantly reminiscent of the private parts of the human body, that we had all come to associate with the Blight. But even if there was little on display that would attract anyone with a full belly, the stalls nevertheless did good business.

But it was the ice that everyone had gathered for. The old to watch, the young to be truly young for a while. Normally, the moat was an odorous soup stirred by every imaginable effluent. But the cold had dispersed all but a ghost of the usual stench and set the liquid smooth as apple jelly. My grim mood was out of place: even the frost-cured faces of the malcontents who dangled from the castle walls seemed to be grinning. I thought of my father, smiling too through the iron cage of an eater machine. In his own happy world. Then I tried to forget.

The flat-footed skaters sprawled, stood up, skimmed those miracle seconds before the next fall. I hardly recognised anyone beneath the dirty bindings, and those I did were servants and underworkers, not fit company for someone of my birth. But I joined in anyway, clumsy as a broken spring. Amid the skating figures there was one that kept returning. We circled. We collided. The bare palms of my hands skidded though a melting patch and I laughed as I hauled myself up from my knees. She was laughing too. Eyes that were green as the ice between a baggy hat and bandages of scarf. She had rag doll limbs, rag doll clothes but I could feel her warmth burning through. And it was just a game as my arms brushed the softness of her breasts as we skated, just a game as she bumped her limbs against mine.

The rim of the sun broke evening over the ice. I tried to catch my breath at the wet edge. The girl skidded over to join me. She pulled the rags down from her face to her sharp certain chin. I saw that she was the girl I had seen sitting on the ash heap above the marsh. And although she was pretty beneath the grime, I felt a flash of resentment that she should break into my dreams. Still, I tried to talk to her even though her accent was thick, like the sound of steamhorse slurry tipped down a chute.

The sky was darkening. The stalls of the fair were stripped to skeletons, fought over by the hungry rooks and the even hungrier rats. The ice was empty. Its glow had almost faded as we picked our way through the slushy earth at the edge of the Meadow. Looking back across the ice, her hand tight as a stone in mine, I thought I glimpsed something blacker than the shadows slide beneath the surface. Maybe some creature. Maybe nothing at all. It wasn't a time for thinking.

That silence in the valley that I had noticed early in the day was now a tight physical presence, something from within a box within a box. The girl and I stood awkwardly together: two scarecrows all but ignored by the rooks bickering over the remains of the fair. She loosened the ties of the blanket she was wearing for a coat and I could see the hollow of her neck, the sweat-glimmered divide of her breasts. The idea of talk was even more useless than before. We had come to that moment that all men and women (children though we still both undoubtedly were) must share without sharing. And I stepped forward in the half-thawed mud. She touched me inside the soft prison of her arms with chilly fingers and I answered without question.

The wind fluted a discord between the empty stalls. It was no use here. We needed to go somewhere. The tower was out of the question; my mother's instruction to make the most of the day certainly wasn't intended to extend to this. There was of course a well-worn tradition of the nobility taking their pleasure with those who couldn't afford to refuse, but the tradition of hypocrisy was stronger still. And this time was different, just as all times have been different for everyone since the Great Beast first spewed out this mineral land.

She grabbed my hand and we hurried across the misnamed Meadow, on into the Pits. The bleached moon rode the wind above the ash heaps but the paths led down, through twists and turns I could never have followed. Here the soot settled, the dirt gathered in drifts, the frost and the snow were never white. Tin roofs and pit props broke across tunnel throats. The sky closed over with rubble. She led me down.

Here, she said, and gestured towards some hole that was no different from the rest, probably worse if you looked closely. I glanced back, aware of mutterings and wet eyes twinkling, but the space was darkness without scale. She tugged me through into giving blackness. There were the gathering odours of mortality as we clawed away layers of our clothing, sharp explorations that became urgent and sweet. Her hot, chewed lips against mine. But for all the blind clamour of my senses there was a part of my mind that refused to dissolve, that was playing over the memory of each moment even before it happened.

The vision of the girl above the marsh, dissolved into this. Nothing was quite as it should be. I pulled her limbs the way I wanted them and she pushed back at me. Inexperienced children though we were, we reached some compromise and took our uncertain pleasure. Everything tunnelled down. It was like the moment of waking when the dream fades. I realised as I fell back and saw the faint moon-glimmer of her flesh that even the darkness itself was less than absolute.

I slept. I dreamed the scent of dappled pine needles, some memory of a summer wind from the east that the Pits had yet to taint. When I opened my eyes I saw the grey slopes of our limbs, entwined but separate. She mewed something half-awake. I smelled tears and realised that she had been crying.

I asked her why.

We began to talk: talking in the darkness is sometimes easier than making love. She told me about her life, the undoing of certainties, the inexhaustible surprises of loss and age. For the first time, I realised that there are visions at the corner of everyone's eyes. Dreams that we dare not turn and face. Just as I had stumbled away from the sight of this girl above the marsh. Just as my father had tried to dissolve his own dreams in anger and bitterness.

We whispered the same words. Our incantations of humanity. Her face was above me, distant and close as the moon, eyes over my eyes, lips over my lips. And her need was inside my flesh, drawn tight beyond release. I loved her. I could feel the world pouring through me, all power and all innocence. And it was mine and I understood through her. For a moment I knew everything.

I slept again, sweetly in her arms. I dreamed of the shadow I had seen beneath the ice. It was sliding between us. When I awoke there was enough light to make out the puff-ball rottenness of the cave. She had rolled away from me, still curled asleep, showing nothing but the bony architecture of her back. I touched her skin. I stroked the notches of her spine. I wanted fire and tenderness, but she didn't respond. She lay breathing lifelessly still. When I pulled her over, her limbs sprawled loose. And she was smiling. Her green eyes wide and staring right through my head and up beyond the clouds.

She was smiling like my father, neither dead nor alive.

I remembered the shadow under the ice. The shadow in my dream.

The Blight had been here, taken her from me. Even as I wept the Pits were clangourously awakening. My grief was drowned in noise before it left my throat.

On hands and knees I dragged my clothes together. The face I had seen like a vision atop that heap of ash gazed at me without seeing. I kissed her ragged lips, the softness of her breasts. I breathed her skin. Her beautiful eyes were staring into a place I couldn't touch or feel or smell or see. I spread her hair in a burnished fan, I settled her limbs, her dirty-nailed hands. She looked beautiful beyond words, but even as I stared at her I grew afraid that the vision would shatter. I backed into the tight grip of the tunnel with a different kind of fear in my throat, almost glad to be away.

I entered a cavern, drizzled by daylight from crevices in the roof, bitter with smoke. I stumbled along the paths that seemed to lead upwards. Whole families huddled around spitting fires. In places I had to climb around these shivering mounds of flesh and clothing. But even when I was close enough to reach into the flames, there was hardly any heat.

Walking without thinking or caring, I soon came to broadening ways and the bright open sky. The shift whistles were starting to scream. Underworkers were emerging from the dirt, crossing the sharp landscape on their journeys from the hole where they lived to the one where they worked. Many more, unseen, made their way underground through the honeycomb soil. The labouring steamhorses, hauling chains, driving pulleys that turned cogs that burrowed darkness, looked well-fed and well-oiled, plump compared to the underworkers who tended them.

The scent of the girl still lingered on my flesh but already the feeling of loss was distant. All the richness had gone. My whole life seemed like a process of loss, as though the Blight had always been here, emptying the air to grey, draining every dream. Drawing and sucking like a leech until, emboldened, it took a form that this world could see.

I wandered out of a choking drift of steam, still unsure of my directions and in no hurry to find my way. Then I stopped and looked around. Scrap iron clawed the rubble. Grasping hands, trying to reach beyond. An underworker was singing a melody to the rhythm of cogs and chains. Gears within gears; worlds within worlds...and then my heart began to pound. Suddenly, I was close to a different dream.

I quickened my pace across the Pits. My way led past a church that pricked the sky amid the chimneys at the edge of the deepmines. A crowd had gathered on the loose mix of bones and rubble that formed the graveyard. As I approached I heard screeching and wailing.

I slowed when I reached the spot, stumbling over uptilted femurs and broken memorials. The people were mostly underworkers, crossing themselves with tattered hands and murmuring imprecations to the saints. When I looked up at the blackened spire I saw why.

A shadow was fluttering from the belfry. It had the texture of loose grey skin; a living flag. I could hear it muttering over the cries of the onlookers, words without meaning that were closer to baby talk than insanity. It was easing its way between the slats like leaves through a gutter. As it did so it began to sob, as though the process caused it much pain.

I stared for a few moments. So this was the fabled Blight, the thing that had made my father smile and robbed me of my love, flapping here, obvious as a dishcloth thrown against the sky. It must have been drawn by the resonance of the bells, driven by whatever hungers possessed it to suck out the potency of cast bronze. Looking up, the sight was sickening without meaning, like the suffering the Blight itself carried. It taught me nothing, not even fear. I pushed my way through the onlookers without glancing back, on across the slagheaps beyond. When I reached a fork in the ways beside the ruins of a mine that led left towards my tower, I turned right.

It was hard work climbing the coalseamed fields where the steamhorses grazed each night. The creatures churned the steep edges of the valley to sand, and twice I had to stop myself tumbling backwards by grabbing barbed wire. It hurt but did little damage. And my luck held when I literally fell across a copperweave nosebag. I shook out the coaldust and hitched it over my shoulder like a sack.

Up above the field boundaries there was nothing but rock and air. I stopped at last to catch my breath and look down over the valley. It was grey. White. Black. Every colour that wasn't a colour. This far off in the chimney haze, even the moat of Castleiron was no longer green. The stench of sweat and sulphur brimmed over the mountains to the ravaged sky. This was my home and reality screamed at me through every pore, but now I was determined to change it. Maybe the dream had gone, but the Blight wasn't going to take me: *I* was going to take *it*.

I began to poke among the rocks, exploring the crevices where agronts sheltered in the day. I found the first one easily, a small thing still purplish from the seed pod. I ripped out its stamen before it had time to scream and stuffed it into my makeshift sack. But I needed many more and the search took hours. I climbed. My limbs were agony and the air raked my cigarette-clotted lungs. But slowly the sack grew heavier. The agronts were sly. They waited for me to commit myself to a lunge across sheer rock before skittering just out of reach. But I was driven. I took risks that the peasants who normally came up here with their sacks and skewers would never have chanced — not if they wished to survive.

And all the while the valley below churned life and sulphur. Faintly, I heard the evening shift whistles. Focusing away from the crevice I was clinging to, I saw that the sun was setting through the teeth of the mountains. My shadow stretched across a nearby peak. I was incredibly high now and the sack was heavy on my back. I could feel one or two of the larger agronts that I had failed to kill outright still squirming. Maybe I had enough. Those I pursued now were old and wary, survivors of many night forays into the valley to dog the sleeping and the unwary. And doubtless they had been hunted many times before. I chanced looking directly down at the swimming drop. I saw that the granddaddy of all agronts was climbing my leg.

A shock went though me. One moment my fingers were scrabbling at the rock. The next I was in air. Flying. It was easy to fall. But quickly my bones thundered and I realised that I couldn't have dropped far, not if I felt pain at all. I dragged myself up. The sack was not far off. The wounded agront was trying to haul itself into hiding on knobbly arthritic roots. I kicked it to stillness.

There was a way down through the rocks. Half-falling, half-walking, I followed. Darkness settled. The steamhorses paused in their rootings for coal to track me with their headlights, the beams moted with soot. They were gentle animals; I remember them now with fondness. That night it was almost as though they were trying to help me find the way. Down into the Pits, where there was always black and fire. Across the slagheaps. To the redbrick tower I called my home.

My mother was sitting in the main hall. A fire was burning but it gave off more smoke that light. I was grateful; it meant that she could hardly see me.

She asked me the questions she thought she was expected to ask. Her son missing for a night and a day. Genuinely, I think she loved me. But her voice was without warmth. The Blight was here too. I could feel it in my own bones, killing even the bruises, the cracked ribs, the pain. Oh where have you been, my son… I stumbled briefly into her arms and let her kiss me, felt her muted wonder at the state I was in. Her breath smelt of coal. There were questions she couldn't ask, questions I couldn't answer. In a hurry for it to end, I broke away, banging the copperwire sack up the stairs behind me.

Passages I knew from childhood. Old friend shadows and grinning cracks in the wall. Places I could shake hands with. The room that my father liked to call his study. Where he escaped from everything but life itself. And now even that. He was stretched out beside the big window where furnacelight and moonlight webbed the darkness. The smile on his face glowed through the iron bars of the eater machine. The smile he could never quite manage on his own.

I was breathing hard, I could smell the tower, bricks and blocked chimneys and forgotten chamber pots gone cloudy ripe under unmade beds. And the hot metal and clinker and oil and coal dust in the stables. And the smoke and sulphur of the mines, the reek of clay freshly exposed to air. And the human smells of the Pits, of dreams forgotten for too long. And the bittersweet reek of corrupted power from inside the high walls of Castleiron. And the faint musty odour of the cigarettes my father used to smoke as he stood looking out.

The eater machine was idling, squatting over his face. The hopper was empty and the liveiron muscles gently tensed and loosened, just keeping in trim. My father didn't need much food. It was hardly a drain on his energy, just lying here smiling.

The open mouth of the copperwire sack gave off the mixed scents of coaldust and agront. I fumbled out the first creature; a small one. I ripped off the fingery roots and fed the fat leaves one by one into the hopper. Then another agront from the sack. Bigger, and still living. Its roots curled tight around my wrist. I plucked out the warm stamen to kill it. The roots shuddered and went dead. I began to pull off the leaves, then thought better of it and simply dropped the whole thing into the hopper. The machine's arms began to move, probing open my father's lips and reaching inside between teeth still stained brown to work his tongue and jaw, pushing chunks of agront inside. I dropped another agront in whole. And again. And another. The juices began to dribble and spray as the eater machine picked up speed. My father's jaw moved jerkily and without volition. Inside his mouth, the gripper pressed the mush down into his throat where the constricting bands around his neck took over. Even to someone like myself who would normally have relished the prospect of eating fresh agront, the sight was enough to tangle my stomach.

The machine slithered and pulsed, happy as liveiron only could be when working. It was impossible for my father to smile now and his eyes gave nothing away as his belly was pumped full. The eager machine had possessed his body, his face. I just kept on feeding the hopper. The remaining agronts began to squirm inside the sack, catching the reek of death, perhaps sensing in their own small way that something more was about to happen. I had to keep the neck tight to prevent them from escaping.

Then movement made me look up. Something fluttering over and over against the stars. Like ash on a breeze, but bigger. I paused in my labours, the torn roots of an agront twisting in my hands. I smiled. It was coming. The Blight was coming.

Then my eyes were snatched down again as my father gave a liquid belch. His body was trying to vomit, throw out the pulp that the eater machine was forcing inside. But the glistening liveiron tensed and redoubled its efforts, pushing in more and more. His back arched. Iron tensed against flesh but it seemed as though there was no competition. The eater machine simply quivered and pulsed harder.

The shadow beyond the window widened. Taking out the stars, the moon, the dogend glow of the Pits. The headlights of a steamhorse briefly ribboned the valley cliffs with gold. Then that too was gone. The Blight thumped gibbering against the window, sucking away most of the light. Its grey mass seethed, searching the panes for weakness. It found a gap. Sobbing, it forced a tendril through. The tendril shuddered, feeling blindly. My father coughed and strained again as the eater machine forced the pulp through his smile, down into his dreamworld. A pane shattered, spraying in. A blade of glass sliced past my cheek. More of the Blight flooded in.

Sound was everywhere now. The Blight. Breaking glass. The squealing of the remaining live agronts. The pump of the eater machine. The clamour of the Pits. And then everything was lost in a larger sound as my father opened his mouth wider than the eater machine could hold. Liveiron splintered and flew like axed wood. My father's jaws still widened. I remembered a steelsnake I had seen eating a rat down by the marshes. I thought of the whole world being swallowed. Then for a dizzy moment I was looking down. Flesh, bone, gristle, bursting apart. Impossibly, there was something beyond. My father's mouth yawned wider. It cracked open his head. It spread, floor to ceiling. There was hardly anything left of my father now, just pink rags, but still his mouth continued to grow. As I fell backwards it began to vomit out a mass that broke louder than any scream.

A billion things happened at once. Many years later a sentry who was standing guard on the parapets of Castleiron at that moment bowed before this golden throne and told of how he had heard a sound that was deeper than thunder and felt movement that shook him through his boots. He said that he knew it was either the beginning or the end of the world. Then he looked across the swarming darkness of the Pits and saw light.

I saw only chaos. Splashing wounds from the glass, the Blight broke fully into the room. It fought its way against the tide as the whole tower rocked and fountained bricks into the sky. The jaws were still stretching. The Blight stretched too. Ragged scraps of it circled like leaves in a whirlwind as it poured itself down into the cavernous mouth. Its gibberings ceased forever and I felt the hot waves of its delight.

As what remained of the Blight and my father joined there was a moment of silence without scale. Like the quiet of dawn, but impossibly amplified. Then a column of light broke from the giving mouth, upwards out of what remained of the tower. It seared the clouds and arched across the mineral night, spreading faster than any eye could follow. Light. Changing everything. My own senses were blasted as I fell backwards and away.

The Giving Mouth widened and poured out sweetness. The Age of the Great Beast ended as it began, but now it was dreams that spewed across the Kingdom. The slagheaps were clothed in meadowgrass. Underworkers were washed from the Pits, beached at the edge of the edge of a forest that swayed. The rooks preened their plumage to blue and circled the rising sun. Castleiron crumbled and silver fish leaped in the crystal moat. The Great Beast closed its jaws forever over the Queen set in her iron throne, then shivered to sparkling dust.

Everything was remade.

I stumbled with everyone else amid the wreckage and beauty on that first morning. I opened my eyes to blue sky. Warm sweet air danced against my face. I climbed to my feet in a ruin, greengold with bricks and ivy. I wandered through an orchard and marvelled at the tall four-legged beasts that whinnied and tossed their manes in the sunlight and blossom. When all had settled and the morning had arrived in full, I found my mother. Her hair was lifting in the breeze and she looked younger than I could ever remember. She was kneeling in a filigree of flowers. Nearby, a stream was chattering diamonds. White clouds chased shadows across the rolling green. She was looking around in wonder. Tears were streaming her cheeks.

I embraced her and cried too.

I could tell you much more; the end of my particular tale is just a beginning. But you probably know more than I about the wonders of this world. And I pray that the truth of its origins do not sour it for you.

Now that I strain my weary eyes I can tell from your face that you hear me without comprehension. You still see only this crotchety old King. You frown as you watch me smoking these leaves that grow so sweetly in the herb garden and yet taste so bitter on the tongue. You puzzle over my habits as you puzzle over my sudden angry moods. But eventually you always turn away and smile and shake your head. You put them down to age. You try to understand, but the wonders of adventure always beckon. On banquet days you sit at my right hand beside this throne set inside the yellowed teeth of this Giving Mouth that even now wafts the sweet air of Paradise against your face and stirs the hair around your noble brow. My chosen successor, you are handsome and proud, wise in the ways of goodness. You look out of that window and see the sweetdark river, forests and meadows tumbling like kites in a dream. You sleep soft and long, and morning is always a surprise. Your days are bright with colour. And you smile with your pretty ones at those stories of times when this Kingdom was cursed. Such tales as are only fit for firelight and the brimming comforts of red wine.

My time is not long. For today, you have heard enough. But soon, before the trees turn to fire and my joints become intolerable, I must take your hand and you must help me down the forgotten stairways of this tower. There in the deepest quietest recesses, where the candles glow and I have decreed that there will be nothing but gold and incense, I will show you a wonder that you will never believe. A beautiful girl who has slept though my life and will sleep beyond yours. Her hands steepled in repose. The green eyes of her smile caught inside dreams beyond anything that even this world will ever show.

And you will let her sleep, for no one would dare to wake her.

A Sun in the Attic

MARY GENTLE

Mary Gentle's fiction almost always perceives reality through a historical context. "A Sun in the Attic" is no different, despite taking place in an alternate universe. With its resolutely feminist slant, the story poses the question of the worth of progress, and the implications of technological innovation in a matriarchal society – all of this while still incorporating the steampunk signature of airships and other "clockwork" devices.

The Archivist sits in a high room, among preserved (and precisely disabled) relics; sorting through notes, depositions, eye-witness accounts, and memoirs.

Outside the window, the city of Tekne is bright under southern polar light. The room is not guarded. There is not the necessity.

In the somewhat archaic and formal style proper to history scrolls, the Archivist writes: In the Year of Our Lady, Seventeen Hundred and Ninety-Six —

Then she pauses, laying down the gull's-quill pen, staring out of the window.

Beyond the quiet waters of the harbour, the slanted sails of the barbarian fleets have drawn perceptibly nearer.

The Archivist turns back to her material.

Tell it as it happened, she thought.

Even if it is not in a single voice, nor that voice your own. Tell it while there is still time for such things...

An airship nosed slowly down towards the port's flat-roofed buildings. Beyond the harbour arm, the distant sea was white and choppy. Tekne's pale streets sprawled under the brilliant Pacific sun.

"It *may* be a false alarm." Roslin Mathury leaned on the rim of the airship-car, protesting defensively. "You know what Del's like, once he's in his workshops."

"That's why you've brought us back from the farm estates a month before harvest, I suppose?"

Roslin busied herself with straightening the lace ruffles at her cuffs and collar. Without meeting Gilvaris Mathury's gaze, she said, "Very well, I admit it, I'm anxious."

The airship sank down over the Mathury roofs, the sun striking highlights from its dull silver bulk. The crew tossed mooring ropes, and house servants ran to secure them.

"I should have made him come to the country with us!" Roslin said.

"No one ever made Del do what he didn't want to," Gilvaris observed. "I should know. He's my brother."

"He's my husband!"

"And mine, also."'

"When I married you, it wasn't to be told the obvious," Roslin said, equally acidly, gaining some comfort from the familiarity of their bickering. "Well, husband, shall we go down?"

The mooring gangway being secured, they disembarked onto the roof of the Mathury town house. The airship cast free, rising with slow deliberation. Its shadow fell across them as it went, and Roslin was momentarily chilled. She saw, as she looked past it, the crescent bulk of Daymoon, blotting out a vast arc in the western sky.

"*Se* Roslin, *Se* Gilvaris." The housekeeper bowed. "We're glad to have you back safely — "

Roslin cut the small elderly man off in mid-speech. "Tell me, what's so bad that you couldn't put it in a message to us?"

"The *Se* Del Mathury worked while you were gone," the shaven-headed servant said. "He made some discovery, or thought that he did; he had us bring food to his workrooms, and never left. I think he slept there."

Roslin nodded impatiently. "And?"

"He saw visitors," the housekeeper continued, "admitting them privately; and received messages. Three weeks ago we brought his morning-meal to the workrooms. He was gone, *Se* Roslin. We've seen and heard nothing from him since."

Light sparkled from glass tubes and flasks and retorts, from coiled copper tubing and cogwheels. A half-assembled orrery gleamed.

Gilvaris turned, pacing the length of the workroom. Boards creaked under his tread. Sunlit dust drifted down from the glass dome-roof, and the swift shadows of seabirds darkened it with their passing. Their distant cries were mournful.

"He might have forgotten to leave word," Roslin offered.

"Do you really think so?"

The caustic tone moved her to look closely at Gilvaris. Unlike his younger brother in almost everything: tall and dark where Del was fair, secretive where Del was open, slow where Del was erratically brilliant.

"No," she said, "I don't really think so. Where *is* he? Is he still in Tekne, even? He could be anywhere in Asaria!"

Gilvaris absently picked up a few bronze cogs and oddly-shaped smooth pieces of glass, shuffling them from hand to hand. "I'll try Tekne Oldport. That's where he commonly gets his supplies. And I'll ask at the university. Also, it might be wise to discover who his visitors were."

Roslin dug her hands deep into her greatcoat pockets, feeling the comforting solidness of her pistols. "Damn, when I see him — "

"If he didn't go willingly? House Mathury has enemies."

Her dark eyes widened. "So we do…"

"Now wait. That's *not* what I meant. I know House Mathury and House Rooke are rivals in trade, but — "

Roslin came over to him, took his hand. "Trust me."

"You shouldn't see Arianne." Gilvaris put an emphasis on the first word.

"Should I not?"

"You don't have the temperament for it."

"And you do, I suppose?"

Gilvaris raised an eyebrow. "I have been told that I resemble my aunt closely."

Roslin bit back a sharp answer. "Don't quarrel. You go to the Oldport, I'll ask questions elsewhere. We can't waste time. I'll never forgive myself if Del gets hurt because we weren't here when he needed us."

A summer wind blew cold through the streets. Roslin walked down to the wider avenues of new Tekne, under the tree-ferns that lined the pavements. Sun gilded the white façades of the city houses. Daymoon was westering, its umber-and-white face blotting out a third of the sky.

She stopped to let a roadcar pass; the engine hissing steam, pulling its fuel car of kelp and a dozen trailers.

House Mathury has enemies, she thought grimly, approaching the wide steps that led up to one of the larger houses. She passed under the archway and entered the courtyard beyond. Servants showed her into the house. As she expected (but was none the less impatient) they kept her waiting for some time.

"*Se* Roslin."

She turned from pacing the hall. "*Se* Arianne."

Arianne Rooke, being a generation older than her, still affected the intricately braided wig, the face-powder and high-heeled boots of that fashion. Her eyes were bright, lively in her lined face; and they gave nothing away.

"It is a pleasure, *Se* Roslin. You should visit us more often."

Her smile never faltered as she ushered Roslin through into a high narrow room. The walls were lined with bookshelves. It smelled faintly musty: the unmistakable scent of parchment and old bindings.

"House Mathury has, after all, connections here."

"Connections? Yes," Roslin said bluntly, refusing her offer of wine and a chair, "you could almost say I'm here on a family visit."

"I don't quite understand."

She looked the woman up and down. Arianne was small and dark and, despite her age, agile. Roslin didn't trust her. She was head of House Rooke; she was also Del and Gilvaris's mother's sister.

"Where's Del?" Roslin demanded.

"*Se* Roslin, I don't —"

"Don't take me for a fool," she said. "Our houses have fought for... but he's one of your own blood! What have you done to him?"

Arianne Rooke seated herself somewhat carefully in a wing-armed chair. Resting her elbows on it, she steepled her fingers and regarded Roslin benignly over the top of them.

"Now let me see what I can gather from this. Your husband Del

Mathury is missing? Not your husband Gilvaris too, I trust? No. It would never do to lose two of them."

Roslin said something unpardonably vulgar under her breath.

"And for some reason," Arianne continued, "you imagine that *I* am responsible? Come, there are far more probable reasons; you as a wife should understand this."

Such delicate insinuations did nothing for Roslin's temper. "I'm not as stupid as you think!"

"That would be difficult," Arianne agreed.

"I ought to call you out," Roslin said savagely, regretting that her pistols must be left with the servants.

"My dear, you're a notable duellist, and I have a regard for my own skin that only increases with age. So I fear I must decline."

Roslin, aware of how much Rooke was enjoying herself, thought: Gil would have done this better.

"You're trying to tell me you don't know anything about what's happened to Del."

"I can but try." Arianne spread her hands deprecatingly. "Would that I did. Would that I could help."

That hypocrisy finished it.

"You listen to me, Arianne. I mean to find Del. And I will. And if you've had anything to do with this, I'll take my evidence before the Port Council, I'll bring House Rooke down about your ears, my friend. Or," she finished, blustering, "I may just kill you."

"Isn't melodrama attractive?" Arianne Rooke observed. "I'm sure you can find your own way out."

She could not know that, when she had gone, Arianne Rooke chuckled a little. Then, sobering, took up pen and parchment to write an order for the immediate and secret meeting of the Port Tekne Council.

"Anything?" Gilvaris asked.

"No. She made me lose my temper, so naturally I didn't learn anything. Except that I shouldn't lose my temper. You have any better luck?"

"Not so far." He sat back on one of the benches. They haunted the workrooms, he and Roslin. "He could be held somewhere. Now we're back here, we may get a demand for money."

Roslin looked round the darkening room. It was the short Asarian twilight: Daymoon had already set.

"Maybe... It doesn't look like there was a struggle here, does it?"

Gilvaris shook his head. "It seems to me that there's equipment missing. I wouldn't know for sure — but it could be so."

She knew he rarely admitted ignorance. Part of the reason for that was a life spent struggling in the effortless wake of a brilliant younger brother; if Del had not loved him so devotedly, Gilvaris's life might have been bitter.

Del, she thought. We're not whole without him.

"What I'm saying is, it's possible he packed and left. He's clever enough to do it without the servants knowing, if he thought it necessary."

"You think he left us?" Roslin said, incredulous. "Damn, you're as bad as Arianne Rooke."

"I don't think he left *us*, specifically," Gilvaris said, unruffled. "I think he left. Those visitors he had: some were tradesmen, and some were from the harbour. But at least one was from the Port Council. They're no friends of Mathury. I think Del's in hiding."

Roslin considered it. "Why?"

Gil shrugged. "Haven't I always said, one day he'll discover something that'll get him into trouble?"

"It's amazing," Roslin said, as they dismounted from the roadcar on the Oldport quay. "I always saw Del as a loner, shut away in those rooms. He knows more people than I do."

"He kept in touch with a lot of colleagues from the university," Gilvaris said.

The wet morning was closing to a rain-splattered noon. They had seen and spoken with, so far, a maker of airship frames, a glassblower, a metalsmith, a windvane repairer, a clockmaker (this being a woman Roslin disliked instantly, knowing that she had been a frequent visitor to House Rooke before Roslin had), as well as printers of newssheets, and at least four sellers and importers of old books. All knew Del professionally and personally. None knew where he was now.

"He was on to something. When he shuts himself up and works

like that…" Roslin shook her head. Gilvaris linked his arm in hers as they walked.

"Metal and glassware. His most recent orders."

"Meaning?" Roslin queried.

"I wish I knew."

A harbour ship chugged past, and the smell of steam and hot metal came to Roslin through the damp air. Viscid water slapped at the quay steps. Out in the deeper anchorages, up-coast ships spread flexible canvas shells. Steamships wouldn't risk leaving Asaria's canals for the cold storm-ridden seas. Down-coast krill-ships were arriving from the southern icefields.

"If he was that desperate, he wouldn't take one of our ships," Gilvaris forestalled her. "I've made enquiries, there's one more chance. A barbarian ship."

Roslin looked where it was moored by the quay, saw low sharp lines, great jutting triangular sails. And thought of Del: intense, impractical, obsessed.

"Would he go? Without a word to us?"

"He would, if he thought that staying would put us in danger."

Roslin blinked. "I — damn, I can't think like that!"

"There's plenty who can."

After a moment Roslin put her free hand in her pocket, gripping the butt of the duelling pistol. They went forward to hail the barbarian ship.

"I have seen no one," the barbarian insisted, in passable Asarian.

He was a tall man, taller even than Gilvaris, with pale yellow skin and bright, braided golden hair. His robes were silk, and from his belt were slung paired metal blades. Roslin recalled that rumour said barbarians fought with these long knives, like servants.

No one? she thought. He's lying.

"Perhaps I can speak to your captain. Will she see me?"

He said, "I am captain here."

"Oh." Roslin sensed rather than saw Gil's amusement. Momentarily at a loss, she glanced round the bare cabin. Cushions surrounded low tables. The table from which the barbarian had risen was covered with parchments and thin ink-brushes. Seizing on this, she commented,

"Skilful work. What do you write?"

"Of my travels."

Roslin studied the script. A scant number of repeated symbols were inscribed from right to left across the page, instead of from top to bottom.

Partly gaining time, partly curious, she asked, "What do you say about us?"

He smiled. "That the southern polar continent of our legends is no legend. That Asaria is a land in which women head the family; that women here take many husbands — where I come from, men take many wives. And that otherwise the strong oppress the weak, the rich oppress the poor; knaves and fools outnumber wise and honest men; and that the machines of peace are very apt to become the engines of war. In short, that Asaria differs very little from any other continent of the globe."

"'Engines of war?'" Roslin queried.

"Why, ma'am, consider this: you have your cars not pulled by beasts of burden, what strong and tireless transport they might make for cannon! And your kite-gliders, they would let you know of the enemies' advance long before he sees you. You have ships that need not wait on wind or tide. You have ships of the air. Consider, there is not a city wall that could stand against you!"

Gilvaris Mathury, a little satirically, said, "Ah, but you see, cities in Asaria have no walls."

The barbarian inclined his head. "Indeed, I have studied your Asarian philosophy: its alternative is to put walls around the mind."

Roslin ignored that. "In your history, sir, say also that in Asaria women love their husbands, and men love their brothers — "

"Man," said Gilvaris, "do you think *we'd* harm him?"

"Let us say," the barbarian said carefully, "that *if* there were such a man, and *if* he were due to arrive here, you would have but to wait until he came to the ship. But say also, that you may not be the only ones he is hiding from, and that — if you are seen waiting — you will not be the only ones to find him."

Seabirds roosting under the eaves of the Oldport houses cried through the night. Roslin lay awake. Gil's arms round her were some comfort, but she missed the complementary warmth of Del.

Lovers: husbands: brothers. It was not in her nature, as it was not in Asarian custom, to compare. Two so different: Del with the obsessed disregard of the world that first attracted her, Gilvaris who had spoken of marriage with House Mathury (and only in that moment had it crystallised, to be without either of them was unendurable).

So she had spoken to her mother, head of house Mathury, and little help did she have from a woman whose three husbands had been acquired at different times from all over Asaria. Roslin, nevertheless, married the brothers. And a season later was, by virtue of the plague, left sole survivor and heir of Mathury, which served to bind them closer than the common.

Beside Gilvaris, aware of his quiet breathing, she knew he did not sleep. They lay awake and silent until Daymoon rose.

"Are we right to be here?" Roslin sat on the edge of the bed, lacing up her linen shirt. She could see from their high window the steps of Oldport South Hill, the fishing boats at the quay. "Can we trust a barbarian?"

"It's all we can do. Can *he* trust us, that's what he'll ask." Gilvaris's voice was muffled as he pulled on his coat. Adjusting the mirror until the polished basalt oval gave back his reflection, he flicked the lace ruffles into place. "It could take time to get a message… *Quiet!*"

For once he moved faster than Roslin. She barely caught the sound of footsteps on the stairs, and he was by the door, pistols raised. There was a sharp repeated knock.

Roslin grinned, relaxing. "That's the landlord. Breakfast, I'd guess, and not Arianne Rooke's cut-throats." Without releasing the pistol, Gilvaris pulled the door open, surprising the visitor with his hand raised again to knock.

It was Del Mathury.

"It's no good yelling at me!" Del protested. "I didn't want to be found. I wouldn't be here now, if the barbarian hadn't said it was the only way to stop you turning all Tekne upside-down."

"What the—"

Roslin's temper cooled. She felt the sting of tears behind her eyes.

"What did you think we'd feel like?" she demanded. "Damn, you might have been dead for all we knew!"

"You knew I'd be all right." His open face clouded slightly. "Didn't you? You didn't think I'd...it was a matter of staying out of sight until the ship sailed. I was going to send a message to you both then, so that you could join me on board."

Roslin sighed, sat down on the chair-arm, and put her arm round him. Gilvaris positioned himself protectively behind Del.

It's like Del not to see the obvious. But you knew that when you married him, she reminded herself.

"Del, love, why would we want to go on a barbarian ship? And for that matter, go where?"

"Somewhere I can work without the Port Council bothering me."

"You're the brilliant one," Gil said. "Tell us why we've got to leave, not Port Tekne, not the up-country farms, but all Asaria?"

"Don't be angry with me, Gil."

"I'm not."

Roslin had a sudden vision of them as children: the elder brother eternally trailed by, and eternally protective of, the younger. She wondered if either of them coveted the other's relationship with her as she coveted their brotherhood before they ever knew her.

"It was made very clear to me," Del said, "when I talked to people, that what I was doing wasn't liked. I don't know why. I don't expect it matters... Gil, Ros, I missed you when you weren't here. You'd better come and see what I've been working on."

Del led them high up among the old deserted houses of the South Hill, below the derelict fort. Roslin was sweating long before they reached the ultimate flight of steps. She saw, across the five-mile span of Tekne, North Hill push out like a fist into the sea, and the kite-gliders and airships anchored on its crest. Inland from Tekne the country went down into flat haze, broken only by the vanes of wind- and watermills.

"We should have stayed on the estate," Roslin grumbled. "You and your machines — Gil's conspiracies — I don't like any of it."

Del, who was perfectly familiar with that complaint, only grinned. He took them up to the top floors of a derelict mansion that jutted out over the streets below. The walls ran with damp, and clusters of blue and purple fungi grew on the stairs. A continuous thin sound broke the quiet: the sifting of old plaster and stone dust in decay. Roslin smelt musty ages there. The sound of the wind died, and with it the shrieks of birds.

At the very top of the house, in an attic with a shattered dome-roof, Del had set up his makeshift workshop. Half of it was in crates, ready to go aboard the barbarian ship; but Roslin could only concentrate on the massive structure of metal and glass that all but filled the room.

"Look at this." Del picked up a brass cylinder. Roslin turned it over in her hands, then gave it to an equally puzzled Gilvaris. Del snatched it back impatiently, and manipulated some of the wheels jutting from it. "No. Like this."

Dubious, Roslin copied him, holding it to her eye. The metal was cold against her skin. Her lashes brushed the polished surface of the glass. She felt Del take her shoulders and turn her towards the window. She saw a white blur, felt swoopingly dizzy; then as her long sight adjusted she made out houses, streets, tree-ferns… And lowered it, and the side of North Hill sprang back five miles into the distance.

Roslin turned the tube in her hands. It was blocked at both ends by glass, one piece of which slid up and down a track inside the tube, adjusted by cogwheels.

Del took it away from her and rubbed her fingermarks off the glass.

"It's a pretty toy," Gilvaris observed, making the same test, "but as to people's concern, I confess I don't understand that."

"The principle can be applied to other things. It's producing the lenses that's most difficult; they have to be ground."

Roslin, gazing at the arrangement of tubes, prisms, lenses and mirrors that towered over their heads, began to make sense of it.

"Hellfire! I bet you can see as far as the barbarian lands," she said.

"Further than that — " Del stopped. Gilvaris held up a hand for silence. "What is it?"

Roslin listened. There was something you couldn't mistake about the tread of armed troops. She moved to look down the stairwell.

She said, "It's Arianne Rooke."

"One would suppose we were followed," Gilvaris leaned over her shoulder.

Roslin saw the first shadow of confusion on Del's face.

"You led them to me," he said.

"Looks like we did." There was movement below in the shadowed stairwell. Deliberately she drew the pistol from her greatcoat pocket, cocked it, aimed and fired.

The report half deafened her. A great mass of plaster flaked off the far wall and spattered down the stairs. The scramble of running feet came to an abrupt halt. Roslin handed the pistol back to Gilvaris to reload. She leaned her elbows cautiously on the rail and called down: "Come up, Arianne. But come up alone — or I'll blow your damned head off."

Arianne Rooke gazed up at the spidering mass of tubes and mirrors and lenses. The late-morning sun struck highlights and reflections from them. Roslin watched her lined, plump face. Her heels clicked as she walked across the floorboards, circling the scope; and she at last came to rest standing with hands clasped on her silver-topped cane. Her braided wig was slightly askew; exertion had left runnels in the dark powder that creased her skin.

"I have thirty men downstairs," she said without turning to look at anyone there. "This must be destroyed, of course."

"You—"

Roslin gripped Del's arm, and he subsided.

Arianne Rooke turned, regarding Gilvaris with some distaste. There was a distinct resemblance between aunt and this one of her nephews. Roslin wondered if that meant Gil would, when he reached that age, be like Arianne. It was an unpleasant thought. And then she wondered if they would — any of them — live to reach Arianne Rooke's age.

"You," Arianne said, "I thought you, at least, had some intelligence, Gilvaris."

"This rivalry between Rooke and Mathury is becoming a little…" Gilvaris reflected, "…excessive, isn't it?"

The older woman inclined her head. "Think that, if you will."

"This won't give you any trade advantage," Del said, bemused. "Or is it that you can't bear Mathury to have something Rooke doesn't?"

Roslin caught Gil's eye, and saw him nod.

"Arianne," she said, "do you know a woman called Carlin Orme? She's one of my husband's colleagues. She has a printing press. You may know her better as editor of the Port Tekne news-sheet."

Rooke frowned, but didn't respond.

"I spoke with Carlin Orme last night," Roslin said. "And with a number of other news-sheet editors. I thought, in fact, that it would be a good idea if someone other than Arianne Rooke followed us here. They'll be interested to see what my husband Del has discovered. And to know that House Rooke is here with thirty armed men."

"My dear," Arianne said, "never tell me that was your idea?"

"Well, no. Gil's the subtle one. I'd settle for something more straight-forward. And permanent."

The last chimes of noon died on the air.

"Call off your people," Rooke said, "and I'll do the same. Quick, now."

Roslin said, "I ought to give them something, *Se* Arianne, if I can't give them the treachery of House Rooke. Why shouldn't Tekne know about this?"

The woman looked round at all three of the Mathury. Roslin waited for the outcome of the gamble.

We have to win here, in Tekne, she thought, glancing fondly at Del. Because that ship's a dream — there's nowhere to go.

"Oh, you children!" Arianne Rooke swore explosively. "You haven't the least idea of… Do you know that I can call on the Port Council to silence you? Yes, and silence Carlin Orme and her like too, if I need. *Se* Roslin, I don't want to have to do that. Your husbands were Rooke before they were Mathury. But I will if I have to!"

"Port Council?" Gilvaris demanded.

For answer, Arianne Rooke drew from under her coat what even they must instantly recognise as being the Great Seal of the Port Tekne Council.

We underestimated you, Roslin thought.

"What *is* all this?" she demanded.

"Delay Carlin Orme." Rooke reached out with her cane to tilt one of the great framed lenses. "I'll tell you — no, I'll show you. I'll show you without any of us having to leave this room."

Arianne Rooke stepped back from the scope, which she had most carefully adjusted. She handled it a sight too familiarly for Roslin Mathury's peace of mind.

"I want you to look through this — *without* upsetting it." She arrested Roslin's hand. Her fingers were cool, almost chill. "Each of you. And while you're doing that, I want you to listen to me."

"So talk." Roslin, hands clasped behind her back, bent to the eye-piece — and forgot all about listening to Arianne Rooke.

It took a moment for her eyes to focus. One side of her field of vision was starred with the sun's glare, and there was the deep purple-blue of Asaria's summer sky. And...

She gazed through the scope at the surface of Daymoon.

All her life it had been familiar, the sister-world that dwarfed the sun in the sky. Now she saw lands, seas, icecaps. The webwork of dry rivers, the arid ochre land; and white cotton that specked the world under it with the minute moving shadows of clouds.

A bright metallic spark travelled across her vision, high over the deserts of Daymoon, a sharp, unnatural shape that fell into shadow as it entered the crescent's darkside. Roslin went cold. Another speck followed. Now she became adept at picking them out, their mechanically perfect flight (and thought, without reason, of Del's workshop and the half-repaired orrery).

"But — " she straightened, blinking. "Then it's true, the legends are *true...*"

"No," Rooke said. "Not now. Now there is nothing there. In all the archives of the Port Council, we have no record of any life. Look at what you do *not* see: patterns, lines, edges. No fields. No canals. No cities."

"But I saw..."

"What you see are machines. Del Mathury, you will most readily comprehend that."

"I thought as much," Del admitted, unsurprised.

"Tell me country tales, servants' tales," Arianne invited Roslin. "What is there on Daymoon?"

Roslin recalled shadows and firelight, and how tall the world is to a small child.

"Daymoon's a fine world. The people live in crystal houses, and their lanterns burn for ever. They build towers as tall as the sky, and fly faster than any airship ever made. Their carriages outrun the speed of the sun. Each woman there is richer than a *ser* of the Port Council, each man also. They cross the seas and span the land, and no disease touches them."

Abandoning the child's ritual, still bemused, she said, "So I was told, when very young. Servants believe it still, and think to go there when they die."

"Which is well, since few of us can be *ser* here in Asaria," Gilvaris commented acidly, straightening from the scope. "Is that what you'd hide, that they've no paradise waiting? That Daymoon is a lie?"

"Daymoon is true. *Was* true," Rooke corrected herself. "And you see what is left. To put it most simply: I wish to keep us from that road, the road they followed to destruction. Del Mathury, worlds have been destroyed by those like you."

Roslin stared blankly. Gilvaris, glancing at Del, thought, No, you're not the first. How many years has the Port Council studied, to be so knowledgeable? And how many years have they kept it secret?

"I have often thought, in all of *that*—" Arianne Rooke's gesture took in light-years, infinity, "—that there must be worlds enough besides us and Daymoon. A million repeated worlds, differing only in small details. No sister-world, perhaps, or no southern Pacific continent, no Asaria or perhaps a barbarian empire of the north, or…many things."

Suddenly practical, she turned to Del. "If you must work, then work *with* the Council."

Del laughed. "'Must' work? If no one made anything new, we'd never change."

"I should not be ashamed to stay as we are now."

"No, I dare say *you* wouldn't." Del was caustic.

Roslin said, "We'd better work out something to tell Carlin Orme."

There was some argument, Roslin hardly attended. She was watching Arianne Rooke, who stood there with one hand on her cane, and the other tucked into her waistcoat pocket, for all the world like a Fairday shyster.

"I'll talk to Orme," Gilvaris announced, cutting off further discussion. "Del, you'd better send word to the barbarian ship."

Roslin quietly moved aside, to stand near Rooke.

"'Machines'?" she said.

"On Daymoon, they mock the dead race that made them. Is that what you'd have over Asaria?"

She heard unaccustomed seriousness in Rooke's voice.

"Do you think you can undiscover things?" Roslin asked. "Silence every Del Mathury yet unborn? You're mad!"

"I'm not mad. But I do have visions." Arianne Rooke laid a dark hand on the scope. "I believe there is a choice at some point. Perhaps now: an age of reason. And then an age of passionate unreason, ending as you have seen… There are scars of war on Daymoon. No, I don't seek to take away the machines, so much as the desire to use them so poorly."

Roslin said, "I don't understand you."

Del, as he went past them, said, "Arianne Rooke, who gave you the right to play God?"

As close to pain as Roslin had ever seen her, the woman said, "Nobody."

Silent for a moment, Roslin watched through the attic doorway as her younger husband went to speak with one of Rooke's armed men.

"How long have you been watching us?"

"Some years. The rivalry between Rooke and Mathury hasn't made it any easier, I'll admit. And for that reason — that you're less likely to believe me — I've taken the rather extraordinary measure of summoning the Port Council to full session. They can confirm what I say."

After a perfectly timed pause, she added, "We shall have to do something for young Mathury."

"For House Mathury," Roslin corrected, at last on sure ground. "Shall we say, a seat on the Council? Gil would be good at that. You see, if Del's going to work with the Council, I think he needs someone there to look out for his interests."

Arianne Rooke chuckled. "You bargain well."

"And you flatter a little, bribe a lot, and hold force as a last card."

"Which is only to say, my dear, that I'm a politician."

Roslin squinted up through the broken roof at the sky. An airship glided soundlessly overhead.

"I don't understand what's been happening here." She met Rooke's gaze. "I'm missing something. Some chance I ought to take, some question I ought to ask."

Motionless, watchful, Arianne Rooke gave the conversation more attention than an outsider might think it warranted, and thought to herself, Can this woman, who (let us be honest) is not altogether *bright*, can she come close to a Del Mathury's curiosity? Because if she can...

Rooke said, "And shall I tell you more, *Se* Roslin?"

A silence fell. The sunlight sparked from brass, mirror, lens. And in the pause, it became apparent that Roslin Mathury could not summon so irresponsible a curiosity; did not desire, or see the need for it.

"No," she said, smiling. "Leave me to run the Mathury estates without your interference. That's all I want. Now do you think we should go and bring a little order out of this chaos?"

Rooke thought, I spoke with a barbarian once, what did he say? "Putting a wall around the mind…"

The Archivist pauses.

That last sentence, true in its way, fails to suggest the whole truth. She carefully erases it.

Outside, bells ring gladly, and pennant ribbons uncoil on the breeze. She blinks away images three generations dead. Sees Tekne, now little changed. Fewer airships, fewer steamcars (but there are always servants to do the work). The only significant change is that there are barbarians in the streets.

But really, one shouldn't call them that. Not with the ser-Lords of all four continents here to celebrate the centennial of the Pax Asaria. And what better to encourage them in Asarian philosophy than a dramatic reading? she thinks, smiling at her own vanity.

Even if such turning points in history are largely guesswork…

In haste to join the carnival, the Archivist inscribes her final lines:

Arianne Rooke, alone and last to leave, adjusted one of the free lenses to catch the sunlight through the broken roof. She walked unhurriedly away. Where the sun focused, a thin wisp of smoke coiled acridly up from the wooden attic floor.

The God-Clown Is Near

JAY LAKE

Steampunk isn't just airships and Victoriana and alternate history. It also re-imagines the tradition of the Golem in literature, remade in a more mechanical context. In this story, Jay Lake uses that trope in one of his delightful yet disturbing Dark Town stories, which represent a new brand of American fantasy: surreal, pulpish, yet undeniably clever and literary at the same time.

"I need you to build me a clown," said Rêve Sueño, interrupting Doctor Cosimo Ferrante at his work.

Ferrante was the finest flesh sculptor in Triune Town, one of the Dark Towns hidden in the blank spaces on the maps of the world. His atelier, high-ceilinged and ornamented in a violently gilded excrescence of rococo frieze work, was practically one of the sacred spaces of the city. Not to be invaded by penny-ante thugs from the Dreamstalker stirps with snakeskin jackets and saw-toothed smiles.

Rêve's brother Traum leaned against the hand-carved door of Ferrante's atelier, propping it open. The hugely-muscled pair could have been twins, except that Rêve's eyes were the color of smoke from a summer fire, while Traum's glowed red as the flame. Otherwise the fair-skinned, dark-haired brothers were as alike as two sharks.

Ferrante had always admired the effect.

Disturbed but not startled — never startled — Ferrante carefully set the dripping scalpel down before he soiled the terrazzo floor, then drew a sheet over his subject. He twisted an alcohol-soaked rag between his fingers, sniffed the resulting odor, then smiled at his visitors. He was whippet-thin to their bulk, but just as tall, and possessed of considerably more gravitas, as befit his profession.

"There are several stirps in Triune Town quite capable of training good clowns from among their members. Had you made an appointment in the usual fashion, I might have saved you the trouble of a pointless interruption."

"*Nothing* I do is pointless," said Rêve. The smoke-colored eyes glinted like steel awls. "I need a clown with unique abilities."

"All clowns are unique." Ferrante smiled. "It is in their nature."

"My clown will be more unique. I need a moral clown, a judge and executioner of unparalleled power and soul-searing aspect."

"A moral clown." Ferrante drummed his fingers against his chin. "Is this for the Dreamstalkers, or are you freelancing?"

Rêve laughed. "Let's just say I've received a higher calling." Even Traum, always silent as stone, smiled.

"I am troubled," Ferrante told his friend Jack over a bottle of absinthe at Valdosta's, a little café along one of Triune Town's winding, messy streets. The place wasn't as large as Ferrante's atelier, perhaps fifteen feet wide and thirty deep, and the ceiling was a riot of brass and copper pipes, through which coffee, tea and stranger fluids ran in some curious alchemy of steam, pressure and taste. Taps and stopcocks lined the walls at random heights, along with a modestly-stocked bar in a curio cabinet at the back of the room beneath the mummified heads of the past three generations of Valdostas *grandpère, père et fils.*

Jack, of the Sloe-Eyed Jacks stirps and therefore achingly beautiful and equally deadly, sipped his green liqueur. Jack was singular and masculine, all of him, man-Jack, woman-Jack and baby-Jack alike, a form of power in the name-riddled society of Triune Town. There was no stirps more deadly or dangerous than the Sloe-Eyed Jacks, which only lent Jack more grace and wit. Even so, Ferrante thought of his particular Jack, a woman-Jack, as Jack the sad, for his Jack always had a slight cast of regret to his face.

"You are troubled by the Dreamstalkers?" Jack asked with a small, secret smile that promised visions of paradise.

Ferrante shook his head clear of Jack's pheromones. "No, not the whole stirps. Just those two idiots, freelancing for some reason. Why would anyone want a moral clown? Clowns are exempt from morality — that is what makes them clowns."

"A moral clown would be the inverse of a sinning priest," said Jack.

He touched his delicate finger to the rim of the absinthe glass, a fractured, bubbly piece of handwork that looked to have come from the lips of a drunken glassblower. "Or perhaps a fallen angel, if one may be permitted a vision so grand."

"One may, of course," Ferrante said, slipping briefly under the spell of Jack's perfect fingertip.

Jack's finger tapped Ferrante's chin. "Dream on, my friend. We are better met over a tablecloth than a bedsheet, trust me. I will see what devilment it is that the Sueño brothers have found for themselves if you will see what specifics and purpose they seek for their little project."

Along with everyone else in the café, Ferrante watched Jack sway out of Valdosta's to the piping of some steam-whistled eagle tucked away amidst the ceiling. He sighed, finished his absinthe, and closed his eyes to await the visions that ever drove his work.

Within the green mists of the drink the leathery head of *grandpère* Valdosta chattered and mumbled in the language of dogs for a very long time, but no wisdom found Cosimo Ferrante.

The next day a pert boy in a slave harness came to the atelier. He had cornsilk hair and lips that society matrons would kill for, but someone had sewn the boy's eyelids shut in a bout of lovely irony.

"Message for you, Doctor," said the slave, walking across the threshold with no hesitation as Ferrante unbarred the door.

So they did not take his vision, thought Ferrante, turning a polished cheekbone over in his fingers. He despised affectation, though it was hardly the fault of this gorgeous boy that the work was not fairly done. "Someone cares for me enough to send me you?" he asked.

The slave tittered, a small laugh that echoed of endless days of harsh-drilled practice. "I bring only this, Doctor," he said, pulling an envelope from a pouch on his harness and offering it straight to Ferrante. "From the brothers Sueño with their compliments."

"I see." Ferrante took the envelope, brushing the boy's fingers. "And do you have time to dally a while? I would tip you for your trouble, but I should need to make a careful anatomical study of you first." Ferrante traced the boy's chest beneath his harness straps.

"I am wanted at Sheep's Cheese Hall at the next hour," said the slave with another titter, "and I have been well-paid by the brothers. Good day, Doctor."

Ferrante nodded, attraction already forgotten, as he went to find his fiche reader. It was a great, huge thing, terribly cranky, imported some years earlier from the Cities of the Map for just this kind of work.

First he had to throw the breakers in the junction box, for the atelier, like all of Triune Town, used very little electricity in the run of everyday business. Then he dragged the reader out of the back closet, removed the dust cover, chased off the mice, wiped down the glass and the lens, after which he cleaned himself. Finally, he actually hooked the thing up and turned it on, which was always a disturbing experience given various mysterious clicks and sharp odors.

All effort was rewarded when the diagrams sprang to life. It was indeed a clown that the brothers Sueño wanted, at least on the surface, but beneath the skin it was something else entirely, a steel-armatured horror of biological toxins, chemical hells and radically overdesigned muscles. Not to mention the cerebral modifications, which were extreme even by the standards of his trade.

Ferrante sucked his breath between his teeth. If this thing could be built, it would be a terror upon the land. The Dark Towns had struggled secretly against the Cities of the Map since before Gilgamesh laid bricks in Uruk, but something like this, produced in any quantity, would mean an open war.

So why did a pair of thugs from a mid-tier stirps want to build so deadly a thing? And where did they get the plans? The engineering was nothing of the Cities of the Map, that was obvious to Ferrante — pure Dark Towns, but with an artistry such as he had never seen.

And Ferrante was the best stylist in Triune Town.

Rêve Sueño had giggled, hinting of a divine revelation, but no one knew better than the folk of the Dark Towns how hollow that promise had ever been. *Besides*, thought Ferrante, *no god would use microfiche.*

Would they?

He met the brothers Sueño in the cabin of one of the high-wheeled carts that plied the streets of Triune Town, drawn by slaves and debtors under the lash of angry men. It was typical of the Dark Towns that while perfectly good busses existed, the old ways kept their hold. Besides, there were advantages to such conveyances, such as privacy.

Rêve sprawled back on the purple velvet upholstery, while Traum peeked out the window curtains, silently watching the traffic. Rêve smoked from a water pipe, and to Ferrante's expert eye was already far gone into whatever state his herbs were taking him.

"What do you intend for this creature?" Ferrante asked without preamble.

"You never question such things," said Rêve. "When the Black Chain stirps wanted conjoined triplets for their centennial party, you produced them with no remark. Why care now?"

"It affects my price," sniffed Ferrante. "I am not in the weapons trade. I deal in amusements and aesthetics, ideally at the same time. You want me to build something dangerous. That incurs risk, both now and later. Hence my need to know."

Rêve giggled. "What risk? If your heart is pure, our clown will leave you in peace."

"And whose heart is pure? Ever?"

Rêve just giggled again, earning a sidelong glance from Traum. Ferrante stared Rêve down, until finally Rêve hiccupped into silence, set the water pipe on the floor and took a deep breath.

"The Dark Towns are failing, Doctor. We all know that. In these past few centuries the Cities of the Map have grown beyond all reason, hemming us in around the world. Our spirit withers." Rêve leaned forward, smoky eyes gleaming in the shadowed cabin. "If we unleash judgment, on ourselves, on the Cities of the Map, on the entire world, the balance will begin to tip back toward us. This moral clown is our savior. You shall be father to a new order, Doctor Cosimo Ferrante."

Ferrante tugged at his stiff collar, his face sweating. Traum no longer watched the street, but rather stared at him, eyes narrowed in speculation. "The cost will be impossibly high…" Ferrante's voice wavered. He wanted to leave the cabin alive. "Protective measures… difficulty…"

"I knew you were our man," said Rêve as Traum stepped over to hug Ferrante in a bone-cracking grip. "Money is the least of our worries. Who do you have in mind for a brain donor? Or will you culture it yourself?"

Ferrante met his Sloe-Eyed Jack at the top of one of the zeppelin masts near the city walls. The gentle peaks of the Allegheny Mountains loomed in the distance, visible even through the obscuring twilight that always surrounded Triune Town. The mast itself towered over them, twisting in a felicitously random spiral as it rose, as intestinally straight as any street below. They stood on the mooring platform, now scattered with the dung of orangutans, and looked out across the staggering spires of their city.

"Money," said Jack, "is like blood. It flows through defined channels, powered by well-known pumps."

"You cut to the heart of the matter," Ferrante said, his imagination seething with the terrible power of Rêve Sueño's moral clown. The god-clown, Ferrante supposed he could call it.

"Hah," said Jack. "Yet here we have money in the hands of two of Triune Town's lesser lights, money which seems to have sprung into being from the shadowed depths of the earth. What would you think were you to exsanguinate a man only to find extra pints of blood in abundance?"

"I would check my equipment," said Ferrante, "assuming either a holding tank already partially filled or a bad measurement."

"So have we done, with the help of the Midas Minions and a few other expert stirps. No one seems to know where the money has come from."

"I know where it's going." Ferrante massaged his eyes, chin on his chest, before looking up again at the distant Alleghenies. "They want to build a god-clown. And it will be terrible."

"I trust you said no."

Ferrante stared at the sky a moment longer. "They blackmailed me with my life."

Jack laid a hand on Ferrante's wrist, the touch thrilling Ferrante to his core. "I will not threaten you. I do not need to. But this god-clown must not be. Work if you have to, but go slowly, make subtle errors. We will pursue their funding sources."

Shuddering, Ferrante nodded. Long after Jack left, his wrist tingled. When Ferrante finally looked down at his hand, he found he had sweat blood where Jack's fingers touched him.

Ferrante stalled for several months. New vats must be ordered from certain companies in Germany. Tissue cultures must be reengineered, restarted, quality-checked. The skeleton will be titanium, not steel. Titanium is not working well, we will go back to steel. The Teflon will not bond correctly in the joints.

No matter what he complained of, the brothers Sueño bought their way through the problem. Jack became less and less available, and currents of dissent began to sweep through Triune Town. Not since the demise of the Mandy Dancers and that unfortunate business with the Homicide Kings had Triune Town been so disturbed.

Though Ferrante had said very little about his project outside his confessions to Jack and the necessary conversations with Rêve, the mouth of rumor whispered throughout the city. One day, on the way to Valdosta's, Ferrante saw a graffito on one of the leather folds of the Shylock Tribe's tower. "The God-Clown Is Near," it read, with a crude cartoon of a pair of oversized lips beneath it.

He ate an entire loaf of anise bread with his absinthe, and for his troubles was chased through his waking dreams by a cloven-hoofed monster in clown regalia.

The core musculature was adapting nicely to the long bones, accepting the Kevlar mesh reinforcement. Ferrante was proud of the adrenal and ATP microglands he had engineered into the myosin-actine interfaces. He had skin growing in separate culture beds, also reinforced with considerable shielding against corrosives and biological toxins. This made the skin almost flat white, with a slight bluish cast, but so be it. Finally, his various testbed tracheae hosted a variety of attempts at the biological and chemical dispersal mechanisms called for in the original plans — the problem of course being to keep the host from poisoning itself.

There remained only the brain. If this creature was a weapon, Ferrante told himself, then the place to sabotage it was in the control system. He had half a mind to ask Rêve Sueño to donate his own brain as the basis, but was afraid Rêve might take him seriously and agree to the thing.

All practical considerations aside, that would leave Ferrante with a lifetime of contending solo with Traum Sueño, something to which he would not look forward.

It was the monster of his absinthe dreams that showed him the answer. He *could* sabotage the god-clown without ruining the elegant work of the design. Ferrante took his surgical kit and his organ cooler and found his way to the Redstreet District and one of Triune Town's slaughterhouses.

———

"I need half an hour of *complete* privacy with a large male goat," Ferrante told the slaughterman, a wiry, dark-skinned fellow from the Judas Goat stirps.

"I can't rightly sell it after you've got jizz all over it," complained the slaughterman.

Ferrante didn't know whether to laugh or weep. "A hundred dollars, and no jizz. I promise."

Jack drifted into the bloodstained hallway, not his own Jack the sad but a man-Jack, just as beautiful.

"It's alright Orpheus," Jack told the slaughterman. "He's with me." Jack glanced at Ferrante. "Give the man his money, Doctor."

Ferrante paid the slaughterman, and shortly found himself alone in a room with Jack and a large, very frightened goat. Even in the horrendous stench of the abattoir, Jack smelled good.

"There's a stirps behind them, one I've never heard of," Jack told Ferrante as the doctor stalked the goat, a glittering glass syringe in one hand.

The goat bleated and charged Ferrante, who dodged nimbly to one side and tried to plunge the syringe in without success. "Yes," Ferrante gasped, resuming his stalking of the goat.

"It's called 'The College.' I don't know what that name signifies." Jack watched Ferrante's foot slip on fresh goat dung. "I don't like not knowing. You should finish the god-clown, then I will trace it."

"You told me to sabotage it," Ferrante said with a grunt, tackling the goat, which promptly kicked him in the gut. He sagged to the sticky floor, retching, but managed to plunge the syringe all the way in to the goat's neck.

"Use your judgment," said Jack, walking to the door. "Be careful." He glanced at Ferrante, sitting on the floor cradling the goat, and smiled. "Remember, no jizz."

Still coughing, Ferrante unwrapped his surgical kit and selected a bone saw. "Go home, Jack," he said.

"Well," said Rêve Sueño. "How is the patient?"

Ferrante threw back the sheet covering the god-clown. It resembled an enormous garden slug in its pale nakedness, folds of flesh rolling along the rib cage and gut, massive thighs, yet with narrow, long-fingered hands like a strangler. There were no genitals, just a little dimpled mound for urination, and the face was broad, almost normal except for the coloration. It was bound to the worktable by wide leather restraints, an IV snaking into one arm.

"He's big," said Ferrante, "to accept all that reinforced muscle. There's also a whole array of bioreactors hooked into the torso and thighs supporting the toxin production and to introduce countermeasures in case of blowback." He smiled at Rêve. "But of course you've read the specs. They *were* yours, after all."

"What about his motley?"

"Carbon-fiber straight from Dupont, dyed in the color scheme you requested." White and blue, with red accents, in fact. "I was even able to get the ruffled collar made with razor-wire reinforcements."

"And the mental templates?"

Ferrante's smile grew bigger. "Exactly as specified." Except they were overlaid on a goat's brain instead of a human's. Even with all the auxiliary tissue he grafted in, and the cortical subprocessors, this wasn't a primate brain at all. Whatever the god-clown saw fit to judge, it would be judging from a different view of the world.

"Turn it on," said Rêve. Traum nodded agreement, then stepped forward to drift his fingers across the god-clown's chest.

Ferrante opened a shunt on the god-clown's IV bag. "Have you gentlemen been spreading the god-clown graffiti in the streets?"

"Us?" Rêve sounded hurt. "Of course not. We're public-spirited fellows. I can't say that some of our society's more excitable members might not have picked up on what is about to happen."

"With a little help from their friends, no doubt," said Ferrante, thumbing open the god-clown's eyelid to check dilation.

The god-clown screamed, an ear-piercing ululation that drove Ferrante to the tile floor of his atelier, hands to his ears in an attempt to block the noise.

Traum Sueño leapt forward to grab the god-clown by its shoulders, but without a break in the scream, it puffed a gray vapor into his face.

Traum collapsed on the ground, writhing and pawing at his nose and mouth, as the god-clown snapped the leather restraints binding it to Ferrante's worktable and leapt up. It slammed Rêve against a wall and ran out the door, still screaming.

Ferrante got up, injected himself with four different antidotes he had prepared for such an eventuality, then checked his erstwhile sponsors.

Traum's eyes showed only white, while cerebral-spinal fluid ran clear and warm from his nose. Ferrante thoughtfully injected an air bubble into the carotid artery before moving on to Rêve. The god-clown had already finished him off, snapping Rêve's neck and crushing the back of his skull.

Never one to waste an opportunity, Ferrante quickly drenched Traum with lye and alcohol to control the biohazard, covered him with a plastic sheet, after which he fetched his bone saws to harvest what he could from Rêve.

His own Jack the sad joined Ferrante for absinthe at Valdosta's a few days later.

"I haven't seen you for a while," the doctor said.

"I've been busy." Jack smoothed the tablecloth with his hands. "So have you."

"So I have." Ferrante looked at his sad Jack. "Is there any more to tell me about the god-clown?"

"The stirps is the College of Clowns," Jack said, "and they are very, very old. I was surprised to learn even what little I did. Consider this — we are concealed from the Cities of the Map, living between and within, and sometimes among, them. The College of Clowns, and perhaps a few other stirps, are just as concealed from us."

"They must be strange," said Ferrante after a moment's thought.

"Everyone is strange," said Jack. "But the mirror shows us only the familiar."

"What of our flawed god-clown?"

Jack shrugged. "He is gone from Triune Town, the brothers Sueño are safely dead, and the College of Clowns has found somewhere else to ply their wiles for a time." His finger stroked the back of Ferrante's hand, sending chills across the doctor's spine. "I might prefer to enjoy my absinthe dreams in more privacy. Shall we return to your atelier?"

Ferrante and his sad Jack made love by the light of mythic beasts rampaging through their dreams on a bed of satin sheets watched over by a canopic jar labeled "Sueño, R." Somewhere in the world the god-clown still screamed, while wrapped in satin Cosimo Ferrante found a soul-searing ecstasy that would haunt him forever.

The Steam Man of the Prairie
and the Dark Rider Get Down:
A DIME NOVEL

JOE R. LANSDALE

for Philip José Farmer

Steampunk can be retro and entertaining while also being very dark. The sometimes shocking "The Steam Man..." by Joe R. Lansdale doesn't just combine all sorts of steampunk tropes – it blows the lid off of them, creating an action-filled story that also horrifies within its very complex structure. Leave it to Lansdale to postulate that the Traveler from H. G. Wells' *The Time Machine* has damaged the space-time continuum, turning him into the Dark Rider. Squeamish readers beware!

Foreword

Somewhere out in space the damaged shuttle circled, unable to come down. Its occupants were confused and frightened.

Forever to the left of the ship was a rip in the sky. And through the rip they saw all sorts of things. Daylight and dark. Odd events.

And dat ole shuttle jes go'n roun' and roun' and roun'.

(1)
In Search Of

The shiny steam man, forty feet tall and twenty feet wide, not counting his ten-foot-high conical hat, hissed across the prairie, farted up hills, waded and puffed through streams and rivers. He clanked and clattered. He made good time. His silver metal skin was bright with the sun. The steam from his hat was white as frost. Inside of him, where the four men rode in swaying leather chairs, it was very hot, even with the steam fan blowing.

But they pushed on, working the gears, valves, and faucets, forever closing on the Dark Rider. Or so they hoped.

Bill Beadle, captain of the expedition, took off his wool cap and wiped the sweat from his face with an already damp forearm. He tried to do this casually. He did not want the other three to know how near heat exhaustion he was. He took deep breaths, ran a hand through his sweat-soaked hair, and put his cap back on. The cap was hot, and though there was really nothing official about his uniform or his title of captain, he tried to live by a code that maintained the importance of both.

Hamner and Blake looked at him casually. They were red-faced and sweat-popped. They shifted uncomfortably in their blue woolen uniforms. Through the stained glass eyes of the steam man they could see the hills they had entered, see they were burned brown from the sun.

It was midday, and this gave them several hours to reach the land of the Dark Rider, but by then it would be night, and the Dark Rider and his minions, the apes in trousers, would be out and powerful.

Only John Feather, their Indian guide, looked cool in his breech-cloth and headband holding back his long, beaded, black hair. He had removed his moccasins and was therefore barefoot. Unlike the others, he was not interested in a uniform, or to be more precise, he was not interested in being hot when he didn't have to be. He could never figure out the ways of white men, though he often considered on them. But mostly he considered the steam man, and thought: Neat. This cock-sucker can go. A little bouncy on the ass, even in these spring-loaded seats, but the ole boy can go. The white men do come up with a good thing now and then.

They clanked through the hills some more, and through the right ear canal of the steam man, also stained glass, they could see the wrecks.

Beadle was always mystified by the wrecks.

Most people called them saucers. They lay in heaps and shatters all over the place. Strange skeletons that weren't quite bone had been found in some of them, and there were even mummified remains of others. Green squid with multiple eyes and fragments of clothing.

There was no longer anyone alive who really knew what had happened, but what had been handed down was there had been a war, and though damn near everybody came, nobody really won. Not the world, not the saucer people. But the weapons they used, they had brought about strange things.

Like rips in the sky, and the Dark Rider.

Or so it was rumored. No one really knew. Story was the saucers had ripped open the sky and come to this world through a path alongside the sky. And that after the war, when the saucer men gave it up and went home, the Earth changed and the rips stayed. What was odd about the rips was you could toss things into them, people could enter them, and things could come out. And there were things to see. Great batlike creatures with monstrous wingspans. Snake-headed critters with flippers and rows of teeth, paddling across the blue-green ether inside the rip. Strange craft jetting across odd landscapes. All manner of things. If you stood near the dark openings, which reached from sky to ground, you could feel them pulling at you, like a vacuum, and if you stepped too close, well then you were gone. Sucked into the beyond. Sometimes the people who were pulled, or went by choice into the rips, came back. Sometime they didn't. But even those that came back bore no real information. It was even reported by a few that the moment they stepped through the rip, they merely exited where they had entered.

Curious.

As for the Dark Rider, no one knew his origin. A disease caused by something from one of the saucers was the usual guess, but that's all it was. A guess. The Dark Rider sucked blood like a vampire, had prodigious strength and odd powers, but had no aversion to crosses, garlic, or any of the classical defenses. Except one. Sunlight. He could not tolerate it. That much had been established.

He also had an army of apelike critters who traveled with him and did most of the shit work. When the Dark Rider was not able to do it, he sent the apes in britches to do his work. Rape. Murder. Torture. Usually by impalement. His method was to have the victim stripped naked and placed on an upright stake with the point in the anus. The pressure of the victim's weight would push him or her down the length of the shaft until the point came out the upper part of the torso. Usually the neck or mouth, or even at times through the top of the head.

Beadle had seen enough of this to give him nightmares for the rest of his life, and he had determined that if it ever appeared he was about to be captured alive by the Dark Rider or his minions, he would kill himself. He kept a double-barreled derringer in his boot for just such a circumstance.

The steam man clanked on.

It was near nightfall when they stomped out of the foothills and into the vast forest that grew tall and dark before them and was bordered by a river. It was a good thing, this forest and river. They were out of wood and water, and therefore out of steam.

Though the night brought bad possibilities, it was also preferable to the long, hot days. They grabbed their water bags, pulled their Webb rifles over their shoulders on straps, and disembarked from the steam man via a ladder that they poked out of its ass. Like automated turds, they dropped out of the steam man's butt and into the coolness of the night.

The white men left John Feather to guard the steam man with an automatic pistol and a knife on his hip, a Webb rifle slung over his shoulder on a strap, a bow and a quiver of arrows, and went down to the river for water.

John Feather knew he would be better off inside the steam man, in case the Dark Rider and his bunch showed up, but the night air felt great and sucked at a man's common sense. Behind him the steam man popped and crackled as the nocturnal air cooled it.

John Feather tapped the ammo belt strapped across his chest and back, just to make sure it was there. He took one of the heavy clips from his bandolier and squeezed it with his fingers, a habit he had developed when nervous. After a time, he put the oiled clip back on the bandolier and wiped his greasy fingers on his thigh. He looked for a time in every direction, listened intently. Normally, though he liked them, he didn't miss the white men much, but tonight, he would be glad to have them back. Safety in numbers.

Beadle, Hamner, and Blake inched down the slick riverbank, stopped at the water, and listened to it roar and churn dirt from the bank. There had been a big rain as of late, and the river was wild from it. The reflection of the moon was on the river and it wavered in the water as if it were something bright lying beneath the ripples.

Beadle felt good outside of the metal man. It was wonderful to not have his ass bouncing and his insides shook, to be away from all that hissing and metal clanking.

The roar of the river, the wind through the pines, the moon on the water, the real moon in the sky, bright and gold and nearly full, was soothing.

He eased one of his water bags into the river, listened to it gurgle as it filled.

"We ought to bring Steam down here, Captain," Hamner said. He had removed his cap, which was pretty much the understanding when nightfall came, and fixed it through his belt. The moonlight shone on his red hair and made it appear to be a copper bowl. "We could camp closer to the water."

"I'm afraid Steam's furnaces may be too cold and too low of fuel to walk another inch," Beadle said. "There's just enough left for us to get settled for the night. It would take an hour to heat him up. At least. I'm not sure it's worth it just to have him walk a few hundred feet."

"It is pleasant here, though," Hamner said.

"Not so pleasant we don't need to get this over with and get inside," Beadle said.

This indirect reference to the Dark Rider settled down on them suddenly, and the need for fresh air, wood, and water was eclipsed by a wave of fear. Just a wave. It passed over them and was tucked away. They had grown used to fear. When you hunted the Dark Rider and his boys, you had to learn to put fear on the back burner. You thought about it too much, you'd never breathe night air again. With the Dark Rider, fear and horror were a constant.

Beadle looked at the nearly full moon and wondered if the Dark Rider was looking up at it too. Beadle had sworn to get the Dark Rider. It's what he was being paid for, he and his team. He had formed Steam Man and Company a year back, and during that time he had killed many of the Dark Rider's ape boys, his minions as Beadle liked to call them, and his employers had been very happy, even giving him the honorary title of Captain. But he hadn't gotten the Dark Rider. There was the real deal. And the big money. The reward for the Dark Rider was phenomenal. And Beadle wanted the bastard, reward or not. He thought of him all the time. He wrote dime novels based on his team's exploits, stretching the truth only slightly. He had made a silent vow to pursue the Dark Rider to the ends of the Earth.

As Beadle looked at the moon, he saw the last of the white steam that was issuing from the steam man's tall, conical hat float across the sky, blurring it, and then the steam dissipated.

"Let's finish," Beadle said.

They made numerous trips with their bags of water, but soon they were famished. Then, leaving John Feather once again to guard Steam, they gathered wood. That accomplished, they took tools from inside the steam man, chopped and sawed the wood and hauled it inside with the water.

As Beadle had expected, the furnaces had cooled. They were lucky they had been able to find water. They might have had to spend a long night in Steam with little to drink until the morning, when it was safe. This way, they could be more comfortable. Even baths could be taken.

"Do you think the Dark Rider is near?" Beadle asked John Feather as they stacked the wood inside the steam man.

"He is always near, and always far away," John Feather said.

This was one of the Indian's odd answers that disturbed Beadle. He knew if he asked John Feather to decipher it, he would merely give him another hard-to-understand remark. It was best to consider the answer given, or just discard it. When John Feather was in this kind of mood, there was no reasoning with him.

Beadle decided to answer his own question, which actually had been foolish, sprung out of fear and the need for something to say. The truth was obvious: they couldn't be too far away from the Dark Rider. Just the day before, they had passed through the burnt and reeking remains of a village with a hundred inhabitants or so with stakes rammed up their asses. Even cats and dogs and three parakeets had been cruci-fied. It was the Dark Rider's calling card. Therefore, he could not be far away. And he always fled to this part of the world, amongst the thick, dark woods with its bad things, near the place where the sky was most ripped and you could see into it and view all manner of strange and terrifying things not seen elsewhere.

Beadle pulled up Steam's ass flap and locked it for the night with bolt and key. While the wood burned and the water heated, they ate a cold supper of beef jerky and hardtack and washed it down with water, then each retired to his own devices. Beadle had wanted to read, but the kerosene lamps made the place smoky and uncomfortable, even with the steam man's vents. After first usage of the lamps and a miserable night of smoke and kerosene stink, they had decided to withhold from using them. He could, of course, read by candle light, but he found this uncomfortable and only resorted to this when he was absolutely bored out of his mind.

He did, however, light a candle and put it in a candle hat and used the ladder to descend into one of the steam man's legs, past the machinery that made it walk, and into the foot where he found a can of oil.

Steam had been well-oiled the night before, but it never hurt to do it again. There was always a fear of rusty devices, gritty gears, a metal rod gone bad. And considering who they were hunting, it wouldn't do to have Steam play out.

When he finished there, he went throughout the steam man with his candle hat and his can of oil, dripping the liquid into all of its parts. He paid special attention to the backup controls in the trunk of the steam man. If the head controls failed, these, though simpler, cruder, could manage the machine's basic movements.

After a time the water was heated, and they drew straws for who bathed first, as the others would have the same water. Beadle lucked out. He got naked and climbed in the tub at the top of Steam's head. He set the timer. He had fifteen minutes before the next bather had a shot at the suds, and he greatly enjoyed every minute of his time.

Deep in the woods, outside his compound, hanging about for lack of anything else to do, the Dark Rider, alias the Time Traveler, alias many other names, turned his face to the moon as he jerked his dick and thought of blood. At his climax he gave up blood and sperm in thick, waddy ropes that splattered on the leaf mold and the body of the dog. He imagined the dog a woman, but it had been days since he had had a woman, tasted a soft throat and sweet blood. He would have settled for a man or child, an old person, but none had been available. Just the dog, and it had been a gamey wild dog at that. Still, feeding on anything made him horny, which was both a blessing and a curse.

Finished, he made the mistake of haste, caught a hunk of dick in his zipper and cursed. The others, who had been patiently waiting for the

Dark Rider to finish, said nothing. You didn't laugh at the Dark Rider, not even if he caught his dick in a zipper. Laugh at him, you might find your face on the other side of your head.

The Dark Rider worked for a while, managed his whang free, put it in his pants and zipped up, looked around for anyone with a smile on their face. Most of his minions, as the dime novels written by his nemesis, Beadle, called them, were looking about, as if expecting someone.

In a way they were. Beadle and his regulators, and that infernal tin man.

When the Dark Rider was certain he was fixed, he nodded to his flunkies, and they waddled forward to take the dog and to lick the blood and sperm on the ground. The toadies began to fight amongst themselves, tearing at the dog, rolling and thrashing about in a hungry fury, ripping at the meat, scattering fur, spewing what blood was left in the critter.

After waiting for a while, the Dark Rider became bored. He took hold of one of the apes and threw him on the ground and pulled his britches down. He took out his dong again and ass fucked the beast. It wasn't very pleasant, and he grew angry at himself for resorting to such entertainment, but he went ahead and did it anyway. Consummated, he snapped the animal's neck and gave him to the others as a gift. Some of the ape men fucked the corpse, but pretty soon they were eating it. The dog just hadn't been enough.

The Dark Rider thought about what he had done. If he kept popping the necks of these little beasts, pretty soon he might have to gather wood for the impalement stakes himself. He'd have to go easier on them. They were not limitless. It was too big a pain to get others.

When they had all bathed and the water was run out of the tub and down the pipes and out what served as Steam's penis — a tube with a flap over it — they settled in for the night, secure in the giant man.

Beadle, in his hammock at the top of Steam's head, dreamed pleasantly at first of a lost love, but then the dream changed, and the Dark Rider came into it. He was dressed, as always, in dark pants and shirt, high black boots, wide black hat, and long black cape. His eyes were flaming sockets, his teeth white as snow, sharp as sin. In the dream, the Dark Rider took Beadle's love, Matilda of the long, blonde hair and sleek, rich body, and carried her away.

Beadle awoke in a sweat. It was a dream too real.

Matilda. Sucked dry of blood, and then, for the sport of it, impaled through the vagina, left for the heat, bugs, and birds. That had been the beginning for Beadle. The beginning of Steam and Company, his hunt for the Dark Rider. His vow to pursue him to the ends of the Earth.

(2)
In the Bad Country

The next morning, early, just as light was tearing back the black curtain, they worked the bellows inside the steam man and made the furnace hotter. The steam man began to chug, cough, sput, and rock with indigestion. They cranked him up and worked the gears and twisted the faucets and checked the valves. When the steam man's belly was volcanic, they climbed into their chairs, at their controls, Beadle in the command seat.

"Let's do it," Beadle said, and he pulled a gear, twisted a faucet, and took hold of the throttle. The steam man began to walk. He went down the riverbank with a clank and into the river with a splash. The water rose up to his waist, and though there was resistance, and Beadle had to give him nearly full throttle, Steam waded the river and stepped up on the bank. The step would have been a climb for a man.

Now the woods were before the steam man. These woods were the known domain of the Dark Rider, and only a few had ever been this far and returned alive. The survivors told of not only the dark woods, but of the wild creatures there, and of the Dark Rider and his white apes, and beyond the forest, a great rip in the sky. Perhaps the biggest rip there was. A rip so big and wide you could see not only creatures inside it, but stars, and at times, a strange sun, blurred and running like a busted egg yolk. Beadle wondered if the Dark Rider would run again. That was his strategy. Hit and run and hide. But would he run from here, his own stronghold? Would he be prepared to stand and fight? Or would he go to ground, hide and wait them out?

The good thing was they had the day on their side, but even during the day, the Dark Rider had his protection.

It was best not to think about it, Beadle decided. It was best to push on, take it as it came, play it as it laid.

Deep down in the cool, damp ground, the Dark Rider lay wrapped in clear plastic hauled from one of many possible futures, plastic used to keep dirt off his clothes.

The grave was deep. Twenty feet. It had been dug by the ape men, or as they were more properly known, the Moorlocks. A sheet of lumber had been placed over the top of the grave to keep out stray strands of daylight.

Nearby, in underground catacombs, the Moorlocks rested. Unlike him they were not destroyed by light, just made uncomfortable. It was their eyes; they were like moles, only not really blind, just light sensitive. He had tried building sunglasses for them from pieces of stained glass and wire framing, but the daylight still affected them. Beneath their white fur, their pink skin was highly sensitive. He had taught them to sew shirts and pants, make shoes from skins, but the sun burned right through their clothes. They had abandoned shoes, shirts, and glasses, but they still wore the pants. Something about the pants appealed to the Moorlocks. Maybe they liked the confinement of trousers better than letting their hammers swing, their snatches grab dust.

As the Dark Rider lay there, hiding from the light, he began to cry. How in God's name... No, fuck God. God had put him here. Surely it was God. Fate. Whatever. But the bottom line was still... Why?

Once upon a time, though which time he was uncertain, he had been an inventor and had traveled the ages via machine. A time machine.

Then there had been the dimensional juncture.

If he could but do that moment over he would not be what he had become. Sometimes, it was almost as if his old self had never been, and there had always been what he was now, the Dark Rider.

And Weena. How he missed her. She had been the most wonderful moment of his life.

Once upon a time, he had lived as an Englishman in the year 1895, wherever that now existed, if it existed. He had been an inventor, and the result of this invention was a machine that traveled through time.

Oh, but he had been noble. Saw himself as a hero. He traveled to the far future where he discovered a world of soft, simple people who lived above ground, were supplied goods by the machinery of the Moorlocks below ground. And they, without wishing to, supplied the Moorlocks with a food source. Themselves.

These simple people were called the Eloi.

While in this future, he met a beautiful and simple Eloi maiden named Weena. He made love to her, and came to love her. She was stolen by the Moorlocks, and after a desperate but futile battle to find and rescue her, he was forced to escape in the time machine. But he had pushed the gear forward, went farther into the future, to a world with a near burned-out sun, populated by crablike creatures and a dull, dead ocean.

He returned then to his own time to tell his tale. But he was not believed when he explained that there were four dimensions, not three. Length, width, depth…and time.

Returning to the era of the Eloi, he discovered Weena had escaped from the Moorlocks, and he decided then and there to become the champion of the Eloi, and within a short time he had taught the mild-mannered people how to do for themselves. He traveled through time and brought to the Eloi animals that no longer existed in their future. He taught them to raise meat and vegetables. He taught them how to fight the Moorlocks.

It was a great time, ten years he judged it.

But then he discovered on one of his exploratory journeys through time that there was a fifth dimension. It existed alongside the others; a place where time took different routes, numerous routes.

Somehow, by his travel he had opened some kind of wormhole in time, and now it had all run together and its very fabric had begun to rip. It was believed in this time that the rips had been caused by squid-like invaders in saucers, but in fact, they were the result of his blunders through the Swiss cheese holes of time.

Returning to the Eloi and Weena, he discovered, through his dimensional traveling, he had not only screwed up time and crosshatched it and connected it in spots and disconnected it in others, but he had also contracted some strange malady.

He craved blood. He was like a vampire. He had to have blood to survive.

Weena stood by him, and he made the Moorlocks his prey. He discovered other side effects of the dimensional plague. He had tremendous strength, speed, and agility and a constant erection.

But there was a great sourness in him, and soon he began to change. Even when he did not want to change, he changed. Day became repellant, and he found that he enjoyed being amongst the bodies of the dead Moorlocks that he fed on. He liked the smell of death, of rotting meat.

Weena tried to help him, make him whole again. But there was nothing she could do. And in a moment of anger, he struck her and killed her. It was the final straw. Gloom and doom and the desire to hold destruction in his hand overwhelmed him. He fell in love with the horrors.

Only the memory of Weena remained clean. He had her body mummified in the deep sands beyond the garden world of the Eloi, and he had her placed in a coffin made of oak and maple. Then he buried it in one of the great gardens and a tree was planted to mark it.

Time took the tree and the garden, and now there was just the dirt and her mummified remains, and even that, eventually, his former joy, and now his nemesis, time, would take.

He had made an old museum his home. It housed the wares of many centuries. It was unique. It was a ruined palace of green porcelain, fronted by a giant sphinx that had been some sort of monument. Below the museum, beneath the sphinx, and other sites, were the Moorlocks' tunnels and their machines. Machines that had ground out simple goods for the Eloi.

He became their king, and in time, the Eloi became their food again. And his.

The machines roared below ground once more.

The Eloi quivered again.

And then came the rip.

Time lies tight between, within, and behind dimensional curtains, and these curtains are strong and not easy to tear, but somehow, presumed the Dark Rider, his machine had violated the structures of time, and by its presence, its traveling through, it had torn this fabric and other times had slipped into the world of the Eloi and the Moorlocks, slipped in so subtly that a new time was created with a past and a present and a possible future. There was not only a shift in time, but in space, and the Wild West of America collided with a Steam Age where inventors from his own time, who had never made such inventions, were suddenly now building steam ships and flying ships and submarines. Time and space were all a jumble.

The disease in him would not kill him. It just made him live on and on with a burning need to kill, maim, and destroy. Perhaps his disease was merely one that all mankind bore in its genes. A disease buried deep in the minds of every human being, dormant in some, active in others, but in him, not buried at all.

Was he not merely a natural device, a plague, helping to monitor a corner(s) of the universe? Was he not nature's way of saying: I'd like to destroy all this and start over. Just take this Petri dish and wash it off and disinfect it?

The Dark Rider liked to believe he was the ultimate in Darwinism, and that he was merely doing what needed to be done with a world of losers. Instead of combating evil, did it not make more sense to merely be evil so that mankind could go back to what it had originally been?

Nothing.

The sun was scorching again, and inside the steam man it was hotter than the day before. Beadle and his companions sweated profusely, worked the steam man forward with their levers and valves. Steam tore at trees with his great metal hands, uprooting them, tossing them aside, making a path through the forest as they went in search of the Dark Rider's lair, which though not entirely known, was suspected to lie somewhere within, or on the other side of, the great forest.

As the hot day wore on, and more trees were ripped and tossed, a road began to appear through the great forest. Inside the steam man it was hotter yet as Hamner and John Feather tossed logs into the furnace and worked the bellows and stoked the flames that chewed at the wood and boiled the vast tank of water and produced the steam that gave power to the steam man's working parts.

The steam man clanked and hissed on, and finally they broke from the trees, and in the distance they could see a great, white sphinx, and near it another building of green stone. Though run down and vine-climbed, both had a majestic air about them.

Beadle said, "If I were the Dark Rider, that would be my den."

John Feather made a grunting noise. The others nodded. The steam man pushed on.

Then the ground opened up, and the steam man staggered and fell in. His knee struck the rim of the trench and he was knocked backward, then sideways, came to rest in that position, one leg deep in the hole, the other pushed up and behind him and on the surface. His left shoulder and head leaned against one side of the trench.

The fall caused logs and flames to leap from the furnace, and Blake's pants leg caught on fire. He came out of his chair with a scream, lost control of his levers and valves, and the steam man faltered even more, its hands clutching madly at the edge of the trench, tearing out great clods of soil. Wads of steam spurted from Steam's hat and his metal body heaved and screeched at the grinding of machinery.

John Feather leaped forward, shut the furnace, threw the guard latch in place. Beadle, thrown from his chair, standing on the side of the steam man, since the floor was now askance, wobbled to the controls, turned off the steam.

"We seem to have stepped into a trap," Beadle said, slapping cinders off his pants.

"Goddamn it," Blake said, from his position on the floor. "It's my fault. I let go of my controls."

"No," Beadle said. "You had no choice, and besides, Steam was already falling. It's the Dark Rider's fault. Let's not brood. Let's assess the damage."

They went up the winding staircase to the steam man's hat and used the emergency opening over his ear. They threw open the door and lowered the flexible ramp.

Outside, in the midday sun, what they saw upset them. But it was not as bad as they had feared. Steam's left leg lay on the back side of the trench, while his other leg and lower torso were in it. His head and chest poked out of the deep ditch, and he was leaning to port. The leg that was bent behind him looked to be solidly connected, stretched a bit, but serviceable.

"Maybe he can climb out," Blake said.

Beadle shook his head. "Not with his leg like that. He may pull himself out, but I think there's a chance he'll twist his leg off, then where will we be?"

"Where are we now?" Blake said.

"In a hole," Hamner said. "That's where we are."

"The tripod and winch," John Feather said.

"Yes," Beadle said. "The tripod and winch."

Inside the steam man, stored in a number of connecting parts, was a tripod and winch device. It was there for moving large trees when heating materials were needed and small wood was not available. So far, it had never been used, but it was just the ticket.

They unloaded and fastened the device together, set the tripod up over the trench, fastened the cables to the steam man, then set about lifting him.

The sun was past noon and starting to dip.

By late day, they had lifted the steam man three times, and each time his great weight had sagged the crane, and he had fallen back into the pit, straining the leg even more.

Finally, in desperation, they cut some of the smaller trees from the forest behind them, and used them to reinforce their apparatus. This was hard business, and the four of them, even with the smaller trees trimmed and topped, had a hard time moving them, pushing them upright and into place, lodging them tight against the ground.

When they had a tripod of trees to reinforce their tripod and winch, John Feather climbed to the top with Hamner, and they bound the trees tightly to their metal tripod with cable.

All set, they checked and tightened the cables, made sure the steam man was solidly fastened, and set about lifting him once more. Shadows spread across the ground as they worked, filled the trench and cooled the air.

Beadle, dirty and sweaty, an itch in his ass, looked up from the winch lever they were working and saw that the sun was falling down behind the sphinx and the building of green stone. "Gentleman," he said. "I suggest we hasten."

(3)
The Dark Rider Awakes

Beneath the green rock museum, in the darkness of his grave, the Dark Rider stirred, removed the plastic and sat up. Almost at the same moment, the Moorlocks removed the wooden cover.

Effortlessly, the Dark Rider leaped from the pit, landed at its edge, straightened, and looked out at the mass of red eyes around him. When he looked, the red eyes blinked.

In a corner of the dark room sat the Time Machine, draped in spiderwebs. All except the saddle, which the Dark Rider used as his throne.

The Dark Rider took his place on the saddle and a Moorlock brought him his black hat. He sat there, and for a moment, astride his old machine, he felt as if he were about to venture again into time and space. A wave of his old self swelled up inside of him and washed him from head to foot. There were warm visions of Weena. But as always, it passed as immediately as it swelled.

His old self was gone, and venturing forth in his machine was impossible. The machine had worn out long ago, and he had never been able to repair it. Certain elements were no longer available. For a while, he searched, but eventually came to the conclusion that what he needed would never be found.

And besides. What was the point? Time and space were collapsing. Not more than a month ago he had come upon men and women from the Stone Age killing and eating a family in a Winnebago.

He and his Moorlocks fought and impaled the prehistorics, and he only lost ten Moorlocks in the process. Once upon a time the loss of the Moorlocks would not have bothered him at all, but with the death of most of the Moorlock women through sheer chance and his own meanness, there were only a few females left. He kept them in special breeding centers in caverns beneath the ground. But though the Moorlocks loved to fight, they did not dearly love to fuck. Oh, now and then they'd rape some of the women they came across, before they impaled them, but it just wasn't the way it used to be. When they got home they weren't excited like they had been once upon a time; so excited they'd mate with the Moorlock women, impregnating them. Nature was trying desperately to play them out.

Thinking on this, the Dark Rider frowned. It wasn't that he cared all that much for the Moorlocks, it was simply that he liked servants. He supposed he could enslave others, but the Moorlocks were really perfect. Strong, obedient, and not overly bright. Other races had a tendency to revolt, but the Moorlocks actually thrived on stupidity and control, as long as they were allowed their little delights now and then.

But he had more immediate worries tonight. The steam man and the fools inside it. But the whole operation might cost him a kit and caboodle of the Moorlocks.

Sighing, the Dark Rider concluded that their loss was one of the necessities of business. Which was, simply defined, fear and destruction and a good solid meal.

One of the Moorlocks waddled up to the Dark Rider with his head held down.

"What it is it, Asshole?"

Asshole was the Dark Rider's favorite of the Moorlocks.

Asshole leaped about, slapped his chest, made some noise.

"They are near?" asked the Dark Rider.

"Uh, you betcha," Asshole said.

"Then, I suppose, we should go greet them. Get Sticks."

Just about everything that could go wrong, had gone wrong. The tripod had turned over. Blake had fallen and sprained an ankle, but was otherwise all right. They cut him a crutch from an oak tree, and he hobbled about, tugging on ropes and struggling to free Steam.

Eventually everything was in place again, and Steam was lifted just enough to free his leg. Beadle climbed back inside and stoked up the dying embers. John Feather climbed in after him and handed him new wood from the stockpile. Beadle put it in on top of the meager flames, then they worked the bellows. The flame flared up and the logs got hot, and still they worked the bellows.

When the fire was going good, Beadle went out on the ramp under Steam's ear and called down to Blake and Hamner. "Crank the winch up tight, then stand back."

When Beadle disappeared back inside Steam, Hamner and Blake took hold of the winch crank together and set to work. They managed to lift Steam even more, allowing his trapped leg to slip into the pit with the other. It was hard work, and when they were finished, it was all they could do to keep standing.

Inside, Beadle and John Feather worked the controls, and Steam climbed easily out of the pit. When he stood on solid ground again, Hamner and Blake cheered, and inside Steam, Beadle and John Feather did the same.

But it was a short-lived celebration. John Feather pointed at one of Steam's eyes, said, "Bad shit coming."

"My God," Beadle said. "Lower the ladder, let them in."

(4)
Sticks A' Steppin'

The Dark Rider's contraption was a man made of sticks and it stood at least twenty feet higher than Steam. The sticks had been interlaced with strips of rawhide, woven and strapped, tied to form the shape of a man. There were gaps in the shape, and through the gaps you could see the apes in trousers, as well as flashes of metal. It made cranking and clanking sounds. And the damn thing walked.

John Feather lowered the ladder in Steam's butt, and Hamner scrambled up, followed by the not so scrambling Blake and his crude crutch.

Once inside they took their seats and ran their hands over their controls.

"Steam is bound to be stronger than a man of sticks," Hamner said.

"Don't underestimate the Dark Rider," Beadle said. "We have before, and each time we've regretted it."

Hamner nodded. He remembered when their team had consisted of several others. Mistakes and miscalculations had whittled them down to this.

"What's the game plan then?" Blake asked.

"We approach him cautiously, feel him out."

"I don't think we'll have to worry about approaching him," Hamner said. "He seems to be coming at a right smart clip."

And indeed, he was.

Sticks and Steam approached one another. From the rooftop of the museum, the Dark Rider watched. He hoped a kill could be made soon. He was very hungry. And he dearly wanted Beadle. The bastard had been chasing him forever. He would impale the others, but Beadle he would have some fun with first. To humiliate him, he would fuck him. Maybe fuck a wound he would tear in his body with his hands, then he'd torture him some, and drink his blood of course, and call him bad names and pull out his hair, and maybe fuck another wound, then he'd have him impaled after boiling his feet raw, coating them with salt and having a goat lick the soles until the skin stripped off.

Well, he might have to lose that part with the goat. He'd already killed and sucked dry every damn goat in these parts, not to mention sheep, a lot of dogs, a good mess of cats, deer, and of course there wasn't a human outside of Beadle and his bunch within a hundred miles. Not a living one anyway. That was the problem with having his kind of urges. You soon ran out of victims. Rats were plentiful, of course, but even for him they were hard to catch.

Then a thought occurred to him. He could get Asshole to do the foot-licking part. He could be the goat. Asshole, like all the Moorlocks, had a rough tongue, and dearly loved salt any way he could get it. With this in mind, the Dark Rider began to feel content and confident again.

Up close, Beadle and his boys could hear machinery inside of Sticks, and they could see into the huge, open eyes, and there they saw the apes in trousers, howling, barking, running about, the moonlight illuminating their little, red peepers.

Inside Sticks, the Moorlocks worked furiously. Most of their equipment ran on sprockets and cables and bicycle gears, and in the center of the stick man, and at the back of his head, were bicycle seats and pedals, and on the seats, peddling wildly, were the Moorlocks. The pedaling engaged gears and sprockets, and allowed the head Moorlock, Asshole, who sat in a swinging wicker basket, to work levers and guide gears.

As the steam man and the stick man came in range of one another, Asshole pulled levers and yelled and barked at his humanoid engines, and Sticks reached out and grabbed Steam by the head, brought a stick and wicker knee up into his tight, tin stomach.

The clang of the knee attack inside of Steam resounded so loudly, Beadle, without thinking, jerked both hands over his ears, and for a moment, Steam wobbled slightly.

Embarrassed, Beadle grabbed at his gears and went to work. He made Steam throw a left, and Sticks took it in the eye, scattering a handful of Moorlocks, but others rushed to take their place.

Blake, who worked the right arm, tried to follow with a right cross, but he was late. Sticks brought up his left arm and wrapped it around Steam's right, and they were into a tussle.

Beadle realized quickly that from a striking standpoint Steam was more powerful, but in close, Sticks, with his basket woven parts, was more flexible.

Blake tried to work Steam's right arm free, but it was no go. Sticks brought his right leg around and put it behind Steam's right, kicked back, and threw Steam to the ground, climbed on top of him and tried to pummel him with both tightly woven fists.

Great dents jumped into Steam's metal and poked out in humps on the inside. Sticks used a three-finger poke (he only had four fingers on each hand) to knock out one of Steam's stained-glass eyes. The fingers probed inside the gap as if trying to find an eyeball, touched Beadle slightly, and disappeared.

Lying on his back as he was, Steam rocked right and left, and inside of him his parasites worked their gears and valves and cussed. Finally it came to Beadle to have Steam's right leg lift up and latch around Sticks's left leg. Then he did the same with the other side, brought both knees together so Steam could crush Sticks's ribwork and the Moorlocks inside.

But the ribwork proved stronger and more flexible than Beadle had imagined. It moved but did not give. He decided it was Steam's turn to grab Sticks's eye sockets. He called out orders, and soon Steam's hands rose and he grabbed at the corners of Sticks's eye sockets with metal thumbs, shook Sticks's head so savagely Moorlocks flew out of the eyeholes.

Moorlocks began to bail through the eyeholes onto Steam's chest, poured in through the busted left eye of Steam.

John Feather leaped out of his harness seat, drew his knife and went at them. Blood flew amidst screams of pain. John Feather slashed and stabbed, killed while he sang his death song. The Moorlocks leaped on top of him. Hamner started to free himself to help John Feather, but Beadle called, "Work the controls."

Sticks's head began to tear and twist off, came loose in a burst of basket work and sticks that flipped and scattered Moorlocks like water drops shaken from a wet dog's back.

Bicycle parts went hither and yon, crashed to the ground. One Moorlock lay with a bicycle chain wrapped around his head, another had a fragment of a pedal in his ass.

Inside Steam, John Feather still fought while Beadle and his crew worked the gears and made Steam roll on his right side. In the process, John Feather crashed about, along with the Moorlocks.

Then Steam stood up. John Feather and the Moorlocks fell back, past the seats and the controls and down the long drop of the left leg to the bottom of Steam's left foot. Beadle heard the horrid crash and winced. It was unlikely there were any survivors, Moorlocks or John Feather.

Beadle steeled himself to his present task, began to walk Steam, stomping fleeing Moorlocks with the machine, spurting them in all directions like overstuffed jelly rolls.

From his position atop the museum, the Dark Rider watched and grew angry. Damn dumb Moorlocks. Never give an ape a vampire's job.

The Dark Rider rushed downstairs with a swirl of his cape. He went so fast, the front of his hat blew back.

Near the anterior of the museum stood the Dark Rider's clockwork horse. It stood ten hands high and was made of woven wooden struts and thin metal straps, and at its center, like a heart, was a clockwork mechanism that made it run.

The Dark Rider took a key from his belt, reached inside the horse, inserted the key, turned it, wound the clock. As he wound, the horse lifted its head and made a metal noise. Lights came on behind its wide, red eyes.

The Dark Rider pulled himself on top of his horse, whom he had named Clockwork, sat in the bicycle seat there, put his feet on the pedals, and began to pump. Effortless, the bicycle horse moved forward at a rapid gait, its steel hooves pounding the worn floor of the museum, knocking up tile chips.

Two Moorlocks who stood guard at the front of the museum jumped to it and opened the door. With a burst of wind that knocked the Moorlocks down, the Dark Rider blew past them and out into the night.

(5)
Things Get Pissy

"The Dark Rider," said Hamner.

Beadle and Blake looked. Sure enough, there he was, bright in the moonlight, astride his well-known mechanical horse. Its hooves threw up chunks of dirt and its head bobbed up and down as the Dark Rider pedaled so furiously his legs were nothing more than the blurs of his black pants.

"He looks pissed off," said Blake.

"He's always pissed off," said Beadle.

Beadle set the course for Steam, and just as the old metal boy made strides in the Dark Rider's direction, a Moorlock, bloodied and angry, came hissing out of the stairway in the left leg of Steam and leaped at Beadle.

Beadle lost control of his business, and Steam suddenly stopped, his left arm dropping to his side and his head lilting. This nearly caused Steam to tip over, and it was all Blake could do to shut down his side of the machine.

The Moorlock opened its mouth wide and bit into Beadle's shoulder. Beadle grabbed it by the scruff of the neck and pulled, but the Moorlock wouldn't come loose. Hamner came out of his seat and jumped at the Moorlock, sticking his thumbs in its eyes, but even though Hamner pushed at the beast's head, causing its eyes to burst into bleeding lumps, still it clung to Beadle.

Beadle beat dramatically at the Moorlock's side, but still it held. Both men hammered at the beast, but still, no go. The old boy was latched in and meant business.

Then John Feather, bloodied and as crazed as the Moorlock, appeared. He had a knife in his teeth. He put it in his hand and said, "Step back, Hamner."

Hamner did, and John Feather cut the Moorlock's throat. With a spew of blood and a gurgle, the Moorlock died, but still its dead head bit tight into Beadle's shoulder.

John Feather sheathed the knife. He and Hamner tried to free the head, but it wouldn't let go. Its teeth were latched deep.

"Cut the head off," Beadle said.

John Feather went to work. As he cut, Beadle said, "I thought you were dead."

"Not hardly," John Feather said. "I got some bumps and my ass hurts, but the Moorlocks cushioned my fall, and I cushioned this guy's."

"Shit," said Blake, who, with his injured leg had not left his chair, "he's on us."

The Dark Rider, moving at an amazing clip, was riding lickety-split around Steam, and he was whirling above his head a hook on a long-ass rope. He let go of the rope with one hand and the hook went out and buried itself in the right tin leg of Steam and held.

The Dark Rider continued to ride furiously around Steam, binding its legs with the rope, pulling them tighter and tighter with the power of the mechanical horse.

Beadle, the head of the Moorlock hanging from his shoulder, struggled at the controls, tried to work the legs to break the rope. But it was too late.

Steam began to topple.

(6)
Steam All Messed Up

Steam fell with a terrific crash, fell so hard his head, containing Beadle and his crew, came off and rolled over the Dark Rider and his horse, knocking Clockwork for more than a few flips, causing it to shit horse turds of clockwork innards. Steam's head rolled right over the Dark Rider, driving him partially into the ground, but it had no effect.

Inside Steam's torso Beadle unfastened his seat belt, fell out of his seat, got up, and wobbled, trying to adjust to the Moorlock's head affixed to his shoulder.

One glance revealed that Hamner was dead. His seat had come unfastened from the floor and had thrown him into Steam's right eye, shattering it, poking glass through him. Blake was loose from his seat and on his crutch. He reached and took a Webb rifle off the wall.

John Feather reached his bow and arrows from the wall, unfastened the top of his quiver and threw it back, slipped the quiver over his shoulder, and took his bow and drew an arrow.

Beadle took a Webb rifle off the wall. Beadle looked at John Feather, said: "Today is a good day to die."

"It's night," John Feather said, "and I don't intend to die. I'm gonna kill me some assholes."

Actually, it was Asshole himself who was approaching the beheaded Steam, and with him was a pack of Moorlocks previously scattered from the remains of Stick.

Beadle and his crew went out the hole under Steam's ear. "I'm gonna die," Beadle said, "I'd rather do it out in the open."

Nearby lay Steam's body, leaking from its neck the remains of the exploded furnace: embers, fiery logs, lots of smoke and steam.

The Moorlocks came in a bounding, yelling, growling rush. Strategy was not their strong point. All they really knew was what the Dark Rider told them, and good, old-fashioned, direct ass-whipping. The Webb rifles cracked. Arrows flew. Moorlocks went down. But still they closed, and soon the fighting was hand to hand. The Moorlocks were strong and would have won, had not their leader, Asshole, leaping up and down and shouting orders, received one of John Feather's arrows in the mouth.

Asshole, still talking in his barking manner, bit down on the shaft, shattering teeth, then, appearing more than a bit startled, turned himself completely around and fell on his face, driving the shaft deeper, poking it out of the back of his neck.

In this instant, the Moorlocks lost courage and bolted.

The Dark Rider came then, called: "Get the fuck back here, or I'll impale you all myself."

These seemed like words of wisdom to the Moorlocks. They turned and began to stalk forward. Beadle picked out the Dark Rider and shot at him, hit him full in the chest. The bullet went through him with a jerk of flesh, an explosion of cloth and dust.

The Dark Rider, though knocked down and dazed, was unharmed.

Slowly, the Dark Rider stood up.

"That's not good," said Beadle.

"No," John Feather said. "It's not. I guess tonight is a good night to die. And while we're at it, if we're gonna go, I must tell you something, Beadle."

"What?"

"I've always wanted to fuck you."

"Huh," said Beadle, and John Feather let out with a laugh and loosed an arrow that took a Moorlock full in the chest, added: "Not!"

Amidst laughter, Beadle began to fire, and the Moorlocks began to drop.

But the ole Dark Rider, he just keep comin' on.

The Dark Rider was on them in a rush. He tossed John Feather hard against Steam's head, grabbed at Beadle, missed, grabbed at Blake who was hitting him with his crutch.

When Beadle regained his feet, the Dark Rider had Blake down and was poking at his ass so hard with the crutch, he had ripped a hole in his pants.

Before the Dark Rider could impale him, Beadle shot the Dark Rider in the back of the head. It was a good shot. No blood came out, just some skull tissue, and the Dark Rider flipped forward and over and came up on his feet, hatless.

He reached down and picked up his hat, dusted it on his knee, and put it on. He looked mad as hell.

John Feather had recovered. He let loose an arrow and it struck the Dark Rider in the chest with a thump, stayed there. The Dark Rider sighed, snapped the arrow off close to his chest.

The Moorlocks surrounded them.

The Dark Rider said, "And now it ends."

Then the Moorlocks swarmed them. Shots were fired, an arrow flew. But there were too many Moorlocks. In a matter of seconds, it was all over.

(7)
Getting the Shaft

They were carried away to a place outside of the museum, stripped nude, tied with their hands behind their backs, then surrounded by Moorlocks.

Though Hamner was dead, he was the first to be impaled. His body was partially feasted on by the Dark Rider and the Moorlocks, then he was raised into the moonlight with a freshly cut wooden shaft in his ass. The end of it was dropped into a prearranged hole. His dead weight traveled down the length of the stake and the point of it gouged out of his right eye. He continued to slide down it until his bloody buttocks touched the ground.

Second, the Dark Rider, out of some perverse desire for revenge, had Steam impaled. A large, sharpened tree was run through the trap door in the steam man's ass, poked through his neck, then the battered, steeple-topped head was placed on top of the stake.

With arms tied behind their backs, Beadle and his Moorlock head, John Feather, and Blake, who could not stand because of his leg, awaited their turn. The Moorlocks were salivating at the thought of their blood and flesh, and Beadle was reminded of a pack of hunting hounds at feeding time. He regretted that he had not gotten to his derringer in time, but the derringer was no longer an issue; like his clothes, it had been taken from him.

The Dark Rider, his hat removed, his face red with Hamner's blood, strands of Hamner's flesh hanging from his teeth, said, "I'm going to save you, Mr. Beadle, until last, and just before you the Indian. And you, what is your name?"

"Blake. Mr. James Blake to you."

"Ah, Blakey. Defiance to the last.

"Moorlocks..." the Dark Rider said.

The Moorlocks all leaned forward, as if listening at a keyhole.

"Gnaw his balls off."

They rushed Blake, and there was an awful commotion. Beadle and John Feather struggled valiantly to loose themselves from their bonds and help their friend, but the best they could manage were some lame, ignored kicks.

Blake was lifted up screaming, and while his legs were held apart by Moorlocks, the others, their heads popping forward like snapping turtles, tore at Blake's testicles, and when they were nothing more than ragged flesh (they got the penis too), a stake was rammed in his ass and he was dropped down on it. He screamed so loud Beadle felt as if the noise was rocking his very bones.

The Moorlocks carried Blake to a prearranged hole, dropped him in, pushed in dirt, and left him there. Courageously, Blake yelled, threw his legs up as high as he could. The movement dropped his weight, and the sharpened stick went through him and out of his throat, killing him quickly.

"That will be the way to do it," John Feather said. "It's how we should do it."

Beadle nodded.

The Dark Rider, who sat in a large, wooden chair that had been brought outside from the museum, said, "My, but he was brave. Quite brave."

"Unlike you," Beadle said.

"Ah," the Dark Rider said, "I suppose this is where you are going to challenge me, and with my ego at stake, and your ass at stake, so to speak, I'm going to take you on, one on one, and the winner survives. If I win, you die. If I lose, well, you all go to the house."

"Are you too much of a coward to do that?" Beadle said.

The Dark Rider removed a handkerchief from inside his vest and wiped Hamner's blood from his face and put on his hat. He tossed the handkerchief aside. A Moorlock grabbed it and began to suck at the blood on the cloth. A fight broke out over the handkerchief, and in the struggle one of the Moorlocks was killed.

When this moment had passed, the Dark Rider turned his attention back to Beadle.

"I don't much care how I'm thought of, Mr. Beadle. Since very little causes me damage, and I have the strength of ten men, it's sort of hard to be concerned about such a threat. And besides, in the rare case you did win, my Moorlocks would eat you anyway. In fact, if I should die, they would eat me. Right, boys?"

A murmur of agreement went up from the Moorlocks. Except for those eating the corpse of the loser of the handkerchief battle. They were preoccupied.

"No, I'm not going to do that," the Dark Rider said. "That would be too quick for you. And it would give you some sense of dignity. I'm against that. In fact, I actually have other plans for you. You will get the stake, but not before we've had a bit of torture. As for the red man, well, I can see now that the stake, if you're courageous like your friend, can be beat. I could tie your legs, Indian man, of course, stop that nonsense. But no. I'm going to crucify you. Upside down. And keep the boys off of you for a while so you'll suffer. As I remember, a saint was crucified upside down. Perhaps, Mr. Red Man, you will be made a saint. But I doubt it."

A cross was made and John Feather was put on it and his hands were nailed and his feet, after being overlapped, were also nailed. John Feather made not a sound while the Moorlocks worked, driving the nails into his flesh. The cross was put in the ground upside down, John Feather's head three feet from the dirt, his long hair dangling.

Beadle was taken away to the museum. The Moorlocks were given Blake's body to eat, all except the left arm which was wrapped in cloth and given directly to the Dark Rider for later.

Beadle was placed on a long table and tied to it. The Dark Rider disappeared for a time, about some other mission, and while Beadle waited for the horrors to come, the lone Moorlock left to watch him played with Beadle's dick.

"Lif id ub, pud id down," he said as he played. "Lif id ub, pud id down."

"Would you stop that, for heaven's sake?" Beadle said.

The Moorlock frowned, popped Beadle's balls with the back of his hand, and went back to his game. "Lif id ub, pud id down…"

(8)
A View from Doom

John Feather, in pain so intense he could no longer really feel it, could see the horizon, upside down, and he could see the ground and a bunch of ants. He had been taught that the ants, like all things in nature, were one, his kin. But he didn't like them. He knew what they wanted. Pretty soon they'd be on the cross, then the blood on his hands and feet. Then would come the flies. With kinfolk like ants and flies, who needed enemies? He could kind of get into accepting rocks and trees as his kinfolk, though he was, in fact, crucified on one of his kin, but ants and flies. Uh-uh.

He heard a squawk, lifted his head and looked up. At the top of the cross, waiting patiently, a buzzard had alighted.

John Feather remembered he had never had any use for buzzards, either. Come to think of it, he didn't like coyotes that much, and the way his luck was running, pretty soon they'd show up.

They didn't, but he did hear flies buzzing, and soon felt them alight on his bloody hands and feet.

When the Dark Rider showed, the first thing he did was light a kerosene lamp, and the first thing he said was, "I suppose we shall remove the Moorlock head. This will give us a wound to work with."

The Dark Rider took hold of the Moorlock's jaws, pried them apart, tossed the head, sent it bouncing across the floor. The assisting Moorlock watched it bounce. He looked longingly at the Dark Rider.

"Do your job here," the Dark Rider said, "and you can have it all to yourself."

The Moorlock looked pleased.

The Dark Rider, who had brought a roll of leather, placed it just above Beadle's head and uncoiled it. It was full of shiny instruments. The first one he pulled out was a long metal probe, sharpened on one end.

He held it up so Beadle could see it. It caught the lamplight and sparkled.

Beadle told himself he would not scream.

The Dark Rider poked the probe into the bite wound on his shoulder, and Beadle, in spite of himself, screamed. In fact, to his embarrassment, he thought he screamed like a girl, but with less restraint.

Inside the great time and space cosmic rip, the metal ship hurtled by again, and inside the ship, or as they called it, the shuttle, peering out one of its portholes, was an astronaut named McCormic. He was frightened. He was confused. And he was hungry. He and his partners, a Russian cosmonaut and a French astronaut, had recently finished their last tube of food and the water didn't look good. Another forty-eight hours they'd be out of it, another three or four days they'd be crazy and drinking their urine, maybe starting to think of each other as hot lunches.

Through a series of misfortunes they had lost most of their fuel and could not return to Earth. They were the Flying Dutchman, circling the globe. They had lost contact with home base. The radio waves were silent. It was as if the world beneath them had died. To add tension to all this, their air supply was draining. It would in fact play out at about the same time as the water supply, so maybe they would never get to drink their urine or dine on one another.

To top it off, McCormic was having trouble with his hemorrhoids, which was their way, to appear only at the least opportune time.

And then, there was the rip.

No matter where they were while circling the Earth, the rip was always to their left. They watched it constantly, saw inside it strange things. The rip made no sense. It fit nothing they knew or thought they knew. McCormic felt certain it was widening, even as they watched.

McCormic turned to his partners. The Russian was sitting on the floor. His name was Kruschev. Like his companions, he had removed his helmet some time ago. He was reading from the Frenchman's copy of *Huckleberry Finn*, in French. He didn't understand the jokes.

The Frenchman, Gisbone, said, "I know what you are thinking, my friend McCormic. I am thinking of the same."

McCormic glanced at the Russian. The Russian nodded. "It is closer than our Earth, comrade."

McCormic said, "It would be easy to use the thrusters. Turn into it. I say we do it."

John Feather thought perhaps the best thing he could do was pull with all his might and tear his hands free. The flesh there was not that strong, and if he could pull them through the nails, and was able to free his hands, then... Well, then he could hang upside down by his feet and die slowly of what he was already dying of, only with his hands free. Loss of blood.

But hell, it was something. He balled his hands into fists around the nails and pulled with everything he had.

Boy did it hurt.

Boy did it hurt a lot.

He pulled the flesh of his palms forward until the nails touched his clenched fingers. He jerked forward, and with a scream and burst of blood, John Feather's hands were free.

At about that time the shuttle, blasting on the last of its fuel, came hurtling through the crack in the sky, whizzed right by him so hard it caused the impaled steam man to rattle and the cross on which John Feather was crucified to lean dramatically.

The shuttle's wheels came down, but it hit at such an angle they crumpled and the great craft slid along on its belly.

John Feather, from his unique vantage point, watched as the ship tore up dirt, smashed through what was left of the smoldering stick man, turned sideways, spun in several circles, and stopped. There was a popping sound from the craft, as if metal were cooling.

After a long moment, the door of the craft opened. John Feather waited for a squid in harness and overalls to appear. But something else came out. Something white and puffy, shaped like a man, but with a bright face that made it look like some kind of insect.

At this moment, John Feather's cross finally came loose in the ground and toppled to the earth with him on top of it. He let out a howl of pain.

Fuck that stoic red man shit.

McCormic was first. He wore his helmet, had his oxygen tank turned on. After a moment, he turned off the oxygen and removed the helmet. He came down the flexible staircase breathing deeply of the air.

"Very fresh," he said.

The Frenchman and the Russian came after him, removing their helmets.

"I believe it ees our Earth," said the Frenchman. "Only fugged up."

From where he lay, John Feather tried to yell, but found that he had lost his voice. That scream had taken it out of him. He was hoarse and weak. But if he could get their attention, whoever, whatever they were, they might help him. They might eat him too, but considering his condition, he was willing to take the chance.

He tried to yell, but the voice just wasn't there. He tried several times.

The men with parts of their heads in their hands, turned away from the ship, walked around it, and headed away from him, in the direction from which he and his friends and the steam man had come.

When they were dots in the distance, John Feather's voice returned to him in a squeak. But it didn't matter now. They were out of earshot.

All he could manage was a weak "Shit."

The Dark Rider had a lot of fun poking Beadle's wound, but he eventually became bored of that, left, came back with a salt shaker. He shook salt in the wound. Beadle groaned. The Moorlock hopped up and down. He hadn't had this much fun since he'd helped eat his first-born young. The Dark Rider smiled, tried not to think of Weena.

After lying there for a while, John Feather sat up and looked at his crucified feet. They hurt like a bitch. It took balls, but he reached down and grabbed both feet with his hands, and jerked with all his might.

The nail groaned, came loose, but not completely. The pain that shot through John Feather was so intense he lay back down. He prayed to the Great Spirit, then to the white man's god Jesus. He threw in a couple words for Buddha as well, even though he couldn't remember if Buddha actually did anything or not. Wasn't he just kind of an inspiration or something? He tried to remember the name of the Arabic god he had heard mentioned, but it wouldn't come to him.

Great Spirit, Jesus, Buddha, all seemed on vacation. The men carrying their heads didn't show up either.

John Feather sat up, took hold of his feet again, wrenched with all his might.

This time the nail came free, and John Feather passed out.

With pliers, one by one, the Dark Rider removed, with a slow wrench, Beadle's toenails.

John Feather found he could stand, but it was painful. He preferred to go forward on knuckles and knees, but that wasn't doing his hands any good.

Finally, using a combination of stand and crawl, he made it to the steam man, looked up at the spike in its ass, saw there was room to enter inside between shaft and passageway. Painfully, he took hold of the shaft and attempted to climb it. It was very difficult. His hands and feet hurt beyond anything he could imagine and the wounds from them slicked the stake with blood.

He fell twice and hit the ground hard before finally rubbing dirt in his wounds and trying a third time. It was slow and deliberate. But this time he made it.

"And this little piggy cried wee-wee-wee, all the way... HOME!"

With that, the Dark Rider jerked out the last toenail on Beadle's left foot.

Beadle groaned so loud, for a moment, even the Moorlock was startled.

"Now," the Dark Rider said, "let's go for the other one. What do you say?"

Beadle was too much in pain to say anything. And besides, what would it matter? He was going to save his breath for groaning and screaming.

Inside Steam, John Feather found water and washed the dirt from his wounds and used herbs and roots from his medicine and utility bag, applied them in a quick poultice, then bound them with ripped sheets from one of the locked cabinets. He made a breech cloth from some of the sheet, found his extra pair of soft moccasins and slid inside of them. His feet had swollen, but the leather was soft and stretched. He was able to put them on without too much trouble, and he found the cleansing and dressing had relieved the pain in his feet enough so that he could stand. It wasn't by any means comfortable to do so, but he felt he had to.

He tied his medicine bag around his waist, got a Webb rifle from its rack, his extra bow and quiver of forty-five thin arrows with long, steel points.

Then he paused.

He put the rifle, the bow and quiver of arrows aside. He looked out of Steam's ass at the shaft that ran through it and out the neck, looked at the head balanced on top.

John Feather climbed down inside the right leg and took a canister off the wall. He carried it to the gap in Steam's ass and opened it, even though the action caused his hands to bleed. Inside was kerosene. He poured the kerosene down the shaft. He took flint and steel from his medicine pouch and struck up a spark that hit the soaked shaft and caused it to burst into flame. Fire ran down the length of the shaft and it began to burn.

John Feather took wood from the sealed hoppers, built a fire in Steam's belly.

"Just two more to go on this foot," the Dark Rider said, "then we start on the fingernails. Then we're going to see if you've been circumcised. And if not, we're going to do that. And if so, we're going to do it really close, if you know what I mean."

"Can I have 'em? Can I have 'em?" the Moorlock asked.

"You can have them, but as it looks to me, you should start on and finish your head."

The Moorlock grabbed the head of his brethren and began chewing on it.

Between bites he said, "Thank you, Master. Thank you."

"Let's do the right thumb first," the Dark Rider said. "What do you say?"

It was a rhetorical question. Beadle knew it was useless to ask for mercy from his enemy. He kept wishing he'd just pass out, but so far, no such luck. This hurt like hell, but was survivable, and therefore stretched out the possibilities. None of them good. It was made all the worse by the fact that the Dark Rider took his time. A little tug here, a little tug there, almost a tug, then a tug, easing the nails out one slow nail at a time.

Not to mention that the Dark Rider liked to pause with his pliers to squeeze the joints themselves, or to pause and poke at the wound in his shoulder.

The Dark Rider seemed to be having the time of his life.

Beadle wished he could say the same.

John Feather worked the bellows. The fire was going nicely. It wasn't normally a wise thing to do, but John Feather doused the interior of the furnace with kerosene, and as a result, a rush of fire burst out of it and singed his eyebrows, but the wood blazed.

John Feather checked the shaft in Steam's ass.

Burning nicely.

He went back to the bellows, worked there vigorously, stoking up the flame. The water in the chambers began to heat, and John Feather continued to work the bellows. Smoke came up through Steam's ass as the shaft blazed and caught solid.

"Now we have the pinky on the right hand... And, there, isn't that better just having it done with?"

Beadle couldn't understand what the Dark Rider was saying. He couldn't understand because he couldn't quit screaming.

The Dark Rider said, "And now let's do that lefty."

Vapor from the pipes pumped up and out of Steam's headless neck. Steam toppled forward and struck the ground hard, throwing John Feather against the side of the furnace, and in that instant, John Feather realized the shaft had burned through. Slightly burned from the furnace, John Feather recovered his feet, closed the furnace door, crawled along the side of Steam and began to work the emergency controls in the mid-body of the machine. They were serviceable at best.

Working these controls, he was able to make Steam put his hands beneath him and right himself.

John Feather clung to a cabinet until Steam was standing straight, then he took his stance on the platform in front of the seats and moved from one position to the other, working levers, observing dials.

It was erratic, but John Feather managed to have Steam lurch forward, find his head, and set it in place. Or almost in place. It set slightly tilted to the left.

John Feather climbed into the head and refastened the steam cables that had come unsnapped when the head came loose. He had to replace one from the backup stock. He tried the main controls. The fall Steam had taken had affected them; they were a little rough, but they worked.

John Feather started Steam toward the museum.

Condensation not only came out of the hole in the steam man's hat, but it hissed out of his eye holes and neck as well. He walked as if drunk.

(9)
Ruckus

The wall came apart and Steam tore off part of the roof too. He grabbed a rip in the roof and shook it. A big block of granite fell from the ceiling, just missed Beadle on the table, passed to the left elbow of the Dark Rider, and got his Moorlock companion square, just as he was sucking an eyeball from the head he had been eating.

Steam ducked his head and entered the remains of the museum.

"I swore what I'd do to you Beadle," the Dark Rider said. "And I'll do it."

With that, the Dark Rider ducked under the table Beadle was strapped to, lifted it on his back, his arms outstretched, his hands turned backward to clasp the table's sides, and with little visible effort, darted for the staircase.

Steam, head ducked, tried to pursue him, but as he went up the stairs the ceiling was too low. John Feather made Steam push at the ceiling with his head and shoulders like Atlas bearing the weight of the world, and Steam lifted.

The ceiling began to fall all around and on Steam.

The Dark Rider was up the stairs now, heading for the opening to the roof. When he came to the opening, he flung the table backward so that Beadle landed on his face, breaking his nose, bamming his knee caps, and in the process, not doing his already maligned toes any good.

The Dark Rider grabbed the table and tore it apart, causing the straps that bound Beadle to be released. He grabbed Beadle by the head, like a kid not knowing how to carry a puppy, and started up a ladder to the roof.

When the Dark Rider reached the summit of the ladder, he used his free hand to throw open the trap, then, still holding the struggling Beadle by the head, pulled him onto the moonlit roof.

To the Dark Rider's right, he saw that the rip in the sky had grown, and that a rip within the rip had opened up a gap of darkness in which strange, unidentifiable shapes moved.

Below his feet the roof shook, then exploded. Steam's crooked head poked through. And then rose. It was obvious the steam man was coming up the stairs, and he was tearing the roof apart.

The Dark Rider picked Beadle up by shoulder and thigh, raised him over his head. The Dark Rider thought the easy thing would be to toss Beadle from the roof.

Game over.

But that was the easy thing. He wanted this bastard to suffer.

And then he knew. He'd take his chances inside the rip. If he and Beadle survived it, he'd continue to make Beadle suffer slowly. Nothing else beyond that mattered. He realized suddenly that Beadle had been all that mattered for some time now, and when Beadle was dead, he would have only the memory of Weena again. Nothing else to preoccupy his thoughts. No more Beadle, no more steam man or regulators.

With Beadle raised over his head, the Dark Rider growled and started to run toward the rip.

John Feather saw through the shattered eye of Steam what the Dark Rider planned. Painfully, he grabbed at the quiver he had discarded, picked up his bow, took a coil of thin rope from the wall, tied it to the arrow with one quick loop, and watched as the Dark Rider completed the edge of the museum's roof, which was where the rip in the sky joined it.

The Dark Rider leaped.

John Feather let the arrow fly, dropped the bow, grabbed at the loose end of the rope and listened to the rest of it feed out.

The shot was a good one. It was right on the money. It went through Beadle's left thigh, right on through, and into his inner right thigh.

John Feather heard Beadle yell just as he jerked the rope with all his might. Beadle came loose from the Dark Rider's grasp in midair and was pulled back and slammed onto the museum roof, but the Dark Rider leapt into the dark rip with a curse that reverberated back into this world, then was nothing more than a fading echo.

The Dark Rider's leap had carried him into a place of complete cold darkness. His element. Or so it seemed.

He passed between shapes. Giant bats. They snapped smelly teeth at him and missed.

In time, he thought it would have been better had they not missed.

Because he was falling.

Falling...falling.

His leap had carried him into an abyss. Seemingly bottomless, because he fell and fell and fell, and if he had been able to keep time, he would have realized that days passed, and still he fell. And had he needed oxygen like normal men he would have long been dead, but he did not need it, and therefore he did not die.

He just continued to fall.

He thought of Weena. He wondered if there really was a plane on which her soul survived, wondered if he could join her there, if she would want him now that he was what he was.

And he fell and he fell...and he is falling still....

But, back to John Feather and Beadle.

John Feather found a knife, dropped the ladder out from under Steam's ear, hobbled down it and out to Beadle. John Feather, while Beadle protested, cut the arrowhead out of Beadle's thigh, hacked the arrow off at the shaft, and using one injured, bleeding foot against the outside of Beadle's leg, jerked it free.

"We're going to have to help one another," John Feather said. "I'm not feeling too strong. My hands are seizing up."

"Did you have to shoot me with an arrow?"

"It was that, or follow him. And if you had gone into that rip, I would not have followed. I'm not that much of a friend."

The two of them, supporting one another, hobbled back to Steam.

Inside, Beadle found spare pants and shirt and boots and put them on. John Feather doctored his wounds again. Then, in their control chairs, they worked Steam and brought him out of the remains of the museum. They saw a few Moorlocks through Steam's eyes, but they were scattering. The sun was coming up.

"We should try and kill them all," Beadle said.

"I'm not up to killing much of anything," John Feather said.

"Yeah," Beadle said. "Me either."

"Without their leader, they aren't much."

"I think we're making a mistake."

John Feather sighed. "You may be right. But…"

"Yeah. Let's take Steam home."

John Feather, in considerable pain, looked through one of Steam's eyes at the landscape bathed in the orange-red light of the rising sun. There were more rips out there than before, and he saw things spilling out of some of them.

"If we still have a home," said John Feather.

Epilogue

The astronauts, who had shed their heavy pressure suits and were wearing orange jumps, stopped walking as a green Dodge Caravan driven by a blonde woman with two kids in it, a boy and a girl, stopped beside them.

She lowered an electric window.

"You look lost," she said.

"Very," said McCormic.

"I suggest you get in." She nodded to the rear.

The astronauts glanced in that direction. A herd of small but very aggressive looking dinosaurs were thundering in their direction.

"We'll take you up on that suggestion," McCormic said.

They hustled inside. The boy and girl looked terrified. The astronauts smiled at them.

The blonde woman put her foot to the gas and they tore off.

Behind them the dinosaurs continued to pursue. The woman soon had the Caravan up to eighty and the dinosaurs were no longer visible.

"How much gas do you have?" asked McCormic.

"Over half a tank," she said. "Where are we?"

McCormic looked at the others. They shrugged. He said, "We haven't a clue. But I think we're home, and yet, we aren't."

"I guess," said the blonde woman, "that's as good an answer as I'm going to find."

The Caravan drove on.

All about, earth and sky resounded with the sounds of time and space coming apart.

The Selene Gardening Society

MOLLY BROWN

Continuing the adventures of Jules Verne's space travelers from *De la Terre à la Lune,* Molly Brown's "The Selene Gardening Society" spotlights the light, playful side of steampunk with its clever and witty banter — a comedy of manners with a steampunk swagger. Who doesn't want to start a garden on the moon? Clockwork *and* environmentally conscious: greenpunk.

Chapter One
J. T. Maston takes up gardening

An open-topped carriage turned up the long drive to one of the grandest houses in New Park, Baltimore. The mansion's doors flew open, a stream of servants filing out into the afternoon sun to greet their mistress, the former Mrs. Evangelina Scorbitt.

Evangelina patted the large box on the seat beside her. It contained her latest purchase: a wide-brimmed hat garnished with a cluster of tall feathers. Despite having invested — and lost — nearly half of the late Mr. Scorbitt's fortune in the Baltimore Gun Club's failed scheme to melt the polar ice cap, she was still one of the wealthiest women in Maryland, well able to afford the occasional new hat. And this hat was something special.

At the age of forty-seven, Evangelina was painfully aware that, even as a girl, she had never been a beauty. But the moment she'd tried on that hat, she'd felt transformed. The milliner insisted she looked ten years younger, and for the first time in her life, this overweight middle-aged woman with hair the colour of dirty straw had actually liked what she saw in the mirror. It was the most wonderful hat in the world, and she couldn't wait for her new husband to see her in it.

Her driver was slowing the horses to a walk when the ground beneath them was rocked by an explosion. Evangelina was thrown back in her seat as the horses reared up, then bolted across the lawn.

She calmly grabbed hold of the side of the carriage as it careered across the grass, pursued by a gaggle of uniformed servants. And every dog in the neighbourhood was barking. "You'd think they'd be used to it by now," she sighed.

She was sitting in front of her dressing table when the house was shaken by another explosion. The maid standing behind her jumped, nearly skewering her with a hat pin. "Sorry, Ma'am."

Evangelina shook her head. The staff were as skittish as the horses. And the neighbourhood dogs were at it again. She told her maid to close the window.

Melting the North Pole had seemed a good idea at the time. There must be limitless supplies of coal in the Arctic — once you got past all that ice. So a plan was devised to straighten the Earth's axis by firing a gigantic cannon set into the side of Mount Kilimanjaro, the idea being that the recoil from the shot would nudge the planet into the desired position.

Despite the cannon's failure to affect the Earth's orbit — due to a slight mathematical error involving the accidental erasure of three zeros — and the loss of all that money, Evangelina continually reminded herself that everything had worked out for the best in the end. Everyone now agreed that melting the polar ice would have drowned half the civilised world, including Baltimore. And so the mistake in calculations became a cause for celebration, and the man who had made it became a hero.

And that hero was none other than Mr. Jefferson Thomas Maston, generally known as J. T.

J. T. Maston was nearly sixty, with an iron hook at the end of one arm (the result of an accident with a mortar during the Civil War), but he was a great man: not only a renowned mathematician, but an inventor (he'd designed the mortar that removed his hand himself). It was not long after their first meeting that Evangelina had decided she wanted nothing more than to be this great man's wife, and it was now a little over three months since Evangelina had got her wish, and had become Mrs. J. T. Maston.

She should have been deliriously happy, if not for one thing: J.T. Maston had taken up gardening.

She found her husband bending over a howitzer in a far corner of the grounds. "I thought that would be a good spot for the azaleas," he said, pointing at a patch of cleared soil between the fountain and the grotto.

She positioned herself directly in her husband's line of sight. "Well?"

"Well what?"

She did a little twirl, raising a hand to indicate her hat. "What do you think?"

"About what?"

She stopped twirling. "Never mind."

Her husband shrugged and turned his attention back to the cannon. "Stand back."

Evangelina covered her ears as the gun went off, discharging a cloud of seeds.

Chapter Two
In which a solution is suggested

"I wouldn't even mention it," Evangelina said, "but the neighbours are complaining, the staff are threatening to leave, and now he's dug up all my rose bushes and is talking about turning the ornamental pond into an onion patch."

The monthly gathering of the New Park Ladies' Gardening Society burbled their sympathy. They were meant to be discussing their annual "Best Delphiniums" award, but the conversation had drifted off-topic.

It was a warm day, and the various scents of lavender, musk, rose, and vanilla emanating from the ladies around her seemed to be fighting a losing battle against the reek of garbage wafting in through the windows of the Methodist meeting hall.

"And he didn't even notice my new hat," she added, fanning herself.

This was greeted with such an eruption of clucking and tsk'ing that Fiona Wicke was forced to bring down her gavel.

Once the most beautiful woman in Baltimore, these days the thrice-widowed chair of the Gardening Society contented herself with being the most fashionable. She leaned back in her seat — at least as far back as the stiff horsehair-padded bustle beneath her dress would allow — and formed a temple with her lace-gloved fingers. "I take it Mr. Maston and Mr. Barbicane are still not speaking?" It seemed everyone in Baltimore knew about the rift between J. T. Maston and the president of the Gun Club. It all went back to those three silly little zeros. The one thing Mr. Impey Barbicane refused to forgive was an error in calculations — even an error that had saved the world — with the end result that Mr. Maston had not only resigned his position as club secretary, but had completely forsworn mathematics.

And taken up gardening instead.

"Therein lies the source of your problem," Fiona said, "and also the solution. Find a way to reconcile those two men, and you shall have your garden back."

"But how?"

"You might distract the men from their quarrel by providing them with a new goal on which to focus their attention."

"As you might distract a vicious dog by throwing it a piece of meat," the Society's first vice-chair (and one of its youngest members), the forty-three-year-old Hermione Larkin, added.

Fiona raised an eyebrow at her vice-chair before turning back to address Evangelina. "Give them a new project to work on and all past differences will quickly be forgotten."

"As your garden will also be forgotten...by your husband, I mean," added Hermione.

"A project?" Evangelina said. "What kind of project?"

Prunella Benton rose to her feet. "Wasn't your husband involved in that expedition to the moon some years back?"

"That's it!" a voice at the back of the room exclaimed. "That's your project, a return to the moon!"

Chapter Three
A delegation

"There is no point in returning to the moon," Mr. Impey Barbicane stated categorically, the beads of sweat on his upper lip betraying his discomfort at being confronted by a delegation of middle-aged women. "The moon is uninhabitable."

"Baltimore was uninhabitable a hundred years ago," Prunella Benton said, dismissing Barbicane's argument with a wave of her hand. "No society to speak of, at any rate."

"My house was uninhabitable until I replaced those awful curtains," Hermione Larkin added, rolling her eyes.

Barbicane, exasperated, turned to his compatriot, Captain Nicholl. Though it was only a few months since Evangelina had last seen them, both men looked older than she remembered. The face below Barbicane's trademark stovepipe hat seemed thinner and more haggard, while Captain Nicholl seemed pale and tired.

Even the room seemed different from how she remembered it. The formerly gleaming clusters of muskets, blunderbusses, and carbines that adorned the walls now seemed dingy and uncared-for, the glass display cases of ammunition were covered in a layer of dust, and the exuberant atmosphere she recalled from her previous visits had been replaced by an air of gloom.

It felt as if everything in the place had somehow become smaller. Even the men seemed smaller.

"It's not the same thing at all," Captain Nicholl stepped in. "There is no air or water on the moon."

"And there are no sandwiches in a forest," Hermione responded. "If you wish to have a picnic in the woods, you bring the sandwiches with you!"

"Sandwiches?" said Barbicane.

"What Mrs. Larkin means is: if a place is not inhabitable, you find a way to make it so," Evangelina explained.

"May I remind you," said Captain Nicholl, "Mr. Barbicane and I have actually orbited the moon, and in our close observations of its surface, we saw no sign of life, and no sign of anything that might sustain life."

Fiona Wicke spoke up at this point. "If, as you say, there is no air on the moon, it is worth bearing in mind that vegetation produces oxygen."

"But there is no vegetation on the moon," Mr. Barbicane responded, a trace of irritation creeping into his voice.

"And there was precious little vegetation in my garden until I planted it," said Hermione.

"Ladies," said Captain Nicholl. "From what I have seen with my own eyes, I am forced to conclude that the lunar soil is incapable of supporting vegetation. You must believe me when I tell you that nothing can survive there. Nothing."

Hermione seemed about to speak again, but Fiona silenced her with a discreet shake of the head. "Just one last question," Fiona said. "Why did you send a projectile to the moon in the first place?"

"To prove it could be done," said Barbicane.

"They were laughing at us," Fiona said as the women emerged into the sunlight. "Not aloud, but inwardly; you could see it in their faces. And they had every right to do so. We were not prepared, we had not thought it through."

A sudden gust of wind sent several sheets of discarded newspaper flapping about the square. Hermione grimaced in disgust as one of the dusty sheets plastered itself across the front of her carefully draped and bustled skirt. "When is someone going to do something about the garbage problem in this city?" she demanded, shaking her skirt free.

Fiona watched the paper blow away down the street, her face creased in thought.

Chapter Four
Fiona thinks it through

"Is Mrs. Wicke at home?" Evangelina asked, handing the maid her card.

Evangelina was left to wait in the front parlour while the maid went to see if her mistress was at home. She was admiring a *cloisonné* vase when she heard Fiona's voice coming from behind her: "I've never really liked that vase, it was a gift from my first husband's mother."

Evangelina's first reaction on turning around was to ask Fiona if she was all right. Though it was half past two in the afternoon, her hair was down and she was still in her dressing gown.

"Yes, yes, of course. I'm fine."

"Are you sure you're all right?" Evangelina persisted, trying not to stare at Fiona's state of undress.

"Yes, yes! I'm glad you came, actually; I want to show you something."

She led Evangelina out into the garden. "What is that?" she asked, pointing at a mound of grass cuttings and kitchen scraps.

"It's a compost heap," Evangelina said. "Are you quite sure you're all right?"

"Take a look at it," Fiona insisted. "What does it consist of?"

"Fiona, I don't need to examine your compost heap to ascertain its contents. I know what's in a compost heap, I have one myself."

"Potato peelings, eggshells, coffee grounds," Fiona began, counting each item off on her fingers. "Apple cores, hedge trimmings — "

"Fiona, what are you getting at?"

"Garbage! It's all garbage! And what is the biggest problem in Baltimore today? The garbage problem."

"So?"

"So we send our garbage to the moon!"

"But that's what I came here to tell you about. Immediately after we left the Gun Club the other day, Mr. Barbicane contacted my husband to tell him about our proposal — which they both found rather amusing — with the end result that Mr. Maston has since been reinstated as club secretary and returned to the pursuit of mathematics, while I have this morning hired two men to repair the damage to my garden. So everything has turned out as planned and we can forget about the moon."

"No, no, you don't understand," Fiona insisted. "This isn't about your husband's rift with Barbicane. This is about making the moon a place where human beings can survive, and it can work! What was Barbicane and Nicholl's main objection to the possibility of making the moon habitable? The lack of an atmosphere. But what I am proposing will create that atmosphere."

"How?"

"Of what does our own atmosphere consist?" Fiona asked her.

Evangelina shrugged. "Oxygen, I suppose."

"I think you'll find some seventy-eight per cent of the air we breathe is nitrogen. And what gas does a compost heap produce in abundance?"

"Nitrogen?"

"Exactly! So...we send our garbage to the moon where it decays into compost, producing nitrogen to enrich the soil, thus enabling the growth of vegetation. The vegetation produces oxygen. Then we throw in some worms, insects, and small animals to produce carbon dioxide, and voila! We have an atmosphere."

Evangelina's mouth dropped open. "Where do you get such ideas?"

"Come upstairs and I will show you."

Evangelina followed her back into the house and up the stairs to a large study lined with overflowing bookcases.

Fiona walked over to a desk piled high with open books and several stacks of handwritten notes. "My second husband, though he made his living in textile sales, had a great interest in science, especially chemistry. I've still got all his books, and have been conducting further research of my own at the public library."

Evangelina picked up one of the handwritten sheets and began reading its contents out loud: "Corncobs, cotton, paper, sawdust, wood chips, straw, hops, restaurant scraps, market scraps, hair, feathers, hooves, horns, peanut shells, seashells, seaweed…. What is this?"

"Just a partial list of things that can be composted, all of which are thrown out every day. When I was at the library yesterday, I found a survey predicting that over the next twenty-five years, the average American city will produce an average of eight hundred and sixty pounds of garbage per capita. With the current population of Baltimore standing at approximately five hundred thousand souls, that makes a total of…" She paused to riffle through her notes. "Ah, here we are: four hundred and thirty million pounds of garbage. Keep in mind this figure is for Baltimore alone, and assumes no further growth in population, which strikes me as unlikely. Now, consider the population of New York, currently standing at over three and a quarter millions—"

Evangelina didn't need to hear any more figures to grasp what Fiona was telling her. "In just twenty-five years, we could turn the moon into a gigantic compost heap!"

"And that is just the beginning," Fiona said, concluding her address to an extraordinary meeting of the New Park Ladies' Gardening Society, called at less than forty-eight hours notice. "Upon his return to earth, the third passenger in Barbicane and Nicholl's projectile, the Frenchman Michel Ardan…"

More than two decades after the Frenchman's only visit to America, the mere mention of the name "Ardan" was still enough to prompt a wave of wistful sighs.

"…remarked that the greatest disappointment of his life was to learn there were no Selenites, but I tell you now that the Frenchman was wrong. Ladies, we are the Selenites!"

The entire membership of the Society — all seventeen of them — rose to their feet to give Fiona a standing ovation.

"Whatever became of Monsieur Ardan?" Hermione whispered to Evangelina.

"He returned to France some years ago," Evangelina whispered back, "and the last I heard, was growing cabbages."

"Cabbages? How perfect! We could invite him to judge our best vegetable competition!"

Evangelina took a slow, deep breath. "Hermione, he lives in France."

Chapter Five
A garden on the moon

"Over the same period, Boston, with a population of approximately five hundred and sixty thousand, will produce well over four hundred and eighty-one million pounds of garbage," Fiona informed the trio of gentlemen seated on the opposite side of the table.

"Four hundred eighty-one million and six hundred thousand, to be precise," said J. T. Maston.

Evangelina sat quietly at Fiona's side. The only reason for her presence today was her role in arranging this second meeting. Until the occasion two weeks previously, when she had burst in uninvited with three other women, Evangelina had been the only non-member — and the only female — ever allowed into the Gun Club premises. This special status had only been granted to her on account of her generous financial contribution to the scheme to shift the Earth's axis. Getting Mr. Barbicane to agree to a second audience with Fiona had not been easy, but once Evangelina became determined upon something, she usually got her way.

Now there was little for her to do except allow the others to talk while she reflected on her surroundings, and she couldn't help being pleased by what she saw.

The firearms on display had been restored to their shining former glory, the glass cases sparkled, and the air of gloom had lifted. And it was all due to the return of J. T. Maston, once again at his usual place, his good hand scribbling furiously as he recorded every word spoken at the table into his notebook.

"While New York, with a population of approximately three and a quarter million is predicted to produce —"

"Two billion, seven hundred and ninety-five million pounds of garbage," said J. T. Maston, entering the numbers in his book with a flourish.

"Correct," said Fiona. "And not only will this raw material cost us nothing, city governments will pay us to take it. The only initial expenses involved would be those of setting up a company and hiring local men to work as our collectors. Once we acquire the garbage, we simply pack it into missiles designed to break open upon impact, and send it crashing into the moon."

J. T. Maston began sketching a design for the garbage missile. "The opening mechanism, here, will require a small explosives charge…"

"Or perhaps just a spring?" Fiona suggested tactfully.

"That would work, too," Maston agreed, modifying his drawing.

"And you plan to follow this garbage with seeds," said Barbicane. "What kind of seeds?"

"Whatever is readily to hand, I should imagine," Captain Nicholl interjected before Fiona could answer. "Surely any plant will do as long it produces oxygen."

"Acorns," said J. T. Maston. "If people are going to live on the moon, they will require wood for building houses."

"Yes, trees must be a priority," Barbicane agreed, "because they take the longest to grow."

J. T. Maston drew a large circle to represent the moon. "We could fit an oak forest in here," he said, marking out a section of the northern hemisphere.

"Apple orchards over there," said Barbicane, indicating a section over to one side. "Pear trees over there, orange groves down here."

"We'll need grasslands for cattle," Captain Nicholl enthusiastically joined in, while Fiona insisted there also be room for the purely aesthetic, "The Selenite garden must be a place of beauty, a new Eden if you like."

"Roses, gardenias, et cetera, over there," said J. T. Maston. "Corn and wheatfields here." He looked up from his fevered sketching. "But how do we water all this vegetation?"

"India rubber," said Evangelina, speaking up for the first time.

"What?" said Nicholl.

"Children's toy balloons made from the sap of the India rubber tree," Fiona explained. "Every shipment to the moon will include a number of these balloons filled with water…thanks to a suggestion from one of our members who caught her grandson throwing a water-filled balloon at the neighbours' cat."

"A garden on the moon," Mr. Barbicane said wistfully. "If only it were possible."

Fiona's eyebrows shot up in surprise. Even Captain Nicholl seemed a little startled.

"But it is possible," Fiona protested, sifting through her notes. "There's much more I haven't gone into yet. Bees, for example. I didn't mention the bees because they don't come in until a later stage. And there'll be worms. Lots of worms…"

"My dear Mrs. Wicke, I am sure that your idea is more than possible in theory, it's just impossible in practice."

"But…"

"The one thing you have not considered is: how on earth do you expect to send all these missiles to the moon?"

"But you've done it before," Fiona sputtered. "The Columbiad cannon…"

"The cannon to which you refer fired one projectile containing three men, two dogs, and a handful of chickens towards the moon on one occasion more than twenty years ago. Firing that one — comparatively lightweight — missile, one time only, required four hundred thousand pounds of fulminating cotton. What you are proposing would seem to involve the firing of an immense number of much heavier projectiles on a daily basis over a period of many years, possibly a century or more. I doubt there is that much explosive in the world, and even if there was, the cost would be prohibitive."

Fiona scoured her pages of notes, searching for an answer.

"But the cannon still exists," said Evangelina.

Barbicane shook his head. "Melted down, years ago."

"And Moon City?" Fiona asked, referring to the Florida base the Gun Club had constructed for that one, long-ago trip to the moon.

"Long since reclaimed by jungle," said Barbicane. "There was no reason to maintain it."

Fiona turned an imploring gaze to Captain Nicholl.

The captain responded with a sympathetic shrug.

"What is going on here?" J.T. Maston demanded, slamming his good fist down on the table. "When did Impey Barbicane ever fail to rise to a challenge? When did Captain Nicholl ever withdraw from the prospect of difficulty with a shrug? These are not the men I know! The men I know do not retreat from problems, they thrive on them!"

"Calm down, Maston," said Mr. Barbicane. "I merely said it was impossible. I never said we wouldn't find a way to do it."

That evening, Evangelina sat down at her roll-top desk to compose an overseas cablegram.

Scorbitt House
New Park, Baltimore

Dear Monsieur Ardan,

We have never met, but my husband has always said he considers you the best of men, and I thought you would want to know what is happening here in Baltimore…

Chapter Six
The great work begins, and a cablegram arrives

Over the next few weeks, a company was formed, workers were hired, and rubbish collection contracts were signed with cities up and down the eastern coast of America. A team was dispatched to the Florida wilderness to begin the rebuilding of Moon City, the ladies of the Gardening Society worked on refining their designs for the Selenite garden, Barbicane and Nicholl attacked the problem of the explosives, and J.T. Maston spent his days and nights at the chalkboard, covering it in strange arithmetical symbols that meant nothing to Evangelina, but which he assured her were absolutely vital to the project at hand.

And the following cablegram arrived:

Le Plessis-Brion
France

Dear Madame Maston,

Thought my travelling days were over, but your news has rekindled the only passion still burning in this old man's heart. Pull of Selene too strong for this Endymion, cannot stay away. Passage booked on steamer *Nereus*, arriving Baltimore seventh September.

Tell Barbicane: explosives problem solved. Explanation on arrival.

Ardan

P.S. Sorry husband did not notice new hat. Am sure it was very lovely.

Chapter Seven
A Frenchman, a Norwegian, and a cannon

The ladies of the New Park Gardening Society gathered along a railing at the dockside, the new-style S-bend corsets beneath their gaily coloured outfits contorting their spines into the latest fashionable silhouette: torso thrust forward as if leaning into a wind. Evangelina stood near the front of the group, feeling rather splendid in her ensemble of leg-of-mutton-sleeved dress, white gloves, lace-trimmed parasol, and hat bedecked with silk flowers.

A short distance away from the women, a committee of Gun Club members waited in loose formation, the men almost indistinguishable from one another in their uniform attire of dark frock coats and stovepipe hats.

At long last, the ship's passengers began to disembark.

The ladies twittered in excitement while the men went through a ritual of solemnly clearing their throats, straightening their backs, and tugging at their waistcoats.

A man emerged from the crowd, heading straight for the line of waiting ladies. Tall and broad-shouldered, with weathered skin and a shock of white hair as thick and wild as a lion's mane, he wore no coat nor hat, and was dressed more like a farmhand than a gentleman in his open-necked shirt and trousers of the coarsest material. Evangelina asked herself if this could possibly be the person she was here to greet, but her doubts were soon dispelled as the men surged forward to shake the oddly dressed stranger's hand and slap him on the back. "Is that him?" she asked Prunella Benton.

Prunella nodded, apparently too overcome to speak.

And then before she knew it, the Frenchman was standing before her, taking her gloved hand in his large, callused paw and raising it to his lips. "My dear Madame Maston, it was your siren call that lured this simple man of the soil away from his little cabbage patch. And now I am, and shall ever remain, your devoted admirer," he said, his dark eyes gazing at her with an intensity that made her feel, for that one moment, as if she was the only woman in the world.

"I... I..." she said.

"Your husband is the most fortunate of men," Monsieur Ardan told her before moving on to give his full attention to the next woman down the line.

A fortyish bearded man in a brown wool suit approached the group, followed by at least a dozen stevedores wheeling an assortment of trunks and crates.

"Ah, there you are at last!" Ardan exclaimed, striding over to the man. He threw an arm around his shoulders and introduced him to the assembled party. "My travelling companion, Professor Stefan Halstein of the University of Christiania."

The professor bowed to the assemblage before turning to say something to Ardan.

"My friend the professor begs your indulgence as he speaks little English, and asks me to present you with his gift of Norwegian pine cones," Ardan explained, indicating one of the crates, "so there may be a little bit of Norway on the moon. While I..." he went on, touching the crate beside it, "have brought you cabbage seeds from France."

The group started to applaud, but Ardan raised a hand for silence. "And herein," he said, denoting the remaining crates and trunks with a sweeping gesture, "lies the solution to the problem of explosives."

"What is it?" everyone demanded to know.

The Frenchman once again signalled silence. "My friend the professor is a pioneer in the field of electromagnetism. Later we will organise a demonstration."

Evangelina sat in a box at the Baltimore Opera House, which Monsieur Ardan and the Norwegian professor had hired for their demonstration. A row of thick wooden planks and metal sheets hung suspended from the ceiling above the central aisle, the seats below them cordoned off. On the stage, Michel Ardan and the professor stood either side of a tiny cannon connected to an array of Leyden jars. Professor Halstein spoke in French; Ardan translated his words into English.

Ardan said something about coils of wire and electromagnetic forces of attraction and repulsion — none of which she understood — then held up a piece of metal so small she could barely see it. "Please keep in mind, the apparatus we are using today is merely a miniature model expressly designed for this indoor demonstration, to fire a projectile barely one pound in weight. The full-sized version of the professor's electromagnetic cannon will not be powered by Leyden jars, but by a steam-driven dynamo the size of this room, and will be capable of firing missiles weighing up to two tonnes, with almost no sound, and no recoil." He then went on to talk about the row of targets hanging from the ceiling. There were thirty of them, fifteen metal and fifteen wood, none less than five inches thick.

Ardan handed the piece of metal back to the professor. The professor popped it down the barrel, then threw a switch. Something inside the cannon began to glow bright red; the only sound was a low, deep hum. The professor threw the switch a second time. There was a sudden sound of metal hitting wood, then metal, then wood, then metal, and then everything went silent once more.

The targets were lowered from the ceiling. Every single one had a big round hole through the middle.

"But where is the projectile?" someone asked. A search was instigated, which continued until one of the men noticed a hole in the wall at the back of the upper balcony. Everyone hurried upstairs and into the lobby beyond the balcony, where they found a hole punched through to the outside of the building. One of the men looked through and reported seeing a broken window in the top floor of a building across the street.

"Tell the professor we need to get started immediately," Mr. Barbicane instructed Ardan.

Chapter Eight
Two years later: a new beginning

It was after eleven P.M., but thanks to the array of dynamos thrumming in the night, the crowded streets of Moon City were awash with light. Even the tall cannon looming over the rooftops at the edge of town had been bathed in light for the occasion, and it was to the cannon that everyone was heading. It was the 31st of December, 1899, and the first Earth-to-Moon garbage missile was scheduled for deployment at the stroke of midnight.

Evangelina and J.T. joined the throng making their way past rows of vast warehouses filled with vats of percolating garbage, to the specially erected stands where the Mastons were to have seats of honour alongside Fiona Wicke, Monsieur Ardan, and the head of the worm department.

By eleven-thirty, everyone was seated and glasses of champagne had been distributed to those in the seats of honour.

Monsieur Ardan dabbed at his eyes as the cannon was levered into position. "Oh, to be a piece of rubbish inside that capsule!"

At one minute to midnight, Professor Halstein placed a hand on the switch, and at midnight exactly, he pulled the switch down.

There was a brief dimming of the lights combined with a whooshing sound, and then someone shouted, "There it goes, the first of thousands!"

Mr. Barbicane raised his glass of champagne. "To the moon, and a new century."

"To the moon, and a new beginning," Fiona said, clinking her glass against his.

Monsieur Ardan and the head of the worm department drank a toast to "the lovely Selene, soon to turn green," then joined in a chorus of "Auld Lang Syne." Evangelina turned to face her husband. "Just think about it, J.T., a hundred years from now, people will be living on the moon."

J.T. Maston turned his face up to the blackness into which the projectile had vanished, his mind already racing into the future. "When we get home," he said, "I really must dig out that ornamental pond."

Seventy-Two Letters

TED CHIANG

With its strange factories, nod to Kabbalistic magic, and alternative biological science, Ted Chiang's "Seventy-Two Letters" takes the idea of the
Golem to new steampunk heights. His extrapolations are not only brilliant
– they lead to a stunning and emotional climax. While some steampunk
skates over the surface of the implications of its invention, Chiang's story
delves into the ethics and politics of the moral dilemma with an unusual
grace.

When he was a child, Robert's favorite toy was a simple one, a clay doll
that could do nothing but walk forward. While his parents entertained
their guests in the garden outside, discussing Victoria's ascension to
the throne or the Chartist reforms, Robert would follow the doll as it
marched down the corridors of the family home, turning it around
corners or back where it came from. The doll didn't obey commands
or exhibit any sense at all; if it met a wall, the diminutive clay figure
would keep marching until it gradually mashed its arms and legs into
misshapen flippers. Sometimes Robert would let it do that, strictly for
his own amusement. Once the doll's limbs were thoroughly distorted,
he'd pick the toy up and pull the name out, stopping its motion in mid-
stride. Then he'd knead the body back into a smooth lump, flatten it
out into a plank, and cut out a different figure: a body with one leg
crooked, or longer than the other. He would stick the name back into
it, and the doll would promptly topple over and push itself around in
a little circle.

It wasn't the sculpting that Robert enjoyed; it was mapping out the
limits of the name. He liked to see how much variation he could impart

to the body before the name could no longer animate it. To save time with the sculpting, he rarely added decorative details; he refined the bodies only as was needed to test the name.

Another of his dolls walked on four legs. The body was a nice one, a finely detailed porcelain horse, but Robert was more interested in experimenting with its name. This name obeyed commands to start and stop and knew enough to avoid obstacles, and Robert tried inserting it into bodies of his own making. But this name had more exacting body requirements, and he was never able to form a clay body it could animate. He formed the legs separately and then attached them to the body, but he wasn't able to blend the seams smooth enough; the name didn't recognize the body as a single continuous piece.

He scrutinized the names themselves, looking for some simple substitutions that might distinguish two-leggedness from four-leggedness, or make the body obey simple commands. But the names looked entirely different; on each scrap of parchment were inscribed seventy-two tiny Hebrew letters, arranged in twelve rows of six, and so far as he could tell, the order of the letters was utterly random.

Robert Stratton and his fourth form classmates sat quietly as Master Trevelyan paced between the rows of desks.

"Langdale, what is the doctrine of names?"

"All things are reflections of God, and, um, all — "

"Spare us your bumbling. Thorburn, can *you* tell us the doctrine of names?"

"As all things are reflections of God, so are all names reflections of the divine name."

"And what is an object's true name?"

"That name which reflects the divine name in the same manner as the object reflects God."

"And what is the action of a true name?"

"To endow its object with a reflection of divine power."

"Correct. Halliwell, what is the doctrine of signatures?"

The natural philosophy lesson continued until noon, but because it was a Saturday, there was no instruction for the rest of the day. Master Trevelyan dismissed the class, and the boys of Cheltenham school dispersed.

After stopping at the dormitory, Robert met his friend Lionel at the border of school grounds. "So the wait's over? Today's the day?" Robert asked.

"I said it was, didn't I?"

"Let's go, then." The pair set off to walk the mile and a half to Lionel's home.

During his first year at Cheltenham, Robert had known Lionel hardly at all; Lionel was one of the day-boys, and Robert, like all the boarders, regarded them with suspicion. Then, purely by chance, Robert ran into him while on holiday, during a visit to the British Museum. Robert loved the museum: the frail mummies and immense sarcophagi; the stuffed platypus and pickled mermaid; the wall bristling with elephant tusks and moose antlers and unicorn horns. That particular day he was at the display of elemental sprites: he was reading the card explaining the salamander's absence when he suddenly recognized Lionel, standing right next to him, peering at the undine in its jar. Conversation revealed their shared interest in the sciences, and the two became fast friends.

As they walked down the road, they kicked a large pebble back and forth between them. Lionel gave the pebble a kick, and laughed as it skittered between Robert's ankles. "I couldn't wait to get out of there," he said. "I think one more doctrine would have been more than I could bear."

"Why do they even bother calling it natural philosophy?" said Robert. "Just admit it's another theology lesson and be done with it." The two of them had recently purchased *A Boy's Guide to Nomenclature*, which informed them that nomenclators no longer spoke in terms of God or the divine name. Instead, current thinking held that there was a lexical universe as well as a physical one, and bringing an object together with a compatible name caused the latent potentialities of both to be realized. Nor was there a single "true name" for a given object: depending on its precise shape, a body might be compatible with several names, known as its "euonyms," and conversely a simple name might tolerate significant variations in body shape, as his childhood marching doll had demonstrated.

When they reached Lionel's home, they promised the cook they would be in for dinner shortly and headed to the garden out back. Lionel had converted a tool shed in his family's garden into a laboratory, which he used to conduct experiments. Normally Robert came by on a regular basis, but recently Lionel had been working on an exper-iment that he was keeping secret. Only now was he ready to show Robert his results. Lionel had Robert wait outside while he entered first, and then let him enter.

A long shelf ran along every wall of the shed, crowded with racks of vials, stoppered bottles of green glass, and assorted rocks and mineral specimens. A table decorated with stains and scorch marks dominated the cramped space, and it supported the apparatus for Lionel's latest experiment: a cucurbit clamped in a stand so that its bottom rested in a basin full of water, which in turn sat on a tripod above a lit oil lamp. A mercury thermometer was also fixed in the basin.

"Take a look," said Lionel.

Robert leaned over to inspect the cucurbit's contents. At first it appeared to be nothing more than foam, a dollop of suds that might have dripped off a pint of stout. But as he looked closer, he realized that what he thought were bubbles were actually the interstices of a glistening latticework. The froth consisted of *homunculi:* tiny seminal foetuses. Their bodies were transparent individually, but collectively their bulbous heads and strand-like limbs adhered to form a pale, dense foam.

"So you wanked off into a jar and kept the spunk warm?" he asked, and Lionel shoved him. Robert laughed and raised his hands in a pla-cating gesture. "No, honestly, it's a wonder. How'd you do it?"

Mollified, Lionel said, "It's a real balancing act. You have to keep the temperature just right, of course, but if you want them to grow, you also have to keep just the right mix of nutrients. Too thin a mix, and they starve. Too rich, and they get over lively and start fighting with each other."

"You're having me on."

"It's the truth; look it up if you don't believe me. Battles amongst sperm are what cause monstrosities to be born. If an injured foetus is the one that makes it to the egg, the baby that's born is deformed."

"I thought that was because of a fright the mother had when she was carrying." Robert could just make out the minuscule squirmings of the individual foetuses. He realized that the froth was ever so slowly roiling as a result of their collective motions.

"That's only for some kinds, like ones that are all hairy or covered in blotches. Babies that don't have arms or legs, or have misshapen ones, they're the ones that got caught in a fight back when they were sperm. That's why you can't provide too rich a broth, especially if they haven't any place to go: they get in a frenzy. You can lose all of them pretty quick that way."

"How long can you keep them growing?"

"Probably not much longer," said Lionel. "It's hard to keep them alive if they haven't reached an egg. I read about one in France that was grown till it was the size of a fist, and they had the best equipment available. I just wanted to see if I could do it at all."

Robert stared at the foam, remembering the doctrine of preformation that Master Trevelyan had drilled into them: all living things had been created at the same time, long ago, and births today were merely enlargements of the previously imperceptible. Although they appeared newly created, these *homunculi* were countless years old; for all of human history they had lain nested within generations of their ancestors, waiting for their turn to be born.

In fact, it wasn't just them who had waited; he himself must have done the same thing prior to his birth. If his father were to do this experiment, the tiny figures Robert saw would be his unborn brothers and sisters. He knew they were insensible until reaching an egg, but he wondered what thoughts they'd have if they weren't. He imagined the sensation of his body, every bone and organ soft and clear as gelatin, sticking to those of myriad identical siblings. What would it be like, looking through transparent eyelids, realizing the mountain in the distance was actually a person, recognizing it as his brother? What if he knew he'd become as massive and solid as that colossus, if only he could reach an egg? It was no wonder they fought.

Robert Stratton went on to read nomenclature at Cambridge's Trinity College. There he studied kabbalistic texts written centuries before, when nomenclators were still called *ba'alei shem* and automata were called *golem*, texts that laid the foundation for the science of names: the *Sefer Yezirah*, Eleazar of Worms' *Sodei Razayya*, Abulafia's *Hayyei ha-Olam ha-Ba*. Then he studied the alchemical treatises that placed the techniques of alphabetic manipulation in a broader philosophical and mathematical context: Llull's *Ars Magna*, Agrippa's *De Occulta Philosophia*, Dee's *Monas Hieroglyphica*.

He learned that every name was a combination of several epithets, each designating a specific trait or capability. Epithets were generated by compiling all the words that described the desired trait: cognates and etymons, from languages both living and extinct. By selectively substituting and permuting letters, one could distill from those words their common essence, which was the epithet for that trait. In certain instances, epithets could be used as the bases for triangulation, allowing one to derive epithets for traits undescribed in any language. The entire process relied on intuition as much as formulae; the ability to choose the best letter permutations was an unteachable skill.

He studied the modern techniques of nominal integration and factorization, the former being the means by which a set of epithets — pithy and evocative — were commingled into the seemingly random string of letters that made up a name, the latter by which a name was decomposed into its constituent epithets. Not every method of integration had a matching factorization technique: a powerful name might be refactored to yield a set of epithets different from those used to generate it, and those epithets were often useful for that reason. Some names resisted refactorization, and nomenclators strove to develop new techniques to penetrate their secrets.

Nomenclature was undergoing something of a revolution during this time. There had long been two classes of names: those for animating a body, and those functioning as amulets. Health amulets were worn as protection from injury or illness, while others rendered a house resistant to fire or a ship less likely to founder at sea. Of late, however, the distinction between these categories of names was becoming blurred, with exciting results.

The nascent science of thermodynamics, which established the interconvertibility of heat and work, had recently explained how automata gained their motive power by absorbing heat from their surroundings. Using this improved understanding of heat, a *Namenmeister* in Berlin had developed a new class of amulet that caused a body to absorb heat from one location and release it in another. Refrigeration employing such amulets was simpler and more efficient than that based on the evaporation of a volatile fluid, and had immense commercial application. Amulets were likewise facilitating the improvement of automata: an Edinburgh nomenclator's research into the amulets that prevented objects from becoming lost had led him to patent a household automaton able to return objects to their proper places.

Upon graduation, Stratton took up residence in London and secured a position as a nomenclator at Coade Manufactory, one of the leading makers of automata in England.

Stratton's most recent automaton, cast from plaster of Paris, followed a few paces behind him as he entered the factory building. It was an immense brick structure with skylights for its roof; half of the building was devoted to casting metal, the other half to ceramics. In either section, a meandering path connected the various rooms, each one housing the next step in transforming raw materials into finished automata. Stratton and his automaton entered the ceramics portion.

They walked past a row of low vats in which the clay was mixed. Different vats contained different grades of clay, ranging from common red clay to fine white kaolin, resembling enormous mugs abrim with liquid chocolate or heavy cream; only the strong mineral smell broke the illusion. The paddles stirring the clay were connected by gears to a drive shaft, mounted just beneath the skylights, that ran the length of the room. At the end of the room stood an automatous engine: a cast-iron giant that cranked the drive wheel tirelessly. Walking past, Stratton could detect a faint coolness in the air as the engine drew heat from its surroundings.

The next room held the molds for casting. Chalky white shells bearing the inverted contours of various automata were stacked along the walls. In the central portion of the room, apron-clad journeymen sculptors worked singly and in pairs, tending the cocoons from which automata were hatched.

The sculptor nearest him was assembling the mold for a putter, a broad-headed quadruped employed in the mines for pushing trolleys of ore. The young man looked up from his work. "Were you looking for someone, sir?" he asked.

"I'm to meet Master Willoughby here," replied Stratton.

"Pardon, I didn't realize. I'm sure he'll be here shortly." The journeyman returned to his task. Harold Willoughby was a Master Sculptor First-Degree; Stratton was consulting him on the design of a reusable mold for casting his automaton. While he waited, Stratton strolled idly amongst the molds. His automaton stood motionless, ready for its next command.

Willoughby entered from the door to the metalworks, his face flushed from the heat of the foundry. "My apologies for being late, Mr. Stratton," he said. "We've been working toward a large bronze for some weeks now, and today was the pour. You don't want to leave the lads alone at a time like that."

"I understand completely," replied Stratton.

Wasting no time, Willoughby strode over to the new automaton. "Is this what you've had Moore doing all these months?" Moore was the journeyman assisting Stratton on his project.

Stratton nodded. "The boy does good work." Following Stratton's requests, Moore had fashioned countless bodies, all variations on a single basic theme, by applying modeling clay to an armature, and then used them to create plaster casts on which Stratton could test his names.

Willoughby inspected the body. "Some nice detail; looks straight-forward enough — hold on now." He pointed to the automaton's hands: rather than the traditional paddle or mitten design, with fingers suggested by grooves in the surface, these were fully formed, each one having a thumb and four distinct and separate fingers. "You don't mean to tell me those are functional?"

"That's correct."

Willoughby's skepticism was plain. "Show me."

Stratton addressed the automaton. "Flex your fingers." The automaton extended both hands, flexed and straightened each pair of fingers in turn, and then returned its arms to its sides.

"I congratulate you, Mr. Stratton," said the sculptor. He squatted to examine the automaton's fingers more closely. "The fingers need to be bent at each joint for the name to take?"

"That's right. Can you design a piece mold for such a form?"

Willoughby clicked his tongue several times. "That'll be a tricky bit of business," he said. "We might have to use a waste mold for each casting. Even with a piece mold, these'd be very expensive for ceramic."

"I think they will be worth the expense. Permit me to demonstrate." Stratton addressed to the automaton. "Cast a body; use that mold over there."

The automaton trudged over to a nearby wall and picked up the pieces of the mold Stratton had indicated: it was the mold for a small porcelain messenger. Several journeymen stopped what they were doing to watch the automaton carry the pieces over to a work area.

There it fitted the various sections together and bound them tightly with twine. The sculptors' wonderment was apparent as they watched the automaton's fingers work, looping and threading the loose ends of the twine into a knot. Then the automaton stood the assembled mold upright and headed off to get a pitcher of clay slip.

"That's enough," said Willoughby. The automaton stopped its work and resumed its original standing posture. Examining the mold, Willoughby asked, "Did you train it yourself?"

"I did. I hope to have Moore train it in metal casting."

"Do you have names that can learn other tasks?"

"Not as yet. However, there's every reason to believe that an entire class of similar names exists, one for every sort of skill needing manual dexterity."

"Indeed?" Willoughby noticed the other sculptors watching, and called out, "If you've nothing to do, there's plenty I can assign to you." The journeymen promptly resumed their work, and Willoughby turned back to Stratton. "Let us go to your office to speak about this further."

"Very well." Stratton had the automaton follow the two of them back to the frontmost of the complex of connected buildings that was Coade Manufactory. They first entered Stratton's studio, which was situated behind his office proper. Once inside, Stratton addressed the sculptor. "Do you have an objection to my automaton?"

Willoughby looked over a pair of clay hands mounted on a work-table. On the wall behind the table were pinned a series of schematic drawings showing hands in a variety of positions. "You've done an admirable job of emulating the human hand. I am concerned, however, that the first skill in which you trained your new automaton is sculpture."

"If you're worried that I am trying to replace sculptors, you needn't be. That is absolutely not my goal."

"I'm relieved to hear it," said Willoughby. "Why did you choose sculpture, then?"

"It is the first step of a rather indirect path. My ultimate goal is to allow automatous engines to be manufactured inexpensively enough so that most families could purchase one."

Willoughby's confusion was apparent. "How, pray tell, would a family make use of an engine?"

"To drive a powered loom, for example."

"What are you going on about?"

"Have you ever seen children who are employed at a textile mill? They are worked to exhaustion; their lungs are clogged with cotton dust; they are so sickly that you can hardly conceive of their reaching adulthood. Cheap cloth is bought at the price of our workers' health; weavers were far better off when textile production was a cottage industry."

"Powered looms were what took weavers out of cottages. How could they put them back in?"

Stratton had not spoken of this before, and welcomed the opportunity to explain. "The cost of automatous engines has always been high, and so we have mills in which scores of looms are driven by an immense coal-heated Goliath. But an automaton like mine could cast engines very cheaply. If a small automatous engine, suitable for driving a few machines, becomes affordable to a weaver and his family, then they can produce cloth from their home as they did once before. People could earn a decent income without being subjected to the conditions of the factory."

"You forget the cost of the loom itself," said Willoughby gently, as if humoring him. "Powered looms are considerably more expensive than the hand looms of old."

"My automata could also assist in the production of cast-iron parts, which would reduce the price of powered looms and other machines. This is no panacea, I know, but I am nonetheless convinced that inexpensive engines offer the chance of a better life for the individual craftsman."

"Your desire for reform does you credit. Let me suggest, however, that there are simpler cures for the social ills you cite: a reduction in working hours, or the improvement of conditions. You do not need to disrupt our entire system of manufacturing."

"I think what I propose is more accurately described as a restoration than a disruption."

Now Willoughby became exasperated. "This talk of returning to a family economy is all well and good, but what would happen to sculptors? Your intentions notwithstanding, these automata of yours would put sculptors out of work. These are men who have undergone years of apprenticeship and training. How would they feed their families?"

Stratton was unprepared for the sharpness in his tone. "You overestimate my skills as a nomenclator," he said, trying to make light. The sculptor remained dour. He continued. "The learning capabilities of these automata are extremely limited. They can manipulate molds, but they could never design them; the real craft of sculpture can be performed only by sculptors. Before our meeting, you had just finished directing several journeymen in the pouring of a large bronze; automata could never work together in such a coordinated fashion. They will perform only rote tasks."

"What kind of sculptors would we produce if they spend their apprenticeship watching automata do their jobs for them? I will not have a venerable profession reduced to a performance by marionettes."

"That is not what would happen," said Stratton, becoming exasperated himself now. "But examine what you yourself are saying: the status that you wish your profession to retain is precisely that which weavers have been made to forfeit. I believe these automata can help restore dignity to other professions, and without great cost to yours."

Willoughby seemed not to hear him. "The very notion that automata would make automata! Not only is the suggestion insulting, it seems ripe for calamity. What of that ballad, the one where the broomsticks carry water buckets and run amuck?"

"You mean *Der Zauberlehrling*?" said Stratton. "The comparison is absurd. These automata are so far removed from being in a position to reproduce themselves without human participation that I scarcely know where to begin listing the objections. A dancing bear would sooner perform in the London Ballet."

"If you'd care to develop an automaton that can dance the ballet, I would fully support such an enterprise. However, you cannot continue with these dexterous automata."

"Pardon me, sir, but I am not bound by your decisions."

"You'll find it difficult to work without sculptors' cooperation. I shall recall Moore and forbid all the other journeymen from assisting you in any way with this project."

Stratton was momentarily taken aback. "Your reaction is completely unwarranted."

"I think it entirely appropriate."

"In that case, I will work with sculptors at another manufactory."

Willoughby frowned. "I will speak with the head of the Brotherhood of Sculptors, and recommend that he forbid all of our members from casting your automata."

Stratton could feel his blood rising. "I will not be bullied," he said. "Do what you will, but you cannot prevent me from pursuing this."

"I think our discussion is at an end." Willoughby strode to the door. "Good day to you, Mr. Stratton."

"Good day to you," replied Stratton heatedly.

It was the following day, and Stratton was taking his midday stroll through the district of Lambeth, where Coade Manufactory was located. After a few blocks he stopped at a local market; sometimes among the baskets of writhing eels and blankets spread with cheap watches were automatous dolls, and Stratton retained his boyhood fondness for seeing the latest designs. Today he noticed a new pair of boxing dolls, painted to look like an explorer and a savage. As he looked them over, he could hear nostrum peddlers competing for the attention of a passerby with a runny nose.

"I see your health amulet failed you, sir," said one man whose table was arrayed with small square tins. "Your remedy lies in the curative powers of magnetism, concentrated in Doctor Sedgewick's Polarising Tablets!"

"Nonsense!" retorted an old woman. "What you need is tincture of mandrake, tried and true!" She held out a vial of clear liquid. "The dog wasn't cold yet when this extract was prepared! There's nothing more potent."

Seeing no other new dolls, Stratton left the market and walked on, his thoughts returning to what Willoughby had said yesterday. Without the cooperation of the sculptors' trade-union, he'd have to resort to hiring independent sculptors. He hadn't worked with such individuals before, and some investigation would be required: ostensibly they cast bodies only for use with public-domain names, but for certain individuals these activities disguised patent infringement and piracy, and any association with them could permanently blacken his reputation.

"Mr. Stratton."

Stratton looked up. A small, wiry man, plainly dressed, stood before him. "Yes; do I know you, sir?"

"No, sir. My name is Davies. I'm in the employ of Lord Fieldhurst." He handed Stratton a card bearing the Fieldhurst crest.

Edward Maitland, third earl of Fieldhurst and a noted zoologist and comparative anatomist, was President of the Royal Society. Stratton had heard him speak during sessions of the Royal Society, but they had never been introduced. "What can I do for you?"

"Lord Fieldhurst would like to speak with you, at your earliest convenience, regarding your recent work."

Stratton wondered how the earl had learned of his work. "Why did you not call on me at my office?"

"Lord Fieldhurst prefers privacy in this matter." Stratton raised his eyebrows, but Davies didn't explain further. "Are you available this evening?"

It was an unusual invitation, but an honor nonetheless. "Certainly. Please inform Lord Fieldhurst that I would be delighted."

"A carriage will be outside your building at eight tonight." Davies touched his hat and was off.

At the promised hour, Davies arrived with the carriage. It was a luxurious vehicle, with an interior of lacquered mahogany and polished brass and brushed velvet. The tractor that drew it was an expensive one as well, a steed cast of bronze and needing no driver for familiar destinations.

Davies politely declined to answer any questions while they rode. He was obviously not a man-servant, nor a secretary, but Stratton could not decide what sort of employee he was. The carriage carried them out of London into the countryside, until they reached Darrington Hall, one of the residences owned by the Fieldhurst lineage.

Once inside the home, Davies led Stratton through the foyer and then ushered him into an elegantly appointed study; he closed the doors without entering himself.

Seated at the desk within the study was a barrel-chested man wearing a silk coat and cravat; his broad, deeply creased cheeks were framed by woolly gray muttonchops. Stratton recognized him at once.

"Lord Fieldhurst, it is an honor."

"A pleasure to meet you, Mr. Stratton. You've been doing some excellent work recently."

"You are most kind. I did not realize that my work had become known."

"I make an effort to keep track of such things. Please, tell me what motivated you to develop such automata?"

Stratton explained his plans for manufacturing affordable engines. Fieldhurst listened with interest, occasionally offering cogent suggestions.

"It is an admirable goal," he said, nodding his approval. "I'm pleased to find that you have such philanthropic motives, because I would ask your assistance in a project I'm directing."

"It would be my privilege to help in any way I could."

"Thank you." Fieldhurst's expression became solemn. "This is a matter of grave import. Before I speak further, I must first have your word that you will retain everything I reveal to you in the utmost confidence."

Stratton met the earl's gaze directly. "Upon my honor as a gentleman, sir, I shall not divulge anything you relate to me."

"Thank you, Mr. Stratton. Please come this way." Fieldhurst opened a door in the rear wall of the study and they walked down a short hallway. At the end of the hallway was a laboratory; a long, scrupulously clean work-table held a number of stations, each consisting of a microscope and an articulated brass framework of some sort, equipped with three mutually perpendicular knurled wheels for performing fine adjustments. An elderly man was peering into the microscope at the furthest station; he looked up from his work as they entered.

"Mr. Stratton, I believe you know Dr. Ashbourne."

Stratton, caught off guard, was momentarily speechless. Nicholas Ashbourne had been a lecturer at Trinity when Stratton was studying there, but had left years ago to pursue studies of, it was said, an unorthodox nature. Stratton remembered him as one of his most enthusiastic instructors. Age had narrowed his face somewhat, making his high forehead seem even higher, but his eyes were as bright and alert as ever. He walked over with the help of a carved ivory walking stick.

"Stratton, good to see you again."

"And you, sir. I was truly not expecting to see you here."

"This will be an evening full of surprises, my boy. Prepare yourself." He turned to Fieldhurst. "Would you care to begin?"

They followed Fieldhurst to the far end of the laboratory, where he opened another door and led them down a flight of stairs. "Only a small number of individuals — either Fellows of the Royal Society or Members of Parliament, or both — are privy to this matter. Five years ago, I was contacted confidentially by the *Académie des Sciences* in

Paris. They wished for English scientists to confirm certain experimental findings of theirs."

"Indeed?"

"You can imagine their reluctance. However, they felt the matter outweighed national rivalries, and once I understood the situation, I agreed."

The three of them descended to a cellar. Gas brackets along the walls provided illumination, revealing the cellar's considerable size; its interior was punctuated by an array of stone pillars that rose to form groined vaults. The long cellar contained row upon row of stout wooden tables, each one supporting a tank roughly the size of a bathtub. The tanks were made of zinc and fitted with plate-glass windows on all four sides, revealing their contents as a clear, faintly straw-colored fluid.

Stratton looked at the nearest tank. There was a distortion floating in the center of the tank, as if the some of the liquid had congealed into a mass of jelly. It was difficult to distinguish the mass's features from the mottled shadows cast on the bottom of the tank, so he moved to another side of the tank and squatted down low to view the mass directly against a flame of a gas lamp. It was then that the coagulum resolved itself into the ghostly figure of a man, clear as aspic, curled up in foetal position.

"Incredible," Stratton whispered.

"We call it a megafoetus," explained Fieldhurst.

"This was grown from a spermatozoon? This must have required decades."

"It did not, more's the wonder. Several years ago, two Parisian naturalists named Dubuisson and Gille developed a method of inducing hypertrophic growth in a seminal foetus. The rapid infusion of nutrients allows such a foetus to reach this size within a fortnight."

By shifting his head back and forth, he saw slight differences in the way the gas-light was refracted, indicating the boundaries of the megafoetus's internal organs. "Is this creature...alive?"

"Only in an insensate manner, like a spermatozoon. No artificial process can replace gestation; it is the vital principle within the ovum which quickens the foetus, and the maternal influence which transforms it into a person. All we've done is effect a maturation in size and scale." Fieldhurst gestured toward the megafoetus. "The maternal influence also provides a foetus with pigmentation and all distinguishing physical characteristics. Our megafoetuses have no features beyond their sex. Every male bears the generic appearance you see here, and all the females are likewise identical. Within each sex, it is impossible to distinguish one from another by physical examination, no matter how dissimilar the original fathers might have been; only rigorous record-keeping allows us to identify each megafoetus."

Stratton stood up again. "So what was the intention of the experiment if not to develop an artificial womb?"

"To test the notion of the fixity of species." Realizing that Stratton was not a zoologist, the earl explained further. "Were lens-grinders able to construct microscopes of unlimited magnifying power, biologists could examine the future generations nested in the spermatozoa of any species and see whether their appearance remains fixed, or changes to give rise to a new species. In the latter case, they could also determine if the transition occurs gradually or abruptly.

"However, chromatic aberration imposes an upper limit on the magnifying power of any optical instrument. Messieurs Dubuisson and Gille hit upon the idea of artificially increasing the size of the foetuses themselves. Once a foetus reaches its adult size, one can extract a spermatozoon from it and enlarge a foetus from the next generation in the same manner." Fieldhurst stepped over to the next table in the row and indicated the tank it supported. "Repetition of the process lets us examine the unborn generations of any given species."

Stratton looked around the room. The rows of tanks took on a new significance. "So they compressed the intervals between 'births' to gain a preliminary view of our genealogical future."

"Precisely."

"Audacious! And what were the results?"

"They tested many animal species, but never observed any changes in form. However, they obtained a peculiar result when working with the seminal foetuses of humans. After no more than five generations, the male foetuses held no more spermatozoa, and the females held no more ova. The line terminated in a sterile generation."

"I imagine that wasn't entirely unexpected," Stratton said, glancing at the jellied form. "Each repetition must further attenuate some essence in the organisms. It's only logical that at some point the offspring would be so feeble that the process would fail."

"That was Dubuisson and Gille's initial assumption as well," agreed Fieldhurst, "so they sought to improve their technique. However, they could find no difference between megafoetuses of succeeding generations in terms of size or vitality. Nor was there any decline in the number of spermatozoa or ova; the penultimate generation was fully as fertile as the first. The transition to sterility was an abrupt one.

"They found another anomaly as well: while some spermatozoa yielded only four or fewer generations, variation occurred only across samples, never within a single sample. They evaluated samples from father and son donors, and in such instances, the father's spermatozoa produced exactly one more generation than the son's. And from what I understand, some of the donors were aged individuals indeed. While their samples held very few spermatozoa, they nonetheless held one more generation than those from sons in the prime of their lives. The progenitive power of the sperm bore no correlation with the health or vigor of the donor; instead, it correlated with the generation to which the donor belonged."

Fieldhurst paused and looked at Stratton gravely. "It was at this point that the *Académie* contacted me to see if the Royal Society could duplicate their findings. Together we have obtained the same result using samples collected from peoples as varied as the Lapps and the Hottentots. We are in agreement as to the implication of these findings: that the human species has the potential to exist for only a fixed number of generations, and we are within five generations of the final one."

Stratton turned to Ashbourne, half expecting him to confess that it was all an elaborate hoax, but the elder nomenclator looked entirely solemn. Stratton looked at the megafoetus again and frowned, absorbing what he had heard. "If your interpretation is correct, other species must be subject to a similar limitation. Yet from what I know, the extinction of a species has never been observed."

Fieldhurst nodded. "That is true. However, we do have the evidence of the fossil record, which suggests that species remain unchanged for a period of time, and then are abruptly replaced by new forms. The Catastrophists hold that violent upheavals caused species to become extinct. Based on what we've discovered regarding preformation, it now appears that extinctions are merely the result of a species reaching the end of its lifetime. They are natural rather than accidental deaths, in a manner of speaking." He gestured to the doorway from which they had entered. "Shall we return upstairs?"

Following the two other men, Stratton asked, "And what of the origination of new species? If they're not born from existing species, do they arise spontaneously?"

"That is as yet uncertain. Normally only the simplest animals arise by spontaneous generation: maggots and other vermiform creatures, typically under the influence of heat. The events postulated by Catastrophists—floods, volcanic eruptions, cometary impacts—would entail the release of great energies. Perhaps such energies affect matter so profoundly as to cause the spontaneous generation of an entire race of organisms, nested within a few progenitors. If so, cataclysms are not responsible for mass extinctions, but rather generate new species in their wake."

Back in the laboratory, the two elder men seated themselves in the chairs present. Too agitated to follow suit, Stratton remained standing. "If any animal species were created by the same cataclysm as the human species, they should likewise be nearing the end of their life spans. Have you found another species that evinces a final generation?"

Fieldhurst shook his head. "Not as yet. We believe that other species have different dates of extinction, correlated with the biological complexity of the animal; humans are presumably the most complex organism, and perhaps fewer generations of such complex organisms can be nested inside a spermatozoon."

"By the same token," countered Stratton, "perhaps the complexity of the human organism makes it unsuitable for the process of artificially accelerated growth. Perhaps it is the process whose limits have been discovered, not the species."

"An astute observation, Mr. Stratton. Experiments are continuing with species that more closely resemble humans, such as chimpanzees and ourang-outangs. However, the unequivocal answer to this question may require years, and if our current interpretation is correct, we can ill afford the time spent waiting for confirmation. We must ready a course of action immediately."

"But five generations could be over a century—" He caught himself, embarrassed at having overlooked the obvious: not all persons became parents at the same age.

Fieldhurst read his expression. "You realize why not all the sperm samples from donors of the same age produced the same number of generations: some lineages are approaching their end faster than others. For a lineage in which the men consistently father children late in life, five generations might mean over two centuries of fertility, but there are undoubtedly lineages that have reached their end already."

Stratton imagined the consequences. "The loss of fertility will become increasingly apparent to the general populace as time passes. Panic may arise well before the end is reached."

"Precisely, and rioting could extinguish our species as effectively as the exhaustion of generations. That is why time is of the essence."

"What is the solution you propose?"

"I shall defer to Dr. Ashbourne to explain further," said the earl.

Ashbourne rose and instinctively adopted the stance of a lecturing professor. "Do you recall why it was that all attempts to make automata out of wood were abandoned?"

Stratton was caught off guard by the question. "It was believed that the natural grain of wood implies a form in conflict with whatever we try to carve upon it. Currently there are efforts to use rubber as a casting material, but none have met with success."

"Indeed. But if the native form of wood were the only obstacle, shouldn't it be possible to animate an animal's corpse with a name? There the form of the body should be ideal."

"It's a macabre notion; I couldn't guess at such an experiment's likelihood of success. Has it ever been attempted?"

"In fact it has: also unsuccessfully. So these two entirely different avenues of research proved fruitless. Does that mean there is no way to animate organic matter using names? This was the question I left Trinity in order to pursue."

"And what did you discover?"

Ashbourne deflected the question with a wave of his hand. "First let us discuss thermodynamics. Have you kept up with recent developments? Then you know the dissipation of heat reflects an increase in disorder at the thermal level. Conversely, when an automaton condenses heat from its environment to perform work, it increases order. This confirms a long-held belief of mine that lexical order induces thermodynamic order. The lexical order of an amulet reinforces the order a body already possesses, thus providing protection against damage.

The lexical order of an animating name increases the order of a body, thus providing motive power for an automaton.

"The next question was, how would an increase in order be reflected in organic matter? Since names don't animate dead tissue, obviously organic matter doesn't respond at the thermal level; but perhaps it can be ordered at another level. Consider: a steer can be reduced to a vat of gelatinous broth. The broth comprises the same material as the steer, but which embodies a higher amount of order?"

"The steer, obviously," said Stratton, bewildered.

"Obviously. An organism, by virtue of its physical structure, embodies order; the more complex the organism, the greater the amount of order. It was my hypothesis that increasing the order in organic matter would be evidenced by imparting form to it. However, most living matter has already assumed its ideal form. The question is, what has life but not form?"

The elder nomenclator did not wait for a response. "The answer is, an unfertilized ovum. The ovum contains the vital principle that animates the creature it ultimately gives rise to, but it has no form itself. Ordinarily, the ovum incorporates the form of the foetus compressed within the spermatozoon that fertilizes it. The next step was obvious." Here Ashbourne waited, looking at Stratton expectantly.

Stratton was at a loss. Ashbourne seemed disappointed, and continued. "The next step was to artificially induce the growth of an embryo from an ovum, by application of a name."

"But if the ovum is unfertilized," objected Stratton, "there is no pre-existing structure to enlarge."

"Precisely."

"You mean structure would arise out of a homogenous medium? Impossible."

"Nonetheless, it was my goal for several years to confirm this hypothesis. My first experiments consisted of applying a name to unfertilized frog eggs."

"How did you embed the name into a frog's egg?"

"The name is not actually embedded, but rather impressed by means of a specially manufactured needle." Ashbourne opened a cabinet that sat on the work-table between two of the microscope stations. Inside was a wooden rack filled with small instruments arranged in pairs. Each was tipped with a long glass needle; in some pairs they were nearly as thick as those used for knitting, in others as slender as a hypodermic. He withdrew one from the largest pair and handed it to Stratton to examine. The glass needle was not clear, but instead seemed to contain some sort of dappled core.

Ashbourne explained. "While that may appear to be some sort of medical implement, it is in fact a vehicle for a name, just as the more conventional slip of parchment is. Alas, it requires far more effort to make than taking pen to parchment. To create such a needle, one must first arrange fine strands of black glass within a bundle of clear glass strands so that the name is legible when they are viewed end-on. The strands are then fused into a solid rod, and the rod is drawn out into an ever thinner strand. A skilled glass-maker can retain every detail of the name no matter how thin the strand becomes. Eventually one obtains a needle containing the name in its cross section."

"How did you generate the name that you used?"

"We can discuss that at length later. For the purposes of our current discussion, the only relevant information is that I incorporated the sexual epithet. Are you familiar with it?"

"I know of it." It was one of the few epithets that was dimorphic, having male and female variants.

"I needed two versions of the name, obviously, to induce the generation of both males and females." He indicated the paired arrangement of needles in the cabinet.

Stratton saw that the needle could be clamped into the brass framework with its tip approaching the slide beneath the microscope; the knurled wheels presumably were used to bring the needle into contact with an ovum. He returned the instrument. "You said the name is not embedded, but impressed. Do you mean to tell me that touching the frog's egg with this needle is all that's needed? Removing the name doesn't end its influence?"

"Precisely. The name activates a process in the egg that cannot be reversed. Prolonged contact of the name had no different effect."

"And the egg hatched a tadpole?"

"Not with the names initially tried; the only result was that symmetrical involutions appeared in the surface of the egg. But by incorporating different epithets, I was able to induce the egg to adopt different forms, some of which had every appearance of embryonic frogs. Eventually I found a name that caused the egg not only to assume the form of a tadpole, but also to mature and hatch. The tadpole thus hatched grew into a frog indistinguishable from any other member of the species."

"You had found a euonym for that species of frog," said Stratton.

Ashbourne smiled. "As this method of reproduction does not involve sexual congress, I have termed it 'parthenogenesis.'"

Stratton looked at both him and Fieldhurst. "It's clear what your proposed solution is. The logical conclusion of this research is to discover a euonym for the human species. You wish for mankind to perpetuate itself through nomenclature."

"You find the prospect troubling," said Fieldhurst. "That is to be expected: Dr. Ashbourne and myself initially felt the same way, as has everyone who has considered this. No one relishes the prospect of humans being conceived artificially. But can you offer an alternative?" Stratton was silent, and Fieldhurst went on. "All who are aware of both Dr. Ashbourne's and Dubuisson and Gille's work agree: there is no other solution."

Stratton reminded himself to maintain the dispassionate attitude of a scientist. "Precisely how do you envision this name being used?" he asked.

Ashbourne answered. "When a husband is unable to impregnate his wife, they will seek the services of a physician. The physician will collect the woman's menses, separate out the ovum, impress the name upon it, and then reintroduce it into her womb."

"A child born of this method would have no biological father."

"True, but the father's biological contribution is of minimal importance here. The mother will think of her husband as the child's father, so her imagination will impart a combination of her own and her husband's appearance and character to the foetus. That will not change. And I hardly need mention that name impression would not be made available to unmarried women."

"Are you confident this will result in well-formed children?" asked Stratton. "I'm sure you know to what I refer." They all knew of the disastrous attempt in the previous century to create improved children by mesmerizing women during their pregnancies.

Ashbourne nodded. "We are fortunate in that the ovum is very specific in what it will accept. The set of euonyms for any species of organism is very small; if the lexical order of the impressed name does not closely match the structural order of that species, the resulting foetus does not quicken. This does not remove the need for the mother to maintain a tranquil mind during her pregnancy; name impression cannot guard against maternal agitation. But the ovum's selectivity provides us assurance that any foetus induced will be well-formed in every aspect, except the one anticipated."

Stratton was alarmed. "What aspect is that?"

"Can you not guess? The only incapacity of frogs created by name impression was in the males; they were sterile, for their spermatozoa bore no preformed foetuses inside. By comparison, the female frogs created were fertile: their eggs could be fertilized in either the conventional manner, or by repeating the impression with the name."

Stratton's relief was considerable. "So the male variant of the name was imperfect. Presumably there needs to be further differences between the male and female variants than simply the sexual epithet."

"Only if one considers the male variant imperfect," said Ashbourne, "which I do not. Consider: while a fertile male and a fertile female might seem equivalent, they differ radically in the degree of complexity exemplified. A female with viable ova remains a single organism, while a male with viable spermatozoa is actually many organisms: a father and all his potential children. In this light, the two variants of the name are well-matched in their actions: each induces a single organism, but only in the female sex can a single organism be fertile."

"I see what you mean." Stratton realized he would need practice in thinking about nomenclature in the organic domain. "Have you developed euonyms for other species?"

"Just over a score, of various types; our progress has been rapid. We have only just begun work on a name for the human species, and it has proved far more difficult than our previous names."

"How many nomenclators are engaged in this endeavor?"

"Only a handful," Fieldhurst replied. "We have asked a few Royal Society members, and the *Académie* has some of France's leading *designateurs* working on it. You will understand if I do not mention any names at this point, but be assured that we have some of the most distinguished nomenclators in England assisting us."

"Forgive me for asking, but why are you approaching me? I am hardly in that category."

"You have not yet had a long career," said Ashbourne, "but the genus of names you have developed is unique. Automata have always been specialized in form and function, rather like animals: some are good at climbing, others at digging, but none at both. Yet yours can control human hands, which are uniquely versatile instruments: What else can manipulate everything from a wrench to a piano? The hand's dexterity is the physical manifestation of the mind's ingenuity, and these traits are essential to the name we seek."

"We have been discreetly surveying current nomenclatoral research for any names that demonstrate marked dexterity," said Fieldhurst. "When we learned of what you had accomplished, we sought you out immediately."

"In fact," Ashbourne continued, "the very reason your names are worrisome to sculptors is the reason we are interested in them: they endow automata with a more human-like manner than any before. So now we ask, will you join us?"

Stratton considered it. This was perhaps the most important task a nomenclator could undertake, and under ordinary circumstances he would have leapt at the opportunity to participate. But before he could embark upon this enterprise in good conscience, there was another matter he had to resolve.

"You honor me with your invitation, but what of my work with dexterous automata? I still firmly believe that inexpensive engines can improve the lives of the labouring class."

"It is a worthy goal," said Fieldhurst, "and I would not ask you to give it up. Indeed, the first thing we wish you to do is to perfect the epithets for dexterity. But your efforts at social reform would be for naught unless we first ensure the survival of our species."

"Obviously, but I do not want the potential for reform that is offered by dexterous names to be neglected. There may never be a better opportunity for restoring dignity to common workers. What kind of victory would we achieve if the continuation of life meant ignoring this opportunity?"

"Well said," acknowledged the earl. "Let me make a proposal. So that you can best make use of your time, the Royal Society will provide support for your development of dexterous automata as needed: securing investors and so forth. I trust you will divide your time between the two projects wisely. Your work on biological nomenclature must remain confidential, obviously. Is that satisfactory?"

"It is. Very well then, gentlemen: I accept." They shook hands.

Some weeks had passed since Stratton last spoke with Willoughby, beyond a chilly exchange of greetings in passing. In fact, he had little interaction with any of the union sculptors, instead spending his time working on letter permutations in his office, trying to refine his epithets for dexterity.

He entered the manufactory through the front gallery, where customers normally perused the catalogue. Today it was crowded with domestic automata, all the same model char-engine. Stratton saw the clerk ensuring they were properly tagged.

"Good morning, Pierce," he said. "What are all these doing here?"

"An improved name is just out for the 'Regent,'" said the clerk. "Everyone's eager to get the latest."

"You're going to be busy this afternoon." The keys for unlocking the automata's name-slots were themselves stored in a safe that required two of Coade's managers to open. The managers were reluctant to keep the safe open for more than a brief period each afternoon.

"I'm certain I can finish these in time."

"You couldn't bear to tell a pretty house-maid that her char-engine wouldn't be ready by tomorrow."

The clerk smiled. "Can you blame me, sir?"

"No, I cannot," said Stratton, chuckling. He turned toward the business offices behind the gallery, when he found himself confronted by Willoughby.

"Perhaps you ought to prop open the safe," said the sculptor, "so that house-maids might not be inconvenienced. Seeing how destroying our institutions seems to be your intent."

"Good morning, Master Willoughby," said Stratton stiffly. He tried to walk past, but the other man stood in his way.

"I've been informed that Coade will be allowing non-union sculptors on to the premises to assist you."

"Yes, but I assure you, only the most reputable independent sculptors are involved."

"As if such persons exist," said Willoughby scornfully. "You should know that I recommended that our trade-union launch a strike against Coade in protest."

"Surely you're not serious." It had been decades since the last strike launched by the sculptors, and that one had ended in rioting.

"I am. Were the matter put to a vote of the membership, I'm certain it would pass: other sculptors with whom I've discussed your work agree with me about the threat it poses. However, the union leadership will not put it to a vote."

"Ah, so they disagreed with your assessment."

Here Willoughby frowned. "Apparently the Royal Society intervened on your behalf and persuaded the Brotherhood to refrain for the time being. You've found yourself some powerful supporters, Mr. Stratton."

Uncomfortably, Stratton replied, "The Royal Society considers my research worthwhile."

"Perhaps, but do not believe that this matter is ended."

"Your animosity is unwarranted, I tell you," Stratton insisted. "Once you have seen how sculptors can use these automata, you will realize that there is no threat to your profession."

Willoughby merely glowered in response and left.

The next time he saw Lord Fieldhurst, Stratton asked him about the Royal Society's involvement. They were in Fieldhurst's study, and the earl was pouring himself a whiskey.

"Ah yes," he said. "While the Brotherhood of Sculptors as a whole is quite formidable, it is composed of individuals who individually are more amenable to persuasion."

"What manner of persuasion?"

"The Royal Society is aware that members of the trade-union's leadership were party to an as-yet unresolved case of name piracy to the Continent. To avoid any scandal, they've agreed to postpone any decision about strikes until after you've given a demonstration of your system of manufacturing."

"I'm grateful for your assistance, Lord Fieldhurst," said Stratton, astonished. "I must admit, I had no idea that the Royal Society employed such tactics."

"Obviously, these are not proper topics for discussion at the general sessions." Lord Fieldhurst smiled in an avuncular manner. "The advancement of science is not always a straightforward affair, Mr. Stratton, and the Royal Society is sometimes required to use both official and unofficial channels."

"I'm beginning to appreciate that."

"Similarly, although the Brotherhood of Sculptors won't initiate a formal strike, they might employ more indirect tactics; for example, the anonymous distribution of pamphlets that arouse public opposition to your automata." He sipped at his whiskey. "Hmm. Perhaps I should have someone keep a watchful eye on Master Willoughby."

Stratton was given accommodations in the guest wing of Darrington Hall, as were the other nomenclators working under Lord Fieldhurst's direction. They were indeed some of the leading members of the profession, including Holcombe, Milburn, and Parker; Stratton felt honored to be working with them, although he could contribute little while he was still learning Ashbourne's techniques for biological nomenclature.

Names for the organic domain employed many of the same epithets as names for automata, but Ashbourne had developed an entirely different system of integration and factorization, which entailed many novel methods of permutation. For Stratton it was almost like returning to university and learning nomenclature all over again. However, it was apparent how these techniques allowed names for species to be developed rapidly; by exploiting similarities suggested by the Linnaean system of classification, one could work from one species to another.

Stratton also learned more about the sexual epithet, traditionally used to confer either male or female qualities to an automaton. He knew of only one such epithet, and was surprised to learn it was the simplest of many extant versions. The topic went undiscussed by nomenclatoral societies, but this epithet was one of the most fully researched in existence; in fact its earliest use was claimed to have occurred in biblical times, when Joseph's brothers created a female *golem* they could share sexually without violating the prohibition against such behavior with a woman. Development of the epithet had continued for centuries in secrecy, primarily in Constantinople, and now the current versions of automatous courtesans were offered by specialized brothels right here in London. Carved from soapstone and polished to a high gloss, heated to blood temperature and sprinkled with scented oils, the automata commanded prices exceeded only by those for incubi and succubi.

It was from such ignoble soil that their research grew. The names animating the courtesans incorporated powerful epithets for human sexuality in its male and female forms. By factoring out the carnality common to both versions, the nomenclators had isolated epithets for generic human masculinity and femininity, ones far more refined than those used when generating animals. Such epithets were the nuclei around which they formed, by accretion, the names they sought.

Gradually Stratton absorbed sufficient information to begin participating in the tests of prospective human names. He worked in collaboration with the other nomenclators in the group, and between them they divided up the vast tree of nominal possibilities, assigning branches for investigation, pruning away those that proved unfruitful, cultivating those that seemed most productive.

The nomenclators paid women — typically young house-maids in good health — for their menses as a source of human ova, which they then impressed with their experimental names and scrutinized under microscopes, looking for forms that resembled human foetuses. Stratton inquired about the possibility of harvesting ova from female megafoetuses, but Ashbourne reminded him that ova were viable only when taken from a living woman. It was a basic dictum of biology: females were the source of the vital principle that gave the offspring life, while males provided the basic form. Because of this division, neither sex could reproduce by itself.

Of course, that restriction had been lifted by Ashbourne's discovery: the male's participation was no longer necessary since form could be induced lexically. Once a name was found that could generate human foetuses, women could reproduce purely by themselves. Stratton realized that such a discovery might be welcomed by women exhibiting sexual inversion, feeling love for persons of the same rather than the opposite sex. If the name were to become available to such women, they might establish a commune of some sort that reproduced via parthenogenesis. Would such a society flourish by magnifying the finer sensibilities of the gentle sex, or would it collapse under the unrestrained pathology of its membership? It was impossible to guess.

Before Stratton's enlistment, the nomenclators had developed names capable of generating vaguely homuncular forms in an ovum. Using Dubuisson and Gille's methods, they enlarged the forms to a size that allowed detailed examination; the forms resembled automata more than humans, their limbs ending in paddles of fused digits. By incorporating his epithets for dexterity, Stratton was able to separate the digits and refine the overall appearance of the forms. All the while, Ashbourne emphasized the need for an unconventional approach.

"Consider the thermodynamics of what most automata do," said Ashbourne during one of their frequent discussions. "The mining engines dig ore, the reaping engines harvest wheat, the wood-cutting engines fell timber; yet none of these tasks, no matter how useful we find them to be, can be said to create order. While all their names create order at the thermal level, by converting heat into motion, in the vast majority the resulting work is applied at the visible level to create disorder."

"This is an interesting perspective," said Stratton thoughtfully. "Many long-standing deficits in the capabilities of automata become intelligible in this light: the fact that automata are unable to stack crates more neatly than they find them; their inability to sort pieces of crushed ore based on their composition. You believe that the known classes of industrial names are not powerful enough in thermodynamic terms."

"Precisely!" Ashbourne displayed the excitement of a tutor finding an unexpectedly apt pupil. "This is another feature that distinguishes your class of dexterous names. By enabling an automaton to perform skilled labour, your names not only create order at the thermal level, they use it to create order at the visible level as well."

"I see a commonality with Milburn's discoveries," said Stratton. Milburn had developed the household automata able to return objects to their proper places. "His work likewise involves the creation of order at the visible level."

"Indeed it does, and this commonality suggests a hypothesis." Ashbourne leaned forward. "Suppose we were able to factor out an epithet common to the names developed by you and Milburn: an epithet expressing the creation of two levels of order. Further suppose that we discover a euonym for the human species, and were able to incorporate this epithet into the name. What do you imagine would be generated by impressing the name? And if you say 'twins' I shall clout you on the head."

Stratton laughed. "I dare say I understand you better than that. You are suggesting that if an epithet is capable of inducing two levels of thermodynamic order in the inorganic domain, it might create two generations in the organic domain. Such a name might create males whose spermatozoa would contain preformed foetuses. Those males would be fertile, although any sons they produced would again be sterile."

His instructor clapped his hands together. "Precisely: order that begets order! An interesting speculation, wouldn't you agree? It would halve the number of medical interventions required for our race to sustain itself."

"And what about inducing the formation of more than two generations of foetuses? What kind of capabilities would an automaton have to possess, for its name to contain such an epithet?"

"The science of thermodynamics has not progressed enough to answer that question, I'm afraid. What would constitute a still higher level of order in the inorganic domain? Automata working cooperatively, perhaps? We do not yet know, but perhaps in time we will."

Stratton gave voice to a question that had posed itself to him some time ago. "Dr. Ashbourne, when I was initiated into our group, Lord Fieldhurst spoke of the possibility that species are born in the wake of catastrophic events. Is it possible that entire species were created by use of nomenclature?"

"Ah, now we tread in the realm of theology. A new species requires progenitors containing vast numbers of descendants nested within their reproductive organs; such forms embody the highest degree of order imaginable. Can a purely physical process create such vast amounts of order? No naturalist has suggested a mechanism by which this could occur. On the other hand, while we do know that a lexical process can create order, the creation of an entire new species would require a name of incalculable power. Such mastery of nomenclature could very well require the capabilities of God; perhaps it is even part of the definition. This is a question, Stratton, to which we may never know the answer, but we cannot allow that to affect our current actions. Whether or not a name was responsible for the creation of our species, I believe a name is the best chance for its continuation."

"Agreed," said Stratton. After a pause, he added, "I must confess, much of the time when I am working, I occupy myself solely with the details of permutation and combination, and lose sight of the sheer magnitude of our endeavor. It is sobering to think of what we will have achieved if we are successful."

"I can think of little else," replied Ashbourne.

Seated at his desk in the manufactory, Stratton squinted to read the pamphlet he'd been given on the street. The text was crudely printed, the letters blurred.

"Shall Men be the Masters of NAMES, or shall Names be the masters of MEN? For too long the Capitalists have hoarded Names within their coffers, guarded by Patent and Lock and Key, amassing fortunes by mere possession of LETTERS, while the Common Man must labour for every shilling. They will wring the ALPHABET until they have extracted every last penny from it, and only then discard it for us to use. How long will We allow this to continue?"

Stratton scanned the entire pamphlet, but found nothing new in it. For the past two months he'd been reading them, and encountered only the usual anarchist rants; there was as yet no evidence for Lord Fieldhurst's theory that the sculptors would use them to target Stratton's work. His public demonstration of the dexterous automata was scheduled for next week, and by now Willoughby had largely missed his opportunity to generate public opposition. In fact, it occurred to Stratton that he might distribute pamphlets himself to generate public support. He could explain his goal of bringing the advantages of automata to everyone, and his intention to keep close control over his names' patents, granting licenses only to manufacturers who would use them conscientiously. He could even have a slogan: "Autonomy through Automata," perhaps?

There was a knock at his office door. Stratton tossed the pamphlet into his wastebasket. "Yes?"

A man entered, somberly dressed, and with a long beard. "Mr. Stratton?" he asked. "Please allow me to introduce myself: my name is Benjamin Roth. I am a kabbalist."

Stratton was momentarily speechless. Typically such mystics were offended by the modern view of nomenclature as a science, considering it a secularization of a sacred ritual. He never expected one to visit the manufactory. "A pleasure to meet you. How may I be of assistance?"

"I've heard that you have achieved a great advance in the permutation of letters."

"Why, thank you. I didn't realize it would be of interest to a person like yourself."

Roth smiled awkwardly. "My interest is not in its practical applications. The goal of kabbalists is to better know God. The best means by which to do that is to study the art by which He creates. We meditate upon different names to enter an ecstatic state of consciousness; the more powerful the name, the more closely we approach the Divine."

"I see." Stratton wondered what the kabbalist's reaction would be if he learned about the creation being attempted in the biological nomenclature project. "Please continue."

"Your epithets for dexterity enable a *golem* to sculpt another, thereby reproducing itself. A name capable of creating a being that is, in turn, capable of creation would bring us closer to God than we have ever been before."

"I'm afraid you're mistaken about my work, although you aren't the first to fall under this misapprehension. The ability to manipulate molds does not render an automaton able to reproduce itself. There would be many other skills required."

The kabbalist nodded. "I am well aware of that. I myself, in the course of my studies, have developed an epithet designating certain other skills necessary."

Stratton leaned forward with sudden interest. After casting a body, the next step would be to animate the body with a name. "Your epithet endows an automaton with the ability to write?" His own automaton could grasp a pencil easily enough, but it couldn't inscribe even the simplest mark. "How is it that your automata possess the dexterity required for scrivening, but not that for manipulating molds?"

Roth shook his head modestly. "My epithet does not endow writing ability, or general manual dexterity. It simply enables a *golem* to write out the name that animates it, and nothing else."

"Ah, I see." So it didn't provide an aptitude for learning a category of skills; it granted a single innate skill. Stratton tried to imagine the nomenclatoral contortions needed to make an automaton instinctively write out a particular sequence of letters. "Very interesting, but I imagine it doesn't have broad application, does it?"

Roth gave a pained smile; Stratton realized he had committed a *faux pas*, and the man was trying to meet it with good humor. "That is one way to view it," admitted Roth, "but we have a different perspective. To us the value of this epithet, like any other, lies not in the usefulness it imparts to a *golem*, but in the ecstatic state it allows us to achieve."

"Of course, of course. And your interest in my epithets for dexterity is the same?"

"Yes. I am hoping that you will share your epithets with us."

Stratton had never heard of a kabbalist making such a request before, and clearly Roth did not relish being the first. He paused to consider. "Must a kabbalist reach a certain rank in order to meditate upon the most powerful ones?"

"Yes, very definitely."

"So you restrict the availability of the names."

"Oh no; my apologies for misunderstanding you. The ecstatic state offered by a name is achievable only after one has mastered the necessary meditative techniques, and it's these techniques that are closely guarded. Without the proper training, attempts to use these techniques could result in madness. But the names themselves, even the most powerful ones, have no ecstatic value to a novice; they can animate clay, nothing more."

"Nothing more," agreed Stratton, thinking how truly different their perspectives were. "In that case, I'm afraid I cannot grant you use of my names."

Roth nodded glumly, as if he'd been expecting that answer. "You desire payment of royalties."

Now it was Stratton who had to overlook the other man's *faux pas*. "Money is not my objective. However, I have specific intentions for my dexterous automata which require that I retain control over the patent. I cannot jeopardize those plans by releasing the names indiscriminately." Granted, he had shared them with the nomenclators working under Lord Fieldhurst, but they were all gentlemen sworn to an even greater secrecy. He was less confident about mystics.

"I can assure you that we would not use your names for anything other than ecstatic practices."

"I apologize; I believe you are sincere, but the risk is too great. The most I can do is remind you that the patent has a limited duration; once it has expired, you'll be free to use the name however you like."

"But that will take years!"

"Surely you appreciate that there are others whose interests must be taken into account."

"What I see is that commercial considerations are posing an obstacle to spiritual awakening. The error was mine in expecting anything different."

"You are hardly being fair," protested Stratton.

"Fair?" Roth made a visible effort to restrain his anger. "You 'nomenclators' steal techniques meant to honor God and use them to aggrandize yourselves. Your entire industry prostitutes the techniques of *yezirah*. You are in no position to speak of fairness."

"Now see here—"

"Thank you for speaking with me." With that, Roth took his leave.

Stratton sighed.

Peering through the eyepiece of the microscope, Stratton turned the manipulator's adjustment wheel until the needle pressed against the side of the ovum. There was a sudden enfolding, like the retraction of a mollusc's foot when prodded, transforming the sphere into a tiny foetus. Stratton withdrew the needle from the slide, unclamped it from the framework, and inserted a new one. Next he transferred the slide into the warmth of the incubator and placed another slide, bearing an untouched human ovum, beneath the microscope. Once again he leaned toward the microscope to repeat the process of impression.

Recently, the nomenclators had developed a name capable of inducing a form indistinguishable from a human foetus. The forms did not quicken, however: they remained immobile and unresponsive to stimuli. The consensus was that the name did not accurately describe the non-physical traits of a human being. Accordingly, Stratton and his colleagues had been diligently compiling descriptions of human uniqueness, trying to distill a set of epithets both expressive enough to denote these qualities, and succinct enough to be integrated with the physical epithets into a seventy-two-lettered name.

Stratton transferred the final slide to the incubator and made the appropriate notations in the logbook. At the moment he had no more names drawn in needle form, and it would be a day before the new foetuses were mature enough to test for quickening. He decided to pass the rest of the evening in the drawing room upstairs.

Upon entering the walnut-paneled room, he found Fieldhurst and Ashbourne seated in its leather chairs, smoking cigars and sipping brandy. "Ah, Stratton," said Ashbourne. "Do join us."

"I believe I will," said Stratton, heading for the liquor cabinet. He poured himself some brandy from a crystal decanter and seated himself with the others.

"Just up from the laboratory, Stratton?" inquired Fieldhurst.

Stratton nodded. "A few minutes ago I made impressions with my most recent set of names. I feel that my latest permutations are leading in the right direction."

"You are not alone in feeling optimistic; Dr. Ashbourne and I were just discussing how much the outlook has improved since this endeavor began. It now appears that we will have a euonym comfortably in advance of the final generation." Fieldhurst puffed on his cigar and leaned back in his chair until his head rested against the antimacassar. "This disaster may ultimately turn out to be a boon."

"A boon? How so?"

"Why, once we have human reproduction under our control, we will have a means of preventing the poor from having such large families as so many of them persist in having right now."

Stratton was startled, but tried not to show it. "I had not considered that," he said carefully.

Ashbourne also seemed mildly surprised. "I wasn't aware that you intended such a policy."

"I considered it premature to mention it earlier," said Fieldhurst. "Counting one's chickens before they're hatched, as they say."

"Of course."

"You must agree that the potential is enormous. By exercising some judgment when choosing who may bear children or not, our government could preserve the nation's racial stock."

"Is our racial stock under some threat?" asked Stratton.

"Perhaps you have not noticed that the lower classes are reproducing at a rate exceeding that of the nobility and gentry. While commoners are not without virtues, they are lacking in refinement and intellect. These forms of mental impoverishment beget the same: a woman born into low circumstances cannot help but gestate a child destined for the same. Consequent to the great fecundity of the lower classes, our nation would eventually drown in coarse dullards."

"So name impressing will be withheld from the lower classes?"

"Not entirely, and certainly not initially: when the truth about declining fertility is known, it would be an invitation to riot if the lower classes were denied access to name impressing. And of course, the lower classes do have their role to play in our society, as long as their numbers are kept in check. I envision that the policy will go in effect only after some years have passed, by which time people will have grown accustomed to name impression as the method of fertilization. At that point, perhaps in conjunction with the census process, we can impose limits on the number of children a given couple would be permitted to have. The government would regulate the growth and composition of the population thereafter."

"Is this the most appropriate use of such a name?" asked Ashbourne. "Our goal was the survival of the species, not the implementation of partisan politics."

"On the contrary, this is purely scientific. Just as it's our duty to ensure the species survives, it's also our duty to guarantee its health by keeping a proper balance in its population. Politics doesn't enter into it; were the situation reversed and there existed a paucity of labourers, the opposite policy would be called for."

Stratton ventured a suggestion. "I wonder if improvement in conditions for the poor might eventually cause them to gestate more refined children?"

"You are thinking about changes brought about by your cheap engines, aren't you?" asked Fieldhurst with a smile, and Stratton nodded. "Your intended reforms and mine may reinforce each other. Moderating the numbers of the lower classes should make it easier for them to raise their living conditions. However, do not expect that a mere increase in economic comfort will improve the mentality of the lower classes."

"But why not?"

"You forget the self-perpetuating nature of culture," said Fieldhurst. "We have seen that all megafoetuses are identical, yet no one can deny the differences between the populaces of nations, in both physical appearance and temperament. This can only be the result of the maternal influence: the mother's womb is a vessel in which the social environment is incarnated. For example, a woman who has lived her life among Prussians naturally gives birth to a child with Prussian traits; in this manner the national character of that populace has sustained itself for centuries, despite many changes in fortune. It would be unrealistic to think the poor are any different."

"As a zoologist, you are undoubtedly wiser in these matters than we," said Ashbourne, silencing Stratton with a glance. "We will defer to your judgment."

For the remainder of the evening the conversation turned to other topics, and Stratton did his best to conceal his discomfort and maintain a facade of bonhomie. Finally, after Fieldhurst had retired for the evening, Stratton and Ashbourne descended to the laboratory to confer.

"What manner of man have we agreed to help?" exclaimed Stratton as soon as the door was closed. "One who would breed people like livestock?"

"Perhaps we should not be so shocked," said Ashbourne with a sigh. He seated himself upon one of the laboratory stools. "Our group's goal has been to duplicate for humans a procedure that was intended only for animals."

"But not at the expense of individual liberty! I cannot be a party to this."

"Do not be hasty. What would be accomplished by your resigning from the group? To the extent that your efforts contribute to our group's endeavor, your resignation would serve only to endanger the future of the human species. Conversely, if the group attains its goal without your assistance, Lord Fieldhurst's policies will be implemented anyway."

Stratton tried to regain his composure. Ashbourne was right; he could see that. After a moment, he said, "So what course of action should we take? Are there others whom we could contact, Members of Parliament who would oppose the policy that Lord Fieldhurst proposes?"

"I expect that most of the nobility and gentry would share Lord Fieldhurst's opinion on this matter." Ashbourne rested his forehead on the fingertips of one hand, suddenly looking very old. "I should have anticipated this. My error was in viewing humanity purely as a single species. Having seen England and France working toward a common goal, I forgot that nations are not the only factions that oppose one another."

"What if we surreptitiously distributed the name to the labouring classes? They could draw their own needles and impress the name themselves, in secret."

"They could, but name impression is a delicate procedure best performed in a laboratory. I'm dubious that the operation could be carried out on the scale necessary without attracting governmental attention, and then falling under its control."

"Is there an alternative?"

There was silence for a long moment while they considered. Then Ashbourne said, "Do you recall our speculation about a name that would induce two generations of foetuses?"

"Certainly."

"Suppose we develop such a name but do not reveal this property when we present it to Lord Fieldhurst."

"That's a wily suggestion," said Stratton, surprised. "All the children born of such a name would be fertile, so they would be able to reproduce without governmental restriction."

Ashbourne nodded. "In the period before population control measures go into effect, such a name might be very widely distributed."

"But what of the following generation? Sterility would recur, and the labouring classes would again be dependent upon the government to reproduce."

"True," said Ashbourne, "it would be a short-lived victory. Perhaps the only permanent solution would be a more liberal Parliament, but it is beyond my expertise to suggest how we might bring that about."

Again Stratton thought about the changes that cheap engines might bring; if the situation of the working classes was improved in the manner he hoped, that might demonstrate to the nobility that poverty was not innate. But even if the most favorable sequence of events was obtained, it would require years to sway Parliament. "What if we could induce multiple generations with the initial name impression? A longer period before sterility recurs would increase the chances that more liberal social policies would take hold."

"You're indulging a fancy," replied Ashbourne. "The technical difficulty of inducing multiple generations is such that I'd sooner wager on our successfully sprouting wings and taking flight. Inducing two generations would be ambitious enough."

The two men discussed strategies late into the night. If they were to conceal the true name of any name they presented to Lord Fieldhurst, they would have to forge a lengthy trail of research results. Even without the additional burden of secrecy, they would be engaged in an unequal race, pursuing a highly sophisticated name while the other nomenclators sought a comparatively straightforward euonym. To make the odds less unfavorable, Ashbourne and Stratton would need to recruit others to their cause; with such assistance, it might even be possible to subtly impede the research of others.

"Who in the group do you think shares our political views?" asked Ashbourne.

"I feel confident that Milburn does. I'm not so certain about any of the others."

"Take no chances. We must employ even more caution when approaching prospective members than Lord Fieldhurst did when establishing this group originally."

"Agreed," said Stratton. Then he shook his head in disbelief. "Here we are forming a secret organization nested within a secret organization. If only foetuses were so easily induced."

It was the evening of the following day, the sun was setting, and Stratton was strolling across Westminster Bridge as the last remaining costermongers were wheeling their barrows of fruit away. He had just had supper at a club he favored, and was walking back to Coade Manufactory. The previous evening at Darrington Hall had disquieted him, and he had returned to London earlier today to minimize his interaction with Lord Fieldhurst until he was certain his face would not betray his true feelings.

He thought back to the conversation where he and Ashbourne had first entertained the conjecture of factoring out an epithet for creating two levels of order. At the time he had made some efforts to find such an epithet, but they were casual attempts given the superfluous nature of the goal, and they hadn't borne fruit. Now their gauge of achievement had been revised upward: their previous goal was inadequate, two generations seemed the minimum acceptable, and any additional ones would be invaluable.

He again pondered the thermodynamic behavior induced by his dexterous names: order at the thermal level animated the automata, allowing them to create order at the visible level. Order begetting order. Ashbourne had suggested that the next level of order might be automata working together in a coordinated fashion. Was that possible? They would have to communicate in order to work together effectively, but automata were intrinsically mute. What other means were there by which automata could exchange in complex behavior?

He suddenly realized he had reached Coade Manufactory. By now it was dark, but he knew the way to his office well enough. Stratton unlocked the building's front door and proceeded through the gallery and past the business offices.

As he reached the hallway fronting the nomenclators' offices, he saw light emanating from the frosted glass window of his office door. Surely he hadn't left the gas on? He unlocked his door to enter, and was shocked by what he saw.

A man lay face down on the floor in front of the desk, hands tied behind his back. Stratton immediately approached to check on the man. It was Benjamin Roth, the kabbalist, and he was dead. Stratton realized several of the man's fingers were broken; he'd been tortured before he was killed.

Pale and trembling, Stratton rose to his feet, and saw that his office was in utter disarray. The shelves of his bookcases were bare; his books lay strewn face-down across the oak floor. His desk had been swept clear; next to it was a stack of its brass-handled drawers, emptied and overturned. A trail of stray papers led to the open door to his studio; in a daze, Stratton stepped forward to see what had been done there.

His dexterous automaton had been destroyed; the lower half of it lay on the floor, the rest of it scattered as plaster fragments and dust. On the work-table, the clay models of the hands were pounded flat, and his sketches of their design torn from the walls. The tubs for mixing plaster were overflowing with the papers from his office. Stratton took a closer look, and saw that they had been doused with lamp oil.

He heard a sound behind him and turned back to face the office. The front door to the office swung closed and a broad-shouldered man stepped out from behind it; he'd been standing there ever since Stratton had entered. "Good of you to come," the man said. He scrutinized Stratton with the predatory gaze of a raptor, an assassin.

Stratton bolted out of the back door of the studio and down the rear hallway. He could hear the man give chase.

He fled through the darkened building, crossing workrooms filled with coke and iron bars, crucibles and molds, all illuminated by the moonlight entering through skylights overhead; he had entered the metalworks portion of the factory. In the next room he paused for breath, and realized how loudly his footsteps had been echoing; skulking would offer a better chance at escape than running. He distantly heard his pursuer's footsteps stop; the assassin had likewise opted for stealth.

Stratton looked around for a promising hiding place. All around him were cast-iron automata in various stages of near-completion; he was in the finishing room, where the runners left over from casting were sawed off and the surfaces chased. There was no place to hide, and he was about to move on when he noticed what looked like a bundle of rifles mounted on legs. He looked more closely, and recognized it as a military engine.

These automata were built for the War Office: gun carriages that aimed their own cannon, and rapid-fire rifles, like this one, that cranked their own barrel-clusters. Nasty things, but they'd proven invaluable in the Crimea; their inventor had been granted a peerage. Stratton didn't know any names to animate the weapon — they were military secrets — but only the body on which the rifle was mounted was automatous; the rifle's firing mechanism was strictly mechanical. If he could point the body in the right direction, he might be able to fire the rifle manually.

He cursed himself for his stupidity. There was no ammunition here. He stole into the next room.

It was the packing room, filled with pine crates and loose straw. Staying low between crates, he moved to the far wall. Through the windows he saw the courtyard behind the factory, where finished automata were carted away. He couldn't get out that way; the courtyard gates were locked at night. His only exit was through the factory's front door, but he risked encountering the assassin if he headed back the way he'd come. He needed to cross over to the ceramicworks and double back through that side of the factory.

From the front of the packing room came the sound of footsteps. Stratton ducked behind a row of crates, and then saw a side door only a few feet away. As stealthily as he could, he opened the door, entered, and closed the door behind him. Had his pursuer heard him? He peered through a small grille set in the door; he couldn't see the man, but felt he'd gone unnoticed. The assassin was probably searching the packing room.

Stratton turned around, and immediately realized his mistake. The door to the ceramicworks was in the opposite wall. He had entered a storeroom, filled with ranks of finished automata, but with no other exits. There was no way to lock the door. He had cornered himself.

Was there anything in the room he could use as a weapon? The menagerie of automata included some squat mining engines, whose forelimbs terminated in enormous pickaxes, but the ax-heads were bolted to their limbs. There was no way he could remove one.

Stratton could hear the assassin opening side doors and searching other storerooms. Then he noticed an automaton standing off to the side: a porter used for moving the inventory about. It was anthropomorphic in form, the only automaton in the room of that type. An idea came to him.

Stratton checked the back of the porter's head. Porters' names had entered the public domain long ago, so there were no locks protecting its name slot; a tab of parchment protruded from the horizontal slot in the iron. He reached into his coat pocket for the notebook and pencil he always carried and tore out a small portion of a blank leaf. In the darkness he quickly wrote seventy-two letters in a familiar combination, and then folded the paper into a tight square.

To the porter, he whispered, "Go stand as close to the door as you can." The cast iron figure stepped forward and headed for the door. Its gait was very smooth, but not rapid, and the assassin would reach this storeroom any moment now. "Faster," hissed Stratton, and the porter obeyed.

Just as it reached the door, Stratton saw through the grille that his pursuer had arrived on the other side. "Get out of the way," barked the man.

Ever obedient, the automaton shifted to take a step back when Stratton yanked out its name. The assassin began pushing against the door, but Stratton was able to insert the new name, cramming the square of paper into the slot as deeply as he could.

The porter resumed walking forward, this time with a fast, stiff gait: his childhood doll, now life-size. It immediately ran into the door and, unperturbed, kept it shut with the force of its marching, its iron hands leaving fresh dents in the door's oaken surface with every swing of its arms, its rubber-shod feet chafing heavily against the brick floor. Stratton retreated to the back of the storeroom.

"Stop," the assassin ordered. "Stop walking, you! Stop!"

The automaton continued marching, oblivious to all commands. The man pushed on the door, but to no avail. He then tried slamming into it with his shoulder, each impact causing the automaton to slide back slightly, but its rapid strides brought it forward again before the man could squeeze inside. There was a brief pause, and then something poked through the grille in the door; the man was prying it off with a crowbar. The grille abruptly popped free, leaving an open window. The man stretched his arm through and reached around to the back of the automaton's head, his fingers searching for the name each time its head bobbed forward, but there was nothing for them to grasp; the paper was wedged too deeply in the slot.

The arm withdrew. The assassin's face appeared in the window. "Fancy yourself clever, don't you?" he called out. Then he disappeared.

Stratton relaxed slightly. Had the man given up? A minute passed, and Stratton began to think about his next move. He could wait here until the factory opened; there would be too many people about for the assassin to remain.

Suddenly the man's arm came through the window again, this time carrying a jar of fluid. He poured it over the automaton's head, the liquid splattering and dripping down its back. The man's arm withdrew, and then Stratton heard the sound of a match being struck and then flaring alight. The man's arm reappeared bearing the match, and touched it to the automaton.

The room was flooded with light as the automaton's head and upper back burst into flames. The man had doused it with lamp oil. Stratton squinted at the spectacle: light and shadow danced across the floor and walls, transforming the storeroom into the site of some druidic ceremony. The heat caused the automaton to hasten its vague assault on the door, like a salamandrine priest dancing with increasing frenzy, until it abruptly froze: its name had caught fire, and the letters were being consumed.

The flames gradually died out, and to Stratton's newly light-adapted eyes the room seemed almost completely black. More by sound than by sight, he realized the man was pushing at the door again, this time forcing the automaton back enough for him to gain entrance.

"Enough of that, then."

Stratton tried to run past him, but the assassin easily grabbed him and knocked him down with a clout to the head.

His senses returned almost immediately, but by then the assassin had him face down on the floor, one knee pressed into his back. The man tore the health amulet from Stratton's wrist and then tied his hands together behind his back, drawing the rope tightly enough that the hemp fibers scraped the skin of his wrists.

"What kind of man are you, to do things like this?" Stratton gasped, his cheek flattened against the brick floor.

The assassin chuckled. "Men are no different from your automata; slip a bloke a piece of paper with the proper figures on it, and he'll do your bidding." The room grew light as the man lit an oil lamp.

"What if I paid you more to leave me alone?"

"Can't do it. Have to think about my reputation, haven't I? Now let's get to business." He grasped the smallest finger of Stratton's left hand and abruptly broke it.

The pain was shocking, so intense that for a moment Stratton was insensible to all else. He was distantly aware that he had cried out. Then he heard the man speaking again. "Answer my questions straight now. Do you keep copies of your work at home?"

"Yes." He could only get a few words out at a time. "At my desk. In the study."

"No other copies hidden anywhere? Under the floor, perhaps?"

"No."

"Your friend upstairs didn't have copies. But perhaps someone else does?"

He couldn't direct the man to Darrington Hall. "No one."

The man pulled the notebook out of Stratton's coat pocket. Stratton could hear him leisurely flipping through the pages. "Didn't post any letters? Corresponding with colleagues, that sort of thing?"

"Nothing that anyone could use to reconstruct my work."

"You're lying to me." The man grasped Stratton's ring finger.

"No! It's the truth!" He couldn't keep the hysteria from his voice.

Then Stratton heard a sharp thud, and the pressure in his back eased. Cautiously, he raised his head and looked around. His assailant lay unconscious on the floor next to him. Standing next to him was Davies, holding a leather blackjack.

Davies pocketed his weapon and crouched to unknot the rope that bound Stratton. "Are you badly hurt, sir?"

"He's broken one of my fingers. Davies, how did you—?"

"Lord Fieldhurst sent me the moment he learned whom Willoughby had contacted."

"Thank God you arrived when you did." Stratton saw the irony of the situation — his rescue ordered by the very man he was plotting against — but he was too grateful to care.

Davies helped Stratton to his feet and handed him his notebook. Then he used the rope to tie up the assassin. "I went to your office first. Who's the fellow there?"

"His name is — was Benjamin Roth." Stratton managed to recount his previous meeting with the kabbalist. "I don't know what he was doing there."

"Many religious types have a bit of the fanatic in them," said Davies, checking the assassin's bonds. "As you wouldn't give him your work, he likely felt justified in taking it himself. He came to your office to look for it, and had the bad luck to be there when this fellow arrived."

Stratton felt a flood of remorse. "I should have given Roth what he asked."

"You couldn't have known."

"It's an outrageous injustice that he was the one to die. He'd nothing to do with this affair."

"It's always that way, sir. Come on, let's tend to that hand of yours."

Davies bandaged Stratton's finger to a splint, assuring him that the Royal Society would discreetly handle any consequences of the night's events. They gathered the oil-stained papers from Stratton's office into a trunk so that Stratton could sift through them at his leisure, away from the manufactory. By the time they were finished, a carriage had arrived to take Stratton back to Darrington Hall; it had set out at the same time as Davies, who had ridden into London on a racing-engine. Stratton boarded the carriage with the trunk of papers, while Davies stayed behind to deal with the assassin and make arrangements for the kabbalist's body.

Stratton spent the carriage ride sipping from a flask of brandy, trying to steady his nerves. He felt a sense of relief when he arrived back at Darrington Hall; although it held its own variety of threats, Stratton knew he'd be safe from assassination there. By the time he reached his room, his panic had largely been converted into exhaustion, and he slept deeply.

He felt much more composed the next morning, and ready to begin sorting through his trunkful of papers. As he was arranging them into stacks approximating their original organization, Stratton found a notebook he didn't recognize. Its pages contained Hebrew letters arranged in the familiar patterns of nominal integration and factorization, but all the notes were in Hebrew as well. With a renewed pang of guilt, he realized it must have belonged to Roth; the assassin must have found it on his person and tossed it in with Stratton's papers to be burned.

He was about to set it aside, but his curiosity bested him: he'd never seen a kabbalist's notebook before. Much of the terminology was archaic, but he could understand it well enough; among the incantations and sephirotic diagrams, he found the epithet enabling an automaton to write its own name. As he read, Stratton realized that Roth's achievement was more elegant that he'd previously thought.

The epithet didn't describe a specific set of physical actions, but instead the general notion of reflexivity. A name incorporating the epithet became an autonym: a self-designating name. The notes indicated that such a name would express its lexical nature through whatever means the body allowed. The animated body wouldn't even need hands to write out its name; if the epithet were incorporated properly, a porcelain horse could likely accomplish the task by dragging a hoof in the dirt.

Combined with one of Stratton's epithets for dexterity, Roth's epithet would indeed let an automaton do most of what was needed to reproduce. An automaton could cast a body identical to its own, write out its own name, and insert it to animate the body. It couldn't train the new one in sculpture, though, since automata couldn't speak. An automaton that could truly reproduce itself without human assistance remained out of reach, but coming this close would undoubtedly have delighted the kabbalists.

It seemed unfair that automata were so much easier to reproduce than humans. It was as if the problem of reproducing automata need be solved only once, while that of reproducing humans was a Sisyphean task, with every additional generation increasing the complexity of the name required.

And abruptly Stratton realized that he didn't need a name that redoubled physical complexity, but one than enabled lexical duplication.

The solution was to impress the ovum with an autonym, and thus induce a foetus that bore its own name.

The name would have two versions, as originally proposed: one used to induce male foetuses, another for female foetuses. The women conceived this way would be fertile as always. The men conceived this way would also be fertile, but not in the typical manner: their spermatozoa would not contain preformed foetuses, but would instead bear either of two names on their surfaces, the self-expression of the names originally born by the glass needles. And when such a spermatozoon reached an ovum, the name would induce the creation of a new foetus. The species would be able to reproduce itself without medical intervention, because it would carry the name within itself.

He and Dr. Ashbourne had assumed that creating animals capable of reproducing meant giving them preformed foetuses, because that was the method employed by nature. As a result they had overlooked another possibility: that if a creature could be expressed in a name, reproducing that creature was equivalent to transcribing the name. An organism could contain, instead of a tiny analogue of its body, a lexical representation instead.

Humanity would become a vehicle for the name as well as a product of it. Each generation would be both content and vessel, an echo in a self-sustaining reverberation.

Stratton envisioned a day when the human species could survive as long as its own behavior allowed, when it could stand or fall based purely on its own actions, and not simply vanish once some predetermined life span had elapsed. Other species might bloom and wither like flowers over seasons of geologic time, but humans would endure for as long as they determined.

Nor would any group of people control the fecundity of another; in the procreative domain, at least, liberty would be restored to the individual. This was not the application Roth had intended for his epithet, but Stratton hoped the kabbalist would consider it worthwhile. By the time the autonym's true power became apparent, an entire generation consisting of millions of people worldwide would have been born of the name, and there would be no way any government could control their reproduction. Lord Fieldhurst — or his successors — would be outraged, and there would eventually be a price to be paid, but Stratton found he could accept that.

He hastened to his desk, where he opened his own notebook and Roth's side by side. On a blank page, he began writing down ideas on how Roth's epithet might be incorporated into a human euonym. Already in his mind Stratton was transposing the letters, searching for a permutation that denoted both the human body and itself, an onto-genic encoding for the species.

The Martian Agent,
A Planetary Romance

MICHAEL CHABON

Sometimes the next generation has to go retro to pay tribute to its roots. When Michael Chabon wrote this story for his *McSweeney's Mammoth Treasury of Thrilling Tales* anthology, he was undoubtedly thinking back to his reading as an adolescent, and creating his own homage. The result is other-worldly steampunk that adds Chabon's own unique prose stylings to classic situations and characters. It also represents the infiltration of steampunk into the mainstream. This is evident even in Chabon's masterwork *The Amazing Adventures of Kavalier & Clay*, with its nod to comics and the nostalgia of reading solely for pleasure.

'Tis theirs to sweep through the ringing deep where Azrael's outposts are,
Or buffet a path through the Pit's red wrath when God goes out to war,
Or hang with the reckless Seraphim on the rein of a red-maned star.
   — *Rudyard Kipling*

1.

The brothers first encountered a land sloop on the night, late in the summer of 1876, that one hunted their father down. It picked up their trail in Natchitoches country, two miles from Fort Wellington, at the ragged southwestern border of the Louisiana Territories and of the British Empire itself. The moon, as many sad partisans of the mutineer George Armstrong Custer were to record, hung fat in the sky, stained with an autumnal tinge of blood that, to some diarists, presaged hanging and debacle. Outside the windows of the coach in which the brothers and their parents rode lay the wilderness, flooded in black water and in a steady-flowing hubbub of night birds, insects, and amphibians. The coach bobbed and pitched as if borne on that current of

bedlam and black water, down a road already ancient when the ancestors of these very insects had jabbed and goaded de Soto's men along it
to their itching feverish deaths. The boot-heels of the coachman, a big,
steady Vermonter named Haseltine, drummed against the front of the
coach, just behind the boys' heads, with the random tattoo of a broken
shutter in the wind. The timbers of the carriage groaned with each jolt
and stone in the road. The respiration of the mosquito-mad team, a
pair of spavined drays for which, two days earlier, they had exchanged
the last of their sovereigns, rattled out behind the coach like a string
of tin cans.

The first shrill call of the steel throat in the distance left a rippling
wake of silence.

— Train, said the little one, or — no.

The cry had sounded too forlorn, too lupine for a train. Before the
little boy even saw the knot of grief that deformed the hinge of the
father's stubbled, powder-burnt jaw, he knew that whatever had
uttered it was hungering for them.

— There are no trains, the older brother said. Not this deep into
Indian country. Don't be a dolt.

— I'm not a dolt.

— A train.

— Please, the mother said, boys.

The little boy seized his brother's shoulder, gathering a scratchy
wool handful of stained cadet gray. *He won't ever be a British officer now,
nor will I.* Though he was a good forty pounds lighter and seven years
the junior, the little boy sent the older brother lurching clear across
the coach, slamming his head against a brass fitting. Before the older
brother could retaliate there was another cry from the valve, louder,
nearer, a blurred double-reeded blat less like the call of a wolf than of
an implacable iron toad. At the sound of it the little boy scooted across
the bench and buried his head in the brother's lap. The brother put
an arm around him and stroked his hair. He pulled an old Ohio River
Company trading blanket with its smell of dog and tallow, amid which
they had huddled for most of the past week, up to their chins.

The mother turned to the father.

— Harry, she said. What is it? Could it be a train?

— Not here, said the father. Franklin is right. Not this close to Tejas.
They were less than ten miles now from the border and freedom —

another fact which melancholy diarists of the failed rebellion would be inclined, in the days that followed, to record.

The father stood up and went to the door of the coach. The night and its furor of animals and bugs blew in and stirred the damp black strands of the mother's hair. Her cheeks were glinting, febrile. All the way from the Yalobusha River to the Red she had thrashed and dreamed fever dreams that to the little boy, whose name was Jefferson Mordden MacAndrew Drake, were unimaginably cavernous, lit with lamps of blood. The proximity of Tejas seemed to have revived her; reasoning conversely, her younger son was certain that if they did not make it across the Sabine River she would die. They were headed for the ferry at Beurre. Jefferson Drake had been in possession of this fact and little else for the past eleven days. The father hung half out of the door of the rocking coach and called upward into the night. The brothers could not hear what he inquired of the coachman, nor what reply he received. But when he sat down again, he hoisted the canvas haversack that had ridden between his feet all the way from Sulla, in the Ohio Territory, and began to take out his guns.

2.

Every lost cause has its sacred litany, each of whose plaints begins with the words "If only." If only Custer could have waited one week more for the road to Ashtabula to clear. If only Phil Sheridan had not been shot by the jealous husband of Mrs. Delaplane. And if only Cuyahoga Drake had made it to Tejas, surely the guns and gold promised by Lincoln...

In a telegram dispatched from Fort Wellington on the Sabine to the C-in-C of Her Majesty's Columbian Army, at Potomac, following the events whose successful conclusion raised him to Command of the Mississippi Army, Lieutenant General H. P. W. Hodge stated that Colonel Harry Drake, fleeing the ruin of the mutiny he had helped to foment, had been spotted by a native Natchitoches scout eleven miles from the Sabine River, eastern border of the Tejas Free Republic. The scout, a half-breed named Victor Piles, turned his mongrel pony toward the squat black turrets of the fort, raising a wild alarm. Word of Cuyahoga Drake's southwestern flight had followed him, more or less delayed by the intermittent drunkenness and indolence of the frontier courier corps, from the moment of his escape from the stockade at Sulla on the Ohio. General Hodge, sad, syphilitic, tormented by hidden sympathy with the mutineers, had been feeding the burners of his shining black pair of Mullock-Treadwell land sloops since early that morning, on the off-chance that Drake and his family might pass through the neighborhood on their way to the rusty yellow Sabine. Wellington was among the last of the southwestern stations to be equipped with steam wagons and had taken delivery of two brand-new Terror-class sloops, the *Dauntless* and the *Princess Louise,* only two weeks before. They had emerged from their crates, to the groaning of hot nails and navvies with crowbars, smelling of fresh paint, leather, packing oil, excelsior. Hodge had fallen in love them at once, with a helpless passion fostered by his remote and lonely billet. When Victor Piles came around crying about the rollicking carriage and dappled nags straining for Tejas down the old Natchitoches road, Hodge agonized over which of his darlings to risk and flaunt in pursuit of the renegade hero of Cleveland and Ashtabula.

In the end Hodge chose the *Dauntless.* She had been among the first wagons rolled out of Mullock-Treadwell's huge new Second Manchester Works, and she more than made up in style and speed what she lacked in seasoning or experience in the field. She was a Model 3 Terror, long and canine, a steel greyhound powered by a hundred-horsepower Bucephalus engine. The relative frailty of her armor-plating was more than compensated for by her maneuverability and by the range and mobility of her big .45 turret-mounted Gatling. Along with her crew of six she could carry a section of infantrymen, eight troopers of the 27th Cajun Fusiliers whom Hodge assigned to the pursuit. The question of whether there would be sufficient additional room in her acrid sweltering hold for a living prisoner remained unsettled as the *Dauntless* huffed, riveted leather treads clattering against the gangway of pine planking, out through the gates of Fort Wellington into the wilderness. The NCO in command of the Fusiliers, a Sergeant Swindell, had the foresight, in case space was wanting, to bring along a length of stout rope.

3.

In her haste to flee, after her husband's escape from the guardhouse at Sulla, Mrs. Drake, née Catherine Mordden, had endeavored to condense the wealth and history of her family into an Indiaman chest. Clean linens, a strand of Yalu pearls, her wedding dress, a Bible that had been the gift of her brother at their last parting. Mufflers and oil-skins for the boys. Biscuit, wine, a small wheel of New York cheese. A plait of Iroquois wampum likely to have no value anywhere that her family might conceivably alight. A hundred-year-old flag of red and white stripes, with a quartered ring of yellowing stars on a blue field, that was her husband's most treasured possession; and a chromolitho-graph of Lieutenant General George Armstrong Custer, at the time of his accession to the Command of Her Majesty's Army of the Great Lakes, in a rosewood frame, which was her own. (Scurrilous rumors spread by the enemies of the Ohioists, and kept alive for decades after-ward by the avid gossip of historians, would link Kitty Drake roman-tically to the Martyr of American Hopes, and even trace the younger of the two Drake boys to Custer's seed.) Half a mile from the ferry at Beurre Landing the sea chest, strapped to the roof of the rattling coach, worked itself out of its bindings and tumbled to the roadbed. It landed on one corner and split in two with the neat snap of a snuffbox spring-ing open. Starry flag, lace, and biscuits were strewn across the road. Pearls skittered like water on a hot stove lid. The portrait of George Custer lay, glass glinting, in the lovely ill-betokening moonlight. For a moment, the expression of the Martyr in the portrait, that steady, slightly mad blue gaze which had always struck the portrait's owner as summarizing all that was brash, vainglorious, strong, fundamentally and conclusively un-English, about her husband's generation of soli-tary horsemen and wanderers and Indian fighters, took on a strangely plaintive air. Custer seemed to be remonstrating with the heavens he contemplated. Then, in a half-musical splintering of timber and glass, the *Dauntless*'s left tread nosed its way onto and over the distilled pat-rimony of the Drakes, flattening what it did not tear or turn to dust and shards.

Then the *Dauntless* spoke.

— Colonel Drake.

It spoke in the voice of its chief engineer, a Sergeant Breedlove, who crouched in the dark roaring stink of its cabin, between the stack of metal rungs that climbed to the gun turret and a small transverse slot that permitted him to peer vaguely out into the Louisiana midnight, clutching a wooden funnel to his lips. The funnel was connected to a length of canvas-covered caoutchouc hose that ran up through a small eye in the roof of the land sloop, where it was joined to the narrow end of a large, slender horn or bell that opened beneath the Gatling like a lily, a black tin corsage.

— Colonel Drake, your mutiny is over. Custer has surrendered to the Crown.

The raspy, rather high-pitched tone of the *Dauntless* and its mushy Yorkshire accent carried easily across the narrowing gap between it and the carriage. The little boy looked at his brother, whose name was Franklin Mordden Evans Drake. Franklin Drake looked at their father.

— It's a trick, he said. Custer would never —

— You will not be permitted to reach the border, said the *Dauntless*. Please, Colonel. Do not force us to open fire.

The father rose from the bench once more to put his grimed face and staring eyes out into the uproar and moonlight of the bayou. He had a measuring gaze that could guess accurately at the weight of bullocks or the height of weather vanes or the wish, however pure or sinful, in the heart of an eight-year-old boy. He hung there for a long moment, leaning on the open door of the coach, estimating the chances and the outcomes. Then he closed the door and sat heavily down.

— Five hundred yards back, he said. A land sloop. Machine gun. A Gatling. A forty-five, I'd say.

— It's a Terror, said Frank with a hint of awe. Semi-amphibious. This late in the summer she could likely swim after us right into the river.

It was all the little boy could do to prevent himself from going to the door to see this marvel. The father noticed.

— No, he said.

The little boy sat back and looked at his brother, who was struggling with his own desire to see the thing that was running them to ground. The carriage rolled on, but its rocking had subsided and there was no question that Haseltine, the coachman, was losing his resolve. He had seen Gatlings and Nordenfeldts used on the Cayugas at Ashtabula and the Lakotas at Poudre and the Russians at Belokonsk. It was all too easy for him to imagine looking down to see the glaucous gray insides of his body lying steaming in his lap.

— Coward, said Cuyahoga Drake.

There was such universal disgust in his voice that for a moment the brothers were unsure whom the epithet was intended to damn. Then the father rose and went to the door once more.

— Haseltine! You damned milk-soaked —

—Harry.

The father turned to find the mother staring at him, her lips pressed together, worrying the worried kerchief tucked into the bodice of her shirtwaist dress.

Colonel Drake opened his mouth. He had sensibly and carefully and with only the most reasoning sort of bravery led the armies of the British Empire in victory after victory against Iroquois and Sioux and Alyeskan Tsarists before taking the first unmeasured step of his career and enlisting for eight brutal and glorious months in Custer's mad attempt to rekindle the extinguished Republic on the shores of Lake Erie. His sons waited for his next words.

—Colonel Drake, said the *Dauntless,* this is the final warning I will make.

In the end, the brothers would remember, their father merely nodded. When he drew his sword it was only to rap with the hilt, twice, against the ceiling of the coach.

Haseltine cursed and forgave the horses in a series of unintelligible barks. The carriage creaked and rumbled. The sand beneath its wheels sighed. Through the windows of the coach the clamor of the bayou, as if their forward progress had tended to slip them past or somehow through it like fingers cupped around a candle, now blew in, a steady, flame-snuffing gust. The mother winced and closed her eyes in pain, as if the discordant productions of nocturnal western Louisiana had triggered one of her megrims. Behind or within that clamor lay the grind of gears, the resolute, dumb, canine chuffing of the Terror's big Bucephalus. Up on the box, Haseltine coughed. There was the scratch of a lucifer.

More to his own surprise, perhaps, than that of those whom he addressed, who knew him better, Jefferson Drake found that he was moved by a spasm of profound outrage.

—We can't just sit here and wait for them to grab us!

Colonel Drake lit his own burled pipe. In more normal circumstances the business with match and tobacco might have served to veil his amusement with his younger son, who disdained generally to sit and wait for anything at all.

—What do you propose, Jefferson?

The boy looked at the two revolvers, two rifles, and eight boxes of cartridges that comprised the family arsenal. There were the pair of

Webleys, a balky old single-shot Rigby won in a game of faro by the same seafaring maternal grandfather whose trunk had foundered on the Natchitoches road, and a captured Lebeau-Courally ten-gauge, its stock engraved with (Mrs. Drake had said) scenes from a book called *Atala* by Chateaubriand, and bearing the monogram of the late General Durmanov. It was exquisite but had been designed for the hunting of snipe and woodcock and could not be relied upon to kill a grown man.

Jefferson Drake was an inveterate reader of novels for boys. In these tales there were ever only three possible destinies available to those who found themselves in such a grave predicament. For Heroic Britons, there were the Fighting Martyrdom, guns blazing, and the Impossible Stand, holding out until help arrived. For a noble enemy — Russian, German, Pathan, the odd renegade Frenchman or Iroquois — there was only Defeat Without Surrender, choosing to end one's own life rather than face the ignominy of inevitable capture. (For "savage" enemies such possibilities rarely arose, for these traveled almost exclusively in Swarms or Hordes, and so never found themselves Surrounded.) Looking at their paltry armaments, and knowing from the grave listening expression on the face of his brother, who was keen on such things, that the approaching Terror must be a formidable piece of machinery indeed, the first two options seemed impracticable, in the first case, and in the second case ridiculous. Then too, they were no longer, for reasons the boy could have just managed to explain without truly understanding, Heroic Britons. They were rebels — mutineers. During those months of rapid victory, barbaric rains, and total failure, the Drake family had passed from that portion of the map of existence tinted proud and homely British red into a blank and hostile territory.

— Take our own lives, the little boy said.

It came out more of a question than he had intended, thin and grave and far too possible. He was hoping to be contradicted, and when the father said, "Nonsense," at once, without even taking his eyes off the glowing bowl of his pipe, the boy was so grateful that he burst into tears.

— Stop that blubbering, the father said.

He turned to the mother with a sharp tone and an air of giving her something useful to do. His tone was not unkind.

— Do button him up.

The mother sat forward and reached across the carriage toward him, trying to draw her son toward her fevered breast. But the boy pulled away, and wiped his eyes on his sleeve.

— I can button myself up.

He saw that his brother was watching him, with a peculiar empty expression that he knew well, and he sat back to wait, feeling obscurely comforted. Frank was always watching him, studying his words and behavior, not with envy or scorn or concern — though these were not unknown elements of his feelings for the little boy — but with a version of their father's measuring gaze that seemed to take Jeff's outbursts and ideas as a form of weather, phenomena that, correctly interpreted, could be exploited as the raw materials to which a masterly hand and chisel might be applied. All the currents of brotherly respect and imitation flowed in the usual direction between them: The younger idolized the older, nearly as devoutly as he did their father. But the impetus for their common undertakings as brothers — for all that it was the older one who arranged and directed them — nearly always derived from some wild remark, from the unreasoned hotheaded dissatisfaction, of the younger of the pair.

— Jeff's right. Give us a gun, Daddy. Let us go. They won't get us. I'll see to that.

— Oh, said the mother, Harry, no.

— We haven't got more than a few miles to go. It's hours yet until daylight. Do you think I can't get myself and one little kid across a few miles of mud and frogs?

— He can, the little boy said. You know he can, Daddy.

The father sat a moment. Each time he drew on his pipe his long nose cast a flaring shadow up the high furrowed dome of his skull. The land sloop was close enough now that they could hear her crewmen shouting at one another to be heard over the racket of the machine they were laboring to control.

— Harry, the mother said. No. They will be cared for. They will not be harmed.

— They will be turned against us, said the father. Perhaps you do not consider this to be a form of harm.

He reached down and picked up one of the Webleys, opened the chamber, and checked it for the third time in ten minutes. Then he snapped it shut, and handed it to his older son.

— Your brother has never had the pleasure of meeting Mr. Lincoln, Franklin. See that you get him to San Antonio.

— Yes, sir. I will look after him, sir.

The boys slid from the bench and crouched down to fill their pockets with boxes of cartridges. Then the little boy went to the door. Afterward he would recall the way his heart pounded with the knowledge that he ought to go and throw his arms around his mother and father and bid them farewell. He was inclined, in later years, to excoriate himself for this omission. The truth, however, was that at the time his mind was such a jumble of agitation, apprehension, and the sheer blind desire to be free at last of that miserable rattletrap box, to be *doing something*, that it was not until he was already out of the coach, and scrambling across the road into a twisted thicket of dwarf-bearded oaks, that it occurred to him that he would never see his parents again. By then the land sloop was less than twenty yards from the coach, and it was too late. He crouched in an inch of sucking water, breathing hard, watching his brother's spidery form in the coach's open door. It was difficult to tell for sure but it looked as though Franklin and their father were gravely shaking hands. No doubt he had kissed their mother as well. Although it was Jefferson who concerned himself with the fine gesture and the act of panache, it was Franklin, who found such things laughable, who was always pulling them off.

There was a thud, a sharp huff of breath, and then Frank came scrambling into the trees, clutching the revolver to his chest. He found Jeff, and they squatted together in the foul-smelling mud, painting their backsides with swamp water, watching as the flame of the land sloop's lantern, mirrored and lensed, reached out to engulf the bayou in a swelling balloon of light.

— Get down, Frank said.

He pushed Jeff facedown into the mud and then lay beside him. The land sloop came, slowing, with a sound like an enormous box of nails and broken crockery falling down a flight of stairs. She stopped. In the moonlight Jeff could read the name, *Dauntless*, picked out in gilt letters on her flank. There was a flat chiming as her rear hatch rolled open, then the scrabble of boots, and then suddenly the roadbed seemed to fill with redcoats. They trotted, rifles aslant, to the carriage. Three of them pulled Haseltine from his seat and threw him to the ground. Several others dragged out Colonel Drake, and then with rough politesse assisted Mrs. Drake to step down. She stood slim and straight-backed, head held up, giving the soldiers a look the boys could not in fact see but could easily imagine. Their father struggled against them and was beaten, once, sharply, with the stock of a Martini. After that he stood, and suffered them to put him in irons.

— Colonel Henry Hudson Drake, in the name of Her Imperial Majesty, Queen Victoria, I place you under arrest on the charge of mutiny and treason against the Crown.

— Shoot! the little boy hissed. Shoot the gun.

— Quiet!

— Let me shoot it, then!

He reached for the revolver, kicking at his brother's shins, blind with rage or with the tears his rage incited. The older brother stuffed the gun into the waist of his pants and wrapped the boy up in his long arms that always seemed capable of encircling the younger one several times around. His left hand he clapped firmly, and for far from the first time in their lives, over the little boy's mouth.

The boy struggled for another moment, then just hung in his brother's embrace, and they watched as their parents and Haseltine were pushed toward the hatch of the *Dauntless*. Their mother was handed up into the hold at once, but the soldiers stood around the two male prisoners for some time, talking in low voices that occasionally broke out into angry hisses and, once, four words, shouted.

— I'll not permit it!

The boys recognized the thick Yorkshire burr in which the land sloop had called to them through the darkness. Then their father and Vernon Haseltine were heaved up into the *Dauntless,* like two buckling sacks of bricks. An order was given, and the iron hatch rolled shut, sealing up their parents within.

The older brother did not relax his grip, or remove his hand from the little boy's mouth, until the glow of the land sloop's lantern, handed from treetop to treetop in the eastern distance, dwindled and finally winked out, and the thump of her engine had been absorbed once more into the universal clangor of the swamp.

4.

At Tir-Na-Nog, the house on a Derbyshire hilltop, fifty miles from the sea, to which their maternal grandfather, Joseph Mordden, had retired at the end of his career as a ship's surgeon, there had stood an oak tree of great age and height. In the branches of this Khyber redoubt, storm-tossed yardarm, donjon, eyrie, pagoda, minaret, and pharos, both boys had spent a cumulative total of perhaps twenty-nine full, long August days during the course of their childhoods. And yet in all that time, it had never occurred to either of them — and certainly they would never have been permitted — to attempt to pass a night in the tree. But both of the boys had seen men under their father's command take off into the bush in a boiling cloud of dogs, in pursuit of deserters, fugitives from conscription, runaway spies. Frank suspected that it would be only a matter of time until a squad returned to look for the sons of Cuyahoga Drake. And so, after leading Jeff in a number of elaborate dog-baffling figures and hieroglyphs in and around the shallows of the bayou, he took hold of his younger brother, by the seat and waist of his breeches, and hoisted him up into the branches of a cypress for the night. The moon had set, and it was too dark for them to reconnoiter a way to the Sabine that would keep them off the road. He pulled himself up after Jeff, and they made their way carefully, dizzied by a medicinal odor, into the dark heart of the tree. The branches were coarse and slender and made an unpromising bed. They spent an hour that seemed like five hoping that the dawn would come and proving repeatedly to themselves and to one another that it was impossible to fall asleep while clinging. In the end they chanced the lower, broader boughs, and somehow fell asleep. Jeff's dreams were tormented by lurching and rocking, the creaking of old bones, the ghostly singing of frogs.

Frank hit him.

Jeff opened his eyes. The intervals among the foliage of the tree were filled with luminous needles and clusters of blue, and fringed with Spanish moss and tufts of mist. Jeff sat up, abruptly. If his brother had not caught hold of his arm he would have tumbled into the fly-rippled water below.

— They're coming.

He said it almost without voicing the words, rolling his eyes to the east. Jeff listened. The day lay in an interval of silence between the conversation of the night animals and that of the morning's birds. It was not long before Jeff heard the voices. He could hear that they were irritable and amused; he could hear that some were British and others bayou French. He could hear the labored, happy gasping of a hound. Frank stuck the revolver into the waistband of his uniform trousers, at the back, and lowered himself, hand under hand, down to the shallows. Jeff started after him.

— I thought you said we'd be safe up here, he whispered.

— Safe from alligators. Not redcoats. I just didn't want the dogs to find us before we had a chance to see where we were going.

— Where are we going?

Jeff nearly stumbled over the body of his brother, so quickly did he fall to the soft ground, and threw himself down alongside Frank. The voices had grown louder, the words intelligible; the men from Fort Wellington were coming their way, their boots sloshing and slurping in the mud. Now Jeff could make out the distant rumble of a steam wagon, idling perhaps, back on the Indian road. Perhaps a pair of wagons. No doubt the troops had been ordered to fan out into the bayou in all directions from the point at which the boys' parents had been taken. Frank was looking wildly around for a place to conceal themselves. The brush was thin, here; now Jeff could make out wavering patches of red moving toward them, beyond the clearing in which they had blindly landed the night before.

The expression on Frank's face was blank, thoughtless.

— Do something, Jeff said. Shoot them, swim for it, do something —

Frank seemed to come out of his fog.

— Give me your penknife, he said.

He cut a pair of the reedy stalks that grew all around them and investigated their cores, which proved to be not quite hollow but filled with a spongy mass through which, as he quickly demonstrated, sucking out his cheeks, a faint but steady breath could be drawn.

— What about the alligators?

— I just made them up.

Jeff looked at him. This was precisely the kind of lie that Frank excelled in; one which claimed that an earlier statement had been a lie. Often such a lie was followed by a third that claimed to invalidate it. Frank handed him a short length of reed, then started to crawl toward a deep pool on the other side of the tree in which they had waited out the night. He stopped and took the revolver from his waist, and tucked it lovingly into a hollow formed by the wild braiding of some thick old roots. Then he lowered himself, wincing broadly to cover the appre-

hension and disgust he felt at so doing, into the black water with its
skin of slime.

5.

Buried in water, Franklin Drake clung to the bottom-mud, clutching a
fistful of slick tangling tree roots for an anchor. Water hissed and whispered in his ears. Air came into his lungs only in recalcitrant sips that
had a taste of stale bread. His circulatory system was protesting this
ill treatment and at first, when he heard the water-muffled gunshots,
he thought they were the pulse of his starved heart redounding in his
ears. He let go of the roots, burst up into the light and air, and saw that
his little brother had killed two men. The dead men lay facedown in an
inch of brown water, near the plaiting of roots in which, five minutes
earlier, Frank had hidden the gun. And Jeff was still shooting, taking
careful aim as their father had taught him, both eyes open, one hand
steadying the wrist of the other, as a dozen redcoats rushed him. A
third fell backward, clutching his throat; then Jeff was swallowed up in
scarlet wool. The gun was twisted from his hands, and he was hoisted
into the air by the collar of his shirt.
   —Jeff.
He thought they were going to kill his brother for what he had just
done. Not five hours and I've already broken my promise, he thought.
He waded out of the pool and up onto the slightly firmer mud, then
lost his footing and went sprawling forward, hitting his head on an
exposed root hard enough to render him almost senseless. There was
shouting, and more shouting, red sleeves, spattered gaiters. Then a
hand with very cold fingers grabbed him by the back of the neck and
jerked him to his feet. Frank stumbled. There was blood in his right eye
and then the smell of blood in his nostrils and finally the taste of it, like
rawhide, in his mouth.
   —Stand up, boy.
   —I'm trying.
The soldier's knee found the seat of Frank's britches. Frank stumbled forward a few feet in the direction of his brother, reaching for
him though he could no longer see him; though he could no longer see
anything at all.

—◆—

6.

A spatulate darkness, shaped like a shark, poured itself along the rues and alleys of the Vieux Carré. It splashed against the sides of houses and shops, then surged up walls of brick and clapboard to flood the Quarter's rooftops — drowning chimney pots, weather vanes, and tin flues — before brimming over the volutes of a cornice and ladling itself once more down an iron balcony into the street. The shadow, thrust by the angle of the rising sun several hundred feet ahead of its source, drifted west, toward the Place D'Armas and Government House. When it reached the pair of squat bell towers that flanked the dark brick barn or upended ark of the St. Ignatius Boys' Home, the shadow started up the side of the campanile, then hesitated, as if uncertain whether it would clear or be snagged on the tooth of the high black iron cross. After a moment, however, the shadow resumed its progress, inching its immense snout forward. It topped and descended the tower of St. Ignatius, drifted across the dairy and some other outbuildings, and flowed over the high stone wall that separated the home's grounds from those of the old Presbytère, which since the Declaration of Reunion had served as the territorial courthouse and bridewell. Here, as if having at last sniffed out what it sought, the great shadow came to a stop, falling halfway across the broad expanse of the jailyard, where it plunged into gloom the crew of Negro carpenters who were working there, effecting last-minute repairs to the old gallows that had once dangled the hooded carcasses of Andrew Jackson and the pirate Jean Lafitte.

In the office of the rector of St. Ignatius, the inveterate gloom, which served so well to cow the reprobate spirit of boyhood that was the ineradicable plague and evil genius of the institution, deepened to an almost nocturnal pitch. A faint aureole of dust bloomed around the globe of the gaslamp atop the escritoire at which the rector, in his dressing-gown, sat perched on a velvet stool. With his left hand Father Paul Joseph de St. Malo reached to turn up the flame in the lamp. His right hand went on scratching away at the page on his blotter. After a moment he looked up, and contemplated the dull patch on the carpet where, moments before, the morning sunlight slanting in through the leaded window had fallen in bright bars and chevrons. He smiled. He was engaged in the composition of a letter to the parents of an inmate who had died, and though he had written countless such missives over the twenty-odd years of his rectorship, and though the deceased boy had been a sniveler, a liar, and good-for-nothing, Father de St. Malo was nonetheless glad for the interruption, which had been foretold, the previous morning, in a cable from Savannah.

The old priest rose and passed through a stealthy door cut into the Spanish cedar wainscoting of his office. In his small, white bedchamber he washed his hands in the copper basin, emptied his bladder into the pot, and took off his dressing gown. He was still buttoning up his best shoes — from the workshop of Scapelli, the papal cordwainer — when Father Dowd, the rector's secretary, rapped softly on the hidden door.

— Did you put him in the garden?

— As you said.

— Did you offer him tea or coffee? Did you set out the *fraises des bois?*

— He declined them. He was not happy to be made to wait. He wanted to be taken directly to them.

The rector, having smoothed the scant hair of his pate with water and scrutinized his nostrils in the glass, opened the door. Father Dowd looked him over with professional detachment, and nodded. Suitable attire in which to meet a newly made O.B.E., a conqueror of the clouds, a hero of Empire and Science.

— I don't imagine he's very happy about anything just now, the rector said. Do you suppose he can have heard this morning's news?

— He said he has spent the last ten hours on his ship.

— Ah. Then I suppose I shall have to tell him myself.

They hurried, the gangly young priest from Cork and the stout Acadian rector, down the long corridor that led to the garden. The garden was the rector's only vanity, apart from his calfskin boots. He trained and reserved an elite crew of boys to turn its earth and pollard its fruit trees and sweep clean its sandy paths. Naturally these were the only boys ever permitted into its confines. The remainder of the wards of St. Ignatius found employment in the kitchen, the laundry, and in the shops, where they learned the manufacture of such useful items as bandages, laces, dippers and basins, simple furniture, toothpicks, and, lately, coffins. As they walked to the door that opened onto the garden, the priests passed — and inspected the labor of — five little boys on their knees, spread down the length of the corridor, going over the soft marble floor with buckets and chamois and rags.

— His ship, the rector said. You saw it?

— It's lovely, said Father Dowd. Looking at it, Father, I confess, it was difficult not to feel a desire to…

— Fly away? From this wonderful place?

They stepped out into the garden. The ponderous late-summer humidity of the last several weeks had diminished and the daylight had a touch of that delicate, wistful clarity that was perceptible only to natives of New Orleans as autumnal. The squash vines were effulgent as a horn section with brass-bright flowers, and a light, lightly rank breeze off the river stripped the petals from the last of the roses. It was, the rector thought, ideal weather for a hanging.

The inventor Sir Thomas Mordden stood beside a white-painted iron chair, his back to the garden door. A silver tray, with tea and coffee and cream from the teat of the home's own cow in silver pots, lay on a white iron table, beside an empty teacup and an appetizing red mound of wild strawberries that looked untouched. The inventor was gazing up at the windows of the dormitory. His hands were clasped behind his back with a suggestion of difficult restraint. He might have been trying to determine if he should call out to the boys he had come to redeem, or if he ought just to scale the wall with his bare hands and climb in through their window. He was a diminutive man, but his shoulders were broad, his legs thick, and the hands that labored to constrain one another behind his back looked capable of governing stone, of discovering fingerholds in the narrowest of chinks. At the sound of the priests' footsteps he spun and showed them a face that was sunburnt and wanted flesh. His pewter hair fell in lank strands, nearly to his collar; the breeze lifted and disarranged it. His suit, though it looked new, fit him poorly, as though it had been chosen in haste or disdain, The hair, the baggy suit, the enormous and snarled sideburns, the irritable cast of his haggard features were more in accordance with the proctor's notions of a Methodist pamphleteer, unkempt, idealistic, and doctrinaire, than of a savant, a renowned engineer, a man of considerable means.

— Father.

— Sir Thomas. May I say that however tragic and unfortunate the circumstances, you are most welcome in New Orleans.

— Thank you.

The aeronaut briefly weighed the hand the rector had offered him, then discarded it as if it suited no purpose of his.

— And may I say that it is with considerable interest and a sense of profound pride that I...that we all...have read of your wonderful experiments over these last several years. The newspapers —

— You may or may not, as you please.

— We read that you anticipate...

— Extraordinary things.

This in the same impatient, haughty tone, lips pursed, as if his nostrils burned with the saltpeter whiff of priestcraft. But Father de St. Malo saw something kindle in the aeronaut's eyes at the thought of the outlandish things he and his assistants were verging upon, in his laboratories in the wolds of Lincolnshire.

— Is it true, said Father Dowd, can it really be true, Sir Thomas, that you believe that it will one day be possible for men to travel to the moon?

Sir Thomas did not look at Father Dowd.

— Father, he said to the rector, I have not come four thousand miles to satisfy the idle curiosity of...of anyone. I am here as a private citizen, on personal business.

He gestured up to the windows of the dormitory. They were startling devices, his hands: large, long-fingered, smooth and nimble, with an unnerving suggestion of self-sentience.

— I wish to see my nephews and then be on our way. We spotted heavy weather off Biloxi. My weatherman believes it to be headed this way. I should like to avoid it if I can.

— You do not plan to pass even one night...

— Indeed I do not.

— But sir, Mrs. Drake...

— Naturally I intend to visit my sister before I leave New Orleans. Though I confess I fail to see that whether I do so or not is any affair of yours. Father.

— Sir Thomas. I regret that I must inform you. Mrs. Drake is dead.

Father de St. Malo turned to his secretary as if to have him confirm this information or to solicit further details, though the provost of the Hôtel-Dieu, Dr. Legac, was a boyhood friend. The rector knew as much as anyone about the death, that morning, of the traitor Cuyahoga Drake's wife.

— She suffered ... she underwent a stroke, Sir Thomas. I am told that her end was swift and painless.

— Swift, perhaps, Sir Thomas said. Not painless. Oh, surely not.

— You have condolences of this house, sir, of the city, and of the whole Empire, I am sure.

Sir Thomas nodded. He took a handkerchief from his vest and dabbed at the corners of his eyes. Then he put the handkerchief away.

— Now I have less reason to tarry in this place than I had five minutes ago, he said.

He consulted his pocket watch, gold, fat as a biscuit, inscribed with tendrils and leaves that entwined the initials V. R.

— The storm may be here in an hour, he said, snapping the watch case shut. Time is short.

— I don't understand.

— It isn't necessary that you do.

— Do you not wish to see — ? The, that is ... the remains? And the arrangements, do you no t —

— The arrangements have already been made. I made them by wire before I sailed from England, when it was made known to me that my sister might not survive.

— I see, the rector said. I suppose your work with engines has schooled you to be thorough in your plans.

— You satirize me.

— Not at all, I merely observe....

— You exhibit considerable interest in my affairs, Father. I take it that when I leave New Orleans, you will be careful to report each of my least little actions and statements to the gossips of the town.

— You do me great injustice, Sir Thomas.

— When you do so, Father, make sure you do not fail to report my wishes for the disposition of the second set of remains.

— The second ...?

— Say that I wish that the body of Henry Hudson Drake be strung up as food for kites and buzzards, and that crows peck out his eyes.

He took out his handkerchief again, and dabbed a fleck of saliva from his lips.

— Sir Thomas.

— Will you not take that down, Father? Will you not forget?

— No, sir.

— Don't misquote me.

— I will not.

— Good, Sir Thomas said, turning toward the door. Now, take me to the boys.

7.

There was a fat white boy named Zebedee who sat on your head and broke wind into your mouth and nostrils, and a black boy named Hob Pistorus, all of whose modicum of unreasoning love was lavished on the shiv he had crafted from an iron bedslat. It could flay a live pig before the squeal was out the mouth, as he liked endlessly to repeat. Some of the so-called boys had rasp chins and hairy loins and were mean as Ohio keelmen. They drank themselves blind on cloudy stuff concocted from rainwater and sawdust, and boasted of having poisoned the predecessor of Father Dowd with rat bait. To the boys of St. Ignatius, Her Majesty the Queen-Empress was a fat, ancient she-toad who gaped from the wall with Jesus and Loyola as Father de Tant-Malodeur laid a whistling switch across their backs; her Empire was nothing more to them than the back of a constable's hand, the gates of the debtor's prison, the news that your father had succumbed to cholera with his entire troop in a cantonment on the Red River. Nonetheless the boys used the excuse of her betrayal by Cuyahoga Drake to plague the disgraced man's sons with taunts, blows, and wretched tricks, and with constant allusions, enigmatic and stark, to ropes, neck bones, hangman's hoods. Falling asleep at night, if it were not to be a fatal error, must be a work of forbearance and discipline; Jeff learned to distinguish and await the several snores and the varied nocturnal mutterings of every one of the twelve other boys who were locked into C Ward with him and Frank each night. After an early bad surprise from Zebedee Louch, Jeff schooled himself to tell the pattern of that boy's imitation snore from the more erratic trend of his real one. And yet if Jeff had been on his own — If it had been either one of the Drake boys left alone with the toughs, cranks, and arabs of St. Ignatius — he might have suffered a much harder fate than, as befell Frank, encountering with the ball of his naked foot the soft dead rat that someone had placed in his boot or, in Jeff's case, dwelling for an unbearable minute in the hot stench of Zebedee Louch's crotch. Each brother scouted the other's perimeters, stood picket on the other boy's flank, kept vigil, whistling outside the shit-house, as the other underwent his lonely tribulations in the sweltering hell of the jakes. They had been assigned to bunks at opposite ends of C Ward, but every night, as soon as the porter snuffed the lamps, Frank would make his way down the long row of iron bedsteads and climb in to lie, tensed, listening to the darkness, alongside Jeff. This was an infraction punishable by a jaunt on the strapping horse. Frank was obliged to rouse himself every morning before light showed in the sky, and creep back in the half-light to his own bare bunk.

The brothers felt themselves and their behavior scrutinized by the priests with a greater than usual degree of intensity, and to the extent that they attempted to baffle or elude inspection they might well have been pleased had they known that the weekly reports on their conduct sent by the Fathers of St. Ignatius to the military tribunal at Sulla were replete with puzzled apologies. Though their conversations were indeed diligently monitored, both by the priests and by Hob Pistorus, the usually reliable C Ward telltale, neither of the Drake whelps was ever heard to make reference — not once — to their parents, let alone to any other conspirator, putative accomplice, or hitherto unknown plan of the mutineers. This all-but-inhuman regimen of silence was broken only on Monday mornings at nine, as if according to some privately evolved protocol on the treatment due prisoners of war, when the older brother would appear before Father de St. Malo, shoulders back, head high, and make what he termed a formal petition that he and his co-captive be permitted to visit their mother in hospital, a request that each week, for a different arbitrary reason, was always denied. Beyond this weekly ceremony, however, it was as if the fate and disposition of their imprisoned and ailing parents meant nothing to them at all.

It was Jeff who had recalled reading, in the *Boys' Own Paper*, a ripping yarn, set in the time of Vortigern and Boadicea, in which shadowy druids spoke without speaking by means of a manual alphabet; it was Frank who had diagrammed their hands, assigning four letters to the tip, phalanges, and base of the thumb, five to each of the fingers, and Y and Z to the pair of knobby hinges at the heel of the palm. By this cumbersome, intimate means, lying beside each other on Jeff's cot in the gray eternity of a night on C Ward, they communicated slow and feverish plans of escape, itemizing careful lists of necessary materiel, alternate routes, means of creating disruptions. With great difficulty they consolidated geographic information gleaned from other boys to sketch on the flats of their bellies a map of New Orleans, locating at the navel the Presbytère where their father languished and just under the left breast the mournful pile of the Hôtel-Dieu. Against the skin and bones of their hands the boys dwelt constantly, if never at great length, on the physical and emotional state of their mother, and speculated, with urgent jabs of their forefingers, on the chances of their father's obtaining, and the likelihood of his accepting, the mercy of the court-martial. They remembered what they could of the history of Raleigh's first acquittal, and attempted to derive a kind of grim comfort from the stoical grace with which earlier rebels of the frontier, Jackson and Crockett and Clay, had gone to their deaths. If the boys fell asleep too soon or too deeply, they knew, they would be set upon, and so each labored to keep the other awake, quizzing him on the colors and orders of Imperial regiments; the stages, battles, and commanders of the great Yukon and Ohio campaigns; the names of dogs and horses their family had owned over the years; the genealogies of Morddens, MacAndrews, Evanses, and Drakes as far back as either could stretch them. They spoke and fretted and argued far into the stillness of the morning. They lay together on Jeff's narrow cot, holding hands.

On the day when the dogfish shadow came snuffling over the housetops of the Vieux Carré, the Drake boys took the extreme liberty of appearing for morning inspection as they had slept, side by side, sitting on the younger boy's bunk. This was grounds for caning but on this awful morning they sensed that for once they might be excused and if not then rules be damned and it would suit them to be caned. They had dressed themselves in the cadet's uniform and the broadcloth suit, laundered by Jeff and patched by Frank, in which the troop of Cajun Fusiliers had first dragged them onto the ward. Drawers, comb, stockings, and two suits of gray shoddy provided by the home lay rolled with regimental precision into a worn duffel on the floor.

The bolt was thrown back and the door to C Ward swung open. The brothers' gazes remained fixed on the tall windows opposite the younger boy's bunk. These windows overlooked the rector's garden but years of salt breeze and soot and some inherent light-denying property of the glass precluded a view of anything but an ashy residue of the morning. Frank sat perfectly still; Jeff swung his skinny legs back and forth, making a swishing sound with the tips of his boots against the rough canvas top of the duffel.

— Franklin, Jefferson, said the rector. Sir Thomas is here.

Jeff started to look toward the doorway but felt or rather struck against his brother's inertness, the inflexibility of his gaze on that impenetrable gray window. He stopped kicking at the duffel and just sat.

— He has come all the way from England to fetch you. That is far more than either of you deserves.

One of the boys snickered and Jeff could feel the steady hard examining stares of the others. The two men came down between the ranks of cots and stood before them. The black bulk of the uncle eclipsed the gray windows. His watch chain dangled before Jeff's eyes. Frank had met the uncle a few times before, at Tir-Na-Nog, but Jeff only once, and that when Jeff was an infant in a dress. Frank said that their father and the uncle had quarreled, then, over the murder of John Brown by the Kansas Separatists. They had come to blows, and parted with rancor and finality.

— Nephews. It is hard to be so ill-met after so long a separation.

Jeff's right hand crept across the blanket of the bunk and sought the fingers of his brother's left. They felt rough and cool and dry.

— Well, the rector demanded, have you nothing to say?

Have you? Jeff worked the words with his fingers against Frank's.

Not to a Tory bastard like him.

— Well? said the rector again.

Jeff looked up into the bony florid face of his mother's brother. The eyes were grave and held pity and fatigue. The lower lip of the mouth was like their mother's, full and sorrowing. The sight of it, the memory of her, of his failure to kiss her that night in the coach, filled Jeff with an obscure anger.

— God save the Ohio Rebellion! he cried.

The boys of C Ward whistled and hooted and crowed. There was the whiz of a hornet at Jeff's ear and then its sting. Jeff pitched forward and the hand he slapped to his temple came away shining with blood.

— Good heavens, the rector said.

The uncle caught hold of Jeff with his left hand, by the shoulder, and set him back upright on the bed, keeping a tight grip on him. He held out his big right hand, closed in a fist. The pale eyes were pink-rimmed, their whites stained yellow as if from exposure to some poisonous reagent or fumes.

— God save you, my boy, he said.

He opened the great white anemone of his hand, palm upward, revealing a smooth red stone.

— I assure you, Sir Thomas, the boy who threw that shall be punished, the rector said. None of them will eat today until he comes forward or is named.

There was a groan from the boys, and then silence. The rector worked at the silence with his glare and the twitching of his jaw. It would not give.

A damp cloth and a wad of bandage were found and applied to the jutting bone behind Jeff's ear, and then the uncle applied a plaster. His ministrations were brusque but patient and in the care he took Jeff sensed or perhaps even remembered a vein of tenderness.

— On your feet, the uncle said, both of you.

They went out of C Ward for the last time, followed by the rector, and stood in the great echoing central stair. It seemed dark for this hour. Jeff looked up to the ceiling of the stairwell, where an iron-ribbed skylight generally let in a portion of the fair sky that mocked, or the foul one that suited, the unvarying gray weather of an orphan boy's day. It was filled with something that Jeff took at first to be the shadow of the bell tower but which then moved — floated — to one side and seemed, ever so slightly somehow, to ripple.

The uncle's hand lay heavy on Jeff's shoulder.

— Let those boys not, he said to the rector, be punished for a display of patriotism, Father. I do not desire punishment.

The rector nodded. Then the uncle pushed Frank and Jeff toward the stairs.

— Up, boys, he said. We must hurry.

— Up? said Jeff.

He dug in his heels, gazing in uneasiness at the rippling shadow that filled the skylight. In spite of the gentle attention his cut had received, he felt a violent spasm of mistrust for the uncle now. Perhaps they were to be pushed from the roof, or thrown to a crowd of ruffians, or consigned to some unknown oubliette in the bell tower, like the poor little princes he remembered from his *Lamb's Shakespeare*.

—We go up?

— Quite a considerable way, the uncle said. As a matter of fact.

8.

Though he was to observe and ship out in dozens of them during the course of his life and career — from the world-spanning, titanic *Admiral Tobakoff*, with its concert hall and natatorium, to the worlds-spanning *Lancet*, hardly bigger than a racing scull, from the trim trans-pacific racer *Gulf of Sinkiang* to the sturdy, homely freight blimps of the Red Star line — Frank would never entirely lose the sense of melancholy majesty that stirred his heart when he first saw an airship, moored in the troubled sky a hundred feet above the St. Ignatius Boys' Home. He was moved by her delicacy, by her massive silence, by the rich Britannic red of her silk gasbag. She was like a divot, bright as clay, cut into in the dull gray turf of the clouds. There was a wind in the southeast and she strained at the guy that moored her to the campanile, and once tossed her nose like a mare sniffing fire. An oblong car of silver and dark wood dangled from her underbelly, part Pullman sleeper, part clarinet, its windows haunted by dark mustached faces.

— The *Tir-Na-Nog*, Uncle Thomas said, as if she were a present he had brought along for his nephews. My own design.

He watched them watching his airship, pale eyes crinkling, face flushed. In the presence of the *Tir-Na-Nog* he seemed fonder of them; he draped his arms across their shoulders.

— There isn't another like her in the world.

A hatch opened in the forebelly of the black gleaming gondola. Two of the mustached lascars peered out. One raised an inquiring hand and the uncle nodded, and taking his arm from Frank's shoulders signaled, palm downward, twice. The blue-capped dark heads disappeared from the hatch and after a moment a large wicker basket dropped into sight and dangled, slowly falling.

Frank held his breath and pressed his lips together so hard they turned white. He suffered, with erotic intensity, from the signal passion of his age: engineering. He reverenced the men on whom was shed the peculiar glory of the second half of the century, when adventure went forth with gearbox, calipers, level, and chain. Thus he was mad to know the organization and capacity of the *Tir-Na-Nog*'s engines. He would gladly have indentured himself, for long years, to studying the system of cable, flap, and rudder that guided her, the science and finesse that regulation of her buoyancy and altitude required. He longed to subject his uncle to a close and niggling interrogation, as they had used to do on long July afternoons at Tir-Na-Nog, to draw fabulous facts and anecdotes out of Sir Thomas Mordden, pioneering aeronaut, penetrator of the trackless bush of the sky, deliverer, as the *Illustrated London News* had once phrased it, "of the key to making Britain the queen not merely of the land and sea but of all the vast empyrean girdle of the earth." But gazing up at the wondrous contraption in the sky in which, most wondrous of all, he was now evidently to take ship, Frank maintained a silence as absolute as that of the *Tir-Na-Nog* herself. Their uncle invited them to marvel; Frank refused. He wanted, if momentarily, then with all his heart, to see their uncle punished. Frank knew that this was unjust of him, that his uncle could not be held responsible for things that had transpired and decisions taken while he was sequestered with his assistants in the famous Mordden Laboratories. Frank knew that in holding his tongue he was only punishing himself.

— Is that the one you flew in to Africa? Jeff said.

— No, I fear the *Livingston* was destroyed upon my arrival there, Uncle Thomas said. He smiled. Hacked to bits by the Mtabebe.

— Can we fly all the way to England in that? Without even stopping? How high will we go?

Frank applied a furtive knee to his brother's bottom, hard. Jeff crumpled and then turned his traitor's gaze to Frank. For an instant he looked angry, but the reproach in Frank's eyes banked his fire and he rubbed at his backside with a sheepish air.

— We ain't going anywhere, Frank said.

The basket scraped the tiled cornice, bounced against the galvanized tin of the roof, and settled. Uncle Thomas took hold of Jeff under the arms, and hoisted him over the side of the basket. Frank stood, fighting against the longing to fly. He would not abandon his mother. He would ensure that there remained at least one man in New Orleans, in the Louisiana Territory, in all the vast Crown Colony of Columbia, to mourn the death of Cuyahoga Drake.

— We shall make London easily, my boy, Uncle Thomas said, as if to Jeff. We could make it as far as Istanbul. The Mordden Mark III is a dreadfully efficient engine.

He looked at Frank, fixedly, his womanly mouth curled at one corner, as if reading the hunger to know that underlay his nephew's stoical demeanor. He scattered specifications like crumbs to a reticent deer.

— There are a pair of them, he said. Four-cylinder compound engines. Vertical coil, parallel-flow flash boiler. Firebox above the boiler coils. Honeycomb condenser with vacuum pumps and complete automatic firing. One hundred and twenty horsepower apiece.

There was a burst of drum clatter from the yard of the old Presbytère, a workman's ragged laugh. Jeff reached for Frank's hand, but Frank would not take it. He did not want his brother distracting him with useless tappings at his palm.

— You won't be abandoning her, Franklin, their uncle said. There is no way that you could.

Frank caught his breath. The laughter of the workmen in the jailyard became general and merry. Down in the workshops of St. Ignatius he could hear the chiming hammers of a coffin being nailed.

— My poor boy, Sir Thomas said. You must accept that I am all the family you have left.

— That's a lie!

— Come aboard the *Tir-Na-Nog*, Frank. One day we shall sail her straight to the moon. To Venus or Mars.

Frank craned his head to try to catch a glimpse of the pale Presbytère; he envisioned his father waving from one of its stone window ledges, putting on a jaunty smile, saluting him. But all he could see was the high bell tower of St. Ignatius, part of a spike-topped stone wall, a rounded stucco corner of the prison, a dusty brown patch of tamped earth in the prison yard, a pair of colored workmen leaning on the handles of two pickaxes.

— Stay if you will, then, his uncle said curtly. He gave a signal, and with a jerk the basket rose off the pitted zinc of the roof.

— Frank!

Jeff threw himself against the side of the basket and tried to climb out, wild, in tears for the first time since the night of Custer's surrender. He managed to get one leg over the side. Sir Thomas caught him by the collar and hauled him back in.

— Frank!

Frank remembered the promise he had made to his father; surely to have broken it would be the greater abandonment.

The basket dragged, skipping, along the roof, and snagged against the cornice. In the instant before it would have freed itself and started upward, Frank crossed the roof and threw himself headlong into it, landing in a heap at his uncle's feet. He stood up, steadying himself. He wiped his hands against the knees of his patched cadet's uniform, and looked levelly at his uncle.

— You're a liar, he said. There is no atmosphere in interplanetary space.

Then he could see the bare tree, the scaffold, the platform with its neat square trapdoor. Sir Thomas gathered Jeff into his arms, and covered his face, hooding his eyes with his great hands.

— We're all liars, Franklin, he said. We lie, and then we wait and hope for time and hard work and the will of God to make us honest men.

They bumped up through the hatch of the *Tir-Na-Nog*, into the dark innards of her gondola. Strong arms hauled them from the basket. They were set on their feet in a bright room, trimmed in brass, paneled all around with windows and the glass faces of gauges.

Sir Thomas Mordden took a yachtsman's cap and settled it onto his head.

— London, sah? said the helmsman.

The captain of the *Tir-Na-Nog* nodded, his smile wistful and aimed curiously at his nephews. He might have been picturing them alighting, one day, on the dark red sand of Mars.

— At present, he said. Yes, London will do for now.

Victoria

PAUL DI FILIPPO

Steampunk never met a more eccentric or gifted practitioner of the sub-genre than Paul Di Filippo, whose heightened sense of invention is at fever-pitch in this comedy of errors and mistaken identity. Add in newt-based life, lots of sex, and you have a bawdy, rollicking tale of Queen Victoria as you've never seen her before. We took this story from his highly rec-ommended *Steampunk Trilogy*, considered a classic of second-generation steampunk.

> "I was tired, so I slipped away."
> — *Queen Victoria, in her private journal*

1

POLITICS AT MIDNIGHT

A rod of burnished copper, affixed by a laboratory vise-grip, rose from the corner of the claw-footed desk, which was topped with the finest Moroccan leather. At the height of fifteen inches the rod terminated in a gimbaled joint which allowed a second extension full freedom of movement in nearly a complete sphere of space. A third length of rod, mated to the first two with a second joint, ended in a fitting shaped to accommodate a writer's grip: four finger grooves and a thumb recess. Projecting from this fitting was a fountain-pen nib.

The flickering, hissing gas lights of the comfortable, secluded pic-ture-hung study gleamed along the length of this contraption, giving the mechanism a lambent, buttery glow. Beyond rich draperies adorn-ing the large study windows, a hint of cholera-laden London fog could be detected, thick swirls coiling and looping like Byzantine plots. The sad, lonely clopping of a brace of horses pulling the final late omnibus of the Wimbledon, Merton and Tooting line dimly penetrated the study, reinforcing its sense of pleasant seclusion from the world.

Beneath the nib at the end of its long arm of rods was a canted pallet. The pallet rode on an intricate system of toothed tracks mounted atop the desk, and was advanced by a hand-crank on the left. A roll of paper protruded from cast-iron brackets at the head of the pallet. The paper, coming down over the writing surface, was taken up by a roller at the bottom of the pallet. This roller was also activated by the hand-crank, in synchrony with the movement of the pallet across the desk.

In the knee-well of the large desk was a multi-gallon glass jug full of ink, resting on the floor. From the top of the stoppered jug rose an India-rubber hose, which traveled upward into the brass tubing and thence to the nib. A foot-activated pump forced the ink out of the bottle and into the system at an appropriate rate.

Fitted into the center of this elaborate writing mechanism was the ingenious and eccentric engine that drove it.

Cosmo Cowperthwait.

Cowperthwait was a thin young gentleman with a ruddy complexion and sandy hair, a mere twenty-five years old. He was dressed in finery that bespoke a comfortable income. Paisley plastron cravat, embroidered waistcoat, trig trousers.

Pulling a large turnip-watch from his waistcoat pocket, Cowperthwait adjusted its setting to agree with the 11:45 passage of the Tooting omnibus. Restoring the watch to its pocket, he tugged down the Naturopathic corset he wore next to his skin. The bulky garment, with its many sewn-in herbal lozenges, had a tendency to ride up from his midriff to just under his armpits.

Now Cowperthwait's somewhat moony face fell into an expression of complete absorption, as he composed his thoughts prior to transcribing them. Right hand holding the pen at the end of its long arm, left hand gripping the crank, right foot ready to activate the pump, Cowperthwait sought to master the complex emotions attendant upon the latest visit to his Victoria.

Finally he seemed to have sufficiently arrayed his cogitations. Lowering his head, he plunged into his composition. The crank spun, the pump sucked, the pallet inched crabwise across the desk along an algebraic path resembling the Pearl of Sluze, the arm swung to and fro, the paper traveled below the nib, and the ink flowed out into words.

Only by means of this fantastic machinery — which he had been forced to contrive himself — was Cowperthwait able to keep up with the wonted speedy pace of his feverish naturalist's brain.

May 29, 1838

V. seems happy in her new home, insofar as I am able to ascertain from her limited — albeit hauntingly attractive — physiognomy and guttural vocables. I am assured by Madame de Mallet that she is not being abused, in terms of the frequency of her male visitors, nor in the nature of their individual attentions. (There are other dolly-mops there, more practiced and hardened than my poor V., to whom old de Mallet is careful to conduct the more, shall we say, demanding patrons.) In fact, the pitiable thing seems to thrive on the physical attention. She certainly appeared robust and hearty when I checked in on her today, with a fine slick epidermis that seems to draw one's fascinated touch. (Madame de Mallet appears to be following my instructions to the letter, regarding the necessity for keeping V.'s skin continually moist. There was a large atomizer of French manufacture within easy reach, which V. understood how to use.)

Taking her pulse, I was again astonished at the fragility of her bones. As I bent over her, she laid one hand with those long thin flexible, slightly webbed digits across my brow, and I nearly swooned.

It is for the best, I again acknowledged to myself, to have her out of the house. Best for her, and above all, best for me and the equilibrium of my nerves, not to mention my bodily constitution.

As for her diet, there is now established a steady relationship with a throng of local urchins who, for tuppence apiece daily, are willing to trap the requisite insects. I have also taught them how to skim larval masses from the many pestilential pools of standing water scattered throughout the poorer sections of the city. The boys' pay is taken from V.'s earnings, although I let it be known that, should her patronage ever slacken, there would be no question of my meeting the expenses connected with her maintenance.

It seems a shame that my experiments had to end in this manner. I had, of course, no way of knowing that the carnal appetites of the Hellbender would prove so insusceptible to restraint, nor her mind so unamenable to education. I feel a transcendent guilt in having ever brought into this world such a monster of nature. My only hope now is that her life will not be overly prolonged. Although as to the proper lifespan of her smaller kin, I am in doubt, as the authorities differ considerably.

God above! First my parents' demise, and now this, both horrible incidents traceable directly to my lamentable scientific dabblings. Can it be that my honest desire to improve the lot of mankind is in reality only a kind of doomed hubris...?

Cowperthwait laid his head down on the pallet and began quietly to sob. He did not often indulge in such self-pity, but the late hour and the events of the day had combined to unman his usual stern scientific stoicism.

His temporary descent into grief was interrupted by a peremptory knock on his study door. Cowperthwait's attitude altered. He sat up and answered the interruption with manifest irritation.

"Yes, yes, Nails, just come in."

The door opened and Cowperthwait's manservant entered.

Nails McGroaty — expatriate American who boasted a personal history out of which a whole mythology could have been composed — was the general factotum of the Cowperthwait household. Stabler, trap-driver, butler, groundskeeper, chef, bodyguard — McGroaty fulfilled all these functions and more, carrying them out with admirable expedience and utility, albeit in a roughshod manner.

Cowperthwait now saw upon McGroaty's face as he stood in the doorway an expression of unusual reverence. The man rubbed his stubbled jaw nervously with one hand before speaking.

"It's a visitor for you, ol' toff."

"At this unholy hour? Has he a card?"

McGroaty advanced and handed over a pasteboard.

Cowperthwait could hardly believe his eyes. The token announced William Lamb, Second Viscount Melbourne.

The Prime Minister. And, if the scandalous gossip currently burning up London could be credited, the lover of England's pretty nineteen-year-old Queen, on the throne just this past year. At this particular point in time, he was perhaps the most powerful man in the Empire.

"Did he say what he wanted?"

"Nope."

"Well, for Linnaeus's sake, don't just stand there, show him in."

McGroaty made to do so. At the door, he paused.

"I done et supper a dog's age ago already, figgerin' as how you wouldn't take kindly to bein' disturbed. But I left some for you. It's an eel-pie. Not as tasty as what I could've cobbled up if'n I had some fresh rattler, but not half bad."

Then he was gone. Cowperthwait shook his head with amusement. The man was hardly civilized. But loyal as a dog.

In a moment, Viscount Melbourne, Prime Minister of an Empire that stretched nearly around the globe, from Vancouver to Hyderabad, stood shaking hands with a baffled Cowperthwait.

At age fifty-nine, Melbourne was still possessed of dazzling good looks. Among those numerous women whose company he enjoyed, his eyes and the set of his head were particularly admired. His social talents were exceptional, his wit odd and mordant.

Despite all these virtues and his worldly successes, Melbourne was not a happy man. In fact, Cowperthwait was immediately struck by the famous Melbourne Melancholia. He knew the source well enough, as did all of London.

Against the wishes of his family, Melbourne had married the lovely, eccentric and willful Lady Caroline Ponsonby, only daughter of Lady Bessborough. Having made herself a public scandal by her unrequited passion for the rake and poet, George Gordon, Lord Byron (to whom she had ironically been introduced by none other than her own mother-in-law, Elizabeth Lamb), she had ultimately provoked Melbourne to the inevitable separation, despite his legendary patience, forbearance and forgiveness. Thereafter, Lady Caroline became so excitable as to be insane, dying ten years ago in 1828. Their son Augustus, an only child, proved feeble-minded and died a year later.

As if this recent scandal were not enough, Melbourne still had to contend against persistent decades-old rumors that his father had in reality been someone other than the First Viscount Melbourne, and hence the son held his title unjustifiably.

Enough tragedy for a lifetime. And yet, Cowperthwait sensed, Melbourne stood on the edge of yet further setbacks, perhaps personal, perhaps political, perhaps a mix of both.

"Please, Prime Minister, won't you take a seat?"

Melbourne pulled up a baize-bottomed chair and wearily sat.

"Between us two, Mister Cowperthwait, with the information I am about to share, there must be as little formality as possible. Therefore, I entreat you to call me William, and I shall call you Cosmo. After all, I knew your father casually, and honored his accomplishments for our country. It's not as if we were total strangers, you and I, separated by a huge social gap."

Cowperthwait's head was spinning. He had no notion of why the P.M. was here, or what he could possibly be about to impart. "By all means — William. Would you care for something to drink?"

"Yes, I think I would."

Cowperthwait gratefully took the occasion to rise and compose his demeanor. He advanced to a speaking tube protruding from a brass panel set into the wall. He pulled several ivory-handled knobs labeled with various rooms of the house until a bell rang at his end, signaling that McGroaty had been contacted. The last knob pulled had been labeled PRIVY.

The squeaky distant voice of the manservant emerged from the tube. "What's up, Coz?"

Cowperthwait bit his tongue at this familiarity, repressing a justly merited rebuke. "Would you be so good as to bring us two shandygaffs, Nails."

"Comin' up, Guv."

McGroaty shortly appeared, bearing a tray with the drinks. A bone toothpick protruded from his lips and his shirttails were hanging out. He insouciantly deposited his burden and left.

After they had enjoyed a sip of their beer and ginger-beer mixed drinks, the Prime Minister began to speak.

"I believe, Cosmo, that you are, shall we say, the guardian of a creature known as Victoria, who now resides in a brothel run by Madame de Mallet."

Cowperthwait began to choke on his drink. Melbourne rose and patted his back until he recovered.

"How — how did you — ?"

"Oh, come now, Cosmo, surely you realize that de Mallet's is patronized by the *bon-ton*, and that your relationship to the creature could not fail to become public knowledge within a few days of her establishment there."

"I wasn't aware — "

"I must say," Melbourne continued, running a wet finger around the rim of his glass, thereby producing an annoying high-pitched whine, "that the creature provides a novel sensual experience. I thought I had experienced everything the act of copulation had to offer, but I was not prepared for your Victoria. Evidently, I am not alone in appreciating what I take to be her quite mindless skills. In just the past week, I've run into many figures of note at de Mallet's who were there expressly for her services. Those scribblers, Dickens and Tennyson. Louis Napoleon and the American Ambassador. Several of my own Cabinet, including some old buggers I thought totally celibate. Did you know that even that cerebral and artistic gent, John Ruskin, was there? Some friends of his had brought him. It was his first time, and they managed to convince him that all women were as hairless as your Victoria. I predict some trouble should he ever marry."

"I am not responsible — "

Melbourne ceased to toy with his glass. "Tell me — exactly what is she?"

Having no idea where Melbourne's talk was leading, Cowperthwait felt relieved to be asked for scientific information. "Credit it or not, William, Victoria is a newt."

"A newt? As in salamander?"

"Quite. To be precise, a Hellbender, *Cryptobranchus alleganiensis,* a species which flourishes in the New World."

"I take it she has been, ah, considerably modified...."

"Of course. In my work with native newts, I have succeeded, you see, in purifying what I refer to as a 'growth factor.' Distilled from the pituitary, thyroid and endocrine glands, it has the results you see. I decided to apply it to a Hellbender, since they normally attain a size of eighteen inches anyway, and managed to obtain several efts from an agent abroad."

"And yet she does not look merely like a gigantic newt. The breasts alone...."

"No, her looks are a result of an admixture of newt and human growth factors. Fresh cadavers — "

"Please, say no more. Although here in a semi-private capacity, I am still a representative of the law."

"It was my intention to test the depths of her intellect, and see if I could educate her. In the end, she proved lamentably intractable. Not wishing to destroy her, I had no choice other than de Mallet's."

"Why, if I may ask, did you name her Victoria? Was it a bad joke? Are you aware that in so doing you might have been guilty of *lèse-majesté?*

Cowperthwait was taken aback. "No, no, it was nothing of the sort. A chance resemblance to the new Queen, a desire to dedicate my scientific researches to her — "

Melbourne held up a hand. "I believe you. You need go no further."

There was silence in the study for a time. Then Melbourne spoke, apparently on an unrelated topic.

"When the Queen came to the throne a year ago, she was incredibly naive and unsophisticated. Not lacking a basic intelligence, she had been reared in a stifling and cloistered atmosphere by her mother, the Duchess of Kent. My God, all she could talk about was horses and tatting! She was totally tied to the apron strings of her conniving mother and the Duchess's Irish lover, John Conroy.

"I soon realized that, in her current condition, she would never do as the matriarch of our nation. It was up to me to form her personality along more regal lines, for the good of the Empire.

"I knew that the quickest way to do so involved becoming her lover.

"I will not bore you with the rest of my tactics. Suffice it to say that I believe I have succeeded in sharpening the Queen's wits and instincts, to the point where she will now make an admirable ruler, perhaps the greatest this sceptered isle has ever known."

"I fail to see — "

"Wait. There is more. I have steadily increased the Queen's work schedule, to the point where her day is taken up with reading dispatches and listening to her ministers. I thought she was bearing up admirably. However, I now fear I might have taken things too fast. The Duchess and Conroy have been bedeviling her lately with picayune demands. In addition, she has been nervous about her Coronation, scheduled for next month. Lately in bed together she has been complaining about feeling poorly and faint, miserable and nauseous. I'm afraid I brushed off these sentiments as idle vaporing."

"Surely you could let up a little on the poor girl...."

Melbourne passed a hand across his brow. "I fear it's too late for that.

"The Queen, you see, has just this day fled the throne."

Cowperthwait could scarcely give credence to his ears. "Impossible. Are you sure she has not been kidnapped, or injured while riding? A search party must be mounted — "

"No, it's useless. She's not lying senseless on some bridle trail somewhere, she's gone to ground like the cunning vixen she is. Certain personal items are missing, including her diary. To rouse a general search would only insure that her abdication became public knowledge in a few hours. And with political matters as they stand, Britain cannot afford even temporarily to be without a sovereign. Schleswig-Holstein, the Landgravine of Mecklenburg-Strelitz, the Spanish Succession — No, it's impossible that we advertise the disappearance. There are members of the nobility who would like nothing better than such a scandal. I am thinking particularly of Lord Chuting-Payne. And besides, I don't want Victoria to lose the throne. I have a conviction about that girl. I think she's going to make a splendid monarch. This adolescent impetuousness should not be held against her."

"Oh, I agree," said Cowperthwait heartily. "But why come to me? How can I help."

"I am asking you to contribute the services of your Victoria. I want her as a stand-in for the Queen, until the real Victoria can be found."

"That's ludicrous," expostulated Cowperthwait. "A newt sitting on the throne of England? Oh, I concede that with a wig, she might deceive from a distance. But up close — never! Why not just bring in another human woman, perhaps of low degree, who would impersonate the Queen and keep silent for a fee?"

"And run the risk of future blackmail, or perhaps of capricious misuse by the actress of her assumed position? No thank you, Cosmo. And despite what people say of me in connection with the Tolpuddle Martyrs, I am unwilling to have such a woman later assassinated to preserve the secret. No, I need a mannequin, someone utterly pliable. Only your Victoria fits the bill. Loan her to me, and I'll handle the rest."

"It's all so strange.... What can I say?"

"Simply say, 'yes,' and the nation and I will be forever in your debt."

"Well, if you put it that way — "

Melbourne shot to his feet. "Wonderful. You have no idea how relieved I am. Why, perhaps my Victoria, weary of playing commoner, might even now be on her way back to Buckingham Palace. But in the meantime, let us go secure your Victoria from her bed at de Mallet's. You understand that you'll have to fetch her, for I cannot be seen bringing her away."

"Oh, of course...."

Only when they were in the shuttered landau driven by McGroaty, rattling across the nighted town, with the womanly newt Victoria seated damply between them, a veil demurely drawn across her elongated features, did Cowperthwait think to tell Melbourne about the peculiar diet of his charge.

"Flies?" said the Prime Minister dubiously.

"Fresh," said Cowperthwait.

"I assume the stables —"

"I can see, sir," complimented Cowperthwait, "how you became Prime Minister."

2

A TRAIN STRAIGHT TO CHINA

The grandstand was draped with gay bunting in gold and blue. Local personages of note, politicians and members of the railroad corporation, sat in orderly rows on the wooden platform, the women in their full bombazine skirts protecting themselves from the summer sun with frilly parasols. A brass band played sprightly tunes. Birds trilled counterpoint from nearby branches. A crowd of farmers and merchants, their wives and children, filled the broad meadow around the grandstand. Peddlers hawked lemonade and candy, flowers and souvenir trinkets.

The place was the small village of Letchworth, north of London; the year, 1834, shortly after the passage of the Poor Law, which would transform the rural landscape, sequestering its beggars into institutions. The occasion was the inauguration of a new rail line, a spur off the London-Cambridge main.

A few yards from the grandstand lay the gleaming new rails, stretching off to the horizon. The stone foundation of the station, its brick superstructure only half-completed and surrounded by scaffolding, stood south of the scene.

On the rails — massive, proud, powerful — rested an engine of revolutionary design. Not far off nervously hovered its revolutionary designer, Cosmo Cowperthwait, age twenty-one.

Next to Cowperthwait stood a fellow only slightly older, but possessed of a much greater flair and obvious sense of self-confidence. This was the twenty-eight-year-old Isambard Kingdom Brunel, son of the famous architect and inventor, Marc Isambard Brunel, genius behind the Thames Tunnel, the first underwater construction to employ shield technology.

The association between the Cowperthwaits and the Brunels went back a generation.

Clive Cowperthwait, Cosmo's father, had been engaged to the lovely Constance Winks. Not long before their scheduled nuptials, at a ball thrown by the Royal Association of Engineers and Architects, Clive had chanced upon his fiancée in a compromising position with the elder Brunel, in a niche partially occupied by a bust of Archimedes. The offended man — doubly incensed by the joint desecration of both his bride-to-be and the ancient philosopher — had immediately issued a challenge to duel. Brunel had accepted.

However, in the interval between the challenge and the event, the two men had chanced to discover the mutuality of their interests. At first frostily, then more warmly, the men began to discourse on their shared vision of a world united by railroads and steamships, a world shrunken and neatly packaged by the magnificent inventions of their age. Soon, the duel was called off. Clive and Constance were married as planned. Marc Brunel became both Cowperthwait's business partner and frequent house guest, bringing his own wife and young son along. Upon Cosmo's birth, he and little Isambard Kingdom ("I.K.," or "Ikky") had been raised practically as brothers.

Now the young Cowperthwait turned to his companion and said, "Well, Ikky, what do you think? She's keeping up a full head of steam, with only a few ounces of fuel. Is it a miracle, or is it not? Stephenson's Rocket was nothing compared to this."

Ever practical, Ikky answered, "If this works, you're going to put an end to the entire coal-mining industry. I'd watch my back, lest it receive some disgruntled miner's dirty pickax. Or what's even more likely, the silver table-knife of a mine-owner."

Cosmo grew reflective. "I hadn't thought of that aspect of my discovery. Still, one can't retard progress. If I hadn't chanced upon the refinement of Klaproth's new metal, someone else surely would have."

In 1789, Martin Heinrich Klaproth had discovered a new element he named "uranium," after the recently discovered celestial body, Uranus. Other scientists, among them Eugene-Melchior Peligot, had set out to refine the pure substance. Cosmo Cowperthwait, inheritor of his father's skills, raised in an atmosphere of practical invention, had succeeded first, by reduction of uranium tetrachloride with potassium.

Casting about for new uses for this exciting element, Cosmo had hit upon harnessing its heat-generating properties to replace the conventional means of steam-production on one of his father's engines. Clive Cowperthwait had reluctantly acceded, and today saw the trial run of that modified engine.

"Come," said Cosmo, "let me instruct the engineer one last time."

The two youths clambered aboard the train. In the cab the crew welcomed them rather coldly. The chief engineer, an old fellow with walrus mustaches, nodded ceaselessly as Cosmo talked, but the young inventor felt he really was not paying attention.

"Now, remember, there is no stoking of this engine, or addition of fuel. Depressing this lever brings the two portions of uranium closer together, producing more heat, while pulling it out increases the distance and diminishes the heat. You'll note that this pin and cowling arrangement prevents the depression of the lever beyond the danger zone —"

Cosmo halted in alarm. "The cowling — it's split and ready to fall off. It seems a deliberate breach of all my safety precautions. Who's responsible for this malfeasance?"

The crew looked idly at the ceiling of the cab. One insolent superfluous stoker whistled an air Cosmo recognized as an indecent folk tune by the title "Champagne Charlie."

Cosmo realized it would be futile to attempt to assign guilt now. "Come with me, Ikky. We must fix this before the trial." The two descended the engine. Some distance away on the grandstand, Clive Cowperthwait had just kissed his wife and moved to the front of the podium to give his speech.

"I am sorry that my partner could not be here today, but I'm sure I can speak long enough for both of us...." There was mild laughter from the crowd.

Cosmo was in no mood to join in the gaiety of the spectators. "Where can I find some tools?" he demanded frantically of Ikky.

"How about the blacksmith's, back in town?"

"Good thinking. Let me tell Father to delay the start of the engine."

"Oh, let's just dash. You know how long your father speaks. We'll have plenty of time."

Cosmo and Ikky hurried toward the village.

While inside the blacksmith's they faintly heard the resumption of the music, which had ceased for Clive's speech. Cosmo and Ikky rushed outside in alarm.

At that instant an enormous explosion knocked them off their feet, shattering every window in the village. A hot wind rolled them along the ground. When they managed to regain their feet, they saw the remnants of a mushroom-shaped cloud towering high up into the sky.

With immense consternation, mixed with not a little trepidation, the pair of friends hastened back toward the site of the dedication.

Still many furlongs away, they encountered the rim of an immense smoking crater that sloped away into a glassy plain, the start of an excavation aimed at Asia.

Cosmo yelled into the desolate smoky waste. "Father! Mother!"

Ikky laid a hand on his arm. "It's plainly no use, Coz. There can't be anyone left alive there. They've all been blown to Jehovah by your invention. I read this as a mark of Providence, which even your father's usual loquacity could not forestall, signaling that the world is not ready for such knowledge, if it ever will be.... You may console yourself with the thought that it must have been a painless death, thank God. In any case, I venture to say we won't find enough mortal flinders to fill an umbrella-stand."

Cosmo was in a state of shock, and could not reply. (Later, his old friendship with Ikky would be forever somewhat strained, as he recalled Ikky's callousness in the light of such a disaster, for which, by any fair measure, he was partly culpable.)

Feeling for some reason that it would be unwise to linger at the scene of the disaster, Ikky dragged his friend away.

Back in London, after a period of a few days' insensibility, Cosmo, now sole heir to the Cowperthwait name, had gradually recovered his mental faculties. One of the first things he had noticed had been the appearance of strange sores on his body. Ikky turned out to be suffering from the same manifestation of their experience, as were the few surviving Letchworthians. With the help of a pharmacist, Cowperthwait had derived a Naturopathic remedy, which, kept continuously against the skin, seemed to stem the plague. (Four years later, the sores would be all but vanished, yet Cowperthwait continued to wear his Naturopathic garment, more out of extreme caution than any scientific reason.)

After attending to his own ills, Cowperthwait realized he must set about arranging a ceremonial funeral for his parents. He was ready to step forth from his home one day to visit a local undertaker. Opening his front door, he was shocked to encounter someone already standing there.

The fellow was on the shortish side of average height, wiry and eager-eyed, dressed in loose American style. He hailed Cowperthwait vigorously.

"Friend, I been observin' of you in your bereavement, as you wander stupefied and pole-axed about this here town, and I come to the conclusion that you are in need of some moral companionship and support. In short, a personal valet."

Cowperthwait knew not what to make of this character. "Are you from the undertaker's?"

"Better'n that, young fellow. I'm from the Yew-nited States of Goddamn America, and I can get anything done that you order."

In his confused and guilty condition, Cowperthwait latched on to this offer eagerly. "What—what's your name?"

"Nails McGroaty, if it please you, Chief. Hell, even if it don't. So-called since I am tougher than my namesake, and twice as sharp. Now you just put your affairs in my hands, and let your mind be at peace. We'll show this town a wake, funeral and reception the likes of which they ain't witnessed since ol' Henry the Eighth threw snake-eyes."

Cowperthwait made up his mind. McGroaty was hired on the spot.

True to his word, the brash American arranged a first-class *cortège* to honor Clive and Constance Cowperthwait. There was enough black crepe to cover Westminster Cathedral.

After this performance, Cowperthwait grew assured that McGroaty was indeed no confidence trickster but apparently just a man in need of a permanent position with a lenient employer. Cowperthwait, apparently, had fit the bill.

McGroaty carried out his new household duties with dispatch. So invaluably, in fact, had he acquitted himself on a hundred occasions since, that Cowperthwait felt him more an older, more worldly brother sometimes, than servant.

The man's selling points were not his personal appearance, nor his insouciant demeanor. McGroaty was flippant, wry and occasionally abusive — hardly the marks of a good servant. He affected a casual dress reminiscent of a frontiersman, a kind of roughneck dandyism. McGroaty neglected shaving, and had never been known to bathe — a failing somewhat mitigated by his liberal use of strong toilet-waters.

McGroaty was, as he liked to remind Cowperthwait at frequent intervals, "one hunnerd and ten per cent American." His colorful history made his master wonder how one nation, even large as it was, could hold millions of such individuals, granted the representative nature of McGroaty's past.

McGroaty claimed to have been with the Stephen Austin expedition into the territory of Texas. ("G.T.T.," or "Gone To Texas," was currently American slang for fleeing the law, and Cowperthwait wondered if such had been McGroaty's motives.) The man also maintained that he had been initiated into the Chickasaw tribe as a warrior, after saving the life of Chief Ikkemotubbe, and had willingly fought against his fellow whites who had sought to remove the tribe from their desirable lands in Mississippi. (A permanent weal on his buttocks, eagerly displayed to any chance female acquaintance, however reluctant she might be to view McGroaty's bare arse cheeks, was alleged to represent tribal scarification.) He bragged that he had been a mooncusser in New England, and would slyly exhibit, upon much cajoling, a small flat ingot of gold known as a "smuggler's bar," which fit neatly into his vest pocket.

Cowperthwait never learned what had made him seek permanent refuge in England, but suspected it was an illicit affair of titanic proportions.

All in all, a man of remarkable dimensions — the shortest of which was culture — and a companion Cowperthwait felt helped to offset his tendency toward dreaming abstraction.

Under McGroaty's stewardship, the years passed rather amiably. Ikky and his father ran the joint Cowperthwait-Brunel enterprises alone, insuring Cowperthwait, as absentee proprietor, of a guaranteed income and allowing him to indulge in his scientific investigations. Needless to say, he had lost all interest in further uranium-based transportation.

He had thought himself safe in turning his attentions to biological matters. What harm could come, after all, of experiments with tiny amphibians?

But woman-sized ones — Cowperthwait was beginning to suspect they were another matter altogether.

3
THE MAN WITH THE SILVER NOSE

In the days following the establishment of the false Victoria on the throne, as May shaded into June, Cowperthwait found himself disbelieving at times that he had ever experienced such a queer witching-hour visit from the Prime Minister, or that the product of his laboratory now sat in the regal seat reserved for the Hanoverian line. It seemed too much like a dream or nightmare born of a visit to one of the opium dens of Tiger Bay or Blue Gate Fields in the Old Port section of the city.

Yet such periods of doubt were dispelled by certain stern and irrefutable facts. The salamandrian Victoria was no longer at de Mallet's. The white velvet cushions in the landau were permanently stained. Dispatches detailing the unfolding of events arrived daily from Melbourne, hand-delivered in laminated and inlaid cases which normally contained official state documents. The functionaries who passed on these missives were members of the Queen's Messengers, those agents entrusted with the most privy of communications.

June 1
Still no trace of the veridical V. I have employed certain confidential agents with the story that they are searching for my illegitimate daughter. Naturally, their first step will be to comb all the most obvious hideyholes, including brothels like de Mallet's. Should they ultimately fail, I might have to bring in the Yard.

In the evenings, with pseudo-V. locked in her room, I search the teeming city myself; so far all to no avail.

Hopefully,
W. L.

June 3
Have kept contacts between V. and her ministers to a minimum. Let it be known that the Queen's "neuralgia" prevents her taking much interest in matters of state. All ceremonial duties are indefinitely postponed. Don't believe anyone suspects the imposture yet, tho' V. did eat an insect in public. I talked coolly right over the general consternation. The Ladies of the Chamber are hardest to put off. Many are the spies of Conroy and others. Have told them the Queen is experiencing an unusually difficult and prolonged menstrual period, and has armed herself with a pistol and threatened to shoot anyone who sees her naked, water-bloated form. The Ladies seemed one and all to comprehend. Yet how long can I believably prolong this...?
    Frantically,
    W. L.

June 5
Still no ray of light. Much of the time I might spend searching is taken up with satisfying V.'s predatory sexuality in order to keep her tractable. Her capacity is awesome. Find myself drained. Losing hope.
    Despairingly,
    W. L.

Cowperthwait read these missives with growing concern. All his experiments were pushed aside and forgotten. Even the eight-legged calves from Letchworth failed to sustain his attention. His mind was preoccupied with Melbourne's dilemma. The nation's dilemma, though the general populace was all unwitting. What would happen if the real Victoria were not found by the day of her Coronation? Would a newt be solemnly consecrated by the Archbishop of Canterbury as the Queen of England? It would be worse for England than the papacy of Pope Joan had been for the Romish Church.

And what of the awful travails the real Victoria must be undergoing? Here was a girl who had never in her short life even been allowed to ascend a staircase by herself, for fear she might stumble and fall. Now she was adrift in the urban squalor that was London. Cowperthwait could not rid his mind of a series of images of degradation and humiliation that were both disturbing and strangely exciting.

In the end the hallucinations threatened to rob him of his sleep, and he realized that he had to do something to rid himself of this excess of nervous humours. Science had temporarily lost its allure. There was nothing for it but to join the search for Victoria himself. Any other option would leave him feeling he hadn't done enough.

It would not do to tell Melbourne, however. The Prime Minister seemed somewise reluctant to further involve Cowperthwait, and the young inventor, as a loyal subject, was not willing to risk being told definitely not to contribute his help.

Thus it was that the nine-fold chiming of the tall time-piece in the hall one foggy evening found Cowperthwait, cape athwart his shoulders, standing indecisively at the door to his Mayfair residence.

Where should he begin to look? Where would a young girl on the run likely end up, here in this metropolis of sin and greed? Other than a brothel — and Melbourne had already had them all searched — Cowperthwait realized he hadn't the slightest idea.

Cowperthwait felt a hand on his shoulder and turned to confront Nails McGroaty. His manservant was dressed for the night chill with a stained bandanna knotted around his otherwise bare throat, and obviously intended to accompany Cowperthwait.

In confirmation McGroaty said, "Don't worry, Coz, it's all jake. I ain't lettin' you go out alone. I knows the whole dismal story, knowed it since that first night when I was a-listenin' at the study door. And though it don't matter nuthin' to me — your precious royalty bein' jest a bunch of whangdoodles to a born demmycratic American — I cain't stand by and let you expose yerself to all kinds of danger. You need a ripsnortin' bobcat sech as myself by yer side, when push comes to shove. As I says to Mike Fink when we was workin' on the same barge up and down the Big Muddy, 'Mike, there ain't nuthin' more important in life than friendship.' That was jest before I walloped the tar out of the mean bastard and tossed him overboard."

Cowperthwait felt vastly relieved, and showed it by warmly clasping McGroaty's hand. "Your noble offer is accepted, Nails. Let's go."

As they were leaving, Cowperthwait's eye fell on a Malacca cane protruding from the elephant's-foot umbrella-stand by the door, and he snatched it up.

"Just in case," he told McGroaty with a wink.

"Air you sure, Guv? You remember the last time — "

"I've fixed it since then."

"Suit yerself."

As they left behind the exclusive district where Cowperthwait maintained his household, the streets became more and more thronged with citizens of every stripe. Blind beggars, elegant ladies, coarse streetwalkers known as "motts," hurdy-gurdy operators, men with dancing bears, a fellow running a movable shooting-gallery where participants banged away with spring-loaded pellet guns at targets moved like Cowperthwait's writing pallet by a crank.... A fight broke out between two match-girls, and one knocked the other into a horse-trough. This was the least remarkable incident Cowperthwait and McGroaty witnessed.

When they reached Oxford Circus, McGroaty indicated that they were to cross the thoroughfare. Cowperthwait hesitated.

The actual streets of London were in many cases running sewers and rubbish bins. Offal and manure presented an obstacle ankle-deep. Springing up to capitalize on this phenomenon were the "crossing-sweeps," homeless boys and girls who, for a token payment, would brush a path across the street for a citizen. Seeing his master's hesitation to imbrue his footwear in the muck, McGroaty now moved to engage such a one.

"You there, ol' carrot-top! C'mon and clear us a path!"

The shoeless youth thus addressed hurried over. His clothes were in rags and he was missing several teeth, yet he flashed a broad smile and radiated a kind of innocent happiness. His one possession appeared to be a broom worn almost to its nubbin.

Doffing his cap, he said, "Tiptoft's the name, gents. Reasonable rates and swift service is me motto. Anytime you're in the neighborhood, ask for me."

Without further ado, the boy stepped squarely into the horrid slop with his bare feet and began to sweep industriously. Cowperthwait and McGroaty followed in his wake.

On the far side of the street Cowperthwait asked, "How much?"

"One penny apiece, if it's agreeable, gents."

Cowperthwait handed the lad a shilling.

The sweep was ecstatic with the over-payment. "Thank'ee, guv'nor, thank'ee! Won't I eat elegant tonight!"

Cowperthwait and McGroaty moved on. The inventor seemed touched by the incident, and at last chose to comment.

"Here you see an example of the trickle-down theory of material improvement, Nails. Thanks to the fruits of the Cowperthwait-Brunel enterprises, I am enabled to endow those less fortunate. A rising tide lifts all ships."

"I done heard that trickle-down stuff compared to a sparrow what gets whatever oats a horse shits out undigested."

"A crude and imprecise analogy, Nails. In any case, someday, thanks to science, the streets of London will be clean of organic wastes, and such poor urchins, if they exist at all, will be maintained by a wealthy and benevolent state."

"Ayup," was McGroaty's laconic comment.

Continuing their walk in silence for half an hour through the clammy streets — Victoria the Imposter would have no need of her atomizer in this weather — Cowperthwait finally thought to ask where they might be heading.

"Well," said McGroaty, "I figger ol' Horseapple is always needing people for the treadmills. Perhaps your little lady was press-ganged there."

Cowperthwait nodded sagely, although he was truly no further enlightened.

Through the cobbled dismal streets, past shabby forms slumped against splintered doors in shadowed entryways, ignoring the out-stretched hands and more lascivious solicitations of the ragged throng, Cowperthwait followed McGroaty. They seemed to be trending toward the Thames. Soon, Cowperthwait could contain himself no longer.

"Exactly where are we heading, Nails?"

"Horseapple's pumping station."

Soon the air was overlaid with the murky odors of the river that flowed through the city like a liquid dump. Water sloshed over nearby unseen weed-wrapped steps. Cowperthwait heard the muffled dip of oars, presumably from one of the aquatic scavengers who made their meager living by fishing from the river whatever obscure refuse they might encounter — not excluding human corpses.

A building loomed up out of the fetid air. Light leaked out of its shutters. A vague rumbling as of vast machinery at work emanated from the structure. McGroaty knocked in a mysterious fashion. While they waited for a response, the servant explained to Cowperthwait the nature of the enterprise run by his friend.

"Horseapple heard they was lookin' for someone to supply water to them new houses out in Belgravia. He greased a few palms with the old spondoolicks, and got the contract. He's been addin' customers right steady ever since. 'Course, every new client means more manpower's needed."

Cowperthwait was astonished. "They're drinking Thames water in Belgravia? Why, this stuff is positively pestilential."

"Oh, it ain't so bad as all that. Since they put the grates up on the intake pipes, nuthin' bigger'n a rat can get through."

The door opened and a belligerent poxed and bearded face thrust out. Squinting, the man recognized McGroaty.

"Come in, come in, Nails. Another volunteer for the treadmills, I take it. Does he need further persuasion?" Horseapple flourished a truncheon.

"Not this one, old man. It's my mate, Cosmo. He's lookin' for a lady friend of his, and thought she might be gracin' your establishment."

"Let him look then. But don't disturb their rhythm. It makes for bad water pressure and the toffs complain."

Horseapple conducted the visitors through some cobwebbed antechambers and into a dimly lit cavernous interior. The building must have been at one time a brewery or warehouse. Now, however, ranked across the quarter-acre or so of floorspace were five dozen wooden treadmills, all hooked by an elaborate system of gears, cams and shafts to a brace of huge pumps. The treadmills were manned by rag-clad wraiths chained to their stations. Whip-bearing overseers marched up and down, applying persuasion whenever a unit flagged.

Cowperthwait turned angrily to Horseapple. "My Christ, man, this is absolutely barbaric! A steam engine or two would easily outperform all these poor wretches."

Horseapple stroked his hirsute chin. "You're talking heavy capital investment now, Carmine. The bleedin' pumps cost me enough as it was. And besides, what would these poor buggers do with their free time? Just drink themselves silly and lie in the gutter. As it stands, they've got a roof over their head and three meals a day, albeit it's usually only whatever's fouling up the grates."

McGroaty laid a hand on Cowperthwait's shoulder. "No time for social reform now, Coz. We got an important lady to find."

So saying, the pair trooped up and down the ranks, looking for the missing Queen. For purposes of comparison, Cowperthwait carried a silhouette that had been published in the daily papers.

No luck. Horseapple invited them to check the sleeping off-shift laborers, which they quickly did, making all haste to escape the urinous and bedbug-ridden common dormitory.

Horseapple saw them to the door. "Remember, Nails — ten shillings a head. The way this city is growing, I'll be forced to double my operations in a year."

The door slammed behind them, and Cowperthwait stood motionless a moment, stunned and disheartened by the experience. With such pits and cesspools of inhumanity, how could he ever hope to imagine the Queen was still alive and unhurt, and able to be found? The task seemed hopeless....

McGroaty was whispering in Cowperthwait's ear. "Don't let on, but there's someone watchin' us. To your left, behind that pile of crates."

Cowperthwait slowly turned his head. A glint of light flashed off something silver.

"I'll handle this," Cowperthwait whispered back. He raised his cane. Then, in a loud voice: "Step forward and declare yourself, man!"

From the shadows emerged the form of a giant. A swarthy native of India, he appeared at least seven feet tall, although some of that height might have been attributable to his voluminous headwrap. Dressed in colorful silks, he bore a long scimitar by his side.

"Holy Andy Jackson!"

"Have no fear," declaimed Cowperthwait, his voice quavering. The inventor raised his cane and pressed a spring catch in its handle. The lower portion of the cane shot off, taking the concealed sword-blade with it and leaving Cowperthwait holding a stubby handle.

The two waited for the Indian to advance and decapitate them both with one mighty blow.

Instead, the thuggee was joined by another figure. The Man with The Silver Nose.

Lord Chuting-Payne.

In his late fifties, Chuting-Payne possessed the athletic build of an Olympian. Impeccably attired, the master of vast ancestral estates at Carking Fardels, he had once been deemed the most handsome man of his generation. That had been before the duel he had fought with Baron Leopold von Schindler of Austria.

One evening in the year 1798, the eighteen-year-old Chuting-Payne, only scion of his line, had been hosting a dinner for various ambassadors, in an attempt to further his political ambitions. Present had been his sovereign, the demented King George the Third. The Austrian Baron von Schindler, somewhat tipsy and of a fractious nature, had criticized with Teutonic wit Chuting-Payne's wine list in front of the royal guest of honor. Humiliated beyond tolerance, Chuting-Payne had immediately challenged von Schindler to pistols at twenty paces.

Von Schindler, revealing himself as coward and caitiff, had fired while Chuting-Payne was still turning, blowing off the man's nose.

Immense quantities of blood streaming down his face, Chuting-Payne had then calmly drilled von Schindler through the heart.

The jewelry firm of Rundell, Bridge & Rundell — the very makers of the new lightweight crown that was to be used in frail Victoria's upcoming Coronation — had been employed to melt down some family sterling and fashion a prosthetic silver nose to replace Chuting-Payne's missing flesh one. They had exerted all their skill, and the resulting simulacrum was a marvel to behold. Affixed by gutta-percha adhesive, the nose was said to be capable of exciting the most jaded of women.

But the attainment of a new nose was hardly the end of the affair. Pressed by the Austrians, King George had sworn out a warrant for Chuting-Payne's arrest. The man had been forced to flee the country. As the tale went, he had ended up in India, in the Province of Mysore, still an independent nation at the time. Turning his back on his own country, Chuting-Payne had allied himself with the Maharaja of Mysore, Tippoo Sahib, and his French backers against the British. He had lived in Mysore for a year, until it fell to a joint attack by British and Mahratta troops.

Escaping from the siege of Seringapatam, Chuting-Payne had then traveled among the other independent Indian nations — Sind, Rajputana, Punjab — until the death of George the Third in 1820. Somehow he had amassed a large enough fortune to bribe King George the Fourth to rescind the long-standing warrant against him. He had returned to his native land over a decade ago, a figure of enigmatic Oriental qualities, sunbrowned and distant, more wog than limey.

Having been mistreated by Victoria's ancestor, Chuting-Payne had conceived a stupendous hatred of their whole line. As Melbourne had intimated to Cowperthwait, the man would like nothing better than to involve the throne in any sort of scandal.

"Mister Cowperthwait, I believe," said the silver-nasaled nobleman, his voice imbued with queer resonances. "I don't think we've ever had the pleasure of meeting. My name I assume you know. Allow me to introduce my servant, Gunputty."

Gunputty bowed. Cowperthwait croaked out something. The bizarre pair completely unnerved him.

"What brings you so far from your retorts and alembics, Mister Cowperthwait? Looking for more amphibious subjects among the slime? By the way, where is your creation lately? I've noticed her absence from de Mallet's."

"She's — I've — that is — "

"No matter. She's not the only unique lady missing. Or so my spies report."

"I — I don't know what you mean...."

"Oh, really? I think differently. In fact, I believe we are both abroad in search of the same thing, Mister Cowperthwait. Lest the *hoi polloi* overhear, we'll just call her 'Vee' among ourselves, shall we?"

"You're — you're hallucinating."

"Far from it, Mister Cowperthwait. Although I must admit that your addlepated clodpoll of a servant, who appears the by-blow of a New World savage on a warthog, does resemble some of my less pleasant nightmares."

"Put up your dukes, Tinface, them's fightin' words."

Chuting-Payne snugged his white gloves for a more precise fit. "Tell your man, Cowperthwait, that the last fellow who engaged in fisti-cuffs with me is now so much wormsmeat, and that he would be well-advised to steer clear of his betters. Gunputty — fetch the carriage. Mister Cowperthwait, farewell for the nonce. I sense our paths will cross again."

In a moment Lord Chuting-Payne's phaeton was rumbling away. Cowperthwait felt his wits gradually returning, and was mortified that he had let Chuting-Payne treat himself and McGroaty in such a cava-lier fashion.

Seeming similarly embarrassed, McGroaty said, "I thought you said you done fixed that cane."

"It acted precisely as I wished," extemporized Cowperthwait. "Had it struck that lascar, it would have knocked him senseless."

"I suggest more diereck tactics in the future, Coz. That air Gunputty don't seem the type to be stymied by no flyin' baton."

"Suggestion acknowledged, Nails."

4
A WOMAN CALLED OTTO

Cowperthwait spread mint jelly across his scone. The transparent greenish substance reminded him of the egg mass of the Hellbender. He still recalled the shivery thrill he had felt upon receiving the crate from his American compatriot, S. J. Gould of Harvard, containing the glass vials packed with fresh Hellbender eggs, nestled snugly in wooden cradles set in sawdust and straw for their transatlantic journey. The many nights of feverish experimentation, the innumerable abortions and teratological nightmares which had to be destroyed, the refinements in technique and purification, all resulting in the unique miracle that was Victoria…. A wave of sadness and nostalgia crossed over him. Would he ever see his progeny again, or would she remain forever immured inside Buckingham Palace, a slave to the needs of the state?

The only solution lay in finding the real Victoria, a creature no less fabulous than her salamandrine counterpart. Where, oh where could she be? In the three days since their visit to Horseapple's, Cowperthwait had racked his brain for any likely burrow she might have found, all to no avail. Even at this moment, Cowperthwait had McGroaty out scouring the city for any possible clue, however wild and far-fetched.

A knock resounded on his study door. Cowperthwait tugged down his Naturopathic corset beneath his dressing gown, adjusted the silk scarf around his neck, and called out, "Yes, who is it?"

The door swung open and McGroaty entered, propelling a scurvy character before him. The fellow clutched a battered cap with both hands in front of him, high up on his chest. This position for his headgear was necessitated by his having a withered right arm only a few inches in length. In compensation, his whole left arm was an overdeveloped bulk of muscle.

"Coz, this here's Shortarm. He runs a sewing shop down in the Seven Dials. Shorty, tell the guv'nor what you told me."

Shortarm attempted to compose his features into a semblance of innocence, but succeeded only in looking like a fox with chicken feathers stuck to its lips. "Wurl, it's like this, see. I got me a daughter, a lurvely gell — "

"He fathered the poor thing on his older daughter, so you might say she's his granddaughter too," interrupted McGroaty.

Cowperthwait winced. "Yes, go on."

"Wurl, she's all of six, so's I figgered she was old enough to start earning her keep. Otherwise, she was gonna find herself eatin' air pie, if you get my meanin'. So I puts her to work in the shop, stitchin' up breeches — "

This time it was Cowperthwait who interrupted. "You know, of course, that in so doing you were in direct violation of Lord Althorp's Factory Act, regarding the employment of minors."

Shortarm wrinkled his brow in genuine bafflement. "Can't say as how I ever heard of no Fackery Axe, sir. And she warn't doin' no minin' of any sort."

Cowperthwait sighed. "Pray, continue."

"Wurl. One evenin' aroun' seven, just as the gells was finishin' their day by receivin' their nightly strappado, in busts these two wimmen. One's an older lady with the pinchy face of a do-gooder, so's I know I'm in for trouble right away. The other 'peared to be much younger, but I couldn't be sure, for she had a veil 'crost her face. And not no lacey thing either, but a piece of muslin with eye-holes in it.

"Next thing I knows, the older bitch — parm me, sir, lady — had me good arm what was holdin' the whip doubled up behind me back, fit to snap. Gord, she was a strong un!

"'Sisters,' she says, 'I'm a-here to offer any of you what wants it sanctuary at my school. Which of you will come with me?' Next thing I knows, all my gells is hollerin' and shoutin', 'Me, me, I'll go, take me!' Even me own two daughters joined in the tragic chorus."

Shortarm paused to sniffle and wipe a tear away. "I can tell you, guv'nor, it hurt me deep inside. To think of all the attention and money and high-quality whittles I done lavished on those gells, and then to have 'em turn on me like that. It cut me to the quick."

"Nails, I fail to see what any of this has to do with our search...."

"Hold on, Coz, it's comin.'" McGroaty prodded Shortarm, who resumed his tale.

"The elder gell turns to the one in the veil then and says, 'Vicky, escort the wimmen to the carriages.' When my shop is empty, she boots me headfirst against the wall. I didn't wake up for half an hour, and there was no way of tracin' 'em by then."

A thrill had shot along Cowperthwait's nerves at the name of the assistant rescuer. Trying not to betray his eagerness, he fumbled in his purse to reward the sweatshop owner, coming up with a five-pound note.

"Gord, a fiver! Thank'ee kindly, sir. This'll be more'n enough to replenish my workforce, so to speak." Shortarm turned to leave, then halted. "Oh, if you find my daughters, you're a-welcome to the older one. She's kinder used up. But as for the younger—" Shortarm smacked his lips obscenely.

Cowperthwait shot to his feet. "Nails, eject this brute before I give him a good thrashing!"

McGroaty picked up Shortarm by his trousers and shirt. "Them's the words I been waitin' to hear, Coz!"

When McGroaty returned from tossing Shortarm out, Cowperthwait was pacing his study, rubbing his hands together. He stopped and grabbed McGroaty by the arm.

"Nails, it all makes sense! The Queen, frustrated by the glacial pace of her government and her remoteness from her subjects, has joined forces with a private benefactress, and now seeks to remedy the ills of her empire firsthand! It's a noble attempt and speaks well of her character, but we must find her and persuade her that she can do more good from her throne."

McGroaty rubbed his whiskery chin thoughtfully. "Ackshully, Coz, it shouldn't be too hard. I can't imagine any sech school as can house dozens of gals can remain much of a secret from its neighbors."

"Precisely, Nails. Let us begin our enquiries."

By that very afternoon McGroaty's inspired ferreting had met with success. Cowperthwait clutched in his clammy hand a pasteboard bearing a name and address in nearby Kensington:

LADY OTTOLINE CORNWALL'S
LYCEUM AND GYNOCRATIC MISSION
NUMBER TWELVE NOTTING HILL GATE
EDUCATION, LIBERATION, VINDICATION
"SORORAE SE FACIUNT ID" — SAPPHO

Cowperthwait hurriedly snatched up a large maple cane from the stand by the door. "Come, Nails, let us be off while it is still light out."

McGroaty eyed the cane dubiously. "Is that a plain walkin' stick, or some new infernal device, Coz?"

Cowperthwait chuckled. "The latter, I fear, Nails. Observe." Cowperthwait opened a breach in the cane, revealing a large-caliber shell. "The trigger is here in the grip. I wager even a superhuman specimen like Gunputty will not be able to easily fend off a charge of this size."

"With any luck, we won't run into that towel-headed furriner at all today. Meanwhile, don't go a-pointin' that cane at no helpless merchant who wants a few pence extra fer his termaters, like you usually do."

The pair exited the Cowperthwait manse. There, on the sidewalk, they encountered a familiar face: the gap-smiled countenance of little Tiptoft, the crossing-sweeper.

"Hullo, kind sir. I seen your man scurryin' about the town and took the liberty of followin' him back here. This seems like a ritzy neighborhood with a lack of sweeperly competition. I shall reside here henceforth."

"God's wounds! You—you can't encamp outside my house like this. This is Mayfair, after all, not Covent Garden. What will the neighbors say?"

"Doubtless they will be forever in your debt, sir, for securing such an asset to clean-footed traffic."

To illustrate his utility, Tiptoft dashed out into the street and begin switching away at a huge pile of accumulated manure, sending showers of offal left and right, bespattering passersby who paused to flourish their fists and utter imprecations.

"Stop, stop, that's enough! Look now, will you take this money and go away?"

"I'm sorry, sir, but I've got me mind fixed on a steady income."

"All right, all right. Let's see—do you have any objections to living in my mews, with the horses?"

"Horses is me bread and butter, so to speak, sir. I do not."

"Very well. You may live in the mews and receive meals and a weekly stipend, provided you ply your trade elsewhere."

"Agreed! And furthermore, it is to be understood that your honor will have unqualified first-call on me services."

The two shook hands on the deal. Then Cowperthwait said, "I cannot spend any more time here dallying. We are in search of a woman."

"I could help there, too, sir."

"No, no, that's fine. Goodbye for now, Tiptoft."

"Allow me to conduct you partway, sir."

With Tiptoft sweeping ahead like a dervish, Cowperthwait and McGroaty proceeded toward Kensington, eventually parting ways with their escort near Hyde Park, where the confluence of traffic provided a fertile field for his broom.

Number Twelve Notting Hill Gate was a large edifice in the early Georgian mode, with freshly washed steps and starched curtains in the windows serving to conceal the interior. Using the knocker, which was shaped to resemble the ancient symbol of the Labrys, or double-headed ax, Cowperthwait sought admittance. The door was soon opened part way by an elderly maid, stopping at the short extent of a stout chain.

"No visiting privileges for menfolk," she said, and slammed the door.

Cowperthwait was both baffled and slightly enraged. "I say — " He resumed knocking. The door opened once more, this time to reveal the snout of a large old-fashioned pistol aimed at his head.

A stern and cultivated female voice spoke. "Perhaps you failed to comprehend my maid's injunction. We do not permit husbands, fathers, brothers, uncles, employers or lovers entrance. When we admitted your wife, daughter, sister, niece, employee or paramour, it was under tragic circumstances which your presence would only aggravate and reinforce. Now, will you depart, or shall I blow your head off?"

Cowperthwait's ire won out over any fear. "Madam, I do not know any of the young ladies in your care, unless possibly it be the one whom I seek. My name is Cosmo Cowperthwait, and I merely wish to speak to you about, um, the missing wife of a friend."

The pistol dropped away. "Did you say Cowperthwait?"

"Yes, that was the appellation."

"Author of the monograph 'Sexual Dimorphism Among the Echinoderms, Focusing Particularly Upon the *Asteroidea* and *Holo-thurioidea*'?"

"The same."

"One moment."

The door shut, the chain rattled off, and the door swung wide.

Revealed was an imposing figure of womanhood. Clad in a strange kind of one-piece white cotton garment that ended at the elbows and knees, the woman stood six feet tall with a deep bosom and large hands and feet. Striped lisle stockings and flat athletic shoes completed her outfit. Her hair was sequestered under a plain mob-cap. Her gray eyes radiated a fierce intelligence. Her full unpainted lips were quirked in a smile, as she dangled the pistol by her side.

"You and your servant may enter, Mister Cowperthwait. But just remember that you are here solely on my whim, and may be ejected — or worse — at any moment, if your misbehavior merits it."

Cowperthwait was somewhat embarrassed at this odd woman's revealing attire, but sought to meet her on her own unconventional terms. "Madam, I assure you that you are dealing with two gentlemen of the highest propriety and social standing."

"When one contemplates the deeds that are daily done in society's name, such a description is no high recommendation. But please enter."

Once inside, Cowperthwait said, "I assume I have the honor of addressing the proprietor of this establishment?"

"Indeed. I am Lady Ottoline Cornwall, and this is my school. Perhaps you would care to see its functioning?"

"Certainly. I have already been intrigued by what I have heard of your recruitment methods."

"Desperate times demand desperate measures, Mister Cowperthwait. I am not one of those who believe that idle bemoaning or passivity will accomplish anything. When I see an evil, I move vigorously to remedy it. There is much wrong with this world, but I limit my scope to ameliorating the sorry condition of womankind. I have pledged my family fortune to this establishment, which is dedicated to helping unfortunate girls from every stratum of society. From the warrens of Lambeth to the drawing-rooms of my own posh precinct I extract the abused and maltreated and try to inculcate a sense of their own worth in them."

Lady Cornwall had brought them to a closed door, upon which she now gently knocked, then opened. Cowperthwait saw inside rows of desks at which sat a class of girls of various ages, all dressed identically with their headmistress. At the front of the room stood a teacher.

Cowperthwait eagerly scanned her face for a resemblance to the missing Queen, but was disappointed.

"Here you see some of the girls at their lessons. Latin, Greek, French, geography, and many more subjects are here covered, particularly the natural sciences. We use several of your monographs in this latter area, Mister Cowperthwait."

Cowperthwait was flattered, and did not know where to look. "I — that surprises me, Lady Cornwall. My papers are not intended for the layman. Ah, laywoman."

"Our girls are up to it. Thank you, Miss Fairbairn, you may get back to your teaching."

Shutting the classroom door, Lady Cornwall continued the tour, bringing them to a capacious ballroom. The large space was fitted out with gymnastic equipment of all sort: barbells, skipping-ropes, punching bags. Bales of hay with targets on them even afforded the possibility for some of the girls to practice archery.

"I do not neglect the physical side of my charges either. Eight hours of sleep nightly in our well-ventilated dormitory, plenty of good food and exercise, along with the wearing of sensible clothing — no stays or contorted footgear here — can work wonders in their self-image."

When McGroaty saw the bows and arrows, his face lit up. "Criminy! I ain't handled a bow nor arrow since leavin' the Chickasaws! Here, now, Missie, you're a-holdin' it all wrong. Let me larn you what Chief Ikkemotubbe showed me."

Soon McGroaty was surrounded by enthusiastic young Amazons. Tongue protruding from the corner of his mouth, he placed an arrow in the bulls-eye. Then he presented his hindquarters to the target and, bending over and firing between his legs, split the first shaft with a second.

Applause and huzzahs filled the air. Lady Cornwall said, "Your servant seems to have found something to occupy him. Shall we adjourn to my private office and discuss what brings you here?"

"By all means."

Seated in Lady Cornwall's sanctum, holding a glass of port sangaree, Cowperthwait regarded the formidable woman before speaking. She had impressed him mightily with the acuity of her intellect and the strength of her mettle. He knew he must choose his words with care, so as not to anger or insult her.

"Ah, Lady Cornwall — "

"Please, I disdain titles. Call me Otto. And I shall address you by your Christian name also."

"Yes, um, Otto, then. Otto, would it be safe to assume that you look with favor and hope upon the ascension of our new Queen to the throne, as an exemplar of competent womanhood?"

Lady Cornwall snorted. "After a year, she has yet to prove that she's more than a poppet to Viscount Melbourne. I yet have my hopes. But she'll have to do more than she's done so far to merit them."

Cowperthwait studied the depths of his sangaree. "Suppose I were to tell you that the Queen, in an assertion of her independence, has run away."

Lady Cornwall jumped to her feet. "I'd shout bravo!"

"Please, Otto, calm down. While the Queen's hypothetical desertion might appeal to your romantic side, if you stop to consider it practically it presents more cause for grief than rejoicing. If we don't want to see the Queen lose the throne, then she must be cajoled to return to it."

Dropping into her chair, Lady Cornwall favored Cowperthwait with a calculated look and said, "How does any of this relate to me and my school?"

Dropping all subtlety, Cowperthwait said, "I have reason to believe that you employ a veiled woman referred to as 'Vicky.' Might it be she of whom we speak?"

"What if I tell you no? Then I suppose you'll demand that I haul poor Vicky before you, so that you can satisfy yourself. Why should I subject poor Vicky to your male imperiousness?"

Cowperthwait had no ready answer to this. Lady Cornwall eyed him piercingly, then spoke. "Cosmo, I respect you as a man of science, a male whose intellect and self-control raises him above the brutish level of his fellows."

Such talk made Cowperthwait nervous. What would she think of him if she knew of the newtish Victoria, and how he had satisfied his base lusts upon it?

"Therefore, I will allow you to speak to my Vicky, but only on one condition. That you accompany me this moment on a mission that will perhaps open your eyes to the real condition of women in this isle. What do you say?"

"Well, if it's the only way — "

"It is."

"I consent."

"Capital!" Lady Cornwall rose and took a dress off a peg and donned it unconcernedly. She changed her shoes, then pulled off her mob-cap, spilling out long auburn curls. Clapping a flat straw hat on her head and grabbing a reticule, she said, "Let's go."

"But my servant — "

"Are you afraid to venture unaccompanied someplace where I am not?"

"By no means!"

"Then we're off."

Leaving by a back door, Cowperthwait and Lady Cornwall made their way to an omnibus stand and were soon on their way cross town.

"Exactly where are we heading?"

"To Bartholomew Close, in the Smithfield Market. The central exchange for stolen goods."

Cowperthwait fingered his cane nervously.

They disembarked at a dilapidated three-story building with gingerbread trim, whose lower floor held a meat-market. The sight of so much raw red meat and the smell of animal blood made Cowperthwait feel faint.

"We are looking for Liza, a flower girl. She normally stations herself here, although I do not see her now. I have been arguing for weeks with her parents, trying to enroll her in the school. I feel they are almost ready to consent."

"What are we to do now?"

Lady Cornwall cupped her chin. "We'll have to visit Liza's home."

Down several noisome alleys they treaded, arriving finally at a ramshackle tenement. Lady Cornwall went confidently in, Cowperthwait tentatively following.

Upstairs, in a darkened hall illuminated only by what light penetrated a small, filthy cobwebbed window, the schoolmistress knocked on a door.

The door cracked open and a bearded, greasy face thrust itself out. "Which family?" said the man gruffly.

"The Boffyflows."

"That'll be one penny for crossing the Swindle establishment, one penny likewise for the Scropeses, and a third for the Snypes."

"Very well. We'll pay. Now let us in."

The man opened the door fully. They entered.

The tiny candle-lit unpartitioned room held four families and their miserable possessions. The high-status Swindles occupied the quarter closest to the exit, and hence had to pay no tolls. Next came the Scropeses, then the Snypes. Lowest in stature were the Boffyflows, who cowered — mother, father, infants and adolescents — in the farthest corner.

Dispensing the pence, they made their way to the Boffyflows.

Father Boffyflow was a lardy fellow sitting in a rickety chair and nursing a black eye. Lady Cornwall accosted him. "Where's Liza?"

"On her doss, snifflin' and sobbin'."

"Why wasn't she at work today?"

"Argh, she warn't makin' nuffin sellin' flowers, so I decided she had to go out as a cripple."

"Cripple — ?" Lady Cornwall hastened to the girl on her pallet and lifted up the slack form.

Liza's fresh wrist-stub was wrapped in bloody rags.

Lady Cornwall wailed. "Oh, that I should have temporized with these savages! Now must I live with this on my conscience for the remainder of my life!"

She made to leave, carrying the unconscious girl. Boffyflow interposed himself, thrusting his stomach against the schoolmistress. "'Ere now, where you takin' my girl — "

Before Cowperthwait could interpose there was a gun-blast, and Boffyflow fell back in his chair, shot in the gut.

Lady Cornwall's hand was in her reticule, which exhibited a smoking hole from the derringer within.

"Anyone else object?" she asked.

Mister Snype advanced cautiously. "No argyment from us, Ma'am, long as we get our pence on the way out."

"Cosmo, see to it."

With shaking hands, Cowperthwait paid the exit tolls. The trip back to Number Twelve Notting Hill Gate passed for Cowperthwait as in a dream. Only when he was once more sitting in Lady Cornwall's office and soothing his nerves with a rum and shrub did reality begin to resume its wonted dimensions.

When Lady Cornwall returned from letting out the female physician who had tended to Liza's wounds, she said, "And now, Cosmo, I'll keep my end of the bargain. Here is the woman you wished to see."

Cowperthwait could hardly contain his excitement at the appearance of the veiled woman. At last, the real Victoria would be restored to the throne and his Victoria would be returned to him....

The woman slowly lifted her muslin veil.

At first Cowperthwait could hardly believe that the face revealed to him belonged to a human, let alone a woman. A mass of keloid scars and twisted discolored flesh, it resembled that of some hobgoblin or creature out of Dante's Inferno.

"A combination of acid and flame, administered by her bawd. Even women may hurt women, you see."

Cowperthwait struggled for something to say commensurate with the horrible injustice of the situation. "I — my growth factor — perhaps it might repair some of the damage. I can't guarantee anything. But regular applications might help."

"Vicky would appreciate that. Wouldn't you, Vicky?" The woman nodded mutely, shedding a tear from one ruined eye.

"Thank you, Vicky. That will be all."

When the girl had left, Lady Cornwall came up by Cowperthwait's side.

"Cosmo, you stood up admirably during that little contretemps at Smithfield Market. And your pity toward Vicky touches me. I would like to reward you, if I may."

So saying, Lady Cornwall grabbed Cowperthwait in a grip of iron, tilted him backward and kissed him in the Continental manner, thrusting her tongue deep into his mouth.

Cowperthwait's cane discharged thunderously into the floor.

5

THE FATAL DANCE

For several days after the visit to Lady Cornwall's Lyceum, Cowperthwait moped about like a love-sick schoolboy. The surprising denouement to his visit, in which Lady Cornwall had revealed the passion which lurked beneath her competent exterior, remained vivid in his mind, obscuring all other matters. Even the notion of finding the missing Queen was cast into shadow.

Cowperthwait had for years dreamed of marriage to a perfect companion. The woman would have to be smart and amiable, literate and lusty, free-minded and foot-loose. Truth to tell, his creation of Victoria had been something of an experiment along crafting the perfect bride he could not find.

Now, in the person of Lady Cornwall, he was convinced he had found her. Smitten by her soul-kiss, he could think of nothing but joining their fortunes and estates together. A woman who could appreciate "Sexual Dimorphism Among the Echinoderms" was not to be found every day.

Seeking McGroaty's opinion of the woman, Cowperthwait was somewhat dismayed by the manservant's undisguised disdain of her.

"She puts me in mind of a sartin Widder Douglas I knew, back in Hannibal, Moe. Always a-trying to reform and change people, which in my book is about as pointless as tossin' a lasso at the horn o' the moon. Plus she's all-mighty bossy. You mark my words — if'n you two get hitched, she'll have you scrubbin' her knickers on washday faster'n spit dries on a griddle."

Cowperthwait would have liked to have McGroaty endorse Lady Cornwall, but if this was not to be the case, then McGroaty would have to simply lump it. After all, an opportunity like this came along only once in a lifetime....

The lone difficulty in Cowperthwait's view lay in how best to broach his proposal. It would have to be handled just right....

When scarred Vicky visited shortly thereafter, for her first treatment with growth factor, Cowperthwait entrusted her with a note for her mistress.

Dearest Otto,
Our adventure is etched in flames upon my cortex. If you could possibly see fit to entertain me again, I would like to consult with you upon making our alliance a permanent one, so that we may offer each other mutual aid and comfort.
    Your earnest admirer,
    Cosmo.

The reply he received with Vicky's next visit was rather brusque.

Dear Sir:
I am not at present of a mind to agree to any such permanent and
exclusive arrangement as, if I read you aright, you are tendering. Let
us submerge our feelings for the nonce, and remain simply friends.
  Otto.

This cold water dashed on his marital hopes threw Cowperthwait
into a blue funk. He spent the next few days homebound, reading and
rereading a passage in Blore's *Exceptional Creatures* about the Giant
Rat of Sumatra. Eventually, however, he realized that such behavior ill-
suited him. Thrusting aside all consideration of personal happiness,
he plunged once more into his quest for his vanished sovereign.

Every waking hour was devoted to the increasingly futile search
for the vanished Queen. Accompanied by McGroaty, the young natural philosopher combed the festering warren that was lower-class
London, silhouette in hand, feverish, sleep-deprived brain alert for
any trace of Victoria.

By daylight and gaslight, aboveground and below, amidst the noisy
market crowds or alone in a rooming house with a work-worn suspect
female, Cowperthwait pursued the mirage of Victoria.

From fish-redolent Billingsgate to the prison hulks at Gravesend,
where convicts lay sickly in bilge-water; from Grey's Inn law offices
where pitiful petitioners pled their cases to tubercular sanitariums
where angels like one named Florence Nightingale escorted him from
bed to bed; from filthy dockside to plush gambling parlor — through
every stratum of the underworld, in fact — guided by McGroaty, whose
knowledge of such places seemed encyclopaedic — Cowperthwait jour-
neyed, footsore and obsessed.

And everywhere he searched, it seemed, a nemesis would greet
him.

Lord Chuting-Payne, the arrogant, evil-tempered enemy of the
throne.

Either Chuting-Payne was there waiting for him; or had just
departed; or arrived as Cowperthwait was leaving. No matter what
hour it was, the cruel and sardonic nobleman, always accompanied
by the silent and forbidding Gunputty, appeared fresh and dapper, as

unruffled as a calm lake. At those times when he and Cowperthwait came face to face, they usually exchanged no more than a brittle *bon mot* or two. Sad to relate, Chuting-Payne could be counted on to triumph in such exchanges, his rapier wit honed by a lifetime among the cynical rich.

Cowperthwait came to loathe the sight of the arrogant Lord with his precious-metal nose that made him seem half machine. He soon regarded the man as his own evil doppelgänger, and the only comfort he could find in Chuting-Payne's continued appearances was that it meant the Lord was having no more luck in his search for Victoria than Cowperthwait was.

Victoria. The name itself began to sound unreal to Cowperthwait. Who was this phantasm, this woman he had never met in the flesh? She lay at the heart of Cowperthwait's life, at the center of the Empire's power. On the one hand, although only on the throne a year, it could be generally sensed that, after a succession of old, doddering Kings, she was already the very lifebreath of a fresh new era, the embodiment of the sprawling political organism that stretched its tentacles across the globe. On the other hand, she was only one woman among millions, no more important in the ultimate scheme of things than the fishwife or costermonger Cowperthwait had just interviewed, no more to be loved and admired than the stoic Vicky whom Cowperthwait continued to treat. (And with some measure of success....)

And what of his own Victoria? Melbourne's dispatches had trailed off, and Cowperthwait had heard nothing of the hypertrophied Hellbender in days. The last missive had not been reassuring.

June 10
I fear the "black dog" of Melancholia has me in its jaws. I and the kingdom are positively undone, unless V. makes her reappearance. Whilst hopelessly waiting, I contemplate the merits of your creature: if only all women could be so tractable...!
　　From Stygian depths,
　　W. L.

Something of the same despondency gripped Cowperthwait. He hoped that the Prime Minister in his funk was not neglecting Victoria's needs, but he had no way of finding out. It would hardly do to approach

Buckingham Palace and ask whether the Queen's skin appeared suitably moist....

Three weeks passed. There were now less than seven days until the Coronation, and no sign of Victoria.

This evening found Cowperthwait preparing to embark one more time on another fruitless round of searching. On the point of setting out, a wave of ennui swept over him. He felt as if all his bones had been instantly removed.

"Nails, I fear I cannot continue this Sisyphean task. At least not tonight."

"Cain't say I blame you, Coz. I'm plumb tuckered out myself. What say we swing 'round to de Mallet's, and take it easy for one night?"

"A capital idea, Nails. Although I fear I'm too weary to endure the embraces of any dozy, the atmosphere should prove congenial."

Leaving the house, they encountered Tiptoft asleep under the front portico. Stepping quietly over the lad, so as not to awake him and be forced to endure a whirlwind of sweeping, they set out for Regent's Street.

At the carven oak door of de Mallet's luxurious establishment they employed the gilt knocker in the shape of a copulating couple and were quickly admitted by the majordomo. Their hats were taken, glasses of champagne were proffered on a golden salver, and soon Cowperthwait and McGroaty were seated in the large ballroom, watching couples dance to the stately strains of Mozart flowing from a gilt pianoforte, and eyeing appreciatively the corseted trollops sprawled on velvet chaises around the four walls.

The only incident momentarily to jar Cowperthwait's composure occurred when he thought he detected a flash of reflected candlelight in an oddly fluted piece of silver borne aloft at nose-height across the crowded room. But if the glint indeed indicated the presence of Lord Chuting-Payne, that spectre did not materialize any more solidly, and Cowperthwait, by dint of his mental discipline, soon succeeded in banishing such fears.

Cowperthwait switched from champagne to Madeira, and the room soon took on an ethereal glow. The candelabra appeared to waver and flare, like will-o'-the-wisps. McGroaty disappeared at one point, presumably to display his Chickasaw scars to some lucky roundheels, and Cowperthwait found himself nodding off to sleep. He dozed for a while and awoke feeling more refreshed than he had in ages. It was at this point that Madame de Mallet approached him.

Tall and buxom, swamped with jewels, perhaps overly made-up for some tastes, in the fashion of an older period, de Mallet was a well-preserved seventy. Rumor had it that she had been a chambermaid to Marie Antoinette (and sometime bedpartner of Louis), and had barely escaped the Revolution with her life.

"M'sieu Cowperthwait, may I interest you in a lady tonight? We have a new addition to the house." Here de Mallet bent lower, and spoke in a whisper. "She is someone *très spéciale, un bijou*. I do not offer her to *tout le monde*, only my favorites. I can guarantee that it will be the chance of a lifetime."

Cowperthwait was momentarily intrigued, but, not wishing to disturb his serenity with the rigors of carnal love, he ultimately declined. With a shrug, Madame de Mallet said, *Très bien*, as you wish."

Feeling a pressure of a different sort emanating from his bladder, however, Cowperthwait said, "I could make use of a chamber pot, though."

Madame de Mallet waved her beringed hand airily. "You are familiar with the house. But piddle," she advised, "with discretion and a minimum of noise, please. *La chamber à côté du pissoir,* it is occupied."

Cowperthwait got unsteadily to his feet. He made his tipsy way up the grand staircase, colliding off various couples in an illustration of Brownian motion which appealed to him.

In the second-floor corridor he began counting doors, but soon lost track. Cowperthwait opened what he recalled to be the correct door.

It was not.

Two women were in the room. One, clothed in a plain chemise, sat at a veneered secretary, her back to Cowperthwait as she vigorously scribbled in a small book. Upon hearing the door open, she cradled her arms around the diary, as if to shield its contents, and dropped her face down upon it.

The second woman, a veritable Amazon, filled the rumpled bed with her Junoesque body. Lying spread-eagled on her back, hands clasped behind and pillowing her head, she wore on her features an expression most obviously betokening sexual satiation.

"Otto!" exclaimed Cowperthwait.

Lady Cornwall was not embarrassed. "Yes, Cosmo, it's I. How may I help you?"

Cowperthwait sank into a handy chair and held his head in his hands. "A daughter of Lesbos. No wonder you had no interest in my proposal. I should have guessed, from your mannish ways. How convenient for your perversion, you keeping all those young helpless chicks as your wards — "

Lady Cornwall leapt from the bed and slapped Cowperthwait across the face. "How dare you impugn my motives! My girls are treated as chastely as nuns. Why do you think I'm buying my love in this place, if you imagine I sate my desires at the school?"

Lady Cornwall sat down on the bed and began to cry. Cowperthwait could think of nothing to say or do except to mutter a useless apology and leave.

Finding the privy, he relieved his bladder. What a farce life was, he thought as he piddled. Missing queens, newts on the throne, Sapphic saviors....

Ruefully buttoning his fly, Cowperthwait returned to the main salon.

The current piece of music was just ending. Cowperthwait was startled to see McGroaty standing next to the piano. A borrowed fiddle was tucked under his chin.

"Ladies and gents, pick up yer feet. Yer about to be ennertained by some authentic Virginny foot-stompin' reels. Hit it, Wolfgang!"

McGroaty immediately began an enthusiastic sawing, the pianist managed to master the beat, and the floor was soon filled with energetically twirling couples. Cowperthwait found himself engaged by a red-haired whore and spun about. Reluctant at first, he found the lively music to be just the tonic his tired blood needed, after the dismaying revelation upstairs, and he was soon performing more spiritedly than anyone. Within minutes the dancers had stepped back to form a circle at the center of which Cowperthwait and his enthusiastic partner performed.

Cowperthwait's head was spinning. He couldn't remember when he had felt so wonderful. Damn all his troubles! By God, he'd give everyone a show! He hoped Otto was watching. Picking up his partner by the waist he began a particularly acrobatic maneuver. At that moment, two things happened simultaneously. From the spectators a disdainful voice said, "What an ignorant and savage display — " At the same instant, Cowperthwait lost his footing and launched his partner out of his sweat-slick hands and through the air.

After Cowperthwait had picked himself up off the floor and dusted himself off, he thought to look for the red-haired girl.

Her fall had been inadvertently cushioned by the body of Lord Chuting-Payne, who in so doing had lost his nose. The dead tissue and gaping holes in the center of face were revealed before the whole room. Strong men fainted and woman screamed.

Chuting-Payne calmly accepted his nose back from Gunputty and stuck it back on his face. Unfortunately, it was upside down.

"Dawn tomorrow at my estate, Cowperthwait. Your choice of weapons."

Watching the misassembled nobleman haughtily depart, Cowperthwait wondered briefly if he could convince Chuting-Payne to agree to flying sword-canes at fifty paces.

6

TREACHERY AT CARKING FARDELS

In the flickering light of a candle, Cowperthwait peered into the looking-glass atop the chiffonier in the hallway and nervously adjusted his cravat. It wouldn't do to meet his predictable death looking less than a fashionable gentleman. He wouldn't give Chuting-Payne the satisfaction of standing over his corpse and uttering some cutting remark about the failings of his haberdasher.

A door creaked. In the mirror, Cowperthwait saw McGroaty appear behind him, carrying a package wrapped in oiled cloth. He turned.

"It done took me some time to find where I laid it up, but here it is."

"Here what is?"

"The key to you blowin' that dirty skunk offen the face of the earth." McGroaty began to tenderly unwrap the object within the greasy rags. Soon lay revealed an enormous weapon, a product of the Colt Arms Manufactory in Connecticut. The gun had a barrel as long as a loaf of French bread, with a bore of commensurate diameter. The chamber appeared designed to hold projectiles the size of Cowperthwait's fingers.

The naturalist attempted to pick up the pistol. He found himself unable to heft it one-handed, and perforce had to grasp the giant's weapon with both. He made as if to draw a bead on the stuffed orangoutang at the hall's end. His arms shook with the effort of supporting the pistol's weight, and the gun barrel wavered through an arc of several inches.

McGroaty was smiling earnestly at Cowperthwait's target practice. (Those teeth of his not missing were chipped.)

"That's the trick, Coz! Yer onto it now! You may not reckon it, but yer holdin' the world's finest Peacemaker. I done toted this little honey all over the globe, and she never let me down once. Hellfire, you don't even got to hit nothin' vital to kill that polecat. Jest whang him in the fingertip and he'll likely die of shock. I blowed the head offen a buffalo with this darlin' from a hunnerd yards away."

Cowperthwait laid the monstrous gun back among the rags. His arms were quivering. "No, Nails, I'm afraid not. It simply wouldn't be sporting, since we haven't its mate to offer Chuting-Payne. And I fear I'd be stone-dead before I could lift your Colt up to fire. No, you'd best fetch my father's set. It's time we were off."

Reluctantly McGroaty wrapped up his gun, breathed a sigh of consternation, as if unable to fathom Cowperthwait's finicky morals, and went off to secure the aforementioned pistols.

Soon he returned with a mahogany box. Cowperthwait lifted the lid. Inside, nestled in velvet depressions, was a brace of small pearl-handled pistols.

The selfsame guns purchased by Clive Cowperthwait in anticipation of his duel with Marc Isambard Brunel.

Cowperthwait shed a tear at the thought of his father and mother, and the whole tragic family history. He thought also of Ikky Brunel, who had just promised him a guided tour of *The Great Western*, the marvelous transatlantic steamship about to have its maiden voyage. Now it looked as if he would never get a chance to witness that marvel of this wondrous age. Ah, life — how bittersweet....

"Very good," said Cowperthwait, closing the lid. "That leaves only a few points of unfinished business. Nails, keep this on your person.

It's my last will and testament. You'll find that you're my sole heir."

McGroaty wiped his eyes. "Reckon I'd better make out my own then, cuz I'll be coolin' my heels in the calaboose afore I swing by the neck."

"Why?"

"Cuz when Chuting-Payne croaks you, I aim to croak him."

"Nails, I appreciate the sentiment, but please don't. It would stain the family honor."

"Ain't nothing you could do to stop me, Coz, but I promise anyhow."

"Very good. Now, here is a letter for Lady Cornwall, along with the last of my growth factor for her ward, Vicky. Please make sure she gets them."

McGroaty overcame his disdain of the Lyceum mistress enough to agree to this.

"Excellent. Finally be so good as to fetch Tiptoft." When the sweep appeared, straws in his hair and rubbing crumbs of sleep from his eyes, Cowperthwait handed him an envelope.

"Tiptoft, here's a draft on my bank for a hundred pounds. You are hereby discharged from my services."

"Hurrah!" shouted the lad. "I'm off to Australia to make my fortune!"

Cowperthwait patted the sweep on the head and saw him out the door. Turning to McGroaty, he said, "Let's depart. We don't want to keep the noble bastard waiting."

In the trap, rattling through the empty pre-dawn London streets, Cowperthwait tried to gauge his feelings. He was remarkably calm and clear-headed, especially considering neither he nor McGroaty had gotten any sleep since the fracas at de Mallet's just a few hours ago. He was surprised to find that the prospect of his imminent death did not trouble him in the least. It seemed, rather, a relief to know that everything would soon be over. The failure of his experiments with the salamander known as Victoria, followed by the frustrating and enervating quest for the human Victoria and his disillusionment with Lady Cornwall, had left him weary and dispirited. There seemed little left in life to engage his interests, and, despite his physiological youth, he felt himself a veritable greybeard. Better to have it over with now, than drag through life with this premature ennui....

Soon they had left the sprawling metropolis behind. In under an hour, they were approaching Carking Fardels, the ancestral estates of the Chuting-Payne family, of whom Cowperthwait's nemesis was the last direct descendant. The sky was lightening in various sherbert tones, birds were trilling, and breezes were stirring the mists that writhed among the underbrush. It looked as if it would be a fine day on which to meet one's demise.

McGroaty turned the trap onto a lane that diverged from the tollroad. Beneath fresh mint-green foliage they rolled, until they came to a large pair of gates. Waiting there was the magnificent figure of Gunputty.

Leaning close to his employer, the American said, "Iffen you can ee-liminate ol' Tinface by some scientific slight-o'-hand, Coz, go for it without worryin' about facin' his second. I got a scheme to sap that fuzzy-wuzzy's will."

Cowperthwait sighed deeply. "Please, Nails, no shenanigans that will spoil my exit from this mortal coil."

"Just leave that human mountain to me, Chief," finished up McGroaty mysteriously. At this juncture, the fuzzy-wuzzy in question leaped silently up as postillion and, clutching the carriage's super-structure, waved them on toward their mortal rendezvous.

Across a dewy field, the trap leaving glistening tracks, and to the edge of a copse of speckled alders. Gunputty disembarked and led the way beneath the trees.

A small discreet clearing was to be found amidst the trees, just wide enough for the requisite paces.

Standing nonchalantly there was Lord Chuting-Payne, dressed in morning-coat and spats. His nose was correctly positioned, and had been buffed to perfection. Cowperthwait could see himself in it.

"I had my doubts as to your showing up," said Chuting-Payne. Cowperthwait let the insult pass. He felt serenely exalted above such pettifogging. "I trust you brought suitable weapons...."

Cowperthwait silently held up a hand, and McGroaty laid the pistol-box in it. Chuting-Payne advanced, opened the receptacle and selected a gun. "A splendid model, if a bit antique. I recall that the last time I used such a gun was to perform a trick for the Earl of Malmesbury. He tossed a deck of cards into the air, and I shot only those which would beat the hand of euchre which he simultaneously flashed before my eyes."

McGroaty spat into the grass. Chuting-Payne sneered. "There will soon be a brighter, more vital fluid staining the lawn here, my man, so don't waste your precious substance. Well, there's no point in delaying any further, is there?"

McGroaty and Gunputty stepped aside. Cowperthwait noticed his man whispering into the lowered ear of the turbaned Titan, and the next thing he knew, the two seconds had vanished behind a tree.

But there was no time to ponder their actions further.

Cowperthwait and Chuting-Payne advanced to the center of the clearing and stood back to back. Mist coiled around their ankles.

"On the count of three, we commence walking for twenty paces, turn — completely, mind you, for I have no second nose to lose — and fire at will. One, two, three — "

The walk seemed miles. Cowperthwait felt a small wild animal striving to claw its way to freedom within him, but suppressed it. Soon, soon....

Twenty paces. Turn.

Chuting-Payne stood negligently, with arms folded across his chest, allowing Cowperthwait first shot. The inventor raised his gun, shut his eyes, and fired.

Lifting his eyelids, he saw a robin fall dead from the tree behind the Lord.

Chuting-Payne smiled and brought his pistol up. "Before you die, Mister Cowperthwait, I just want you to know that I have found our common Grail. And the scandal I intend to cause with what I have learned will topple the throne, and more than adequately recompense me for the insults I have suffered. Now, address your prayers to your maker, Mister Cowperthwait."

Chuting-Payne aimed confidently at Cowperthwait, who closed his eyes again, for the last time.

The shot rang out.

Miraculously, Cowperthwait felt nothing. How grand.... He had been right not to fear.... Paradise, hello!

Cowperthwait opened his eyes.

Chuting-Payne lay dead on the turf, the back of head blown off in a gory mess.

It dawned slowly on Cowperthwait what must have happened. "McGroaty! Goddamn you, McGroaty, you promised! That was hardly sportsmanlike!"

Out from the trees stepped a figure.

It was Viscount Melbourne. The Prime Minister clutched a smoking pistol.

"William — I don't — How? Why?"

The dapper nobleman calmly removed the spent cartridge from his gun and substituted a fresh one. "I could hardly let Chuting-Payne continue to live now, Cosmo, could I? After what he just said about his plans to embroil Victoria in a hideous scandal. Not after all the work the two of us have put into keeping her name unsoiled. And besides, I rather like you, and owed you a favor. I consider that debt discharged."

"But I thought you said you didn't believe in assassination."

"That was of women, boy. Entirely different set of rules for the other sex. No, I fear Chuting-Payne's treasonous intentions earned him his death. And besides, without heirs his estate devolves to the throne. I've had my eye on it for years."

A thought occurred suddenly to Cowperthwait. "The Queen! He knew where she was! Now the knowledge is gone with him."

Melbourne seemed queerly unconcerned. "Yes, rum bit of luck, that. But I could hardly wait any longer to bag him."

A sudden malaise swept over the young scientist, leaving him disinclined to press the matter further. All he wished now was to be home in bed. Thoughts of those welcoming counterpanes brought up an associated matter, which he now put to the Viscount.

"My creation — it's been so long since I've had any news from you. Is she flourishing? Does she ever seem to — to pine for her old surroundings?"

Melbourne sought to brush the matter aside. "She does well. Her needs are simple, and easily fulfilled. Most of them, at any rate … if you know what I mean, eh?"

Cosmo opened his mouth to adjure the Minister not to overtax the chimeric creature, but Melbourne cut him off.

"Well, you'd best be heading home. Oh, don't worry — there'll be no legal repercussions. The Crown will handle matters."

From out of the woods there appeared McGroaty, accompanied by Gunputty. Melbourne raised his pistol, anticipating deadly action from the servant on behalf of his wronged master. Cowperthwait too fully expected that the loyal Indian servant would attempt to revenge his master's death.

But instead, the Indian merely beamed a bright smile their way!

Picking McGroaty up like a child, he trotted eagerly toward them.

"Nails, what — ?"

"Everything's jake, Coz. I just finished explainin' something mighty beneficial to ol' Ganpat here. That's his real name, by the way, after some heathen god or other. I managed to instill some demmycratic ideals in him, made him see that iffen his master was to die, he'd be a free man, able to make his fortune with his good looks and exotic ways. We're plannin' to get him a job with P. T. Barnum, who's blowin' in through town soon. He does a mean snake-charmin' act."

Cowperthwait sighed. A regrettable lack of remorse all around here.

But life must go on, he supposed.

Mustn't it?

7

WHAT EVERYONE ELSE KNEW

Cowperthwait slept for a day and a half. His dreams, if any, were painless, and vanished upon waking.

Standing over him was McGroaty, bearing a tray heaped high with lavishly buttered scones, a decanter of tea, and a lidded crystal pot full of fresh strawberry jam.

"I thought you might need some vittles by now, Coz."

Cowperthwait sat up in bed, plumping the pillows behind himself. "Quite right, Nails. Time to fortify the body before attempting to tackle the problems of the mind that yet beset us."

"I couldn't'a phrased it no better myself."

Cowperthwait dug hungrily into the repast. He was amazed at his hunger, having expected to bear some lingering anxiety and consequent loss of appetite over the death of Chuting-Payne. However, even the resemblance of the strawberry jam to Chuting-Payne's spilled brains was not sufficient to dismay him.

As he ate, Cowperthwait pondered the problem of Victoria.

Chuting-Payne had claimed to know her hiding place. It was obvious the knowledge was fresh, for during a recent meeting last week — at the establishment of a Jewish money-lender reputed to occasionally harbor runaway children — Chuting-Payne had been as obviously ignorant as ever.

Therefore, he must have discovered it just prior to the contretemps at de Mallet's —

De Mallet's. Cowperthwait ceased to chew. An image of the old bawd materialized vividly before his slack-jawed face.

"Someone *très spéciale....* the chance of a lifetime...."

It couldn't be — could it? De Mallet's establishment was the first place Melbourne would have searched. The only reason Cowperthwait hadn't bothered himself was that certainty. And yet —

Tossing back the blankets, Cowperthwait sent his breakfast flying. "Nails! Nails!"

McGroaty ambled in unconcernedly while Cowperthwait was attempting to insert both lower limbs into a single trousers-leg.

"Nails, we must hurry with all dispatch to Madame de Mallet's."

McGroaty winked. "Takin' care of some other needs now, I reckon."

"Oh, Nails, you're hopeless. Just ready the transportation." Soon Cowperthwait found himself admitted by a sleepy and disheveled majordomo into the empty parlors of Madame de Mallet's. (McGroaty was waiting outside; should Cowperthwait's hunch prove correct, it would hardly do to have the uncouth ruffian present to embarrass the delicate sensibilities of the woman he now fully expected to meet.) The gilt fixtures and flocked wall-coverings appeared tawdry in the light of day that diffused through the drawn heavy drapes. There was a nauseating odor of spilled champagne and stale bodily exudations. The place wore a face far different from its glamorous nighttime image. Cowperthwait wondered which manifestation, if either, was closest to reality.

Hand on the staircase rail, Cowperthwait was hailed by the servant. "Ey now, Guv'nor, you can't disturb the girls at this hour —"

"Oh, shut up, man! I'm not here for a roger. For Agassiz's sake, why is everyone so blasted fixated on their privates?"

In the upstairs corridor something drew Cowperthwait unerringly toward the room that had once held the salamander Victoria. At the door, he knocked softly. A feminine voice responded.

"Is it night already? I feel like I've hardly slept. Come in, then, come in, I'm ready...."

Cowperthwait twisted the handle and entered.

The chamber was curtained from the daylight, and lit only by a single candle. The match that had just ignited the tallowed wick was being puffed to extinction by the pursed lips of the woman in bed.

Woman, yes. Now she was plainly girl no longer.

Victoria's long hair was a soft brown, halfway between the flaxen color of her youth and the foregone darker shade of her maturity. Her face was round and still somehow innocent, her nose and chin somewhat pronounced. She would, Cowperthwait suspected, never look more radiant. These looks, he knew, were slated to be soon captured by the court painter, Franz Winterhalter.

The Queen possessed a commanding gaze which Cowperthwait now found hard to disengage from his own. At last doing so, he took in the rest of Victoria's *dishabille.*

She lay with the covers thrown back, wearing the sheerest of peignoirs. Her bust and hips were full, giving some hint of a future stockiness, and she looked ripe for bearing many children. Cowperthwait was suddenly certain that it would not be long before a new little Prince or Princess graced the land.

Yet this maternal aspect of Victoria was still implicit, not dominant. At the moment, she looked anything but motherly. Her exquisite body yet unmarred by any pregnancies, she was as inviting a woman as any Cowperthwait had seen.

On a card-table in a corner was a partially completed dissected picture, one of the puzzles Victoria enjoyed assembling. Next to it rested her inevitable diary.

Cowperthwait dropped to one knee. "Your Majesty—"

Victoria's voice was throaty. Cowperthwait knew she had trouble with septic tonsils. "You can forget all titles now, silly boy. I'm not queen here. In this house, there are others who know so much more than I, and deserve that title. But I'm learning. Come here, and I'll show you."

Victoria lifted her arms out imploringly. Shocked, Cowperthwait stood and came to sit on the edge of the bed where he could press his case more convincingly.

"Your Majesty, I realize that the demands of your high office have caused you untold grief, and that it is only natural you would seek to forget all your troubles by adopting a wanton's role. But you must realize that the nation needs you. The Coronation is imminent. And do not forget the personal anguish you have caused your Prime Minister. Viscount Melbourne is beside himself, wondering where you are."

"Whatever are you talking about, you foolish man? It was Melbourne who put me here."

Cowperthwait felt as if his brain were about to tear itself apart. "Melbourne — ?"

"Yes, Lambie told me it would be part of my education. And he was so right. Why, I've met many of the most important figures in the country, on more intimate terms than I could ever achieve in the sterile corridors of state. Writers, artists, members of Parliament, educators. Men and women both. Why, there were even some common laborers who had saved up their money for ages. And the talk has been almost as stimulating as the loving. The secrets I've learned, the bonds I've forged, the self-confidence I've cultivated, not to mention the tricks I've learned that will certainly please my darling Albert when we've married — These will stand me in good stead for my whole reign. I shan't have any trouble getting my way from now on, I feel. Oh, I've enjoyed it so! It's a shame it's almost over."

Cowperthwait tried to find his tongue. "Then you have no intention of abdicating — ?"

"Of course not! I'm returning to the Palace tomorrow, for the Coronation rehearsal. It's all arranged. Now, forget all this talk of matters politic, dear boy. Come here to your little Victoria, and let her make everything all better."

Victoria flung her arms about Cowperthwait, pulled him down and began unbuttoning his fly.

At first hesitant, Cowperthwait soon began enthusiastically to comply.

After all, one simply did not casually disobey one's sovereign, however demanding the request....

It was no trouble to break into Buckingham Palace under the cover of darkness. Security was quite primitive. As an example, in December of that year 1838, "the boy Cotton" would finally be apprehended, after inhabiting the Palace uncaught for several months. Twelve years of age, he was perpetually covered in soot, having often concealed himself in chimneys. He blackened the beds he chose to sleep in, broke open sealed letters to the Queen, stole certain small geegaws and food, and when caught was found to be wearing a pair of Melbourne's trousers.

Cowperthwait did not encounter "the boy Cotton" as he made his way down the echoing passages that night toward the Queen's private bedroom. He followed the directions Victoria had graciously given him earlier that day, after their bout. Cowperthwait had explained his involvement in the subterfuge surrounding Victoria's absence. It turned out the Queen knew nothing about the mock-Victoria occupying her bed with Melbourne, and he thought he could detect no small jealousy on her part. He did not envy Melbourne the explaining he would have to do tomorrow.

At the same time, Cowperthwait was quite angry with the way the Prime Minister had duped him. He was now determined to secure his Victoria, and have it out with the man.

Only once did Cowperthwait encounter anyone, a patrolling Beefeater whom he avoided by ducking into a niche holding a bust of Ethelred the Unready.

At last Cowperthwait stood outside the royal bedchambers. Without knocking, he let himself in.

Melbourne lay abed with the salamander. When the newt saw Cowperthwait she let out a croak of joyous recognition and slithered out of bed. Completely hairless, her sinuous form combined mammalian and amphibian characteristics in an unearthly beauty. The wig she used to impersonate the Queen graced a stand across the room.

Melbourne leapt naked out of bed, his burly hairy body a gross contrast to the ethereal, sylphlike splendor of the Hellbender.

"Sir," uttered Cowperthwait, "I know all! You have tricked me in a dastardly fashion. I suppose you had the interests of the country at heart, but I believe there was also a component of unholy lust in your actions. I now reclaim my ward, and leave you to your conscience."

Cowperthwait took Victoria's hand and turned to go.

Melbourne grabbed her other hand and held on. "No, don't take her. You're right, I am besotted with this creature of yours, have been from the moment I first had her at de Mallet's. I couldn't stand the notion of others enjoying her. The Queen's sojourn away, already long planned, seemed the perfect excuse to arrogate the newt to myself. I can't do without her now!"

"Sir, let go," Cowperthwait urged, tugging on Victoria. "Do not make me employ force with you!"

Melbourne did not listen, but instead continued to pull on the newt. Cowperthwait pulled back, and there ensued a tugging match which soon grew to ferocious proportions.

Without warning Melbourne suddenly shot backward onto the bed.

Looking down, he found himself holding Victoria's severed twitching arm, from which dripped a pale fluid.

"My God!" cried the Prime Minister. "Where have my brutish lusts led me!" He dropped the limb and, cradling his head in his hands began to weep.

Cowperthwait looked at the Prime Minister with disgust. "You have abused a helpless animal, and now feel the appropriate pangs. Let it be a lesson to you that even the highest worldly powers are not exempted from common morality. You may take comfort from the fact that Victoria will quickly regenerate her arm, as she still possesses that newt-like faculty."

Tossing a blanket around the uncomplaining creature, Cowperthwait said, "Come, dear, let us go." He left Melbourne weeping.

In the hansom cab heading home, cradling Victoria's elongated head against his chest, Cowperthwait mused aloud.

"I could wish it were Lady Cornwall by my side at this moment, dear Victoria, but what good would such impossible longing do? No, it is you and I, poor thing. You and I once more."

Cowperthwait stroked her head, and Victoria butted it against the underside of his chin.

"Ah, my dear, you have been through many rigors in your unnatural life. And much as any man loves his creations, I can only hope that your existence is not further prolonged by very many days. If only I knew your natural span...."

And with that sentiment echoing in the coach, the vehicle rolled on through the night —

— through the decades —

— through sixty-three years, until February 1, 1901, when the same city thoroughfare, draped with purple and white banners (Victoria had in her will asked that the black hangings she abhorred be banned) was thronged with weeping crowds watching the horse-drawn gun-carriage bearing the short coffin of their elderly Queen make its slow way from Victoria Station to Paddington Station, on its way to the mausoleum at Windsor.

Among the mourners was a hunched figure dressed in black, her face veiled from sight. She was accompanied by an elderly bald man with a moony face, leaning on a cane whose hairline joint revealed it to be of a deadly nature. The duo was soon joined by a gap-toothed old codger who was slyly tucking a wallet not his own into his breast pocket.

"So long ago," said Cowperthwait. "But the cards at Christmas never stopped coming."

"Wimmen air like elleyfants," said McGroaty. "They never forget."

And as if in silent agreement, Victoria pulled back her veil and snapped a passing fly from the air.

Reflected Light

RACHEL E. POLLOCK

Reprinted from the highly recommended *SteamPunk Magazine*, Rachel E. Pollock's "Reflected Light" represents a strand of activist, political steampunk, putting the reader in the point of view of factory workers in a strange other world. Remade mechanical hands, mysteries involving the disappeared, and an account recorded on a wax cylinder figure prominently in this intriguing piece.

Nicquossee Artifact Collection: Vick Flinders record diary, wax cylinders 1–4
Reference subject: Fardelle "Della" Dicely
Archivist's note: Cylinder condition is denoted "fair," as some minor scratches have obliterated short sections (3 seconds or less) of playback quality. Cylinders will be demoted to "degraded/discard" status after 10 known playback instances. Please confine perusal to attached transcript unless granted playback permission by sanctioned government agency. Current number of known playback instances: 7.

Cylinder 1

They say Della Dicely's run mad. Up and walked off the job two weeks past and none know whence she's gone. Nobody's ever walked off the job, not in our shop, not that I've ever heard. They say when she returns, if she returns, Nonnahee's set to kill her slow. Puts my mind at unrest, that prospect.

Me and Della, we worked side-by-side in this smithy since we was wee younglings, she a piece longer than I. I don't know as I'd call her friend; don't know if Della rightly has friends. Don't know as any of us do. Perhaps she'd be my comrade, my collaborant or fellow or helpmate...something indicating the closeness grown by common labor, the community of the machines.

See, me and Della... But now I reckon I ought to say only "me." I'm a leatherworker; not a carcass-skinner nor a hide-scraper nor an oil-tanner, but a leathersmith proper. I assemble the hides into whatever is requested each morning by the Nonnahee jobman — mostly working-gear. I make toolbelts and knife-sheaths, heavy gloves and cart-age pouches.

Della's favorite thing to make was the welders' leathers — long-sleeved backless shirts and the front-sides of trousers, customized exact to fit the bodily shapes of the men and women they protected. Some say she was the best in the business, and I believe it. Would you feature? Jack-a-Ron Dantsy himself brought his entire gang of weld-ers in, had Della kit them all out, even he himself! Jack-a-Ron Dantsy! I like to have died just to cower in the corner of the same room as the man, but Della? No sir. Walked right up to him, shook his hand just as cool as you please — *shook his blamed hand!* — then whipped out the twine and began to measure him off. She's got brass, Della does.

Not me though, I'm as dull as the dishwater. I just keep my head down and my shoulder to the wheel. Jack-a-Ron Dantsy aside, I'm not much for the high geometry of custom work, even for [*section lost: flaw in wax surface*] sit with a stack of stock patterns, bags and pouches and spannermen's toolbelts, and crank them on out. Leathersmithing, it's hard work, but we're grateful for it. Beats other work, that's for true; at least at the end of the day I've got a pile of things I've made, me with my own hands. What can the railman say, or the stoker? He's moved cars around the yard, shoveled how many piles of fuel? Necessary jobs, honest work to be sure, but I wonder: for the railman, for the stoker, where's the satisfaction in it? Or perhaps they need no sense of accom-plishment in their work, care for none. It's possible; but me? Give me leathersmithy any day.

Cylinder 2

They tell us we're at the bottom of the chain of progress, leathersmiths, working with hide instead of metal, but Della, she figured out that was a lie. That's something she told me before she ran off to wherever: *We ain't the bottom at all. We're an integral part of the cycle.* We make the leathers that protect the welders that build the machines that form the basis of the world of the Hollowland. And what do we use to make those leathers? Machines. And what must the welders have in order to build machines? Our leathers, to protect them from the flying slag and swarf. We may be small cogs, but remove even one tooth of one gear and the machine won't run properly. We, Della told me, are *important*.

I've been a leathersmith all my life, ever since I was tall enough to reach the foot-pedals of the stitching machines. Even before that, [*section lost: flaw in wax surface*] belting through a strap-cutter, finished ornamental edges with the crank-pinker, and traced out patterns to be cut upon hides with bits of colored wax.

It was as a youngling learning the trade from Della that it happened, that which I can never myself forgive, the horrible happenstance that rendered me forever in her debt, [*section lost: flaw in wax surface*] chasing the smoke of atonement.

Hap you ever to see a strap-cutter? It takes two working in tandem to operate, and I worked it that day partoned to Della, both of us green young things but I far the greener stripling. She was showing me how it worked, what my business was and what was hers, when the accident happened. She had the blade and I the hide, and as she pulled the cutter-handle toward her, slicing through the leather so swift and smooth, I got excited and gave the hide a quick little tug, a fillip that sent the cutter through the end and oh! Her hand was caught and the world swung round and I tasted the bile of horror at what I'd done.

At first I cried far more than she — so much blood on the floor and the sight of Della's finger lying there like some cave worm grubbed up from the depths. It shook my teeth a-rattle and no mistake. Della though made neither sound nor weepage until the foreman cauterized the tiny nub with a fire-iron; then she screamed but good, and then the tears came, big and trembly.

"No, Vick, no guilt," she said. "It was not your fault."

That Della could say a hundred-thousand times, but it would always be a lie.

[*three-second pause in the recording*]

Two weeks in the shop without Della have seemed two years at least, mayhap two lifetimes, as we've not only lost her skill and turnout toward the workload, but we've lost her stories as well. Me, I haven't a head for spinning of yarns and no matter — that lies in the province of talekeepers. Della, she's talekeeper for Dicely Clan.

Della knows more tales than hairs on a hide fresh-skinned, and not just Dicely Clan stories neither, nor just those of our people, the Nicquossee. She even knows Sallagee legends and Geriyan epics and oh! Great Builders, but I love the tales she tells of the Lunjinfolk. (She learned those from Dantsy Clan, some first-hand from Jack-a-Ron himself!) I never thought about how swiftly passed our days when the work sped through the machines in the nimble hands of Della's stories, but now she's gone, the melody and rhythm of her tale-telling has been replaced with naught but the steady repetition of chunking machines, their whirring flywheels and laboring treadles punctuated only by the occasional startling arrhythmia of an explosive burst of let-off steam. Our minds are left to occupy themselves, and mine seems only able to caper and slog an ever-tightening spiral around the central figure of lost, mad Della.

I miss her.

In her presence, I, dull Vick, shone with reflected light.

Cylinder 3

Today the world has changed.

My world has changed, at least, for today, my goodman Lundy brought home a piece of godwork, a contraption that has sparked in me a fire, for it flings wide a door that leads to my salvation!

My Lundy's a manufactor — he assembles small machines that do breadbasket-sized tasks in a shop equal-scale of our smithy. He doesn't design the machines, only puts them together according to schematics drawn by the Nonnahee engineers. (The Nonnahee would never allow us to create abstractly, not in any official capacity.) But Lundy, he's a bit of a secret contraptor, bringing home broken parts of things salvaged from the refuse, which is of course forbidden, trashpicking is, but he's friendly with some of the rustmen and slagworkers at the manufactory, [*section lost: flaw in wax surface*] other way when he pockets a broken flywheel or a crushed oilcan. He's a good fellow, Lundy is, and careful about keeping his bricolages hidden from Nonnahee eyes, so I don't begrudge him his devotion to tinkerage; it trumps a fleshly mistress certain.

Twice before Lundy's brought home nigh-fully-functioning machines gifted to him by Garl Spitshine, his particular slagman friend. In what repugnant rotting heap or chemic sludge Garl finds them, I don't know and do not wish to; I fear perhaps he steals them, and I prefer to remain ignorant of that for true. I only know the glee they bring my dearheart Lundy, and, admittedly, a-times myself as well.

The first such contraption was an odd thing with a crank and a stamper-plate and a drawer of tiny lead shapes, neatly arranged. Lundy replaced the bent crankshaft and showed me its true purpose: printing small paper tickets with words in the Nonnahee language. What use this is to Lundy is a mystery to me — he cannot parse the symbols, but he does love cranking out reams upon reams of those gibberish-tickets and I must admit, there is some satisfaction in building up a rhythm turning its crank, watching the little papers move through and emerge with their rows of neat marks. We burn them — often before their ink's dry — for fear of their discovery.

The second such requisition ran off with my heart, however — the device upon which I set down these thoughts: the wax cylinder recorder. It was housed in a splintered wood case (replaced by Lundy), the gears inside missing teeth like oldsters. Its horn was crushed, its mandrel bent, the stylus crumpled like a stomped reed. As with the ticket-printer, Lundy scavenged and repaired and fiddled around with the odd little thing until he coaxed it back to life.

I'll never forget the night he brought it to me, showed me the means by which it worked. There was the machine, hunkered on our rustic table, and there was Lundy, grinning like a new father as he produced a brownish waxy tube, held on the spindle of his own two fingers. He cranked the handle, placed the cylinder on the mandrel, positioned the reproducer, and set it a-running. I couldn't believe my ears when, out of the mouth of the machine, came Lundy's voice:

"Please know this, love: I taught these gears to speak that they might convey the contents of my heart. You have all of it, always." Then the machine laughed in Lundy's peculiar arpeggio.

I stood there, my jaw hanging open, catching flies. Lundy's laugh came echoing out of his own mouth and I, too, couldn't stifle my...oh dear, I've digressed a whole cylinder away.

Trifles aside and I must rush to the point: today Lundy brought home a mechanical hand.

Archivist's note: Though this diary entry at first may seem spontaneous, the voice that speaks the dialogue of Lundy Flinders "through" the machine is in fact that of Flinders himself, leading this scholar to believe that Vick Flinders planned the entry in advance and coordinated its recording with her husband. An alternative possibility is that Flinders replicated the wax cylinder recorder in toto, and Goodwife Flinders utilized a second phonograph to play Flinders' original recording on cue. The clarity and volume of the dialogue however leads this scholar to discount that hypothesis.

Cylinder 4

It is now several days since, as Lundy and I like to say, the Advent of the Palm, and oh! More to relate!

The poor hand, as the ticket-press and phonograph before it, arrived a wretched mangled thing. As per usual, Garl is the means of its shady deliverance; but I don't care if he stole it off a one-armed Nonnahee while he slept. Looking upon it fills every twitching corner of my mind with soft light and cool salve. Lundy has been tinkering with it each night since, well into the wee hours, and I, though I have no head for contraption, help him with what tasks I may — matching cogs from his collection to the broken ones he extracts and cleaning those he salvages intact. I do not shirk from elbow-grease, no, not I, diligent Vick.

Lundy's prognosis is grim for the sad twisted mitt, but he is often a raincloud to my sun. He claims preference of the shadow's view, but truth-told he is buoyed by my brightsiding. I knew the moment I clapped eyes upon the little wreck, if any tale of the world is written by any people's gods, Garl was meant to give that hand to Lundy, and Lundy is meant to make it work again.

Oh, but I cannot keep it to myself: I have news of Della Dicely!

Hap I may have been too bold, but yesterday after half-shift I went to the dockyard, where Della's sister Spondee works as a braider and a knotsmith. I found her easy enough — Spondee is tall and mannish-built — but spent a long while loitering, looking for my courage. I am so poor at conversing! Not so Spondee, for she shot me a narrow glance and stalked right over, demanding my business on the docks. Certain I seemed a halfwit for I feared to speak her name aloud, but [*section lost: flaw in wax surface*] managed to convey with gesture and lipshaping that I worked in Della's smithy. Spondee's eyes flew wide at that. She hissed me silent, grabbed my hand and stalked the length of the nearest pier, pulling me stumbling behind her.

At pier's end, with only ships' timber and hull-iron and a few wheeling sea-birds to eavesdrop, a fire-eyed Spondee favored me with crypticism:

"You'll find [*section lost: flaw in wax surface*] railyard at night, in the broken glass among the cinders."

Her eyes went flat and cold, and then she stalked away, leaving me shivering in the rank, oily spray of the sea. I though, I could dance I was so full of joy! Della must be hiding in the railyard somewhere, and I count the days until I shall go and find her.

As soon as Lundy and I have repaired the clockwork hand, I shall take her a lamp, beckon her forth from the dark cavern of madness, if mad she be, with the crook of a shining brass finger.

Archivist's note: The cylinder diary ends here. It is well-documented fact that Fardelle "Della" Dicely possessed only nine fingers, having lost one to an accident in her youth, but she was never known to wear any type of prosthetic. Though multiple sources recount "Della" Dicely's return to the Hollowland and her subsequent coup to overthrow Nonnahee domination and emancipate the Four Peoples, the fate of Vick Flinders beyond the scope of these recordings is unknown.

Minutes of the Last Meeting

STEPAN CHAPMAN

A brilliant and endlessly creative example of steampunk that takes as its basis an alternative Russia of the Tsars, including nanotechnology and huge mechanized cavalry, Stepan Chapman's "Minutes of the Last Meeting" is a tour de force of sustained imagination. Moving from viewpoint to viewpoint, the story introduces marvel after marvel in the best tradition of steampunk invention.

> "The Tsar has eight million men
> with guns and bayonets.
> Turn and look at the forest of steel and cannon,
> where the Tsar is guarded
> by eight million soldiers.
> Nothing can happen to the Tsar."
> —*Carl Sandburg*

On the afternoon of March 16, 1917, midway between Petrograd and the German front, a steam engine made its laborious way through the mountain passes of Latviya.

Icy steel rails cut across a waste of jagged granite. The soot-encrusted engine pulled eleven cars behind it.

In the cab of the engine stood a short barrel-chested man with bristly gray hair and a walrus mustache. His name was Ivan Klosparik. After glancing at his pressure gauges, he returned his gaze to the rails ahead. Ivan was the tsar's personal engineer, and he took his work seriously.

Ivan was far from his home and his wife. This being wartime, most of Russia's men were far from home. Ivan had grown up in a tiny oats-and-barley town in the lowlands of Taymyrskiy, half a continent away from these desolate crags. Ivan disliked high altitudes. They made his teeth ache.

Ivan watched the tracks through the plexithane windscreen of the cab. The silver tracks and wooden ties wound their way through bleak diagonals of rock and snowdrift. The engine passed a painted steel pole that served as a distance marker.

Ivan pulled off one of his gloves and keyed the train's position into the gauge panel. The train system blinked its acknowledgment on the panel's cathode slate. Ivan shivered and put his glove back on. The wind made a muffled whine. It got in under the cuffs of Ivan's overalls and chilled his bones.

The train approached a stretch of track that curved to the left. Ivan sat himself on the sill of the open window in the left wall of the cab. He held on to the window frame and leaned into the wind. He ran his eyes along the length of the train as it rounded the curve. Everything appeared to be in order.

Behind the engine rolled the coal car, bearing one passenger, Ivan's stoker. Behind the coal car came the gunnery car with its armory of antiaircraft rockets and grenade launchers stored inside. The forward gunner's turret was mounted on its roof. Inside a plexithane bubble, the gunner sat with his hand on the stock of a rotary-mounted Gatling gun. The gunner swiveled restlessly in his chair, scanning the terrain with his binoculars, searching for the slightest sign of ambush or sabotage.

The turret made Ivan feel a little more secure about transporting the tsar and his family through these desolate mountains. But not completely secure. Too many things could go wrong in this world. And the tsar had too many enemies.

The gunnery car pulled the barracks car, quarters for the tsar's honor guard. The barracks car pulled the wireless car, which bore an elaborate radar dish on its roof.

Fifth came the tsar's personal coach, a lushly appointed smoking den which was also the mobile headquarters for all of Russia's armies in the Great War.

Sixth came the coach of Tsarina Alexandra. Then came the recently constructed clinic coach. The clinic coach served as a hospital for the sickly young Tsarevich Alexius and as quarters for the physicians and nurses devoted to his care.

Then came the car for the servants of the imperial family. Then the scullery car. Then the generator car, which supported the rear gun turret. And last the caboose, where Ivan and his stoker slept when they got off duty — and where their relief workers were sleeping now. Since the outbreak of war, all the windows were painted black to discourage snipers.

The train straightened out and crossed a trestle bridge over a gorge. Ivan returned to his station and checked the boiler's pressure readings. Ivan disliked bridges. It was far too easy to plant bombs in them. But of course the Imperial Intelligence Entelechy would never allow such a thing.

Ivan believed three things as matters of faith. One thing was that the Lord worked in mysterious ways. Another thing was that he would meet his wife in heaven, after they died. The third was that the surveillance abilities of the IIE were utterly infallible. Ivan's convictions were all that kept him going on days like this.

Ivan took a pack of cigarettes from his shirt pocket and lit one, shielding it from the wind. He surveyed the ragged mountainside to the right of the tracks, and the valley that dropped away to the left. Nothing but rock and snow. The earth might be uninhabited save for this one old steam train.

Ivan glanced over his shoulder at the gunner's turret. If hostilities did arise, that young man up there would be the first target. And Ivan would be the second.

Ivan told himself to stop worrying. His gastric condition would act up if he wasn't careful. And if he lost his position and his salary, how would his wife stay alive back in Taymyrskiy? He mustn't worry so much, and that was that.

Ivan sighed deeply and watched the tracks, savoring his misery.

Nicholas II sat on cushions of crimson velvet in an armchair of carved mahogany. He was attempting to read an extremely dull intelligence report in a celluloid binder.

Tactical maps and classified documents were piled on every level surface. From this cork-paneled coach, wherever it roamed, Tsar Nicholas commanded his generals in the field. Some of his generals were battling the German infantry. Others were engaged in an internal war against the conspiracies of traitors.

The socialists were making loud noises about their glorious revolution. And it was widely known that the *Zemstva* faction within the imperial *Duma* was funding them. Everything was falling apart. Nicholas's hold over the *Duma*. Military discipline behind the lines. Mother Russia herself. The only constant was this endless war against Kaiser Wilhelm.

Nicholas smoked his briar pipe and read the cautious reports of his spies among the Bolsheviks. He *should* be reading reports on the parliamentary infighting in Moskva. But the posturings of the radicals made better reading. The radicals were all quite mad, but they actually believed in something.

Only madmen would oppose the holy rule of the autocracy. Didn't they realize how easily the IIE could protect Nicholas from their murderous plots? There was no man or woman anywhere in Russia who could escape from the spying eyes of the IIE. That paper clip might be one of its secret cameras. That fly speck on the spittoon might be one of its microphones. Any flea in any mattress, any weed beside the road, might be a spy for the Entelechy. Naturally, under such conditions, everyone reported to the authorities regarding everyone else as often as possible. That went without saying.

Three generations of the autocracy had sheltered beneath the wing of the IIE's protection. Who, then, would oppose the tsar? Only madmen.

But Russia was filled with those. Half of the nation was going mad from the bloodshed and the famine. The other half had been mad to start with. Surely the second coming of Christ was at hand.

Nicholas was a bitter, jaded man. Part of his mind was always frightened and angry, while the other part remained passive and bored. His stormy side raged inside his head, while his passive side never stopped complaining. Life was too much for Nicholas. Why couldn't all these ratty little Bolshevik firebrands leave his world alone? Why couldn't they let it shake to pieces by its own momentum?

Nicholas threw the celluloid binder across the compartment. It bounced off a lacquered screen. Damn reports. Damn everything.

In the tsarina's suite, Alexandra sat on her bed, wearing a green silk dressing gown. The room was filled with embroidered sofas, footstools, armoires, and trunks for her keepsakes. A room out of the nineteenth century. She closed her eyes and wished herself back to her father's *dacha* in the country. But the train rumbled under her, and reality intruded.

She was riding a train in the age of high technology and mechanized warfare. She was an aging woman with four children. She had spent her health and her happiness to give the tsar a son. And when the son had come at last, it had been poor Alexius with his hemophilia and his heart murmur. And now all Europe was at war.

This was no century for a woman of refined sensibility.

Dr. Ostrokov sat at the steel desk in his private office, forking up a plate of fried calamari and potato noodles. He chewed his food and took a swallow from his last bottle of vodka.

Ostrokov's brain seemed to be spinning in his skull. He tried to withdraw his attention from the problem of Alexius's heart. The thirteen-year-old tsarevich was dying by gradual stages of congenital blood disease and cardiac complications. His current condition was comatose but stable. Nature's way of sedating the terminally ill.

Ostrokov tried to relax. After all, it wasn't as though he were a folk healer in some Slavic fairy tale. It wasn't as though he would be boiled in oil if he failed to repair the heart of the young prince. At worst he'd be sent to the German front.

Ostrokov closed his eyes and tried to control his blood pressure. There was only so much that he and his interns and their ultramodern toys could do for the wretched child. The boy's pulmonary function would never be sound. His gamma gobulin count would never increase. Medical science couldn't perform miracles.

Alexius was like the damned war. He went on and on, year after year, beyond all endurance, refusing to die. But perhaps he'd emerge from his coma. Perhaps he had suffered no serious brain damage. Or perhaps he was already brain dead.

Dr. Ostrokov felt that his head would explode. He took another swallow from his vodka bottle, screwed on the cap, and returned it to a desk drawer. He decided to look in on Pod and the other microbots. Dealing with the surgical machines always steadied his nerves.

He stepped from his office into a corridor and moved along, holding a handrail, past the nurse's station. He paused beside the sickroom and peered through a viewing lens. Alexius lay on his back under a white quilt inside an oxygen tent. The boy looked like death. The back-wash of blood from the right ventricle had to be corrected, and soon. The valve replacement was scheduled for two P.M. Only an hour away. If Ostrokov and his team didn't lose the boy today, Alexius might last another season.

Train travel was bad for the tsarevich, but Nicholas insisted on keeping his heir at his side. If pawns of the Grand Duke Michael were to snatch Alexius, then Michael would attempt to seize the throne as regent. Or so Nicholas feared.

But Nicholas was a hopeless paranoid. Alexius would be perfectly safe anywhere in Russia. The IIE made certain of that. For a century now, no tsar nor any member of the dynastic family had been assassinated or deposed or captured. So this clinic coach was a product of mere neurosis. There was no other logical diagnosis.

Yet the orders of a tsar could not be questioned. So Alexius went where his father went. And what could Ostrokov do about it?

Ostrokov entered the surgical cabin. One of the interns was review-ing telemetry files at a data desk. The intern saluted Ostrokov. Ostrokov nodded. Then he stood with his back to the cabin hatch, surveying his domain.

Here was his operating theater, the finest in the land. It resembled the cockpit of a submarine. Perched on racks, high against the walls, cross-connected black boxes aimed their narrowcasting funnels at the sickbed in the next compartment. A pilot's chair stood on a pedestal — with sensing gloves, leg frames, and a spherical white helmet as big as a pumpkin.

Stuck to the cabin's blackened windows were schematics of the var-ious microbots now stationed within Alexius's sickly heart. Here was a slender conical Digger. Here was a cross section of a Gaffer, showing its three stovepipe legs and its long spindly arm. Here was Anchorlegs standing on its suction cup — the largest machine of the eight, a sort of animate toolshed.

And here was a portrait of Pod, the team leader, a small and feeble creature composed mostly of brains and radar. It was Pod that Ostrokov piloted. Sometimes he felt that he became Pod.

All across the battered face of Europe, hospitals were overflowing with broken men and women who'd be lucky to receive morphine, let alone reconstructive surgery. But the hemophiliac tsarevich had his own private microsurgical unit. Scalpels and sutures were useless for cardiac work on Alexius. But with nano-scale technology from China, Ostrokov could operate by remote control.

The surgeon sat down in the pilot's chair and strapped himself into the proprioception gloves and leg harnesses. The cabin was hot and stuffy. Without proper ventilation, the heat from the coal stove was trapped inside. In China, they could build intelligent devices five molecules thick. In Russia, when a tractor broke down, a peasant would call a priest to sprinkle holy water on its motor.

In Russia, women were used as land mine sweepers. The prime minister of Britain had offered the tsar a shipment of modern metal detectors. "No thank you," the tsar's chief of staff replied. "We already have a system in place. We send out parties of excess war widows. The exploded widows give their lives for Mother Russia. And as a collateral benefit, the food shortage is relieved."

And as for ventilating a train compartment, oh no, that was far too difficult a problem for sluggish Georgian brains.

Ostrokov lowered the chair's helmet onto his head and fitted the cathode visor to his eyes. He sat for half a minute, listening to the train wheels and preparing himself. Then he kicked a pedal and opened his tight-beam link with Pod.

His auditory nerves were the first to accept the input. A vast hiss engulfed him, like the churning of a river over a waterfall. Then a deafening boom drowned out the hiss. The atrio-ventricular valve was slamming shut.

In the strained and weary fibers of his legs, he could feel the blood tide slowing and reversing. Turbulence yanked him to and fro. This was the systolic backwash that was killing the boy. It went on and on. Time was slower on the inside. Time *had* to move more slowly for tiny creatures, because they had to move so fast. Only molecules moved faster. Dr. Ostrokov was unbelievably huge and slow, like Alexius's heartbeat. But the helmet was accelerating his brain, tightening every synapse, to allow him to keep up, for just a few seconds, with Pod and the others.

His eyes began to see through Pod's radar bowls. Here was the flat roof of Anchorlegs beneath him. Here were Pod's spindly legs, clutching the roof against the pull of the blood rush. Here, glowing like red coals through the blood plasma, were the navigation beacons on his knees. Out there, looming over him, were the slick corrugated concavities of the auricle.

And there were the three Gaffers, clinging to the muscle wall. Their pincers were anchoring the replacement valve between them. The Gaffers had constructed the smooth white saucer from raw polymers of polyprotonol and felt justifiably proud of it.

Soon the Cutters would cauterize a thousand capillaries and carve loose the leaking flesh valve. There must be no slips, no snags, no hemorrhaging. Each phase must go quickly and cleanly. Simple. Simple as cherry pie. About as simple as threading a strand of egg yolk through the eye of a needle while walking on stilts, blindfolded, while circus clowns shoot water at you from a high-pressure fire hose.

Pod yearned to complete the implant and to escape from this colloidal hellhole. The work was maddening. It wasn't the work itself so much as the waiting for orders. Already Pod had spent decades inside this patient, centuries, millennia — merely awaiting further orders. Why wouldn't Ostrokov let them finish the job? Must they all die of old age inside this sickly boy's chest?

Pod felt Ostrokov looking over his shoulder, also waiting. Pod respected Ostrokov, who'd proved himself a perceptive and level-headed supervisor. Not like those clumsy interns of his, who were far too eager to help.

A great groaning echoed through the heart. As the semilunars squeezed shut, the atrio-ventriculars eased opened. A tide of purple blood poured down from the vena cava, through the auricle and into the ventricle. The noise of the blood wind numbed Ostrokov. His brain was too slow. He ought to be conserving himself for the operation. He had to get out.

Ostrokov kicked the release pedal and gradually returned to his body. Tsarina Alexandra was standing beside his chair. Her hand was resting on his shoulder. The intern had gone away. Ostrokov disengaged himself from the chair, stood up, and bowed. Alexandra stepped into the surgeon's arms and pressed her cheek against the white linen of his shirt.

"We mustn't," Dr. Ostrokov whispered. "Someone will see us."

"I'm afraid, Jacob."

"Everyone is afraid."

"Hold me, Jacob."

"Not here. Look around you. Your son is dying."

"My son has been dying since he was born. Kiss me, Jacob."

"We mustn't."

"Ah, but we must," Alexandra told him, placing her hand over his heart. "The world is ending. And when the world ends, lovers must kiss."

Jacob held Alexandra and kissed her tenderly. As they kissed, the microcamera concealed in the tsarina's wedding ring swiveled to observe them. The camera transmitted its image to a buried relay station in Pskov. The relay station boosted the image to Petrograd and the IIE complex.

In an artificial cavern a kilometer below the city of Peter the Great, the Imperial Intelligence Entelechy lived its paralyzed life and thought its cybernetic thoughts and looked on while Alexandra kissed the Jewish surgeon.

The IIE observed and mused. Within the huge black egg of its polished obsidian shell, a hundred tons of circuitry hummed with the microvoltages that rippled glimmers of perception through its involuted mass. The stone egg rested at the center of a disk of black pumice under a dome of black chitinite. A swarm of data cables radiated from the disk.

Above the IIE's cavern, in a monolithic office building, beehives of analysts decrypted radio traffic around the clock. They fed the best data down the cables, to the 999 vesicles of the simul-processing superbrain.

The IIE's first vesicle gazed upon the tsar, who was smoking his pipe, while its fifth vesicle watched the tsarina. Its eleventh vesicle was peevishly listening to a phone conversation between two of its field agents in Moskva. The tap was loud and clear. Vesicle Eleven could hear every word that Linkroda wheezed at Gorodni, and each of Gorodni's stoic grunts.

Provost Officer Linkroda of Kirov was complaining to Operative Gorodni concerning the chaos in Linkroda's district. Gorodni, meanwhile, was pumping Linkroda for inside material on a recent industrial disaster.

GORODNI: *Nerve* gas? Yesterday you said *tear* gas. What will it be tomorrow, Linkroda?

LINKRODA: Does the official story matter? Kirov will be uninhabitable for two decades.

GORODNI: Yes, it *matters*, damn your soul. When the riot mongers are inciting the serfs to revolt, these things matter. To whom besides myself have you spoken the words "nerve gas"?

LINKRODA: Before I answer that, Vaslav, you tell *me* something. To whom do you report these days?

GORODNI: Provost Officer, let me offer you some advice. A government man does well to keep his eyes turned downward. When his gaze turns upward, his superiors may begin to feel defensive.

LINKRODA: Nonetheless, Vaslav, are you never tempted to boast? Everyone says that you report directly to *Citizen Tridd*. (Inside the IIE, an alarm went off. Linkroda's dossier was called up for red-tagging.)

GORODNI: Watch what you say.

LINKRODA: Oh, I beg your pardon. I had no idea that the very *mention* of the reclusive Tridd was forbidden. In the future I will avoid all reference to the awe-inspiring genius of the secret police. The name of the incomparable Tridd is a name that must only be whispered in the shadows. Still, one hears rumors. Is he truly the tsar's most trusted advisor? Is he secretly ruling in Nicholas's place? Only great power can buy such absolute silence. You must tell me, Gorodni. I have to know. You've seen him. I know you have. You've seen Tridd's face. Tell me. I don't matter. I'll die soon from the gas I swallowed. Tell me about him.

GORODNI: You're raving. You're drunk. Tridd is a myth. A Gothic fiction. Your clearance level is higher than mine, Linkroda. If *you* can't track him down, then why do you think—

LINKRODA: Ah, but perhaps he found *you*, Gorodni. Perhaps you're *his*. Though I can't think why he would choose a man who lies as badly as you. Perhaps your failings endear you to him.

GORODNI: God save you, Linkroda. You're a complete romantic. Do you suppose that you'll get to the bottom of the wild rumors? Be realistic. We're all just glorified thugs at our level of the service. People like us don't get to the bottom of anything. Our job is simply to keep the masses happy. They aren't happy unless they're spied on and bullied. It gives them more to complain about.

LINKRODA: You talk like an insurrectionist.

GORODNI: I call things by their names. Go to bed and sober up.

Gorodni hung up the phone. He leaned on his desk, massaged his brow, and smiled. Tridd again. However disgusted Gorodni felt with his career in disinformation, he never tired of hearing about Tridd. Tridd the invincible! Tridd, the psychotic mastermind! Tridd, who preserved the tsar's crumbling empire by means of sheer brain power. Tridd of the endless rumors. The Slavs were suffering food shortages, fuel shortages, and shortfalls of cannon fodder, but there was never any shortage of rumors.

Gorodni relished the tales of Tridd. He collected them for the IIE. His favorite story described a boy with a freakish head.

Tridd, so they said, had been a child polymath with an eidetic memory and an uncanny grasp of game theory. The child was recruited to the service of the State. At puberty, his skull began to swell. When his head grew bigger than a medicine ball, Tridd had to wear a foam collar, lest the weight of his brain break his neck. As the years progressed, his head grew as big as a hayrick, then as big as a barn.

The secret police commandeered a derelict cathedral for him. Within it they constructed a steel scaffold to support the young man's skull. As Tridd's cranium budded off new lobes, the men tore down walls and built annexes to make room.

As his brain enlarged, Tridd's musculature withered. Unable to breathe without mechanical aid, he was enclosed from the neck down within an iron lung. His shrunken body, mounted in its plexithane cylinder, protruded from one side of an ever-expanding orb of brain and bone. His face, neck, and body became a pitiful parasite, hanging from a living boulder.

Gorodni thought it a very pretty story, this version of Tridd. It was a tempting invitation to paranoia. But true? About as true as Baba Yaga the Witch. And Gorodni was in a position to know this for certain. Why? Because Gorodni had invented Tridd. Tridd was Gorodni's most successful disinformation campaign. Years ago, as a lowly cipher clerk, he submitted the idea of Tridd to the IIE. The exceptional success of the legend won him promotions. Naturally he was Tridd's most devoted mythographer.

Gorodni leaned back in his chair and put his feet on his desk. From one corner of the ceiling of his office, a harvestman spider watched him.

From behind the ten eyes of the spider, the IIE's eleventh vesicle also watched Gorodni and wondered what he was thinking. Perhaps one of the payrolled psychics upstairs in Petrograd would know. V-Eleven couldn't begin to guess.

V-Eleven switched over to its sensor in Officer Linkroda's office, an ashtray on a cluttered desk. Linkroda was fat and bald, his shirt untucked. He dialed his phone. V-Eleven traced the call.

Linkroda rang the phone of his daughter, Anya Tamarova Linkroda, at the IIE complex. The cathode slate on her phone announced the source of the call. Anya let the phone ring. Linkroda hung up, frowning. He returned to his typewriter and his disaster report. V-Eleven lost interest in Linkroda and switched over to the pen holder on Anya Tamarova's desk.

Anya was a salaried psychic observer. She sat in a small cubicle in a large room, surrounded by more than a hundred other licensed sensitives. Facing her desk were monitors for eight remote cameras. Anya sat in a swivel chair, her back straight, her pen poised above her logbook. A plain woman with limp brown hair, in a simple gray dress with a starched white collar. She turned her gaze methodically from one screen to the next.

She stopped at the seventh screen and leaned forward. She began to take notes in shorthand. She was seeing something that only a psychic observer would see. An old woman and a… what? A child? A midget?

They were standing beside a railroad track in the middle of nowhere, about twenty miles south of Petrograd. Anya was watching this place because the tsar would be passing it. The two phantoms just stood there staring south along the track, as if they were waiting for a train.

Anya keyed her screen control to enlarge the central section of the image. The old woman was a typical toothless crone with a mole on her chin and hair growing out of it. She wore a threadbare black dress and a red shawl. But the child or elf or whatever he was…. His skin was green. And his nose was nearly half a meter long and tapered to a point. He wore a tailcoat of bright green, a plaid vest, and no shoes. That creature was definitely something from a fairy tale.

Then it came to Anya: so was the old woman. Anya recognized her now. Anya's pen danced across the pages of the logbook. BABA YAGA. LEGENDARY WITCH. CHILD SNATCHER. CANNIBAL.

The IIE's eleventh vesicle disconnected itself from the pen holder and floated in a void of utter silence. Perhaps all would be well. Perhaps the war would end soon. Perhaps the IIE could turn back the Huns, if it threw a sufficient quantity of lives into the blast furnace of the battlefields. Perhaps it could forestall the onrushing revolution and win safety for the tsar. Perhaps it could win the chess game for one more year.

But there was one thing the IIE could never do. It could never lift the awful black weight of its depression. And no one would ever love it, the way the tsarina loved Dr. Ostrokov. No one would ever be proud of it, the way Gorodni was proud of Tridd. No one would ever feel curious about it, the way Anya felt about her apparitions. Not even that.

While the IIE's eleventh vesicle was feeling sorry for itself, its seventy-ninth vesicle was punching up the feed from Spy Cricket #0018320-D.

The mechanical cricket was hanging from an oat stalk beside a deserted dirt road near Cherblinsk. Off to the west, the road crossed a wooden bridge over an ice-choked river. A bony black cow stood in the middle of the bridge and chewed her cud. Nothing besides the cow had used the bridge all day. To the east lay frozen beet fields. The cricket stared vacantly across the fields and used its hind legs to scrape the frost from its plasticene wing casings. Somewhere a dog was yapping.

The cricket heard the whir of steam autos approaching. It clambered onto the tassel of the oat stalk and angled its eyes toward the crest of the road. A low-slung passenger coupe sped into view. A black van pursued it — a police wagon with a rotating beacon on its roof. Eight rubber tires jounced across rutted mud. The van overtook the car and tried to run it off the road. The car accelerated out of harm's way. The two vehicles raced toward the bridge.

The cricket focused one eye on the autos and angled the other toward the black cow. The cow chewed her cud and stared down at the dirty ice on the river. She never turned her head, never took notice of the noise.

The van and the car were side by side as they crossed the bridge, grinding their fenders together. The car slid over icy planks, tearing down a row of railing posts. Its grille smashed into the black cow. The car and the cow fell from the bridge and down through shattering ice into the frigid murk of the river. The spy cricket heard footsteps running across the ice.

The van skidded to a halt on the far side of the river. Then it turned around, drove back toward the bridge, and parked. A squad of men in khaki uniforms jumped out with rifles slung over their shoulders. They fanned out to surveil the river. The tail end of the car was still sticking up through a hole in the ice. One of the men fired a volley of bullets through it, shattering the windows. There was no sign of movement. A blackbird flew up from some oat grass and soared away. The car sank a little deeper, cracking more ice.

A man in civilian clothes stepped down from the cab of the van — a slight Asiatic man with a thin mustache. He wore a leather jacket and a fur cap with ear flaps. He stamped his feet and squinted at the ice. Citizen Taka had hounded down his quarry, but apparently she'd drowned. This was unfortunate. He'd been instructed to bring the dissident in for questioning.

He walked to the edge of the river. The black cow was visible under the ice, floating on its side, already frozen solid, staring up at Taka from one doleful brown eye. Spy Cricket #0018320-D watched Taka, while Taka looked at the cow, and the cow looked at nothing.

Downstream, unseen by Taka's men, Astra Leonova, agent of the International Workers' Revolution, crept on her hands and knees across the ice, toward the dead reeds and brown moss on the shore. She crawled in among the reeds, gasping for breath and shaking from the cold. The skirts of her red velvet dress and her fur overcoat had been soaked before she could jump clear of the car.

Astra slid into a hollow and propped her back against a driftwood log. Her dress creaked, stiffening into ice. She fervently hoped that Taka would think her drowned. If she kept herself hidden, and no crickets spotted her, she just might get away alive. But to stay where she was meant frostbite and death. Her breath made white arabesques in the still air, like Chinese dragons with white wings and white claws.

She groped the pockets of her coat, hoping to find her cigarette lighter. She'd left it in the coupe. She did find the silver-plated cigarette case that had been given her by Leon Trotsky. She would've preferred the lighter. Her hands and her feet were numb. She fumbled open the cigarette case. Inside it, miraculously still dry, was the cellophane packet that contained her cocaine. What incredible good luck! *This* would keep Astra awake.

She tore open the packet, dipped in a finger, and poked the finger up a nostril. She repeated the process until the packet was empty. She began to feel warmer.

The sun struck a glare from the river ice. It glittered through rustling rushes. Astra's legs trembled on mossy mud. The mud resembled a drapery of ochre velvet and olive green damask, painted in the style of Goya.

Citizen Taka scuffled his boots behind her. Astra turned her head.

"Pardon me, Miss Leonova," said Taka. "We've come to arrest you."

Astra rose to her feet with a stiff dignity. As they walked toward the black van, Taka offered his arm to her. The gesture reminded Astra of a man who had once been her lover — an Irishman named Dunleavy. She wondered what sort of a war Evan Dunleavy was having.

Dr. Dunleavy, as it happened, was not so far away.

Dunleavy drove his steam auto along a different rural road near Cherblinsk. He was taking a drive in the country to relax. Dunleavy was under a lot of pressure. He was the head of the tsar's research effort toward the construction of a trans-uranium warhead.

Dunleavy was on his way to the ruins of a historically significant church. He was an architecture enthusiast when he wasn't pursuing theoretical physics or designing bombs. His colleagues among the rocket scientists found it droll that such a great mind as his should indulge in such a pedestrian hobby. But he persisted, making rubbings of carved stone facades and collecting books on mythical Russian saints. The eccentric Irishman, they called him.

Dunleavy smiled, steering his auto around a bend. For no good reason, his mind had thrown up the recollection of a woman he'd met years ago at a party in Moskva. Her name was Astra. Astra Leonova, the wild-eyed radical. What a beautiful woman she'd been. But Dunleavy had little interest in romance, and less interest in politics. The great passion of *his* life was the trans-uranium effect.

He'd been at the University of London, studying particle theory with Marconi, when he'd first read Tesla's 1909 paper on the radioactive meteor crater in the Tunguska Steppes. Tesla had done a month of field studies then returned to New York, fearing for his health. But Dunleavy did more. In 1910, he traveled to St. Petersburg and petitioned the Imperial Commissariat of Science for the funding for an extended study at the Siberian crater. The Commissariat funded Dunleavy's project because of one crucial fact: In 1909, Kaiser Wilhelm II had initiated a trans-uranium project in Prussia.

Eight long years later, the Kaiser's physicists were stymied. The documents photographed by the IIE's houseflies in Berlin told the story. Hoffman was being too doctrinaire on the heavy water question. The German's inflexibility had killed his chances for a breakthrough. Whereas Dunleavy had delivered the goods.

He knew that he could produce the trans-uranic effect with his implosive device. He knew in his bones that the device would work. It would release the awesome energies of solar fire, here on earth. Someday nuclear fission might serve as the power source for a golden age of universal plenty. A golden age would put the socialists right out of business.

Dunleavy stopped his car beside the open gate of a wrought-iron fence that enclosed a snowbound churchyard. The car's boiler vented excess steam into the frosty air. Evan climbed to his feet and stretched his back — a tall, lanky, fair-haired man in a bearskin coat and muddy boots. He walked through the gate, leaving a trail of footprints in the snow. He shaded his eyes and gazed up at the stonework of the church.

Yes, this was certainly worth seeing. The men who'd carved this facade had truly believed in their God. Men like that no longer walked the earth. Dunleavy thought of entering the church to rummage through the wreckage of the pews for shards of stained glass. Then he walked toward the graveyard beside the church's western gallery. He stepped over a low wall of river rocks and took a walk among the yellowed weeds and the headstones.

Eshmahkies crossed his mind. Eshmahkies were goblins of Slavonic folklore, reputed to be fond of graveyards and empty crossroads. Eshmahkies were dangerous. They could put you to sleep with their magic and bite your nose off. Eshmahkies were the tooth fairies of frostbite. The only useful thing about them was that if you could trick one of them into trimming his fingernails, he was then obliged to work as your serf until his nails grew back.

Dunleavy pondered his own personal eshmahkie, trans-uranic fission. He had tucked this sleeping fire into ten gleaming warheads atop ten of the tsar's missiles. But the risk of even testing the new weapon was enormous. The IIE's modeling of a nuclear detonation showed a significant chance that the explosion would ignite the earth's atmospheric hydrogen and burn the whole planet to a crisp.

Surely the tsar would give Dunleavy more time for study. Surely the tsar would refrain from playing Russian roulette with the life of every living thing that crept or swam or flew. Yes, Nicholas was fighting a desperate war. Yes, he was said to be a weak and impulsive man, haunted by the failures of his life, like most men. But surely he feared God sufficiently to refrain from a premature test blast. Surely he wasn't insane.

No, nothing was sure. When Dunleavy considered the eshmahkie he'd invented, he could only wonder. Could he trick it into trimming its fingernails? Or would it bite off his nose?

Dunleavy stared at the bare branches of the trees. All that tangled complexity. He pulled his coat tighter around his shoulders. He walked back toward his car, profoundly depressed, depressed as only an Irishman or a Russian could be. He scratched his nose.

As the fingertip of his kidskin glove rubbed his nose, Epidermal Mite #011847-B scrambled to the sheltering pit of a sebaceous gland. The mite crouched there until the hand went away. Then it crept back to skin level and crouched there, blinking in the sunlight. It adjusted its iris settings and resumed its transmission.

The IIE was bored to tears with the mute perambulations of the gloomy physicist. It switched its 283rd vesicle to a different sensor.

Roughly half a kilometer west of the Riga-to-Petrograd railway track, Mikhail Bakunin sat on an empty crate and focused his binoculars on the ballast mound under the tracks. He was a burly man with long black hair, wearing a leather greatcoat and a woolen cap. He was sitting in a camouflaged foxhole, among other foxholes that were occupied by the men of his anarchist cadre. The mountain wind moaned through the crate. Bakunin whistled through his teeth.

The satchel charges were still in place. If the contacts didn't freeze, and if the attack went as planned, the tsar's train would never reach Petrograd. And if Bakunin's key agent was successful with her task, then the tsar would be a dead man within the hour. If, if, if. Bakunin pulled a handkerchief from a coat pocket and blew his nose.

As the saboteur blew his nose, the tiny red eyes of Spy Flea #44382-G were staring at the back of his neck. Somewhere behind those eyes, the 665th vesicle of the IIE watched every move Bakunin made.

The cardiac surgery in Alexius was finally underway. The boy lay in his sickbed under a white quilt, as usual. The tsarina sat in the observer's booth. Nicholas had declined to attend.

Dr. Ostrokov sat in the telemetry chair, sweating like a pig. Two interns sat at banks of consoles and watched the boy's vital signs wriggle across oscilloscope screens.

Inside Alexius, Pod and Ostrokov had become indistinguishable. He was living in an undersea cavern within the chest of a giant.

The three Gaffers had lowered the polyprotonol valve into position above the faulty valve of flesh. The three Cutters had completed their oval incision through the transverse septum. They had severed the final muscle fibrils and cauterized the last arteriole with their laser lamps. Now the Cutters were stationed in nooks they'd carved for themselves in the valve tissue, holding the valve in place, ready to release it.

When they let go, the diastolic blood surge would flush the leaky valve into the ventricle, with the Cutters inside it. The Gaffers would lower the artificial valve and glue it into place. Down in the ventricle, the Cutters would anchor the excised valve and slice it into bits for the lymphocytes to gobble. Then Pod would declare the operation a success.

Pod waited and listened. The systole thundered on. The plasma turbulence boiling up from the incision shook the Gaffers on their stovepipe legs. The turbulence tugged at the white saucer in the Gaffers' pincers. The valve cusps sprang open.

Pod tight-beamed the Cutters: "Do it!"

The rushing of the blood tide was a keening banshee to his sonar. He pressed himself tight against Anchorlegs's back. The Cutters retracted their arms. The flesh valve dropped away and left a gaping hole in the septum. The Gaffers swayed on their tripods in the whirling blood maelstrom. Pod spoke to the Gaffers: "Lower away."

The Gaffers lowered the white oval toward the rim of the chasm. As the gap narrowed, the plasma suction got meaner and more erratic.

"Keep it level. Hold back, Number Three. Resume now, Three.

Steady on. Almost there. Three, you're off-center. Widen your tripod. That's better."

An awful black blob of congealed blood, microns across, careened from the vena cava. A clinging mass of jelly buried Gaffer Three. A direct hit.

A clot, thought Pod. *This is all we need.*

"Don't move!" Pod called out to G-3. "Hold onto the valve! Maintain your footing. Nobody move. I'm coming. I'll dig you out."

Pod climbed down the side of Anchorlegs and scurried awkwardly toward G-3 across the wall of the auricle, on his six match-stick legs. Too late. The clot was bigger than G-3, and the drag of its surface area was too much for Three's suction feet. Three lurched forward, crashed against the valve, and was swept down the hole.

"Let go!" Pod screamed at Three as it disappeared. "Let go of the valve!"

No use. Three was down in the ventricle. It hung from the rim of the valve, swinging wildly on its twisted arm.

"Help!" it bleated.

G-1 and G-2 lost control of the valve. Three's pincer dragged it sideways into the hole. It jammed there, gouging trenches into the carefully excavated septum, mangling the hemophiliac tissue. Pod crept as near as he dared to the brink of the incision.

"Let go!" he called down the hole. No use. Surely the tsarevich would die.

But maybe not. What if Pod cut Three's arm from its pincer? Pod could see the pincer stubbornly clinging to the saucer. Pod's clipper was strong enough to sever the joint. But could he reach that far over the rim of the hole?

Pod was a cumbersome top-heavy thing, like a fat black tick. But if he moved his suction cups right up to the edge…if he unfolded all six sections of his clipper armature…if he could just keep his footing long enough….

Pod's feet began to slide. The wound swallowed him.

As he tumbled into the ventricle, he grabbed Three's arm. The drag of the two robots pulled the valve even deeper into the two bleeding ruts in the boy's heart.

But only for a moment. Pod applied his clipper to the nearest arm joint and snapped it. Three went spinning toward the semilunar valve and the pulmonary artery beyond. Pod tumbled after Three.

The artery forked and forked again. Pod lost wireless contact with his team, as he was carried out of range of Anchorlegs's relay station. Back at the surgical site, G-1 and G-2 were on their own. Pod had a more immediate problem.

His location sensor put him in a secondary pulmonary now. If he couldn't snag the endothelium soon, he'd wind up blocking an arteriole. Either way, he was out of the action. He'd have to wait for the autopsy team to retrieve him.

Just then he sailed past G-3. It was jammed headfirst into the arterial tunica, kicking its suction cups, with its broken arm trailing down the artery and flapping in the current. This was Pod's chance. He grappled onto Three's arm again. It held him in place like a rappelling rope, as the rapids rushed past him. Pod anchored himself to the vessel and sighed with relief.

Then there was nothing left to do but *wait*. Pod shut down his radar and tested his battery. It was low. But his resonator was still pulling ultrasound from the hummer in the tsarevich's bed. So in time his battery would recharge. He scanned the radio bands and tuned in the voice of a human. The human was announcing the war news at a rate of roughly one word per second. Meaningless. Incomprehensible. As for Alexius, the prognosis was grim. The procedure had blown up in their faces. Well, these things happened.

A kilometer north along the tracks, Mikhail Bakunin watched the train's approach through his binoculars. He was crouching in his camouflaged trench, where he'd have a good view of the detonations.

He shoved down a plunger handle. A hundred meters ahead of the locomotive, the bedrock under the track ballast exploded into a flurry of dust and rubble.

Ivan Klosparik braced himself and yanked up on the red rubber handle of the brake lever. As the lever lodged in its safety bracket, brake shoes shrieked against the spinning of flanged wheels. The train slowed to a crawl and stopped. The blast crater and twisted rails were still twenty meters distant from the engine's cowcatcher. Ivan crossed himself.

—◦—

In the surgical cabin, the helmet-accelerated Dr. Ostrokov roused himself from his telemetry trance just long enough to kick a foot pedal. He visualized Anchorlegs. It hadn't any arms, but its transmitter was stronger than Pod's.

"Come in, Anchorlegs."

A raspy baritone voice came on the channel. "Is that you, Dr. Ostrokov? Pod is gone." Two more voices broke in. "What are we to do, Doctor?" "Yes, Doctor, what shall we do?"

"Stay calm. The bleeding is greater than anticipated, but you Gaffers have a lot of mono-foam in your tanks. We'll drag the valve sideways, clear of the hole. Then we'll slide it back into position. Later we'll seal off the bleeding. The bleeding can wait. Stay calm. We can still make this work."

Ten milliseconds later, the valve slid into its proper position. A hundred milliseconds after that, the bleeding was completely stanched.

"It's like a miracle, Doctor." "We really beat the odds, didn't we?" "Doctor? Do you copy? Dr. Ostrokov? Do you read?"

"I'm still here," said Ostrokov. "I *think* I'm here."

Those were the last words he ever spoke. And no human heard them. Strapped in his chair, he began to quiver from head to toe. When the interns pulled him free, he went into a *grand mal* epileptic seizure on the floor of the surgical cabin. He died of suffocation. He had swallowed his tongue.

Ivan hung his upper body out of the engine and glared at the track that lay behind the train. Back at the control box, he shifted the drive chain into reverse and pulled down the brake lever. The flywheels engaged their rods, and the train rolled backward.

Bakunin depressed another plunger. A second charge detonated behind the train. Ivan slammed on the brakes again. The train squealed to a halt, trapped like a rat. The wind howled down the mountain pass.

Ivan had expected the second explosion. Now he waited for the assault. The traitors must be planning to take the tsar alive. Otherwise they'd have simply derailed the train. But Ivan wasn't the tsar, so he'd soon be dead. It was a misfortune for Ivan, and a sad thing for his wife. But if duty required that he die, he'd go down fighting.

A bullet whizzed past the roof of the locomotive. Then came the distant report of a rifle from the high ground to the east. Ivan sat down on the iron grate of the cab's floor. His stoker jumped into the cab from the coal car and hunkered down beside him. Ivan lit a cigarette for the two of them.

From atop the gunnery car, the forward turret gunner returned fire. Bakunin's men responded with rifles from the east and the west. The plexithane bubble repelled the flying slugs, but as it did, it cracked. Now the riflemen would aim for the crack. This could go on all day. But then the night would fall.

Alexandra rushed into Alexius's sickroom and knelt at the bedside of her comatose son, while bullets whistled past outside the coach. A line of blood ran down from the corner of the boy's mouth. Alexandra pushed aside the oxygen tent and pressed her silken handkerchief to his jaw. With all the jolting of the train, Alexius had bitten his tongue. Why had the train stopped? And why all the gunfire? Some sort of a drill?

Alexandra turned to the window of the surgical cabin. The intern at the bank of monitors was shouting in a strangulated voice. Where was Jacob? Soldiers were running through the passageway.

A rifle slug tore through the car, shattering two windows. Alexandra threw herself across her son, as if her body could shield him. Icy mountain air flooded the sickroom. The return fire from the two Gatling guns was deafening. The tsarina gathered the boy's quilt around him and lifted him from the bed. She dragged him to a corner of the car and sat on the floor, holding him on her lap.

The interns shot a syringe of barbiturate into Ostrokov's corpse. Above their heads, the boots of one of Bakunin's men hammered on the roof of the coach. The man charged the rear gun turret. A hail of bullets sent him skidding in the opposite direction. His body fell with a dull thump onto a coupling.

More attackers appeared from behind boulders and rushed at the train down slopes of loose scree. The tsar's soldiers ran to and fro along the roofs of the train, repelling boarders with their sidearms. The anarchists' punctured bodies littered the stones, in serf's tunics and ragged boots, bleeding to death.

Ivan Klosparik had killed a few of them with his pistol. Now the coal shoveler was dead, shot through the belly and hanging in Ivan's arms like a sack of potatoes. A puddle of blood edged up against the firebox and hissed.

The situation was hopeless. Ivan was next. The master computer in Petrograd must have fallen asleep. It would probably deploy half the armored might of Russia. But too late to save Nicholas. Too late to save Ivan. So much for the infallibility of the IIE.

All across Latviya, the teletypes were chattering. From Pskov to Ludoni, from Luga to Vyra, word of the emergency was relayed.

Under Petrograd, the IIE watched in horror and could hardly believe what it saw. It saw the interns as they tried to resuscitate the dead doctor. It saw the tsarina clutching her son in a corner of the sickroom. It looked down the barrels of the Gatling guns and watched the anarchists as they fell, clutching their riddled guts.

How could this be happening? The IIE's 665th vesicle had been specifically assigned to track surveillance. Why hadn't it alerted the other vesicles? And why had it erased itself? What madness had possessed it?

The IIE no longer felt sad or weary. Now it was furious. But how could it intervene? Bakunin had outmaneuvered it. He'd caught the train far from reinforcements. The nearest town was Vishniy, more than ten kilometers away. What was available in Vishniy? The IIE speed-scanned its vehicular lists. A fire engine, a tractor for snow removal, and a hand-pumped railroad maintenance wagon. Useless.

All that the IIE could do was to launch a massive force of jet blimps and stilt tanks from the bases under the Neva River delta. Equally useless. But the IIE transmitted the orders anyway.

It could only hope that Bakunin would delay the tsar's assassination. Either way, the IIE would lop off Bakunin's hands, douse him with gasoline, and roast him in a public square. And after the socialist beast's claws were pulled, the IIE would go after its head, Vladimir Lenin, and crush his skull in a vice.

The scramble orders flew from the obsidian egg, out through shielded cables to the control towers and command bunkers that ringed Petrograd. On the shore of the Gulf of Finland, scores of aircraft hangars cranked open their roofs. A fleet of hydrogen-propelled dirigibles rose into the sky and skimmed away, bearing south at full throttle.

Adding futility to overreaction, the IIE deployed an entire division of stilt tanks. From their garages on the banks of the Neva, the tanks galloped east. Their copper-plated hoofs thundered across the poorer districts of Petrograd, trampling flat the make-shift shelters in their path. A hundred strong, the tank pilots rode to the aid of their tsar.

The pilots formed a narrow phalanx on the plain outside the city. They wheeled to the south and rode their tanks along the railroad tracks that wound into the mountains. Their hoofs crushed rocks and flattened sections of the track as they raced to the tsar's rescue. But too late, the IIE feared. Too late.

The IIE's rage deflated. The stone egg moaned in its subterranean cavern. The shame of its failure was killing it. Perhaps Russians built their machines to fall apart. Perhaps the IIE itself was no different from some rusted-out tractor. Perhaps even the holy dynasty of the tsars was just a defective machine like all the others.

The IIE reviewed its channels of sensoria. Here was Nicholas in his study, trying to muster up some reaction. Here was Alexandra, slumped in her corner in shock, ignored by the soldiers as they rushed to and fro. Here was the tsarevich, slumped in her lap, his head against her breasts. Starvation statistics. Troop placements. The trans-uranium bomb project. Loyalty files of E. Dunleavy and A. Leonova. Various committee reports.

The Second Sub-Committee For the Evaluation of Budgeting Considerations Connected With the Kiev Municipal Sewer Question was called to order by the Chair. Role was taken, and a quorum was confirmed. The minutes of the last meeting were read and approved by a voice vote.

There was nothing to hold the IIE's interest. Just the usual litany of disasters.

Sitting at her desk, directly above the obsidian egg, watched constantly by her pen holder, Anya Linkroda knew exactly why Vesicle 665 had betrayed the IIE and then destroyed itself.

The IIE's primary logic circuits were immune to any cyber-infection, but not to Anya's mind. Anya's mind could play all sorts of games with the Entelechy's sanity and could cover its tracks all the while. The IIE had no defense against psychic attack from such a strong sender as Anya.

And it had no reason to suspect that Anya *was* a sender. No senders were allowed near the data complex. But Anya's father had schooled her from infancy to conceal her gift. She had been registered with the secret police as a passive psychic, a specialist in clairvoyance and premonition.

So no one knew who was secretly driving the IIE toward suicide. No one, that is, besides her father and Bakunin. And the IIE was deteriorating fast. She could feel it collapsing from within. Anya had accomplished her task. Think of it. Drab unassuming punctilious little Anya Tamarova. Bakunin would be pleased with her.

The IIE stared at the blank face of the comatose Alexius. The boy sprawled like a pale marble statue across his mother's lap. Nothing in the image moved or changed. Crescendos of boredom swept over the IIE, but some perversity in it prevented it from turning aside. *Nothing was happening.* The IIE felt that it was driving itself insane.

It was unfortunate for the IIE that it couldn't perceive entities of the Other World, the way Anya could. If its cameras could have seen into the noosphere, it would have witnessed the lively conversation that overlaid the unmoving tableau of mother and child. It would have seen Baba Yaga the Witch standing beside the tsarina — Baba Yaga, the whiskery crone who bakes children in her oven for meat pies. It would also have seen a little green man in a three-piece suit who was sitting with his legs crossed, on top of Alexius's chest.

Baba Yaga was all smiles today. She was chatting with her pet eshmahkie, Mr. Gogol. She felt happy because she was anticipating a fine big dinner — a dinner of massive proportions.

"Let's eat him *now*," Baba Yaga suggested. "Why not? You can have the liver. I'll be gobbling down that tender young heart. And spitting out the plastic. Come on! *Let's.* It will take Alexandra's mind off her troubles."

"Soon," crooned the eshmahkie. "Wait for nightfall. You'll have more than you can eat at one sitting."

"Impossible," snapped Baba Yaga, licking her chops.

"I'm right, and you know it," said Mr. Gogol. "Nicholas wants to convene the *Last Meeting*. Only the Irishman can stop it. And he won't. He's too curious to see what his precious bomb will do."

"I want to eat the boy," Baba Yaga insisted. "Right now! And a bite of his mama's pretty *tits*. I want to eat *all* of them. I don't even care if I throw up."

"Soon," sang the eshmahkie. "Very soon."

Not far away, Nicholas sat on a Persian rug with his back against a mahogany chair. He was speaking by wireless directly to the IIE. He was shouting into the microphone, which disrupted the clarity of the transmission. But the IIE heard and understood.

The nuclear bomb was to be launched immediately into the stratosphere over the Urals and detonated. Only the new bomb could demonstrate to the insurrectionists that Nicholas was still the autocrat of Russia, and that he would preserve his holy dynasty by any means necessary.

"These treacherous scum must be shown the facts in large print. The sight of a nuclear fireball will teach them to tremble before me. And the Huns as well! They'll see it too!"

The IIE's primary vesicle said Yes Sir and Of Course Sir and I Understand Sir. Meanwhile its fifth vesicle radiophoned the switchboard of the secret installation at Cherblinsk. The switchboard patched V-Five through to General Bulgakov, who received his orders like a soldier and rang off.

Bulgakov phoned the dacha which served as quarters for Dr. Dunleavy. The dacha switched the call to a cellular handset in Dunleavy's steam auto. Dunleavy answered on the second buzz.

"Dunleavy, this is Bulgakov. Come to the control tower at once. The tsar has ordered the launching of a trans-uranium missile."

"But we haven't — "

"I know all that, Doctor. Meet me at the tower. *Immediately.*"

Dunleavy turned his auto around. His heart was pounding. Instead of following his orders, he stalled for time by driving to the airfield. He needed to make a personal inspection of the missile before it went up. He would only be delayed a few minutes. Then he'd proceed to the control tower and count down the launch.

The missile called Oven was being moved to its firing pad by a carrier module. The carrier looked like a gray metal tarantula laboring along with a silver tower on its back. Oven was the tower, and its minaret was the experimental bomb. The other nine nuclear missiles were peeking from slots in their silos. Dunleavy climbed from his auto and approached the ferro-concrete pad of the launch dish. He squinted up at Oven and shouted into the wind.

"Oven! Are you ready for this?"

"Am being as ready as ever will," Oven called down in its bad Russian. "About the hydrogen not to worry, Doctor. Entire atmosphere to ignite is the chemically impossible. No problem!"

Dunleavy turned back to his auto. He hoped that Oven was right. If not, the tsar was to blame. Dunleavy had warned him.

As Dunleavy was climbing into his auto, a prison wagon sped across the asphalt of the airfield and parked nearby. Citizen Taka, chief of security for the base, climbed from the cab with two of his goons. Dunleavy and Taka cordially detested one another. The Asian saluted the Irishman, then addressed him.

"I saw your auto, and I thought that I might ask you a question. We have captured a saboteur who was attempting to cut her way through the electrical fence. According to our records, she seems to be an acquaintance of yours. Perhaps you can identify her. Would you mind having a look?"

"I'm pressed for time," Dunleavy answered. "If the woman is a spy, then kill her. I have to go."

One of the goons dragged Astra Leonova from the back of the van. Her hair was stiff with blood. Her dress was soaked, as if they'd hauled her from a river. She faced Dunleavy and met his eyes.

His heart went out to her. But Astra had loved her crazy politics more than him. And Dunleavy had loved particle physics more than life itself. So they had gone their separate ways. And here she stood, on a wind-swept airfield, today of all days. Evan hardened his heart and started his auto.

"I don't know her," he told Citizen Taka. "Never saw her before."

At that moment alarm sirens wailed from the four corners of the launch site.

"Am about this terribly sorry," shouted Oven. "But have received overriding ignition an order. Must go now."

The jet stream from the rocket engines burned Astra and the four men to ashes and melted their vehicles to slag.

The launch trajectory was perfect.

In the Other World, Baba Yaga cackled, and Mr. Gogol played his flute.

Ivan Klosparik sat against one wall of his engine cab. Dread lay heavy on his heart. Wave after wave of Bakuninists were assaulting the train. The sky was growing dark.

Ivan saw two black boots standing beside him. He looked up, not even trying to raise his pistol. Mikhail Bakunin was in the cab with him. Bakunin aimed his sidearm and blew off the top of Ivan's skull. Klosparik slumped onto his side on the iron grate.

Bakunin turned and walked toward the coal car. His men had secured the gunnery car. In the barracks car, they'd piled the bodies of the soldiers like coats piled in a closet. Bakunin crossed coupling after coupling and kicked open door after door, ignoring the respectful nods from his men.

At last he came to the sickroom. There he found Nicholas and two more of the royal family under guard. Nicholas turned on Bakunin, shouting in tones of outrage, although his voice shook with fear.

"You have no right!" he declaimed. "I am the tsar!"

"So much the worse for you."

Bakunin stuck his gun barrel under the tsar's nose and blew Nicholas's brains out. Blood and brains spattered Alexandra and her son like a light summer rain. Mikhail bowed to the tsarina with mock solemnity.

Two of his men laughed. Alexandra spat on the floor.

The top of Ivan Klosparik's skull was shot away. But Klosparik was made of sturdy peasant stuff. He refused to die. He thought that he wouldn't bleed so much, if he could manage to stand up. This made no sense, but Ivan chose to believe it anyway.

His hands clawed at the slick steel of the control box. One hand found the brake level and dragged it down. Ivan hung from the lever and tried to haul himself to his feet. His arms trembled. Then the life went out of him, and he fell in a heap. As he lay dead, the train began to roll slowly forward.

Bakunin felt the coach sliding under his boots. He ran from the sickroom. His men snatched up their rifles and hurried after him. Alexandra held perfectly still.

Alexius turned his head and focused his eyes on the face of his mother.

"Mama?" he said. "Mama? Did they fix my heart?"

Then he couldn't make out her face anymore. A strange white light was shining into the car through the smashed windows, and even through the windows that were painted black. It was brighter than any light Alexius had ever seen.

The coach lurched. Alexandra held Alexius tight against her chest. Beneath her, metal wheels were screeching against the tracks.

The train picked up a little speed, just as the fail-safe brakes were activating. The locomotive came to the bomb crater and derailed. The coal car pushed it off the embankment. It slid down the side of the gorge, dragging the rest of the train behind it. Bending steel groaned like the end of the world. Shouting anarchists jumped from the couplings. The clinic coach, servants' car, scullery car, generator car, and caboose went snaking down the side of the gorge.

At the bottom of the gorge, Ivan's locomotive splayed sideways across a granite outcrop. The boiler blew. Bearing shoes, frame trunnions, draw-bar pins, sand pipes, throttle racks, reach sockets, and wash-out plugs went hurtling in all directions.

A strange white light breathed gently on the falling train. The steel glowed as red as burning coals. The light breathed gently on the corpse of the tsar, and on the sick boy and his mother, and on Bakunin and his men. It blew them all into a fine red mist.

After the mountains came Petrograd. Like a magical wind from the heart of the sun, the strange light transformed the city into a tornado of whirling wood splinters and glass flecks.

Anya Linkroda stood up from her chair. She felt as if an electric shock had gone through her. Petrograd was burning out there. Some of the psychics around her were weeping. Bakunin hadn't warned her about anything like this.

The flesh evaporated from Anya's bones. As her bones became a spray of ashes, the IIE suddenly realized how cruelly she had played with it. Then it felt its coolant systems failing. The great black egg was dying. Dying felt pleasant. This must be how humans felt as they fell asleep.

In Moskva, in a cellar under the Kremlin, Officer Linkroda was torturing Operative Gorodni, using a samovar of scalding coffee, a screwdriver, and pliers. Linkroda was hoping to extract information concerning the mysterious Citizen Tridd. Gorodni's hands were held by two carpenter's vices, and Linkroda was working feverishly on his scalp with the jaws of the pliers.

"Where do they keep Tridd?" Linkroda demanded.

Gorodni couldn't stop laughing. Tridd was certainly a convincing tale. And this was Gorodni's reward. He had lied too convincingly.

As Gorodni's mind struggled to tear itself away from the pain, it showed Gorodni a vision of poor Tridd. Tridd's skull loomed in its scaffolding, bigger than a whale. Tridd's shriveled body hung from one side of it like a pale ugly grub inside a test tube.

A vibrant white light pierced the windowless cellar. Linkroda dropped his pliers.

Gorodni kept his mind on the pale grub with Tridd's face. It writhed in agony, lashing itself to and fro, faster and faster. It smashed its plexithane cylinder to pieces against the skull and sent the pieces flying. It twisted loose from the skull and fell free. But it never hit the floor.

Linkroda and Gorodni rode away from the Moskva Kremlin, on the back of a crimson wind.

The hydrogen in the stratosphere above Russia caught fire. It roasted Mother Russia alive. A crackling concrescence of hydrogen and oxygen towered over Eurasia like the Firebird of legend. Then the blaze spread. It burned down Germany and Greece and Arabia and Mongolia. It burned down India and Burma and China and Japan.

The oceans hydrolyzed, releasing more hydrogen and more oxygen, to fuel the rising flames. The elements of water and air conspired with the solar fire, to roast all Earthly flesh.

Tides of red mist swept the globe and bled into the vacuum. Earth turned as black as a cinder and as dead as her moon. Tiny robots tumbled in the currents of combustion, wondering what could possibly have gone wrong. Scarlet winds blew through the filing cabinets of the

Kremlin. All of the dossiers crumbled to ashes. Human history ended, that day in March of 1917.

Perhaps in an age yet to come, the great-great-grandchildren of Pod and Anchorlegs would tell their children long involved fairy tales about the mighty tsar Nicholas and the clever Citizen Tridd. Or about the romance between Dr. Dunleavy and Astra Leonova. But the humans had told their final story. The tsar had resigned.

Now the stars of the heavens are falling to earth like snow. Baba Yaga and Mr. Gogol are dancing a minuet amidst the fireworks.

Jesus and his younger brother, Lucifer, stand atop the embers of the planetary bonfire. They embrace in tears. They begin to dance a waltz.

My story has ended. There are no more engineers or tsarinas. No more spies or physicists. No more heart surgeons or hemophiliacs or bears or ballerinas. There's no one left to tell lies about.

In a matter of minutes, hydrogen and oxygen have concluded their final meeting.

Excerpt from the Third and Last Volume of *Tribes of the Pacific Coast*

NEAL STEPHENSON

Teetering on the border between steampunk and cyberpunk, Neal Stephenson's "Excerpt..." takes place in the same universe as his novel *The Diamond Age*, but much later. Featuring a battle in a shopping mall and nanotechnology that seems descended from steampunk, it's a fitting story to end with – and a perfect transition to Tachyon Publications' *Rewired* anthology.

> Excerpt from the Third and Last Volume of *Tribes of the Pacific Coast*, a memoir of the West Coast Ethnographic Expedition of 21xx, as related by one of the participants, Professor S– H–

For three days we bivouacked in the ruins of the galleria, sleeping on the floor of what had once been an amusement arcade, strewn with the luridly painted hulls of primitive mediatrons long since gone cold and gray. One of the galleria's glass-walled lifts was stalled at the third and highest story and provided a superb observation point over the parking lots to the south. It was from this quarter that Captain Napier anticipated the attack, so there we posted a twenty-four-hour watch. Tod, our native guide, was astonished that the glass walls of the lift were still intact, and ran his hands over them until drawing the wrath of Captain Napier: "The glass is only useful insofar as it is transparent! Go find a rag in one of the old clothing stores and wipe away your fingerprints lest they conceal the approach of some deadly intruder!" Tod cringed away from this reprimand, backed out of the lift, and scurried off in the direction of a store that had not yet been looted to the floor slab.

To our astonishment, Captain Napier turned and kicked one of the walls forcefully! Dr. Nkruma and I averted our eyes, half expecting to be struck by jagged fragments. To our surprise, though, the glass absorbed the impact as if it had been granite or marble. Captain Napier evinced some mischievous amusement at our reaction. "We who grew up in the Diamond Age know glass only as a constituent of the rubble of an earlier era," he said. "As children, who of us did not cut his hand or foot on a fragment of glass while exploring some old ruin, and thus form a pejorative opinion of that substance that, until the development of our modern crosslinked diamondoids, constituted every window in the world! And yet a careful perusal of late twentieth-century architecture will remind you that glass was frequently used in applications where ruggedness was of paramount importance — as is the case in this elevator, where loss of a pane would obviously pose a lethal risk to the occupants. Our friend Tod, I would wager, has amused himself of many an idle afternoon throwing rocks through the windowpanes of unused buildings, and come to view an unshattered pane as an affront to his athletic prowess; and yet I would wager that he could throw rocks against the wall of this elevator all day without effect."

During the course of these remarks, Dr. Nkruma had begun to stroke his goatee, as he often did when in a reflective mood. "Governmental potentates of the previous century were frequently shielded from the effects of kinetic-energy weapons by barriers of thick glass," he said, "but I had not been aware that such technology had come into commercial use." He gave the glass wall an experimental kick or two, as, I must confess, did I. Soon, Tod had returned, proudly displaying a handful of yellowed paper towels as if they were rare parchments from an archaeological site, and commenced vigorously scrubbing the glass; but once again Captain Napier had to admonish him. "Remember that glass is softer than our modern replacements for it, softer even than many of the microscopic dirt particles that are spoiling our view so, and that when you scrub it thus you are grinding those particles into the surface and thus doing more harm than good." Tod, it must be recorded, listened to this disquisition in something of a daze. Captain Napier's attempts to lift our native companion out of his abysmal ignorance spoke well of the former's noble spirit but were probably too late to improve the latter's situation. "In other words, Tod," our leader finally said, noting Tod's lack of comprehension, "you must first wash the glass with copious amounts of water, and scrub only when the gritty stuff is removed." This instruction, expressed as it was in relatively concrete terms, was clear as crosslinked diamondoid to Tod, who immediately bustled away in search of a bucket. I was surprised by his unwonted diligence until I recalled the facts of our situation, and reflected that Tod, with his relentlessly practical and earthbound mentality, must appreciate that small matters such as the clarity of the glass surrounding our sentry post might soon make the difference between life and death for all of us. The 4Wheelers might be content with simply dispatching Captain Napier, Dr. Nkruma, and myself, but Tod they would no doubt perceive as a traitor to their tribe, and kill only after they had given him ample cause to beg for the favor. My mind went back, as it had frequently in the last few days, to the sight of poor Britni Lou, dragged to death behind a 4Wheeler's pickup simply for the crime of smiling at me during one of the 4Wheelers' ceremonial meat-roastings.

The ruggedness of the northern approach to the galleria precluded a frontal assault from that direction. During our day-long retreat through that treacherous landscape of crumbling reinforced-concrete ramps and bridges we had used our supply of explosives to good effect, detonating one sheet charge after another, crashing down entire ramps on top of other ramps in a process that Captain Napier, in characteristic black humor, referred to as "civil de-engineering." If the 4Wheelers wanted to approach from that direction, they had two choices: pick their way on foot through the briar patch of snarled iron rebar that sprouted from the still-settling rubble, or drive their vehicles through the narrow defile we had left as the path of our own retreat. As one unlucky motorist had already discovered, this path was now strewn with mines capable of flinging the burning wrecks of their primitive four-wheeled conveyances a dozen meters into the air.

The south parking lot was too vast for us to mine with our limited supply of explosives. My readers may perhaps be forgiven for not appreciating the vast extent of this space. At first glance it appears, to the modern eye, to be a vacant plain, inexplicably wasted by the architects of the galleria. On closer inspection one descries a faint grid of yellow lines, like marks on a poorly erased chalkboard, and this leads the unwilling mind to the realization that the territory is not a natural formation but a man-made slab of pavement of inconceivable size. As when we look at the Pyramids or the Great Wall, we are impressed not by the work itself, which would be a trivial job for modern engineers, but by the simple fact that men bothered to do it at a time when doing it was much more difficult.

When one considers that as many as twenty thousand customers might have flocked to that place at one time; that nearly all of them came alone in automobiles; that each of these, if it were registered today, would be categorized as a full-lane conveyance, requiring a berth of some twenty square meters; and that half of the parking lot was used not for parking spaces but for traffic lanes; then the reader may begin to appreciate the dimensions of this asphalt steppe, and of our current dilemma. Time had woven a fine, intricate net of cracks across the slab, providing opportunities for various weeds that some-day might subsume the entire substance of the parking lot into the soil. For the nonce, it was still fairly level, and for the 4Wheelers with their special lorries equipped for travel on rough landscapes, it might have been smooth as a windowpane.

We deployed an array of sentry pods in the airspace above the lot, but from the original complement of some ten thousand pods with which we had set out from Atlantis/Seattle we were now down to no more than a thousand, and these so low on power that, if the wind blew hard for a few hours, they would spend themselves out just fight-ing to keep their assigned stations. Captain Napier deployed them anyway just for the impact they would have upon the morale of the superstitious 4Wheelers. What we would have given, at that point, for an extra megawatt-hour of power, stored in a usable format? Our abil-ity to store energy in tiny spaces, and to move it expeditiously through superconductors, has given us a light regard for it, and we have for-gotten that in more rustic settings we might have to burn a hundred trees or spread solar panels over hundreds of hectares in order to gather enough energy to recharge a fingernail-sized battery. Now, as we approached the end of our six-month expedition, with the towers of Los Angeles nearly in sight, we found ourselves in mortal peril from a foe we might have brushed away like so many insects had we not been running low on batteries.

Readers of a critical bent may ask why we did not simply pack more, but those patient enough to have absorbed the present narrative in its full length know of the many surprises we encountered on our way, which could only have added to the length of the expedition; in particular the three months we spent among the nearly extinct techno-shamanistic neo-Pagan tribes of the Humboldt region, trying one desperate stratagem after another to rid our bodies of the insidious nanosites with which we had been deliberately infected, while concealing from them at all costs our secret portable Source. Our disguise as itinerant missionaries, combined with the fact that we had to assume we were constantly under surveillance, made resupply impossible once we had departed the safe confines of Atlantis/Seattle.

Now our miniature Source, so cleverly disguised as a religious statuette, awaited our command. We had water to give it, and air was of course plentiful. Unlike our giant industrial Sources that draw directly upon the mineral wealth of the sea, this one compiled only systems made from nitrogen, oxygen, hydrogen and carbon, and the nanotechnological designs in its secret library used those four species exclusively. Despite this rather severe limitation, the crack engineers at Protocol Enforcement had devised an ingenious set of programs that, with the appropriate input of energy, would cause the matter compiler in our little statue's pedestal to produce small but extremely useful devices of all descriptions — including, of course, weapons.

Perhaps unfortunately for those of us who enjoyed a certain sort of romantic literature as youths, the days are long gone when the weapon was an extension of the warrior's hand, its effectiveness a function of his prowess in the martial arts. Now, as often as not, combat is a function of matching energy against energy, mass against mass, and the stealth of microscopic intruders against the depth and diligence of the defenses intended to stop them. Fortunately for us, and for all tribes that respect Protocol, the 4Wheelers did not have access to this latter type of weapon. Even their energy supplies were mostly limited to solution-phase systems, and so we did not have to concern ourselves with centrifugal rounds ("cookie-cutters") and the other fiendish systems used, in the modern world, to deliver energy into human flesh.

But mass they had, in the form of their seemingly endless fleets of steel-framed four-wheeled vehicles dating back to the Elizabethan era. Hence the 4Wheelers, despite their general technological weakness, had the ability to mount a most impressive sort of mechanized cavalry charge across the proper sort of terrain. The parking lot spread out below us could not have been more perfect for their purposes, nor more difficult for us, with our nearly extinct energy supply, to defend.

Our days and nights in the galleria, then, were spent in a kind of deliberate regression to an earlier technological era. Granted, I might have turned my knowledge of engineering to writing a new program that would cause the matter compiler to generate destructive nanosites of some description. But now that the 4Wheelers knew we were, in fact, secret agents of Protocol Enforcement, they would be sure to protect themselves with Nanobar before approaching our position. As has been discovered by many of the disreputable engineers whom it is our sworn duty to eradicate, Nanobar can be pierced if one has no respect for Protocol, but the engineering challenge is far from trivial. Our system lacked the development tools, and I lacked the time, to undertake such a programme.

Guns of the sort used in the previous century would, paradoxically, have been even more difficult to engineer on short notice, as the secrets of their design have passed from the domain of the engineer into that of the historian. Such weapons rely on the density of the projectile, but our compiler could, of course, not produce lead or any other dense element. And the explosives used to propel the bullet would have required a large energy input to produce.

The modern reader may, therefore, be amused to know that, before the final assault of the 4Wheelers, we had regressed, not merely out of the Diamond Age, but backwards through the Atomic and Industrial eras all the way to medieval times, when weapons drew their energy from the warrior's muscles. As the compiler's library contained a large repertory of springs, I was able to cobble together a sort of handheld catapult, made entirely of lightweight hydrocarbons, designed to launch small bolts about six inches in length. Each bolt was tipped with a rather wicked four-bladed head. Those blades, of course, came straight from the matter compiler and thus possessed a degree of sharpness incomprehensible to any medieval armorer, who would have sneered at the insignificant weight of the projectile, thinking that it could never possess sufficient momentum to cut its way through an opponent's defenses. But the powerful springs provided by our new technology propelled these bolts with such velocity that, in our initial test firings, they were able to penetrate half an inch of steel. It is almost superfluous to relate the depth of the impression made upon Tod by this wonder.

As Tod reeled about our makeshift fortress uttering a seemingly endless string of astonished commentary, Captain Napier, Dr. Nkruma, and myself, without exchanging any words, judged (and here I must beg the reader's forgiveness for conjuring up what is morbid and distasteful) what effect such a weapon might have when directed, not against a steel plate, but against a human being.

Captain Napier reviewed my innovation in favorable terms, which modesty forbids me from repeating here, and, so, after equipping each of the four of us with a launcher, I programmed the compiler to generate ammunition as rapidly as possible. Tod, whose anxiety over our situation had mounted almost to a state of catalepsis, suggested that we create a battery of launchers, and set them up as man-traps near all the entrances to the galleria. I must confess that I found this in some respects to be a tempting idea, but Captain Napier quashed it without hesitation, pointing out that an unused trap might lie in wait for an indefinite period of time and one day strike down an innocent curiosity-seeker.

Our little Source worked valiantly day and night, compiling the bolts half a dozen at a time, releasing its vacuum with a hiss when a batch was finished. Those of us not on sentry duty in the elevator made some pretense of sleeping; but I only lay awake listening for that periodic hiss from the compiler, much like a nervous parent listening to the breathing of a newborn infant.

The attack came just before dawn. Dr. Nkruma was on duty in the elevator, but his vigilance was wasted; the roar of the massed internal-combustion engines on the far fringe of the parking lot penetrated the entire galleria so that all of us were on our feet before he could even sound the alarm. Captain Napier brought us together in the arcade to rehearse the order of battle one last time; to remind us of our solemn duty to the Crown, namely, that given the knowledge each of us stored in our heads, we must never be taken alive by those who would wield the power of modern technology without first bowing to the rule of Protocol. Finally, Captain Napier approached our Source, which to anyone not familiar with its inner workings looked like nothing more than a rather lurid statue of the Virgin Mary, and uttered the code words that initiated its self-destruct programme. By the time we left the room, the Source was a pillar of white fire rising from the bare concrete floor. We went each to his station and steeled ourselves for the onslaught of the 4Wheelers.

The first wave consisted of vehicles that were even more decrepit than normal by the standards of the 4Wheelers, and peering through my field glasses I soon understood why: they were empty decoys, sent out to test our grid of security pods. Not knowing false from real attackers, the pods swarmed down like African bees, futilely expending their final energy supplies. Several of the vehicles exploded as our pods detonated their fuel tanks, but most of them continued to lurch mindlessly across the parking lot, eventually veering into one another or crashing into the galleria itself. Thus did the 4Wheelers clear a path for their true assault, which was a primitive and gaudy spectacle: half a dozen squadrons of several vehicles each, flying colorful flags, converging upon the galleria's several entrances according to some scheme no doubt engineered by King Karl himself.

I will not test the reader's patience by explaining in full the details of the strategy by which Captain Napier hoped to throw back this assault, other than to say that it inevitably relied upon deception, guerrilla tactics, and various psychological gambits we supposed would have a profound impact on the 4Wheelers. In any case such details are not relevant, as very little of our plan was ever implemented. We had foreseen every eventuality except one: that the 4Wheelers would have access to some technology not far below the level of ours. Before any of us had laid eyes on the foe, we had been incapacitated by powerful electrical shocks, delivered by microscopic agents that had been insensibly placed in our own bodies.

Karl himself was kind enough to provide an explanation some time later, when we awoke in his dungeon — the basement of a former office building. Captain Napier, Dr. Nkruma, and I were tightly secured to four-by-eight-foot sheets of three-quarter-inch plywood by means of innumerable ropes and straps. Tod was nowhere to be seen, and it is up to the reader to imagine his fate. Karl entered the dungeon after all of us had been awake long enough to exchange brief accounts of our experiences, which differed from one another only in details. "Them dee-coy cars tole us all we needed to know 'bout yer dee-fenses in depth, namely, that there *was* no depth to the sucker," he crowed, "so once we got into the building, all we had to do was ree-lease the hunter-dee-liverers, and when they found y'all, they nailed each and every one of yew with a nice little ol' nanosite that split in two. The two halves floated round in yer blood 'til they was a certain distance apart and then ZAP! because, ya see, they was exactly the same 'cept for about ten thousand volts' difference between 'em."

"Impossible!" I exclaimed, "such technology is to be found only within the Protocol-respecting phyles."

"Oh, it ain't that hard," Karl leered, "when you got buddies like PhyrePhox and Marshal Vukovic here. Ain't that right, fellas?"

To our utter astonishment, into the room stepped the man calling himself PhyrePhox, whom, as attentive readers will recall, we had encountered under very different circumstances two months previously. On his heels was none other than Marshal Vukovic of the Greater Serbian Expeditionary Force, whose bloody quest for stolen technology was already the stuff of legend.

"Hello, my missionary friends," PhyrePhox cackled, grinning maniacally through his tangle of red dreadlocks, "I see that you are still diligently spreading your gospel. Now perhaps you will preach to us about the inner workings of that pretty Source you carried!"

"This is impossible," I said. "The 4Wheelers, CryptNet, and Greater Serbia — allies!?"

"And that ain't all," Karl said, "we also been getting help from your buddies, the — "

"Silence!" Marshal Vukovic cried, whirling toward King Karl. "Remember that our agreement specifies complete discretion as to the extent of the network."

"It ain't indiscreet to be talkin' to three dead men, 'sfar's I'm consarned," said Karl, whose rustic affect barely concealed his resentment at Vukovic's reprimand.

"They are not dead yet," said PhyrePhox, "though the system that they represent is doomed. New Atlantis, Nippon, and the lesser phyles who have been foolish enough to join together under the Protocol, together represent a dying race of dinosaurs. They control the world by controlling information — information about the potential surfaces defined by certain atoms, and how they may be merged together in order to create structures collectively known as nanotechnology. But information wants to be free — is doomed to be free — and soon it will be available to all, despite the best efforts of Protocol Enforcement to restrict it! Our network is on the verge of breaking forever the monopoly of the Protocol-respecting phyles!"

Throughout this tirade, Captain Napier leveled a steady gaze upon the frenzied PhyrePhox, and the confident smile on his lips did not waver even when those dreadlocks, like a nest of red snakes, were writhing in his face! "Your words have a familiar ring," Captain Napier said, "we read them in the business plans and prospecti of the Second Wave startups thirty years ago — before they went out of business or merged with the titans they had sought to overthrow. We heard them from the Parsis, the Ismailis, the Mormoos, the Jews, the overseas Chinese, before they saw that nanotechnology promised enough wealth for all, and signed the Protocol. And now we hear the same words again from a motley assortment of synthetic phyles, who would have us believe that the very system that has brought undreamt-of prosperity to most of the world is in fact nothing other than an insidious system of oppression. Ask the peasant in Fujian province, who once labored in his paddy from dawn to dusk, whether he is oppressed now that he can compile his rice directly from a Feed, and spend his days playing with his grandchildren or in a ractive on his mediatron!"

"When that man worked in his paddy he was self-sufficient," retorted PhyrePhox, "he belonged to a community of workers who produced their food together. Now that community is destroyed, and he is dependent on your Feed like a baby on his mother's teat."

"And are we meant to believe that your conspiracy will somehow save this peasant from the dire fate of eating three square meals a day?" Captain Napier shot back.

"Instead of a Feed, that peasant will have a Seed," said PhyrePhox, "and instead of planting grains of rice in his paddy he will plant that Seed, and it will grow and flourish into a Source of his own, whose proceeds he can use as he sees fit — instead of relying on a Source owned by foreign strangers a thousand miles away."

"It is an idyllic picture," said Captain Napier, "but I fear it leaves out a great deal. This Seed of yours is more than a food factory, is it not? It is also potentially a weapon whose destructive power rivals that of the nuclear bombs of Elizabethan times. Now, as you have evidently realized, I live on Atlantan territory where the possession of weapons is strictly controlled. The children and women of Atlantis can walk anywhere at any time without fear of violence. But I was not born into this happy estate. No, I grew up a thete, living in an off-brand Clave where the ownership of weapons was completely unregulated, and as a boy exploring my neighborhood I frequently came upon dead bodies striped with the lurid scars of cookie-cutters. Now you would place technology a million times more dangerous into the hands of persons without the education, the good sense, the moral backbone" — here Captain Napier shot a defiant glance at Marshal Vukovic — "to use it properly. If this plan succeeds we are all doomed; so if you intend to torture us for the information you crave, then have at it! For we have all taken a solemn Oath to our God and our Queen, and we will gladly die rather than break it."

At this defiant peroration (which I must confess did much to revive my own faltering strength of purpose) PhyrePhox flew into a perfect frenzy of rage, and had to be restrained by Karl the 4Wheeler and one of his minions lest he slay the helpless Captain Napier on the spot! "Very well, then!" he cried. "You shall be the first, as you are the military man here, and I suspect that the information we seek is to be found with the others. We shall test your endurance, Captain, and let your two companions view the spectacle, and see if they have any fine speeches to deliver after they have seen you systematically reduced to a gibbering wreck!"

Without further ado, Marshal Vukovic gestured theatrically to a technician, who pressed some mechanical knobs and levers on a control panel. Captain Napier cried out involuntarily and bucked against his straps as a surge of electrical current shot through his body.

A respect for basic decency forbids me from detailing the dark events of the next few hours; suffice it to say that Captain Napier was as resolute as Karl, PhyrePhox, and Marshal Vukovic were cruel, and that in this fashion they matched each other volley for volley until my comrade hung loose and unconscious in his web of bonds. One of Karl's minions was dispatched to obtain a bucket of water. As we all awaited his return, the three conspirators spoke in low tones in the opposite corner of the room while Dr. Nkruma and I exchanged a long glance, no words being required to convey our thoughts: which of us would be next, and would we be as strong?

We were startled out of these frightful ruminations by a sudden alarm in the adjoining corridor. One of Karl's guards glanced out the door, cried out in abject terror and slammed the door, shooting the bolts to lock us all inside. Through the heavy door we could hear the sounds of a brief but vicious struggle outside. Then, to our astonishment, a fountain of smoke and powder erupted from the concrete-block wall, and when it cleared away we could see the terminal six inches or so of a narrow, gently curved blade which had apparently been thrust all the way through the masonry! The blade sliced downward through concrete, mortar, and reinforcing steel, describing a roughly oval shape about the size of a man, and sending forth a shower of dust that soon threw a dense haze over the lights and set us all to coughing. Karl, PhyrePhox, and Marshal Vukovic, now trapped in their own dungeon, could do little more than watch dumbfounded, and ready their weapons to defend themselves against this mysterious onslaught. They did not have to wait for long; in a few seconds the ellipse was complete, and heavy thuds sounded from the opposite side. The oval slid into the room and collapsed onto the floor with a tremendous crash and cloud of dust, and standing in the opening thus created we were delighted to see none other than Major Yasuhiro Ozawa of Nippon's Protocol Enforcement Contingent, dressed in full battle armor and wielding the astonishing concrete-cutting sword! Behind him was a full platoon of others similarly equipped. Ignoring the furious commands of their now-impotent leaders, most of our captors threw their weapons down at once, and in short order Captain Napier's torturers had been arrested while Major Ozawa was kind enough to turn his sword to the easier work of cutting us free. "It is much like a chainsaw, but on the nanometer scale, of course," he explained in impeccable English. I could not help but be glad that such a dangerous technology was firmly in the disciplined and reliable hands of the Nipponese, and not encapsulated in a Seed that anyone could grow in his vegetable patch.

While a Nipponese doctor tended to Captain Napier, Major Ozawa explained that our distress spore — the pollen-sized message-in-a-bottle that I had engineered at the suggestion of Dr. Nkruma — had wandered into the immunological field of a Nipponese floating world hovering just off the coast of Los Angeles. Because of its unfamiliar shape it fell under the eye of a Defense Force engineer, who, in the course of unraveling it, found the message hidden inside. Under the care of Major Ozawa's doctor, Captain Napier soon returned to consciousness, though a full recovery would take somewhat longer. Agents of Protocol

Enforcement serving both the Emperor and the Queen were at this moment striking at many nodes of the web spun by PhyrePhox, King Karl, Marshal Vukovic, and their associates, so for the moment there was little for us to do. We exchanged bows with our saviors, toasted our respective monarchs with an excellent sake thoughtfully provided by Major Ozawa, and then embarked on the most important part of our mission: reuniting ourselves with our families, and delivering a full report (of which this account may be considered only an executive summary) to Her Royal Highness Queen Victoria II of New Atlantis, to whom this work is humbly dedicated.

The Steam-Driven Time Machine: A Pop Culture Survey

RICK KLAW

When I was a child in the seventies, it seemed like the 1961 Ray Harry-hausen special effects-laden *Mysterious Island* played constantly on the TV. Not that I minded. Michael Craig leads a crew of Confederate P.O.W. escapees as they pilot a hot air balloon toward points unknown. Crash landing on an apparently deserted island, the castaways encounter giant animals: a crab, a flightless bird, bees, and a cephalopod, all presented in Harryhausen's dynamic stop-motion animation. The group discovers the presumed dead Captain Nemo, who had mutated the animals as part of an experiment. Throw in the pirates that attack the island and you have the recipe for a near-perfect movie. By nine years old, after many repeated viewings the film entered my personal zeitgeist, informing my later tastes and many of my creative decisions.

Mysterious Island was my first exposure to steampunk, long before K.W. Jeter coined the word in the late 1980s:

> Personally, I think Victorian fantasies are going to be the next big thing, as long as we can come up with a fitting collective term for [Tim] Powers, [James] Blaylock and myself. Something based on the appropriate technology of the era; like "steampunks," perhaps... (*Locus*, #315 April 1987)

Featuring interviews with Jeter and Blaylock plus a cover by Tim Powers, the Winter 1988 issue of *Nova Express* introduced me to the term "steampunk." By that time Powers and Blaylock were both part of my reading repertoire. Jeter joined a few years later.

Among many of the advantages of living in Austin as a young science fiction fan in the late eighties and early nineties was the strong and fairly well organized creative community. The local science fiction literary convention, ArmadilloCon, birthed, though probably as a surrogate, the Cyberpunk movement, as it was the first North American convention to feature William Gibson, Bruce Sterling, Lewis Shiner, and Pat Cadigan as guests of honor. Austinite Lawrence Person's previously mentioned 'zine *Nova Express* further encouraged science fiction critical studies with insightful interviews and reviews by professionals and fans alike.

Some twenty years later, pop culture has embraced steampunk. Publishing, film, and even the Internet embolden the term as a branding tool. Nary a week goes by without *Boing Boing* (*www.boingboing. net*), the venerable group blog, posting about some sort of steampunk inspired gadget, cartoon, or essay. A search of their archives generates almost 1500 articles. Subjects vary greatly: laptops, keyboards, watches, *Transformers*, planes, *Car Wars*, submarines, and so on. Many articles showcase functioning modern technology using steampunk methods and materials. Others present actual working machines from the 19th century. Images presenting artistic depictions of steampunk, paintings, sculptures, architecture and the like. Reinterpretations of popular shows such as *Star Trek* and *Star Wars* litter the listings. Original short films featuring steampunk tropes offer many amusing and sometimes exciting diversions.

The user-generated online encyclopedia *Wikipedia* (*en.wikipedia. org*) contains lengthy, extensive entries for both "steampunk" and "List of steampunk works," citing an array of sources. The English language version of the Polish site *Retrostacji, Steampunkopedia* (steampunk.republika.pl) offers the most comprehensive steampunk works chronological bibliography available on the web along with numerous links to steampunk-inspired videos. Sadly, the site stopped updating in February 2007.

Using the collaborative wiki-method, *Æther Emporium* (*etheremporium.pbwiki.com*) claims "to provide a onestop resource and archive for all things Steampunk." Potentially very interesting, the sparse site supplies some intriguing information and views from the nascent steampunk subculture. Another online cultural source, *SteamPunk Magazine* (*www.steampunkmagazine.com*), dedicated to "promoting steampunk as a culture, as more than a subcategory of fiction," produces a PDF format magazine and for-sale print version under the auspices of the Creative Commons license, an agreement that allows anyone to share and distribute the work as long as it is not for commercial or financial gain. Each of the three currently produced issues contains fiction, features exploring different aspects of the subgenre, and interviews with steampunk luminaries.

Even *Wired* (*www.wired.com*), home of the techno elite, lists some 930 archived pages about the subgenre. Often sharing similar coverage with its cyberculture cousin *Boing Boing*, the subjects run the pop culture gamut. Oddly, the domain name steampunk.com works as the home for The Speculative Fiction Clearing House, a portal for science fiction websites. The site has only a tangential relationship with the subgenre.

Back in the late eighties, I encountered my first steampunk roleplaying game. Featuring Victorian space travel and steam-powered devices, *Space 1889* (1988) was the first primarily steampunk RPG. At the time, I immersed myself in the RPG community, envisioning myself more of a gamer and possibly role-play games creator than an essay or even a fiction writer. This delusion lasted for about two years, after which I decided to devote my creative energies toward other writing and editing pursuits.

Prior to *Space 1889*, steampunk elements frequently cropped up in games. Most *Dungeons & Dragons* campaigns contained various steam-powered devices, usually projectiles or vehicles. Hero Games' pulp-era adventure game *Justice, Inc.* (1984) featured many steampunk-type props, most notably steam-powered robots. *Cthulhu by Gaslight*, Victorian era rules for the Lovecraft-inspired *Call of Cthulhu* game, premiered in 1986. While set in the 1890s, the supplement relied less on steampunk — beyond an odd section on time travel — and more on real-world settings.

In the ensuing years, steampunk routinely appeared in RPGs. Within the popular gaming universes such as Warhammer, *GURPS*, and *Dungeons & Dragons*, steam-driven devices and Victorian-era tropes became commonplace. The cross-pollination of the American Old West and anachronistic devices thrived within several games, chiefly *Deadlands* and the Japanese title *Terra the Gunslinger*.

Even LARPers got in the act. Premiering May 21, 2004 near Baltimore, MD, with a three-day episode, *Brassey's Game*, a steampunk live-action role playing game (LARP)[1], involved approximately thirty players in Victorian garb, who relied on heavy character interaction. The initial campaign ran for six weekend-long episodes. Six other stand-alone *Brassey's Game* episodes took place during the first campaign. Since its introduction, several other groups from various parts of the U.S., using modified versions of the original rules, participated in their own *Brassey's Game* events.

Another element of my seventies childhood, *The Wild Wild West*, the first, best, and longest-running steampunk television series, forged my future love of the weird western. The show related the adventures of two Secret Service agents — James West, a charming, womanizing hero, and Artemus Gordon, inventor and master of disguise — as they protected, often in secret, the United States, its interests and citizens. In four seasons from 1965–1969, the duo encountered all sorts of odd villainy including a brilliant but insane dwarf, recurring archvillain Dr. Miguelito Quixote Loveless, and bizarre weaponry such as cue stick guns and a triangular steam-powered tank with a barbed tip. Combining the best elements of traditional westerns and James Bond, *The Wild Wild West* spawned two late-seventies TV movies with the original cast, a dreadful 1999 big-screen movie, two separate comic book series (1960s Gold Key and 1991 Millennium Publications), and four novels, as well as influencing a generation of writers including Joe R. Lansdale, Norman Partridge, and Howard Waldrop.

The Adventures of Brisco County, Jr., the direct thematic descendant of *The Wild Wild West*, premiered on August 27, 1993, starring the cult actor Bruce Campbell of *Evil Dead* fame as the title character. Set in the 1890s, Brisco attempts to capture the members of the Bly Gang, the cutthroats responsible for his father's death. The series sported an intriguing cast of characters: Lord Bowler, bounty hunter and rival, lawyer Socrates Poole, Dixie Cousins, con-woman and Brisco's great love, and inventor/scientist Professor Wickwire, brilliantly portrayed by John Astin and supplier of Brisco's steampunk-like gadgetry. Even with clever story lines, the show lasted for only one season.

Perhaps the most unexpected use of weird western steampunk tropes occurred in the second season of the animated *Adventures of Batman & Robin*. "Showdown," with a Joe R. Lansdale teleplay from a

---

1 A form of role-playing game where the players physically act out their characters' actions.

story by Kevin Altieri, Paul Dini, and Bruce W. Timm tells of the immortal Batman villain Ra's al Ghul's 1883 confrontation with the DC Comics gunslinger Jonah Hex. The battle centers around a plot to blow up the nearly-completed tracks of a transcontinental railroad using dirigibles loaded with cannons and other explosives.

Because starring in one *Wild Wild West*-inspired short-lived TV series is never enough, Bruce Campbell portrayed the title character for two seasons in the disappointingly inane *Jack of All Trades* (2000). Jack Stiles, a secret service agent stationed by President Thomas Jefferson on the fictional French-controlled island of Palau-Palau, defends American interests while serving as the aide to a French aristocrat. Jack employs many steampunk-type weapons and gadgets. Loosely based on the classic 1919 novel, Sir Arthur Conan Doyle's *The Lost World* amazingly ran for three seasons (1999–2000) with poor special effects, bad acting, poorly crafted storylines, and some minor steampunk elements. The 1982 *Q.E.D.*, set in Edwardian England, lasted for only six episodes. *Voyagers!*, a time travel adventure series with periodic steampunk bits, managed twenty-two episodes over one season (1982–1983). Steampunk materials appeared in several episodes of the various *Doctor Who* incarnations.

Under the premise that Jules Verne actually lived the adventures that he wrote about, *The Secret Adventures of Jules Verne* (2000) delivered steampunk action with airships, steam powered devices, and even a steampunk cyborg. Playing upon the inherent metafictional possibilities, several episodes featured "real life" authors and personalities such as Samuel Clemens, Queen Victoria, Alexander Dumas, Cardinal Richelieu (a time travel episode), and King Louis XIII. The promising show never jelled and was canceled after one season.

The Japanese have also embraced steampunk television, albeit the animated variety. Based on the long-running manga *Fullmetal Alchemist*, set in an alternate late-20th-century society that practices alchemy and uses primarily early-20th-century technology, enjoyed a fifty-one episode run (2003–2004) and a 2005 anime feature film. *Steam Detectives* (1989–1990) follows the adventures of a young detective in a reality where the only source of energy is steam power. Set on a floating world with stylized Victorian fashions, *Last Exile* (2003) relates the story of airship pilots Claus and Lavie and their involvement in a plot about a mysterious cargo.

Another steampunk show derived from the works of Jules Verne, *Nadia: The Secret of Blue Water* (1989–1991) inspired a feature film sequel (1992) and a manga series. Set in 1889, circus performer Nadia, young inventor Jean Ratlique, and the famed Captain Nemo attempt to save the world from the Atlantean known as Gargolye who is bent on restoring the former underseas empire. Translated into eight different languages, the series achieved worldwide popularity.

Based on a series of popular video games, *Sakura Wars* relates an alternate 1920s reality that uses steam primarily to power all sorts of modern devices. Developed into numerous video games on several platforms, a manga, a TV series, five OVA[2] tie-ins, and a feature length movie, *Sakura* remains a uniquely Japanese cultural phenomenon.

Back in the seventies, *Mysterious Island* opened my eyes to new worlds as I encountered many more steampunk films. The 1930s Universal monster pictures with lighting-powered monsters, chemically induced madmen, and animal-mutating mad scientists exploited the yet undefined genre. Beneath a Victorian backdrop, Victor Frankenstein empowered his creatures in both *Frankenstein* (1931) and *Bride of Frankenstein* (1935) using the highly unlikely method of electrocution. In the latter film, Dr. Pretorius joins forces with Frankenstein, attempting to create life through alchemical means. Director James Whale recognized the inherent Victorian melodrama and he treated the films accordingly, thus creating two masterpieces.

Two of H. G. Wells' science-gone-amok novels inspired a pair of 1933 Universal movies. *The Invisible Man*, directed under the masterful hand of James Whale, relates the story of a man who goes mad after imbibing his own creation: an invisibility potion. Starring Charles Laughton and Bela Lugosi, *The Island of Lost Souls* adapted *The Island of Dr. Moreau* for the first time. The story of Dr. Moreau and his rebellious mutations, like that of the Invisible Man, speak to the Victorian notions of science and sadism. *The Island of Lost Souls* has been remade poorly twice, as *The Island of Dr. Moreau* (1977, 1996).

Fittingly, the first film recognized as steampunk was the 1902 fourteen-minute French animated short *Le Voyage dans la lune (A Trip to the Moon)*, based on Jules Verne's *From the Earth to the Moon* and H. G. Wells' *The First Men in the Moon*. Wildly popular upon its release, the

---

2 Original video animation, a phrase coined by the Japanese for direct-to-video films.

Georges Méliès film — one of his hundreds of fantasy films — achieved canonical status within science fiction.

Hollywood rediscovered Verne with a vengeance in the 1950s and 1960s, making numerous film adaptations including the steampunk films *20,000 Leagues Under the Sea* (1954), *The Fabulous World of Jules Verne* (1958), *Journey to the Center of the Earth* (1959), *Mysterious Island* (1961), *Master of the World* (1961), *Five Weeks in a Balloon* (1962), and tangentially *Captain Nemo and the Underwater City* (1969). Wells was not far behind with most notably *The Time Machine* (1961). One of producer George Pal's special effect spectaculars, *The Time Machine* thematically remained close to the source material, especially the portrayal of the machine itself. An awful version of Wells' book was made in 2002.

The seventies witnessed a severe drop in steampunk-related films as whiz bang space science fiction became the norm. A notable exception, the entertaining *Time After Time* (1979) suggested that Wells invented a time machine and traveled to 1979 in pursuit of Jack the Ripper.

In 1986, Hayao Miyazaki released his groundbreaking anime *Castle in the Sky* (a.k.a. *Laputa: Castle in the Sky*). A magical *tour de force* featuring floating cities, airships, and pirates, the film follows a young girl, Sheeta, and boy, Pazu, on their quest for the mystical missing city of Laputa. Miyazaki returned to steampunk in 2001 with his masterpiece *Spirited Away*, the highest grossing movie in the history of Japan. Easily the most awarded steampunk work in any medium, *Spirited Away* won the Academy Award for Best Animated Film, the Amsterdam Fantastic Film Festival Silver Scream Award, the Nebula Award for Best Script, the San Francisco International Film Festival Audience Award for Best Narrative Feature, five Mainichi Film Concours Awards, two Awards of the Japanese Academy, four Annie Awards, and many others. Miyazaki's eagerly anticipated follow up was the steampunk *Howl's Moving Castle* (2004), based on Diana Wynne Jones' popular young adult novel. Successful both financially and critically, *Howl's* plays as a traditional European fairy tale but with steampunk elements.

Sadly, with a few exceptions, Miyazaki's works represent the abnormal in modern steampunk. While movies such as *Vidocq* (2001), *The League of Extraordinary Gentlemen* (2003), *Hellboy* (2004), *Van Helsing* (2004), *Around the World in 80 Days* (2004), *Steamboy* (2004), and *The*

Brothers Grimm (2005) display strong stylings, they all fall short on substantive storytelling.

The third and perhaps weakest of Terry Gillam's Trilogy of the Imagination, *The Adventures of Baron Munchausen* (1988), recounts the legendary tales of the eponymous Baron. Littered throughout with steampunk tropes and devices, Gillam displays a magical world in this delightful, if overlong film.

The French duo Jean-Pierre Jeunet and Marc Caro created the strange, surrealist masterpiece 1995's *The City of Lost Children* (*La Cité des enfants perdus*). Unable to dream, a mad scientist steals the dreams of children. The kidnapping of a circus strongman's little brother leads to some bizarre and fascinating confrontations between the strongman, the children, and the scientist. Beautifully imagined within a late-19th-century industrial city complex, *The City of Lost Children* magically envisions a dark steampunk society.

The disappointing film version of *The Golden Compass*, the first novel of Philip Pullman's extraordinary trilogy, His Dark Materials, premiered in 2007 amidst a maelstrom of controversy, as various Christian groups — most notably the Catholic League — urged their members to boycott the movie, citing the story's perceived anti-Christian bias. The protestors had little to worry about, since director/screenwriter Chris Weitz stripped the original tale of any complexity and relevant subtext, presenting a dull lifeless movie. Even with the gorgeous visual effects (particularly of the dæmons and the airships), superior acting (especially Dakota Blue Richards' authentic portrayal of a fierce twelve-year-old girl), and a $200 million budget, *The Golden Compass* offered yet another 21st-century steampunk film failure.

Some thirty-five years after my initial discovery, steampunk still fascinates. I eagerly await to read about the new devices listed on *Boing Boing*. Even given the poor quality of most steampunk movies, films with airships and Victorian stylings still excite me. Clearly I am not alone as evidenced by the sheer amount of steampunk material continually being produced and the very existence of this anthology. *Vive la vapeur!*

My Favorite Steampunk Books and Movies
Rick Klaw

BOOKS

1) *The Exploits of Engelbrecht* by Maurice Richardson (1950)
2) *Anno Dracula* by Kim Newman (1992)
3) *The Anubis Gates* by Tim Powers (1983)
4) *The Golden Compass* (1995), *The Subtle Knife* (1997), and *The Amber Spyglass* (2000): the His Dark Materials trilogy by Philip Pullman
5) *Infernal Devices* by K.W. Jeter (1987)
6) *Stress of Her Regard* by Tim Powers (1989)
7) *The Ragged Astronauts* by Bob Shaw (1986)
8) *The Diamond Age* by Neal Stephenson (1995)
9) *Homunculus* by James Blaylock (1986)
10) *The Warlord of the Air* by Michael Moorcock (1971)

MOVIES

1) *Spirited Away* (2001)
2) *The City of Lost Children (La Cité des enfants perdus)* (1995)
3) *Howl's Moving Castle* (2004)
4) *The Time Machine* (1961)
5) *The Mysterious Island* (1961)
6) *Castle in the Sky* (1986)
7) *Time After Time* (1979)
8) *20,000 Leagues Under the Sea* (1954)
9) *Journey to the Center of the Earth* (1959)
10) *The Adventures of Baron Munchausen* (1988)

The Essential Sequential Steampunk: A Modest Survey of the Genre within the Comic Book Medium

BILL BAKER

Even a cursory examination of the comics medium will reveal a wealth of tales employing the settings, themes and devices which are staples of the steampunk genre. Quite simply, whole chapters, if not an entire book, could easily be devoted to the various manifestations of steampunk in the English-, European-, and Asian-language comic markets. Given this situation, it quickly became obvious that some fairly severe restrictions had to be instituted in the selection process determining which books to include, lest this article expand well beyond the boundaries of its allotted space.

Bearing those facts in mind, what follows is a short list of what this reporter considers some of the better examples of steampunk graphic novels chosen from the ranks of the current American mainstream comics market. Each one of these works represents, in its own way, a pure manifestation of the steampunk genre in the comic book medium. Further, all works cited are currently in print and readily available at comic shops and book stores, be they based in the virtual or physical world, as well as at many local libraries. This ensures that the interested reader can easily satisfy any cravings for the rich and varied pleasures offered by the sequential steampunk narratives included in this survey.

It's only fitting to begin with the series that the editors of this very anthology cited as a prime example of a steampunk comic. Written with taut precision by Ian Edginton and drawn with evocative grace by D'Israeli, *Scarlet Traces* and *Scarlet Traces: The Great Game* relate what happens in the aftermath of the failed Martian invasion chronicled by H. G. Wells in *The War of the Worlds*. In the first volume, we discover that England has risen from the ashes and rubble of near defeat to resume its position as a world power by harnessing the secrets of the derelict Martian technology. In short, *Scarlet Traces* presents a land where the glory of Empire and Victorian sensibilities, including such warts as the colonial mindset and rigid class structures inherent to those systems, have not only survived, they remain the accepted and unquestioned norm. Thus, while there is much to be commended in this oddly familiar landscape, it is a land where the plenty enjoyed by the moneyed few masks something truly terrible and inhuman operating at the very heart of the Empire.

This point is driven home by the opening sequence as an alcoholic veteran of the Navy who miraculously survived the alien invasion stumbles across the bloodless bodies of several young women washed up along the Thames. However, as the victims are from the lower classes, these deaths result in little official notice despite the increasing ill-ease of the populace. It's not until Captain Robert Autumn, a retired soldier and gentleman adventurer from the upper class, aided by his friend and manservant, former Sergeant Major Archie Currie, begin to investigate the disappearance of the latter's niece that the authorities seem to take any real notice. It soon becomes apparent that someone well placed in the government is using their agents to silence or even kill all parties involved with these investigations. This sets up a confrontation between these opposing parties, and leads to a horrific revelation that has the power to destroy not only lives, but the restored Empire itself. The final pages of this volume bring the divergent plot threads together to create a climax that, while tragic, is all but inevitable.

The second volume, *Scarlet Traces: The Great Game*, takes place four decades after its predecessor. The English Empire has a firm and unwavering grip upon much of this world, and has been attempting to extend its reach to include the home world of the Martian invaders. However, all is not well. Despite the fascist government's best efforts at home, abroad and across the void, the interminable war effort has taken a real toll on the populace and economy. Worse yet, homeland terrorism is on the rise and serious questions concerning the fate of all those sent to fight on the Red Planet — troops who rarely, if ever, return home to their friends and family — have begun to surface.

Enter Charlotte Hemming, a fearless photojournalist on a quest to deliver factual news unimpeded by the government's demands that the truth of the situation be suppressed for the greater good. After narrowly escaping a deadly attack by government agents, she obtains the necessary faked documents to travel to the front lines and discover firsthand what is really happening on Mars. However, not all goes as planned, neither for Hemming nor for those who would prevent her from arriving safely at her destination. Still, she does make planetfall, just in time to bear witness to an act of genocidal desperation. Shortly thereafter, she uncovers certain truths which were never meant to be widely known. For something completely unexpected and ultimately terrifying has been discovered on the Red Planet, a revelation that could easily lead to the extinction of the human race. Again, the various questions and concerns raised by the narrative are all addressed and brought to an effective, logical and wholly satisfying conclusion by this tale's end. In sum, the *Scarlet Traces* books are a well written and strikingly drawn series of adventures, and worthy successors to Wells's work.

The Adventures of Luther Arkwright, also published by Dark Horse, is considered a modern classic of the comics medium, and with good reason. This graphic novel centers on the dimension-hopping exploits of the title character, an albino possessed of superhuman mental powers as well as the singular ability to navigate between the various planes of existence comprising the Multiverse. Aided by a group of like-minded agents guided by a supercomputer and the manifestations of the three women he loves who inhabit the various versions of Earth, Luther embarks on a mind- and genre-bending quest to prevent the evil Disruptors from gaining control of Firefrost, an object capable of controlling or even destroying all of existence.

Combining elements from Eastern and Western religious traditions, modern narrative techniques like stream of consciousness and elements lifted from both classic and popular tales of heroic struggle, this is one of the most accomplished and entertaining novels, illustrated or otherwise, of the past decade. Bryan Talbot, the sole creator of this multilayered and highly complex tale, works real visual and verbal magic as he guides the reader through the various levels of action, reality and meaning to a conclusion that is wholly satisfying and, ultimately, utterly transcendent. Quite simply, this is a masterpiece of sequential storytelling, and one which offers rich rewards upon each rereading.

Those craving a more linear adventure firmly set within a historical context need look no further than *The Five Fists of Science* from Image Comics. This clever and satirical tale pits Mark Twain, Nikola Tesla, and Baroness Bertha von Suttner, all of whom are trying to sell an immense engine of destruction to any and all buyers, against the combined opposing interests of Thomas Edison, Guglielmo Marconi, John Morgan, and Andrew Carnegie. The art of co-creator Steven Sanders suits the story perfectly, only serving to heighten and punctuate the drama and humor inherent to Matt Fraction's lean script. The result is a smart, savvy, and truly wild ride through the corridors of a history that might have been. Add in the fact that the design and packaging of this book are worth the price of admission alone, and you have a must-read for fans of fast-paced and witty action-adventure yarns.

Girl Genius, "A Gaslamp Fantasy with Adventure, Romance and Mad Science," is a series which avails itself of more than the technologies inherent to steampunk to tell the life story of a young woman of talent making her way in a strangely altered world. The stories by Phil and Kaja Foglio have drawn upon devices and techniques from sources as varied as science fiction, romance, and young adult literatures to create something that is completely original.

Girl Genius opens on the worst day of Agatha Clay's young life, when her mentor at Transylvania Polygnostic University is killed by Baron Wulfenbach, the tyrannical ruler of all Europe, and she's kidnapped to work in the Baron's laboratories as an assistant. Unbeknownst to Agatha or Wulfenbach, she's the last surviving member of the Heterodyne clan, legendary creators of steampunk technology and bitter foes of all evil scientists. Escaping from the Baron's airborne Castle Wulfenbach where she's been held captive, Agatha flees with Krosp — the intelligent, talking King of the Cats — to find her way in the world and discover the means to avenge her family's demise at the hands of the Baron.

Phil Foglio's art is the perfect foil for the scripts, providing backgrounds which lend weight and the right amount of realism to his cartoony, highly expressive characters. This allows emotionally resonant moments of the script to really hit home without slowing the forward momentum of the plot. This all makes for a series which is fun and fast moving, yet thoughtful and truly addictive. Hardcore fans are especially appreciative of the fact that the Foglios post three new pages a week on *www.girlgenius.net*, allowing them to enjoy Agatha's exploits between releases of the collections.

The final three series in our whirlwind tour of the sequential steampunk world were conceived and largely written by Alan Moore, perhaps the most influential and significant single creator of comics for the past thirty years. Having reconfigured horror, superhero and crime comics with his work on *Swamp Thing*, *Watchmen* and *From Hell*, respectively, Moore decided to refocus his protean powers by conceiving an entire line of comics. This resulted in America's Best Comics, a small group of titles which all spring from a seemingly simple question: "What might have happened if Superman and the other superheroes had never been created, and the comics medium had continued to be largely influenced by the pulps and fantastic fiction?" While all of the ABC books are highly entertaining and worth seeking out, there are three of them, *Tom Strong*, *Tom Strong's Terrific Tales*, and *The League of Extraordinary Gentlemen*, that are of particular interest to this survey.

Tom Strong, the character and the book, launched and set the tone for the entire imprint. The first issue opens with a young boy who lives in Millennium City, a fantastic metropolis teeming with flying cars, cyclopean architecture, and other scientific marvels, receiving his very own copy of *Tom Strong* #1. After boarding a cable car which will take him to school, the youth begins reading the comic. Both he and the reader are then ushered back in time to the West Indies at the end of the Victorian Age. There we discover Tom's parents aboard a sailboat foundering in a terrible storm. They quickly find themselves stranded on a seemingly deserted tropical isle named Attabar Teru, the sole survivors of a shipwreck. After salvaging what supplies they can and burying their small crew, Sinclair Strong assembles and activates Pneuman, a steam-powered manservant. With their mechanized servant's aid, they set up household in the confines of an extinct volcano. Soon, Susan Strong gives birth to their son, but complications threaten to end his life just as it has begun. And that's when the fledgling parents discover that they are not the sole inhabitants of Attabar Teru, for the island is home to an indigenous tribe who not only save Tom, but give aid to the couple.

The natives also provide Tom, who is raised in near-total isolation according to scientific methods inside a chamber with increased gravity, with Goloka herb to increase his mental abilities and extend his lifespan. However, tragedy strikes again when, years later, an earthquake shatters the Strong household. Tom, who has become a teenaged paragon of health with a mind to match, is the sole survivor of this second tragedy. Adopted by the natives, he lives among them developing his skills until he reaches maturity, when he leaves them to rejoin civilization. There he begins his career as an adventurer and a crusader who strives to wipe out evil wherever it appears. Still, Tom occasionally returns to his tropical home to reconnect with his roots and visit with friends and the relatives of his native-born wife.

Throughout this first chapter, Tom's origin story is interrupted to return to the "reality" of the young lad reading the comic to show his reaction to the tale and, coincidentally, what is transpiring in his world. It's quickly apparent that Tom Strong isn't merely a fictional character, but an actual, living resident of the same metropolis as the boy. By the end of the first issue, both the fictional youth and the actual, real-world reader have not only been enlightened to the particulars of Tom Strong's background, but also his cultural place in the "real" world of the series. Even more importantly, the reader is introduced to the various metafictional concepts and radical narrative possibilities offered by the comics medium, ideas which underlie and are continually explored throughout this and all the other installments of the ABC books. The apparent ease with which Moore and Chris Sprouse, the artist of *Tom Strong*, pull off this incredibly difficult hat trick not only bolsters the series' metafictional reality, it also foreshadows the wildly inventive exploration of the fictional world as well as the comics medium itself in this and the other ABC books.

The second title created by Alan Moore of particular interest to this brief survey is an anthology called *Tom Strong's Terrific Tales*. Whether the focus is upon a Young Tom Strong's coming of age, the adventures of Tesla Strong, his daughter, or the otherworldly escapades of Jonni Future — a second-generation space- and time-warping heroine following in the footsteps of her uncle, the original incarnation of that character — this title's short stories continue to build upon and explore the complex metafictional framework established within the pages of *Tom Strong*, all the while playing with the possibilities inherent to the ABC line's fictional steampunk reality and the comics medium itself. In the final analysis, although these two titles might not have resulted in tales quite as profound or groundbreaking as some of Moore's other work, both series offer hours of incredibly inventive and well-wrought fun. As such, they make for a great, even joyous, reading experience.

Which brings us to *The League of Extraordinary Gentlemen*, the third title created by Alan Moore, and the final title in this survey. It's also the only series bearing the ABC imprint which wasn't part of that line's shared fictional world. However, it marks perhaps the most radical use of the metafictional technique seen in that entire line, as it essentially encompasses, and potentially draws upon, all the literary world's fictional characters and settings.

The essential idea underlying it is fairly simple: What would happen if all the various fictional worlds and their denizens all inhabited the same space? Wouldn't the villains hatch and set into motion various plots to control some nation or the entire world? Well, then, wouldn't there be the need for a group to oppose and prevent those evil machinations? This line of inquiry surely would lead to the founding of an organization which would span the ages and draw its members from the varied stories, heroic and otherwise, who would act to circumvent evildoers' plans. And so, The League of Extraordinary Gentlemen was born.

The first two books of the series feature a version of the League from the late Victorian Era, a group consisting of Allan Quatermain, Captain Nemo, Hawley Griffin, also know as the Invisible Man, Dr. Henry Jekyll and his alter ego, Edward Hyde, and their leader, Mina Murray, a survivor of vampiric depredations by Count Dracula. Brought together by Campion Bond and taking orders from a mysterious personage known only as "M," in their first adventure these worthies strive to prevent an attempt by the Asian villain called the Doctor to conquer the world. In order to complete their mission, they must overcome personal differences and prejudices, along with disruptive forces from without, which threaten to derail their mission from the very start. Their second adventure pits them against a seemingly unstoppable extraterrestrial invasion force from Mars. Again, this version of the League must battle their alien-born enemies while they deal with betrayals of the worst kind from within their ranks — efforts which leave the League's members dead or emotionally shattered, and perhaps beyond all hope of recovery.

A third volume, *The Black Dossier*, uses a variety of narrative and visual devices, including 3-D comics, to recreate a top-secret report on the actions of the various incarnations of the League over the course of the past few centuries, including their activities during the reign of

Big Brother and earlier, equally fantastic Royalist eras. Throughout all of these adventures, both Moore's scripts and the wonderfully twisted depictions of the settings and characters by artist Kevin O'Neill provide the reader with thrilling action and suspense, as well as rich insight into the characters' natures and the shape of their shared metafictional world. Moore and O'Neill have both stated that they plan to keep producing new installments in this series for the rest of their professional lives. Given the virtually limitless possibilities offered by the underlying concept powering *The League of Extraordinary Gentlemen*, all lovers of fine illustrated fantastic fiction will have reason to celebrate for years to come.

It's my hope that, despite the stunted nature of this survey, I've presented ample evidence that there exists a wide variety of finely crafted and uncommonly interesting steampunk comic books which are readily available to entertain the curious reader. I also hope it's clear that, if none of the works discussed appeal, there's an incredible amount of other titles, available in English and various other languages, which are worthy of your attention. To paraphrase the Bard, "There are more things in this world of graphic novels, dear reader, than are allowed in my survey." With that thought in mind, I'd like to urge you to embark upon your own investigative voyage, and discover all the steam powered sequential worlds which await you.

Bibliography of works cited

Edginton, Ian. *Scarlet Traces* and *Scarlet Traces: The Great Game*. Illustrated by D'Israeli. Milwaukie, OR: Dark Horse, 2003, 2007.

Foglio, Phil and Kaja Foglio. *Girl Genius* volume 1–6. Illustrated by Phil Foglio. Seattle, WA: Airship Entertainment, 2005-2006.

Fraction, Matt. *The Five Fists of Science*. Illustrated by Steven Sanders. Berkeley, CA: Image Comics, 2006.

Moore, Alan. *The League of Extraordinary Gentlemen*, vol. 1 & 2; *The League of Extraordinary Gentlemen: The Black Dossier*. Illustrated by Kevin O'Neill. La Jolla, CA: America's Best Comics, 2000, 2003, 2007.

Moore, Alan. *Tom Strong*, book 1–6; *Tom Strong's Terrific Tales*, book 1–2. Illustrated by Chris Sprouse and various. La Jolla, CA: America's Best Comics, 2000-2006.

Talbot, Bryan. *The Adventures of Luther Arkwright*. Illustrated by
  Bryan Talbot. Milwaukie, OR: Dark Horse: 1997.

Further Sequential Steampunk Reading
While this short bibliography by no means represents anything like a
comprehensive, or even extensive, listing of the various titles of interest
that are currently in print, the following collections and original graphic
novels represent some of the best examples of steampunk-influenced
comics available on the North American English-speaking comic book
market today. As with those titles cited in "The Essential Sequential
Steampunk," all of these books are widely available via book stores,
comics shops and libraries. — *Bill Baker, November 2007*

Amara, Phil. *The Nevermen* and *The Nevermen: Streets of Blood*.
  Illustrated by Guy Davis. Milwaukie, OR: Dark Horse Comics,
  2001, 2003.
Augustyn, Brian. *Batman: Gotham by Gaslight*. Illustrated by Mike
  Mignola. New York, NY: DC Comics, 2006.
Broadmore, Greg. *Doctor Grordbort's Contrapulatronic Dingus
  Directory*. Illustrated by Greg Broadmore. Milwaukie, OR: Dark
  Horse Comics 2008.
Ellis, Warren. *Planetary: All Over the World and Other Stories* and
  Planetary: The Fourth Man. and Planetary: Leaving the 20th
  Century. Illustrated by John Cassaday. La Jolla, CA: WildStorm,
  2000, 2001, 2005.
Gaiman, Neil. *Marvel 1602*. Illustrated by Andy Kubert. New York,
  NY: Marvel Comics, 2004.
Kelly, Joe. *Steampunk: Drama Obscura* and *Steampunk:
  Manimatron*. Illustrated by Chris Bachalo. New York, NY:
  WildStorm, 2001, 2003.
Klein, Grady. *The Lost Colony: Book No. 1: The Snodgrass Conspiracy*
  and *The Lost Colony: Book No. 2: The Red Menace*. Illustrated by
  Grady Klein. New York, NY: First Second, 2006, 2007.
Millar, Mark. *Jenny Sparks: The Secret History of The Authority*.
  Illustrated by John McCrea. La Jolla, CA: WildStorm, 2001.
Moore, Alan. *Tomorrow Stories: Book One*. Illustrated by various.
  Tomorrow Stories: Book Two. Illustrated by Kevin Nowlan and
  various. La Jolla, CA: America's Best Comics, 2003, 2004.

Morrison, Grant. *Sebastian O*. Illustrated by Steve Yeowell. New York, NY: Vertigo, 2004.

Biographical Notes

Authors

BILL BAKER is a veteran comics journalist who has contributed interviews and feature stories, reviews, and news reportage to various magazines, including *Cinefantastique/CFQ*, *Comic Book Marketplace*, *International Studio*, *Sketch*, and *Tripwire*. He has also worked as an interviewer and reporter for a number of websites, including Comic Book Resources and Wizard World. Baker lives in Michigan and has a blog at *specfric.blogspot.com*.

JAMES P. BLAYLOCK has won both the Philip K. Dick Award and the World Fantasy Award for his fiction. Considered one of the original steampunks, his work has appeared in all of the major magazines, with books including the novel-length version of the story in this anthology, *Lord Kelvin's Machine*, *The Paper Grail*, *The Digging Leviathan*, *Land of Dreams*, and many more. Readers can visit his website at *www.sybertooth.com/blaylock/index.htm*.

MOLLY BROWN has written a science fiction thriller for teenagers, a novelization based on the *Cracker* television series, a short story collection, and the humorous historical whodunit, *Invitation to a Funeral*. Several of her stories have been optioned for film and/or television. Her website at *www.mollybrown.co.uk* features an online tour of Restoration London.

MICHAEL CHABON is one of the most celebrated writers of his generation, having won the Pulitzer Prize for *The Amazing Adventures of Kavalier & Clay*, among several other awards. His *Wonder Boys* was made into a movie starring Michael Douglas and Tobey Maguire. His latest novel, *The Yiddish Policemen's Union*, has been published to substantial critical acclaim. Chabon has also edited three anthologies, including a volume of *The Best American Short Stories*. For more information on Chabon, visit his website at *www.sugarbombs.com/kavalier*.

STEPAN CHAPMAN was born in 1951 in Chicago, Illinois, and studied theatre at the University of Michigan. In 1969, his first published story was selected for *Analog* by John W. Campbell. In the '70s, his early fiction appeared in four of Damon Knight's *Orbit* anthologies. He has performed in plays in the USA and England, and his comedies for children were produced for the Edinburgh Drama Festival. In 1997, the Ministry of Whimsy Press released his first novel, *The Troika*, which won the Philip K. Dick Award. His short fiction has appeared in several hundred literary magazines and in *The Year's Best Fantasy and Horror*. He maintains a website at *www.stepanchapman.com*.

TED CHIANG has won the Hugo and Nebula awards for his short fiction. He also won the Sidewise Award for Alternate History for the story collected in this anthology. An acknowledged master of the short form, Chiang's latest story is "The Merchant and the Alchemist's Gate," released as a book by Subterranean Press and also appearing in *The Magazine of Fantasy & Science Fiction*. He lives in Bellevue, Washington.

PAUL DI FILIPPO is the author of hundreds of short stories, some of which have been collected in these widely praised collections: *The Steampunk Trilogy, Ribofunk, Fractal Paisleys, Lost Pages, Little Doors, Strange Trades, Bablyon Sisters*, and his multiple-award-nominated novella, *A Year in the Linear City*. The popularity of Di Filippo's short stories sometimes distracts from the impact of his mind-bending, utterly unclassifiable novels: *Ciphers, Joe's Liver, Fuzzy Dice, A Mouthful of Tongues*, and *Spondulix*. He has been a finalist for the Hugo, Nebula, British Science Fiction Association, Philip K. Dick, *Wired* magazine, and World Fantasy awards. Paul lives in Providence, Rhode Island. For more information, visit his website at *www.pauldifilippo.com/index. php*.

MARY GENTLE is an English fantasy writer, with novels that include *Ancient Light, Rats and Gargoyles, The Architecture of Desire*, and her masterwork, *Ash: A Secret History*. The critic Nicholas Gevers has said of Gentle that she is "one of the most important and idiosyncratic contemporary British speculative fiction writers," whose work displays "vast imagination, profound understanding of the forces and perceptions governing history, and comprehensively sympathetic insight into war and its effects on human psychology."

RICK KLAW produces reviews and articles for the *Austin Chronicle*, *Monsters & Critics*, *Moving Pictures*, *RevolutionSF*, *SF Site*, *The Greenwood Encyclopedia of Science Fiction and Fantasy*, and other venues. His brief forays into short fiction have appeared in *Electric Velocipede* and *Cross Plains Universe*. Klaw's writings were collected in *Geek Confidential: Echoes from the 21st Century* (MonkeyBrain). Klaw currently lives in Austin, Texas, with his wife, an enormous cat, an even bigger dog, and a modest collection of books. He dreams of finding a copy of *Zeppelin Stories*, June 1929, featuring the mythical Gil Brewer story "Gorilla of the Gas Bags."

JAY LAKE lives and works in Portland, Oregon, within sight of an 11,000-foot volcano. He is the author of over two hundred short stories, four collections, and a chapbook, along with novels from Tor Books, Night Shade Books, and Fairwood Press. Jay also co-edited six volumes of the critically-acclaimed *Polyphony* anthology series from Wheatland Press. His latest novel is *Mainspring* (Tor), picked up as an SF Book Club selection. In 2004, Jay won the John W. Campbell Award for Best New Writer. He has also been a Hugo nominee for his short fiction and a three-time World Fantasy Award nominee for his editing. Lake can be reached via his website at *www.jlake.com*.

JOE R. LANSDALE has been called "an immense talent" by *Booklist*; "a born storyteller" by Robert Bloch; and the *New York Times Book Review* declared that he has "a folklorist's eye for telling detail and a front-porch raconteur's sense of pace." He's won five Bram Stoker Awards, a British Fantasy Award, the American Mystery Award, the Horror Critics Award, the "Shot in the Dark" International Crime Writer's Award, the Booklist Editor's Award, the Critic's Choice Award, and a *New York Times* Notable Book Award. Lansdale lives in Nacogdoches, Texas, with his wife, Karen, a writer and editor. For more information, visit his website at *www.joerlansdale.com/todaysfeature.html*.

IAN R. MACLEOD is the author of *The Light Ages* and *The House of Storms*, which portray an alternate England powered by magic. His first novel, *The Great Wheel*, won the Locus Award for best first novel. An accomplished short story writer, MacLeod's collections include *Breathmoss and Other Exhalations* and *Voyages by Starlight*. He has won the Sidewise Award and the World Fantasy Award. For more information, visit his website at *www.ianrmacleod.com*.

MICHAEL MOORCOCK has written in more modes and genres than any living writer. From being a godfather of modern steampunk to his mainstream literary novels, including *Mother London*, he has demonstrated a range and talent rarely equaled. Moorcock has won the World Fantasy Lifetime Achievement Award, among many others. For more information on Moorcock's many current projects, visit him at the multiverse: *www.multiverse.org*.

JESS NEVINS is the author of *Heroes & Monsters: The Unofficial Companion to the League of Extraordinary Gentlemen*, *The Encyclopedia of Fantastic Victoriana* (a World Fantasy Award finalist), and the forthcoming *Encyclopedia of Pulp Heroes*. You can find more information about Nevins on his website at *www.geocities.com/ratmmjess/*.

RACHEL E. POLLOCK is a frequent contributor to *SteamPunk Magazine*. Her work has also been published in the *Harvard Summer Review*, the *Southern Arts Journal*, the *Costume Research Journal*, and the anthology *Knoxville Bound*. She is a lecturer on costume production at the University of North Carolina at Chapel Hill and author of the craft artisanship blog *La Bricoleuse*, which can be found at *labricoleuse. livejournal.com*.

NEAL STEPHENSON is the author of the bestselling Baroque Cycle (*Quicksilver*, *The Confusion*, and *The System of the World*) as well as the novels *Cryptonomicon*, *The Diamond Age*, *Snow Crash*, and *Zodiac*. He lives in Seattle, Washington. For more information, visit his website at *www.nealstephenson.com*.

Editors

ANN VANDERMEER has been a publisher and editor for over twenty years who currently serves as the fiction editor of *Weird Tales* and as a guest editor for *Best American Fantasy*. She is the founder of the award-winning Buzzcity Press. Work from her press and related periodicals has won the British Fantasy Award, the International Rhysling Award, and appeared in several year's best anthologies. Ann was also the founder of *The Silver Web* magazine, a periodical devoted to experimental and avant-garde fantasy literature. A *Best of the Silver Web* anthology is forthcoming from Prime Books. Books published by Buzzcity Press include the Theodore Sturgeon Award finalist *Dradin, In Love* by Jeff VanderMeer and the International Horror Guild Award-winning *The Divinity Student* by Michael Cisco. Ann has partnered with her husband, author Jeff VanderMeer, on such editing projects as the World Fantasy Award-winning *Leviathan* series and the Hugo Finalist *The Thackery T. Lambshead Pocket Guide to Eccentric & Discredited Diseases*. She is co-editing the following anthologies as well: *The New Weird, Fast Ships, Black Sails; Last Drink Bird Head*; and *Love-Drunk Book Heads*.

JEFF VANDERMEER is the author of the best-selling *City of Saints and Madmen*, set in his signature creation, the imaginary city of Ambergris, in addition to several other novels from Bantam, Tor, and Pan Macmillan. He has won two World Fantasy Awards, an NEA-funded Florida Individual Artist Fellowship, and, most recently, the Le Cafard cosmique Award in France and the Tähtifantasia Award in Finland. He has also been a finalist for the Hugo Award, Bram Stoker Award, International Horror Guild Award, Philip K. Dick Award, and many others. Novels such as *Veniss Underground* and *Shriek: An Afterword* have made the year's best lists of Amazon.com, the *Austin Chronicle*, the *San Francisco Chronicle*, and *Publishers Weekly*. His work, both books and short stories, has been translated into over twenty languages. *The Thackery T. Lambshead Pocket Guide to Eccentric & Discredited Diseases* may be his most famous anthology, and is considered a cult classic, still in print along with his *Leviathan* original fiction series. Recently, VanderMeer began to experiment in other media, resulting in a movie based on his novel *Shriek* that featured an original soundtrack by rock band The Church and a PlayStation Europe animation of his story "A New Face in Hell" by animator Joel Veitch. Currently, VanderMeer is writing a noir thriller called *Finch*.